# Montana

W.R. BENTON


LOOSE CANNON ENTERPRISES
AUBURN, CA

*Ingram Edition*
*ISBN 978-1-944476-92-2*



This book was produced in the USA

www.loose-cannon.com

# Books by W.R. Benton

W. R. Benton is a master story teller, with over 60 books, eBooks, and audio books to his credit. His mountain man book, *"War Paint,"* set in 1820, is soon to be a feature motion picture. Known for his action and adventure, Benton makes many readers feel as if they are actually a part of the book. He tells of the kind of bad guys you love to hate, with good guys you root for from the very beginning.

Explore WR Benton's books, visit

http://www.amazon.com/author/wrbenton/

To learn about new paperback releases

join our mailing list:  http://www.wrbenton.net/newsletter.htm

# Dedications

To my special friend, Juanita Duryea. She is a true Southern Belle and an exceptional woman, with a heart of pure gold. She is a rare gem, loved by everyone, and appreciated by all. She makes me smile with her humor and love of life.

To Bo Porter, a super cowboy from way back and special friend. I salute him as both a hell of a man and my friend, because good friends are hard to find. I love this quote on his Facebook page: "You must speak straight so that your words may go as sunlight into our hearts. Speak Americans. I will not lie to you; do not lie to me." — *Cochise*

To Wesley Parker, a fellow United States Air Force Veteran, and a good friend. May God continue to bless you. If push comes to shove, you'll find me standing beside you, brother.

# A Word from the Author

The period following the American Civil War brought more people west than at any other time in our history. Southern men, unable to find jobs in their states, moved west with their families or alone, hoping for a better life. Northerners also moved west for many reasons, and for a majority of Americans who came, it was with the dream of being successful, owning land, horses, cattle, or finally owning a home. While some found a better life, many others did not—they found death.

This great migration was not limited to only white Americans, but to all of us, white, black, yellow or Hispanic. Some, like Isaac, were men of color and had been living there for years, long before the movement started. Be assured, regardless of a man's color, religion or beliefs, the trip was rough, and establishing a home in Montana was tough. It took a special person to move to a remote corner of the country, build a home, and then develop it to the point it was self-sustaining, much less bringing in a profit.  To make life harder, there were always Indians, illnesses, accidents, wild animals, and other threats.

However, settlers soon discovered the land was rich and if a man and his woman were willing to work hard, they would reap a great harvest come fall. Then again, if they didn't work, someone would likely find their white bones following a hard and cold winter, because the land was as unforgiving as it was generous.

I don't necessarily agree or disagree with the way America gained access to Indian lands, but as Luke states in this book, "It ain't fair, but that's the way life is. The strongest have always taken what they want, and they're doin' it now." But, it's important to remember times were very different then; our society, attitudes, and values were much antithetical than today. They were a tougher people and given to doing what they felt was right at any moment, hoping God would approve. Keep in mind; most Americans believed it was our destiny as a nation to one day posses all the land from Mexico to Canada. Some went so far as to say it was God's will and we should do what it took to make it happen.  My great-grand-mother was one of those who honestly thought it was our God given right to possess all this land, regardless of who owned it previously.

You'll find in this book most of my characters have a strong resignation to God's will, and rarely did they question why someone died or if an injured person would recover, because it was in God's hands. Many people living today, with our health care system, may find this strange and even primitive, but in those days it was very common. There was acceptance of God and most, even those who were unbelievers, had a deep respect for the Holy Bible, and our Lord. Religion was important to the common man and woman, who had no one else to turn to during times of trouble. It's a part of our society that is missing today, and I feel strongly it need not be. While all the characters in this book and most locations are pure fiction, Bannack, Montana and Rolla, Missouri are or were real towns. Our descriptions of both towns is accurate, and I grew up in Rolla, so I know the town well. Bannack is now a ghost town, the last residents leaving in the 1970's and can still be visited. During the Civil War, the Union used Rolla as a supply depot, and most Yankees considered the area south of town to be "rebel country." I was born about eight miles south of town in a small place called Vida. I went to a small one-room schoolhouse during some of my primary years, and later attended high school in Rolla. Vida had a feedlot, a small country store, and that was about it, unless you counted the trailer park on the southwest side of Highway 63. I have chosen Rolla for this book because it was a rough area during the war, experiencing a Union occupation, while many of the men were gone fighting for the south. The James boys, Younger's, Quantrill, and "Bloody Bill" Anderson all knew all the land around the small town well.

This book is a tall tale of the settling of Montana and while it's a work of fiction, it could have happened in much the way I have written it. Life was cheap and difficult, with most folks dying before the age of 50, and there was no promise of a better life if you lived longer. As Ty Fisher, in W. R. Benton's book *Mountain of Death* said, "I ain't never had no easy life, so why should I expect the good Lord to give me one now?"

*W. R. Benton*
*Jackson, Mississippi*
*November 12, 2015*

# CHAPTER 1

## The War

**C**orporal James Thomas didn't feel the heavy cast-iron cannonball that instantly removed his head from his body. His lifeless form fell to the ground and twitched until his system shut down a minute later. Sergeant William Sanders ran by the body of his lifelong friend, but couldn't stop. Bugle calls sounded and the loud booms of cannons filled the air overhead with white cotton balls of death that rained red-hot steel to the ground. Hundreds of rifles sounded and they all fired at the same time, adding more confusion to the already dazed Sanders.

Grasping his rifle tighter, he pointed the long sharp pointed bayonet at the Yankee lines and gave a bloodcurdling Rebel yell, running faster toward his enemy. Men fell to his left and right, but he remained untouched.

"Down!" Screamed Captain Fall from the front.

Bill fell to the ground, but many others did not hear the warning and a second later a swarm of lead bees flew into them. Some men screamed, while others grunted as they fell, and yet others made not a sound. Grapeshot, he thought as he heard the Captain order the troopers forward, before the Yanks had a chance to reload the cannon.

Nearing the field gun, a tall red haired Yank ran at him and Bill swung his bayonet hard, striking the Yankee's gun barrel, knocking the man off-balance. Pulling his rifle back, he brought the bayonet up and into the Yank's soft belly, seeing a look of surprise come over the man's face. The long knife stuck in bone and the man danced wildly on the end of the rifle. Unexpectedly a bullet struck Bill in the side, grazing the skin, causing him to pull the trigger on his rifle. He saw the Yankee blown off the bayonet by the muzzle blast and heavy .54 caliber lead slug.

As he quickly reloaded, he glanced around and saw most of the men in vicious hand-to-hand combat with the blue-bellies. Seating a minié-ball, he replaced his ramrod and moved toward a Yank gunner attempting to place a new load of grapeshot in the cannon. Since the man's back was to him, he rushed forward and ran the long blade into his kidney. The Yankee screamed in pain and fell forward to the grass, dropping the bag of shot.

Turning, Bill ordered, "Ya three men, help me turn this cannon around. We'll give them Yanks a taste of their own medicine."

The four turned the cannon, Bill loaded the bag of grapeshot down the barrel, and one of the men lit the fuse on the big gun. A second later, the cannon jumped from the ground and a huge cloud of smoke covered the area. Screams of pain and anguish came from Union lines.

"Move it slightly to the left now, boys!" The general called out from behind them.

They moved the cannon, powder and shot loaded, and the gun fired. Ten minutes later, out of ammunition, the four ran forward.

Bullets zinged and pinged all around as he moved. He was afraid to stop for a second, because it would mean his death. He knew moving targets were harder to hit. Forward and onward was set in his mind, regardless of the battle or any injuries sustained.

A bullet kicked his hat high into the air, but he continued to run, pausing once to aim at a young Yankee lieutenant. When he squeezed the trigger, the man went down hard, unmoving. Reloading, he scanned the battlefield and saw the Union troops were pulling back.

"Hold yer fire! Ya damn fools, hold yer fire!" The First Sergeant screamed as he walked up and down the battlefield.

"They're runnin'!" Bill's friend James yelled as he walked beside him.

"Ya hit?" Bill asked.

"I don't think so, but ya took a hit or something along yer side."

"Ball grazed me, but it ain't much of an injury, just a light graze."

"Better have the sawbones look at it. Iffen it starts to fester, ya'll play hell gettin' it cleaned and it'll cause a lot of pain, too. Here's yer hat, I found it a ways back."

"I'll pour some whiskey on my wound and be fine."

Then taking his hat from James he said, "Thanks. A bullet knocked it off my head."

"Okay, men!" The First Sergeant called out, "Move into defensive positions and let's make this place home for the night. Sergeant Sanders!"

"First Sergeant!"

"Yer squad will pull picket duty until dark. Keep yer eyes open, 'cause the Yank's might counterattack. That's what I'd do iffen I was them."

"Okay men; let's move out about a hundred feet. I want no loud talkin', playin' grab ass, or smokin'. Iffen you want tobacco, chew."

"We always get the crap details!" A man named Patton complained as he picked up his pack and started moving forward.

"Ya got a complaint, Patton?" Bill asked as he turned to face the man.

"No, just tired is all. We been in battle three days in a row, and I'm beat."

"We all are, but we've a job to do."

With nothing more said, the men moved into positions in some hardwood trees. Sitting on a boulder, Bill glanced around and saw it was a beautiful day. The sun was shining, there was a light breeze, and flowers were even blooming.  It's too nice a day to die.

Bill Sanders was a big man, six feet and six inches, two hundred and twenty pounds, with huge muscles the result of his previous profession. He had been a blacksmith before the war and operated a very successful business, but with the battle of Wilson's Creek, his life had changed. His father had lost an arm and his older brother killed, so Bill joined the 3rd Missouri Infantry out of anger. At first, he figured he had a score to settle with the Yanks, but the thought quickly died and now he fought to stay alive. His quest for revenge died a long time ago.

Removing his hat and pushing his long brown hair back he thought, I wonder if Clara yet waits for me?

Clara Sue Wade was his bride to be and he'd left her behind to go off to war. It was over two months since the last letter, but Bill knew it was normal with the war going on. Some of the men had been in the unit for over two years and not a single letter yet. The problem, as most of the men saw it, was the army was constantly moving and delivering mail was a nightmare. Nonetheless, the lack of mail made the situation much more difficult for the men.

In her last letter, Clara had spoken of the hardships at home and struggles they had to face from day to day. Most of the men were off to war and the women had to work hard to turn a patch of rocky ground into a life-giving garden. She'd spoken of how the Yanks had ridden through and taken all the livestock they could find. Her family had lost all of their fowl, cows, pigs and half the garden to the men in blue and no amount of pleading would stop them. She'd written they were living on wild greens, deer, squirrels, and rabbits.

"We're near Pilot Knob, ain't we, Bill?" Old man Franklin asked unexpectedly from a nearby log. Franklin was near fifty-five and didn't have to be in the infantry, except the Yanks burned his farm and killed most of his family, so he remained where he was.

"Close, I think we're only about five miles from Fort Davidson."

Scratching his chin, Franklin asked, "That close?"

"Mayhap, I ain't real sure. The word I have is General Price wants us to take the place."

"I ain't real partial to attackin' no damned fort. Sounds like a good way fer a man to get his ass killed."

"Likely. It's a goat-ropin' affair too, like most of these battles. Hell, we lost twenty men today and we're likely to lose twenty times as many iffen we go against a fort."

"Well, there's enough of us to take the blame thing iffen Price wants it badly enough, only he'll pay for the fort in blood—our blood."

"We've got over 12,000 men, or so I heard, so we should be able to do the job fast enough."

"How many men do ya reckon the Yanks got?"

"I don't think a fort could hold more than a couple thousand men, but he could have some men dug in outside the walls of the place."

"Yup, I hear ya. I just wonder how many of our men have guns."

"Some of our boys ain't got guns, but I ain't sure how many. Why all the interest in battles all of a sudden?"

Lowering his head, Franklin said, "This fight today scared the hell right out of me. I thought I was a dead man and more than once."

"You've been in big battles before."

"Yep, I have at that. Only there was something about this one that got my attention. Sims was kilt running along side of me and Wilcox took a wicked saber cut to his neck. There was a feelin' I got and it petrified me. It was like I knew I was goin' to die and could do nothin' to stop it."

"But ya didn't die."

Looking up, the old man said, "Nope, but I could have."

"We all could have, but we didn't. I was scared too, and any man with half a mind was afraid, but we still did what needed doin'. Besides, you don't have to be here. All you have to do is see the Captain and you'll be sent to the rear."

"And what, be called a coward? I'm stayin' right where I am, no matter how scared I get."

"You've been in the infantry since '61, nobody will call you a coward! For God's sakes, man, get out iffen you can. I surely would."

Gazing into Bill's eyes, the man asked, "Do ya really think I should?"

Nodding his head, the Sergeant replied, "Yep, I do and the sooner the better. The feelin's you had might have been the good Lord warnin' you! Ain't no man gonna call you a coward either, not with me around. Go and do what you should have done from the start."

Standing, the old man grinned and said, "By golly, I'll do just that." Then, sticking his hand out he said, "Been nice servin' under ya, Sergeant Sanders. Iffen I don't return, ya take care of yerself and keep low in the comin' battles."

As they shook, Bill replied, "I'll do that! Now, get to the Captain and take care of this." As the old man walked away, Bill thought, I wish I could do that, but he's an old man. A man his age shouldn't even be in the army.

At dusk, First Sergeant Andy Watkins walked to Bill's side and said, "Sergeant Thornton and his men will be here to relieve ya directly. Ya know, it's too quiet and it makes me nervous. The Yanks should have counterattacked, but they didn't and that causes me to wonder why."

"Too many of us, I guess."

"Maybe, just maybe, but it ain't like 'em at all."

Bill pushed his hat back and asked, "Where do you want us to go once relieved?"

"Find ya a spot over on the left side."

There came a bright flash of lightning behind them and when they turned, thunder cracked loudly in the evening air. Bill saw dark, almost black, clouds rolling in and he knew they were in for rain.

Grinning, the First Sergeant said, "Have your men use their shelter halves and maybe they'll stay partly dry tonight."

"Most ain't got none."

"That's our supply system, out of everything! How in the hell do they expect us to fight a war, when we ain't got half the stuff we need? Check with the supply Sergeant and see if any of the shelter halves from the dead Yanks were turned in."

Bill laughed and asked, "Are you sure you want me to do that? I'm willin' to bet you right now, he ain't got a one."

Shaking his head, the First Sergeant replied, "Likely he ain't, but ask anyways. Iffen he ain't got none, hunker down under the trees."

At that point, a group of men dressed in gray and butternut entered the woods, and Bill heard Sergeant Thornton say, "Y'all can get back to camp now, we're your relief."

Walking to Thornton, Bill said, "Glad to see you made it through the battle!"

"She was a rough one, I'll tell ya that much."

Turning, Bill spoke to his men, "Move back boys, and let's call it a night."

Returning to the First Sergeant, Bill asked, "Ya goin' back with us?"

"Nope, I'm gonna stay out here fer a spell. I'll be in later."

The full darkness made walking through the woods slow, as each man tried to avoid roots, rocks and fallen limbs. More than once Bill heard a man fall and then break out cursing.

Too early for a moon and with this rain comin' there won't be one tonight, he thought stepping over a large log.

The camp had hundreds of small fires and from the dark woods, they looked like fireflies in the blackness of night. Breaking from the forest, Bill told Corporal Jenkins to see to the men, while he tried to find some supplies.

He found the supply Sergeant, a thin man named Moss, in front of a large tent handing out the evening rations. From what Bill could see, the meal consisted of about three ounces of hog jowl, half a cup of corn meal, even less coffee. The coffee, thanks to the union blockade, wasn't real and was made from a mixture of acorns and chicory.

Seeing Bill approach, Most called out, "Hey, Bill, I see ya survived the earlier battle!"

"That I did, but it was touch and go for a while there."

Having a man take his place on the serving line, Moss walked to Bill and asked, "What brings ya heah?"

"The Sergeant Major sent me over to see if you have any shelter-halves from the Yanks that died today."

"Nary a one, so I 'spect the men on the line kept what they needed. Hell, I didn't even get a pair of boots or a hat. Times are rough for the South, ole son, and it ain't lookin' no better tomorrow either.

Ya might as well take your supper rations while your heah."

Looking down at the meager meal, Bill said, "I can see times are gettin' rough by my supper rations. You know, I can remember when we had some decent pork, beans, and even baked bread with our meals. But, hell, I ain't seen that in over two years."

Shaking his head as he wiped his hands on a dirty cloth, Moss replied, "Ya'll never see them days again. We're 'bout beat is my thoughts on this war."

"There's still some fight in us, but not for long. We can fight without some things, but food, bullets and powder ain't one of them.

"Sergeant Sanders!" A voice called out in the darkness.

"Over here, on the left side of the serving line."

Captain Fall neared and said, "Private Franklin will not be rejoinin' your squad. Due to his age, he's been assigned duties other than fightin'."

Bill laughed, pulled off his hat, and replied "Suh, that's fine. He did one hell of a job for a couple of years there."

Fall, his white teeth showing in the pale moonlight as he smiled, said, "Well, his fightin' days are over, unless the brown stuff hits the stump. In the mornin', I want your men to lead the company as we move forward."

"Where we headin'?" Moss asked, hoping to get a hint at least.

"I can only tell you that we're moving toward Fort Davidson."

"We gonna take that place?" A Corporal moving through the chow line asked.

Shrugging, Fall replied, "I don't even know if that's our intended objective."

"I'll tell you what, for the 25th of September, it's goin' to be a wet one!" Bill said, and then put his hat back on.

Fall, lowering his voice, said, "We're going right through Pilot Knob and the Arcadia valley, rain or no rain, and our scouts say the place is just swarmin' with Yankees."

"Well, suh," Bill said with a frown, "if that's the case, I'd better get back to my men and send them to the chow line. They'll need time to cook and get a good night's rest iffen there's a battle tomorrow."

"Yes, that would be smart. Remember, I want you in front in the morning."

"Yes, suh, we'll be there," Bill replied and then started walking back to his squad.

When he neared camp, he called out, "Corporal Jenkins, get the men to the chow line and do 'er now!"

"I was just goin' to do that. What's up?"

"There ain't much grub and if we want to eat, we need to get there now before it's all gone. I got mine, but it ain't much. I'll tell you what's goin' on directly."

"Y'all heard the man! Get your rations and then get your asses back here, I don't want to have to come after none of ya."

When the men had left, Bill moved to a fire he shared with Jenkins, and pulled a small cast iron skillet from his pack. Placing the skillet on a few coals, he dropped the meat into the pan, and then leaned back to listen to it sizzle as it fried. A few minutes later, he sat up and turned the meat with the tip of his pocketknife.

The night was warm, but between lightning strikes, he could see dark clouds overhead, and there wasn't a hint of a breeze. Last night, brilliant stars had sparkled like diamonds in the black sky, but he suspected tomorrow would be a wet day. He was growing tired of war, as well as the army, but he wasn't the kind of man to desert. He'd sworn an oath to the South when he joined and to Bill Sanders, his word was binding. Either he would see this all the way through or he'd die fighting for a cause everyone knew was already lost.

I wonder if Clara has waited for me as she promised. The way things are going in this war, she might not even be alive. I wish she'd write, so I'd know more about what's goin' on and that she's safe. Well, my meats done, maybe eatin' will take my mind off home.

Pulling his meat from the pan with the tip of his knife blade, he stirred the cornmeal in the grease and watched it cook. As it bubbled in the hot oil, Bill finished his pork in two bites. After a few minutes, he removed the pan from the fire and spooned the blistering hot cornmeal into his mouth. His supper soon finished, he placed his Southern coffee in a tin cup and placed it near the fire to boil, knowing he'd not drink it all. The South had tried many substitutes for real coffee and in Bill's opinion, none of them were worth a damn.

The men began to return and each complained about poor rations.

James shook his head and said, "Poor doin's fer a man's supper. I do declare my hogs back home ate more than I'm gettin' these days."

Corporal Jenkins laughed, dropped his meat into his skillet, and then in a serious tone said, "Yup, it's a shame we wasn't kept back followin' the battle, or we could have gone through some Yankee packs. They've always got food on 'em."

Isaac Mossland, a new Private from Mississippi, gave a weak smile and asked, "Is our food always this bad?" Then suddenly dropping his meat, he added, "Good God, there's worms in the hog jowl!"

"Usually is," Bill said with a flat voice.

Gazing into Bill's eyes, Isaac replied, "I ain't eatin' that! Good God, that's stuff I'd not feed a dog!"

Jenkins laughed again and said, "Y'all be eatin' it within a week! There ain't nothin' else to eat, son, unless ya take it from a dead Yank."

"That's what I'll do, then. No wonder y'all are so thin and look like hell warmed over, it's the food!"

Smiling, Bill replied, "Food, little shelter from the weather, marchin' all the time, and little rest."

"I weighed two hundred pounds when I joined the army," James said, "and now I'm down pretty close to a hundred and twenty." He reached over and turned his meat with a roughcast pewter fork.

A bright flash of lightning reached across the sky, breaking into numerous long white fingers as if searching the black horizon. It lit up the countryside. A sharp crack of thunder sounded and rain began to fall harder, soaking the men in seconds.

"Move up under some of the bigger trees!" Bill ordered as he picked up his cup and began to walk toward a large pine.

"It won't do no good, I'm as wet as a big ole catfish!" James yelled out and then laughed.

"Cut the chatter and keep yer voices low!" Jenkins commanded as he made his way to a big oak tree.

Sitting near Bill, Isaac asked, "I guess we aint' got no dry clothes, do we?"

"Son, the only clothes owned by the whole glorious Southern army are bein' worn right now."

"Damn it! Why didn't people tell me things were this bad!"

"Would you have stayed home then?" Bill asked, interested in the young man's response.

A couple of minutes of silence followed, as Isaac gave the question some thought, and then in a voice just above a whisper he said, "No, I would have joined anyway."

"I figured as much.

# CHAPTER 2

**M**orning came without rain, although it still dripped from trees and the ground was muddy. The air was chilly but not overly cold, as the men awoke and did their morning toilets. Fires began to burn; men coughed, and started cooking what little breakfast there was. The ration issued for breakfast was the same as for the supper meal, only less.

Isaac said nothing as he threw his meat in a skillet and placed it on a bed of red coals. He knew the complaining would accomplish little, except to have the men label him a squawker and he didn't want that.

Returning from the woods, where he'd made water, Bill was approached by the First Sergeant, "Sanders, get your men up and movin' toward Ironton. You're to walk right into the place iffen ya can."

"What if we meet a large force?"

"Hold and wait. We'll not be far behind ya, and we'll rush forward iffen ya run into anything ya cain't handle on your own."

"Okay, men, you heard the First Sergeant! Let's move!" Bill called out as he put his pack on, adjusted his belt, and picked up his rifle. Watching his men don their gear, he waited until they were ready and then moved north.

As they walked, Bill ordered, "Andrews, you move forward about two hundred feet and Higgins, you bring up the rear. Keep your distance about the same as Andrews, two hundred feet."

The two men moved to their assigned positions and as Bill glanced around, he saw his men were ready. Unlike some squads, his had weapons and ammunition, so they'd not have to kill Yanks to get supplies. Some of the units walked into battle with nothing, taking weapons they needed from the dead of both sides.

They were walking on a road pointing north, and Bill suspected it lead to the small town. It was badly rutted by wagon wheels and muddy, so most of the men walked beside it; the potholes and ruts were filled with water. None of the men had any desire to be anymore wet than they already were, because the overnight rain had drenched them.

The sun looks to be comin' out, Bill thought, and then said, "Spread out some, you're all too close together."

Isaac was growing scared; this was his first full day with the unit, and already they were walking into battle. He reached inside his coat pocket and pulled out a deck of cards, along with a half-pint of whiskey. He raised the drink and emptied the whiskey bottle, and then threw both into the woods along the road. He didn't want to walk onto a battlefield with sinful things on his person.

He lowered his head and prayed, "Lord, I ain't much of a man and I guess I ain't never really tried to follow your Word. I'm askin' you to forgive my sins as I march into battle and pray ya'll hear my plea. I won't make any promises to you that I know I won't keep, how-some-ever, I will try to be a better man and read the Good Book a little each day. I ask you, God, to protect me in the comin' fight. This I ask in the name of Jesus, amen."

"What are you doin' over there, Isaac, prayin'?" James asked as he met the younger man's eyes.

"Yup, I figured it can't hurt none."

"It don't, but I ain't so sure it helps much either. Oh, I pray before every fight, only I've seen others pray and still get killed in horrible ways."

"It was their time to die," Jenkins ejected.

"Maybe or maybe not, I ain't sure about religion at times."

One of the old timers, a man named Kelly, said, "Two things I never talk about, God and politics. Ain't no two men agree about neither one very often. But, by golly, I do believe in the good Lord and what happens is all his doin's."

"Amen, brother!" Private Wicks offered his two cents to the conversation.

When Bill looked at the man, he appeared completely serious and for as long as he'd known Wicks, he'd never spoken much. Funny how you can spend years with a feller and hardly know 'em, while another man you might know better than anyone in the world in one night. Wicks ain't much of a talker anyway, so it's hard to get to know the man.

They walked for almost four miles, when Bill saw Andrews running toward him and then heard the sound of rifle shots. The running man spun and fell, got up and started running again.

"Yanks!" Andrews yelled and fell once more.

"Move forward to Andrews, and then get into defensive positions!" Bill commanded as he started to run to the man.

At that point, four blue uniforms broke through the trees, hesitated a few seconds and then fired. Kelly let out a loud scream, fell to his knees, but stood almost immediately.

"Fire!" Bill yelled and instantly the morning stillness was shattered by the sound of eight rifles. Two of the Yanks fell immediately, but instead of stopping to help or fight, the other two turn turned and ran.

"Let's all move forward and check them shot Yanks, but Kelly, you stay here and look after Andrews. Iffen you can, doctor you both up."

"I'm not hit hard, grazed my arm."

Bill nodded and then said, "Come on, let's check those men out."

Both of the Yankees were dead, and Bill allowed his men to strip them of anything they wanted.

Some took food, others ammunition, while a couple took shoes. Each man took what he felt he needed the most, but all got a little something.

Holding up a big piece of salted beef, Jenkins said, "Well, I never cared much for salted beef, but this will go down nicely tonight!"

"If you live," Private Mays commented as he placed the balls and powder he'd taken in his knapsack.

"Hurry up and let's get movin' again. Y'all know them blue bellies will report our little fight." Bill was growing impatient.

Walking back to Andrews, they discovered he'd taken a ball through the fleshy part of his shoulder, a few close nicks, and would be going to see the doctor, instead of attacking Yankees.

Bill scanned the area and said, "Kelly, you take Andrews back, and while you're there have the sawbones look you over, too. Iffen you're able, try to rejoin us."

"I'll do that, only Sergeant, I think we just ran into a small picket line. There's a passel of Yanks ahead, so keep your butt down."

Shaking the man's hand, he said, "Get movin' and get Andrews back, like I said."

When the two hobbled off, Bill led his men down the road, knowing good and well a battle waited at Ironton.

Less than a mile later, they saw a sign for the small town, and came under immense fire from a large group of Yankees. The men in blue had waited patiently for Bill's squad to move in close and then fired a barrage, killing Private Wicks and wounding three others, including Corporal Jenkins.

"Fall back!" Bill yelled as he turned and ran for the safety of the wood line behind him.

Kneeling and looking from behind a big oak, Bill saw the dead Wicks and Private Parker near the union lines.

"Why wasn't Parker brought back?"

The bleeding Jenkins replied, "Too close! He was too close to those damned Yanks is why!"

"Anybody see how badly he was hit?"

Private Mays, who'd been with the squad since the war started, said, "He's gut shot. Ain't no use to risk a feller's life to save a man hit like that. He'll die no matter what we do."

"How bad were you hit?" Bill asked.

"Took some lead in the fleshy part of my thigh. It hurts like hell, except I'll live."

Turning to look at Jenkins, he asked, "And, you?"

"Left forearm was hit solid and I think my fightin' days are over."

"Break the bone?"

"Yup . . . and with . . . your okay, I'll head . . . back to . . . see the doc." Jenkins managed to get out.

"Take Mays and tell the First Sergeant I'm runnin' low on men up here. Let 'em know I got one dead and four wounded."

Standing, Jenkins had Mays slip his arm around his neck and like two lovers, they moved toward the rear.

James said, "They're lucky in some ways. If the bullet hit the bone in the Corporal's arm, it'll come off and he'll go home. Mays will have to heal, and with a thigh wound, it will take a good month or more."

Bill met his eyes and said, "They could both get festered and be dead in less than a week. No, I don't think they're lucky by a long stretch."

Hearing movement behind him, Bill turned to see Higgins running for the small group. When he neared he said, "First Sergeant said for ya to wait up, he's got a bunch of men comin' up to take care of these Yanks."

"That all he said?"

"Said fer me to stay with y'all 'til he gets heah."

"Dig in, boys, and let's wait for the First Sergeant."

Less than ten minutes later, First Sergeant Watkins walked into the trees and asked, "Where's all them Yanks?"

Pointing with his right hand, Bill said, "In that next grow of oaks, right in front of those two men of mine."

"How many do ya reckon are in there?"

"I guess two or three squads, but too many for me and mine to take on."

Turning his head, Watkins yelled out, "Fix bayonets!"

When the clinking of metal on metal ceased, he said, "Men, we're gonna take that clump of woods in front of us. When I give the order y'all charge the tree line."

Shaking Bills hand, Watkins said, "You and your boys stay here, ya've done enough for a spell. Once we clear this nest of blue birds out, you drop back behind us. We're only a mile or less from Ironton right now and there will be a big group of Yankees there."

"Good luck, Andy."

"You, too."

Standing and checking his rifle, First Sergeant Watkins looked around and then yelled, "Charge!"

Bill watched as over a hundred Confederates, dressed in gray or butternut, ran from the woods toward the Yankee lines. Sunlight flashed from their long bayonets and loud rebel screams filled the air. Shots started coming from the Union lines instantly and Southerners began to fall. Smoke filled the small meadow between the lines and for many long minutes, no one could tell what was happening.

Hearing loud shouts of joy coming from the men Watkins had led to the trees; Bill knew the Yanks had been over-run or retreated. There still came an occasional pop as someone fired a rifle across the way. Then, there came a loud silence.

"Move forward men, but watch for any playin' 'possum or sharpshooters!" Bill ordered as he stepped from the trees.

The small group made their way over the field to the wood line to find the Yankees had broken and run. There were six dead men dressed in blue and four rebels. Watkins was sitting on a log when Bill neared. The Southerners were going through the packs and clothing of the dead men, taking what they needed.

"What now?" Bill asked.

"Like I said, you fall in behind us and we continue to the town."

"How come you're leadin' this group? Where's Captain Fall?"

"A sharpshooter shot 'em jus' before we left and seriously injured the man. Hit 'em in the chest and iffen he survives he's the lucky one! Colonel Hicks sent me in his stead."

"I hope the man lives, he's a good officer."

The First Sergeant shrugged his shoulders and said, "I have a hard enough time keepin' me alive to worry about someone else. I've grown cold toward death and while I don't want to die, I don't fear it. Now, let's get movin'."

They ran into snipers and small groups of Yanks all the way to the town of Ironton, which made the trip a slow one. Watkins complained each time they had to stop and clear out a small bunch of Yanks, but there was no other way to do the job.

On the outskirts of the town, Bill moved forward and asked, "How do you want to do this?"

"Hell, I ain't never took a town before. I guess we'll have to kick in every door and clear the houses."

"That's just what I was thinkin' too. Be slow, only I don't see any other way to do the job."

"Well, let's get this show on the road. John! Take your squad on the left side of the street and check every single house! Frank, you do just like him, except you take the right side. I don't want any civilians hurt, if it can be helped, but take no chances."

As the two squads broke from the main group, Bill heard one of the men saying the 23rd Psalms as he moved forward. Suddenly, hearing horses behind them, the First Sergeant turned his head, and then called out, "Steady men, those horse soldiers are ours!"

Walking to the commander of the cavalry unit, Watkins saluted and said, "Well, iffen it ain't Colonel Jefferson! How in the hell are ya, suh?"

"I'm doin' right fine, First Sergeant. What's goin' on here?" A portly Colonel with a long yellow plume sticking out on one side of his hat asked.

"Clearin' a town, but me and my boys ain't never done it before. I ain't real sure how the jobs done, either. We plan on clearing each house, one by one."

"That's the only way it can be done as far as I know, shy of burning the place down. Since this is part of 'Little Dixie' I don't think that would be such a good idea."

Private James Waterman, who was standing near, laughed and said, "Ya'd have a handful of pissed-off Southerners on your hands then, First Sergeant!"

"Waterman, get back to your position, and do 'er now!" Watkins ordered, shook his head and asked, "What can I do for ya, suh?"

"It's what I can do for you. My unit has been order to spearhead this advance to Fort Davidson and clear out any major resistance we find. So me and my men will ride through the streets in this town and see if the Yanks have really left. If any are still around we're sure to take a few shots."

"Well, that's all fine and dandy, but iffen they're holed up good we'll never get 'em out."

"Sure we will, because I have a small cannon along, and while I don't like the idea of destroying Southern property, I'll do it to save lives."

Gesturing toward the town with his hand, Watkins said, "Have at it, suh."

Turning in his saddle the Colonel commanded, "Columns of two! Fo'ard at a walk! Ho!"

The horse soldiers entered the town and were soon lost to sight. Bringing up the rear was a small cannon mounted on a caisson.

A little later, shots erupted, followed by yells and finally the sound of a cannon firing. The waiting Confederate soldiers gave loud yells and threw their hats into the air. The rifle fire intensified and the cannon fired once again before it grew silent. Suddenly, there was heard a loud explosion, followed by screams and then more gunfire. Bill watched as his two squads pulled back from the houses and moved toward the horse soldiers at a run. A few second later, they entered a side street and were lost from view.

Watkins waited ten minutes and during that time, the firing never slowed. Finally, he stood and ordered, "Every man of you, listen to me. It sounds like the Colonel bit off more than he can chew, so we're goin' to go and help 'em out. At a run now boys, let's go!"

The men ran into the small street and as they moved, Bill hoped any civilians would have the sense to stay away from windows. It was then a small girl waved from an upper window and a shot rang out. The wood beside her head splintered and Bill watched as a woman quickly pulled the child from the opening.

"That was a kid! Damn it; confirm your targets before you shoot! I want no innocents killed! Is that clearly understood?" Watkins snapped in a loud voice.

A loud, 'understood!' echoed among the rough pine structures as the men responded. Each carried his rifle at the ready, knowing just around the corner the Colonel and his men had met a large force of Yanks.

As they ran, James moved beside Bill and asked, "Why hasn't that cannon fired?"

"Destroyed or put out of action, I'd guess."

"I don't know of anything except other cannon that could do that."

"The Yankees use grenades now and they allow a man to throw an explosive. They're a small bomb with a fuse."

"Hell, sounds like a big firecracker to me."

"Kind of, except when they explode the metal case the powder is in blows out in all directions, killing men or destroying equipment. When it explodes, it breaks into little pieces and becomes deadly."

They rounded the corner and in the street were bodies, most of which wore gray, and Bill saw the Colonel was laying flat behind his dead horse shooting at a brick house. Only a couple of horses stood and less than a handful were down, which meant most ran away when the firing started. Watkins looked the situation over and said, "Second and third squads, I want you to flank that house and take the pressure off of the Colonel. Fourth squad, you start firing at the windows in the place and don't let up until I give the order. Now move!"

The rest of the unit ran forward and dropped to the ground near the Colonel. A bullet struck cobblestone inches from Bill's head, making a loud zinging as it ricocheted into the air, so he moved to the left where the body of a big bay mare lay. It was then the squad started firing at the house and windows shattered, shutters splintered, and pockmarks appeared in the bricks. Screams of pain came from within the small structure and one man ran out the front door, only to fall in seconds. He'd taken three bullets to his chest and was dead before he struck the ground.

Suspecting his flankers had broken into the house, Watkins yelled, "Cease fire! Cease fire!" The shots slowed and then finally stopped.

Then a rebel kepi on a bayonet appeared from a front window. All of the men in the street creased firing when a Southern voice call out from the building, "It's all clear in heah!"

Colonel Jefferson stood on weak legs and ordered, "I want the two squad leaders from the house to report to me."

Watkins and Bill moved to stand beside the Colonel as two men, barely out of their teens, walked from the building. Saluting the Colonel, one of the squad leaders said, "We killed what we could, but some skedaddled out the back door. Of course, ya'll saw the fool who went out the front door. I have our men gathering up the grenades they had, and I think we can use them to our advantage at some point today. We're also gatherin' up supplies, but there won't be much, they didn't have no packs."

Looking at Watkins, the Colonel said, "I suggest you save the grenades. General Price wants to take Fort Davidson, so they'll come in handy if we attack the place."

"Yes, suh, I agree with ya." The young squad leader replied, and then wiped his wet face with a soiled cloth.

Turning, Watkins yelled out, "Let's get wounded treated, from both sides, and continue on our march. Those too badly hurt to walk will have to make their way to the rear as best they can, or wait for the army to catch up. Sergeant Gilmore, I want a tally of the dead and wounded from both sides."

"Will do, Sergeant Major!"

At that point a runner moved to the Colonel, saluted and said, "Big battle just finished on the courthouse lawn, with the Yanks withdrawin' toward the fort. We have heavy losses, many more than the Yanks."

"But the courthouse is in our hands?"

"Yes, suh."

"Good, very good."

Bill turned to the dispatch runner and asked, "How many is heavy losses?"

Lowering his head, the man said, "Over forty killed and another fifty wounded. The yard in front of the courthouse looks like a butcher shop. They're still lookin' fer Yanks when I left, but I think they lost about a half-dozen men."

"Suh," Sergeant Gilmore said with a salute, "the Yanks left three dead and one wounded. Our dead count is fifteen, with twenty wounded. Of our wounded, two are not expected to live."

"Send them to the rear with your squad goin' along as an escort. Once they're at the hospital, I want you to come directly back. Is that understood?"

"Yes, suh."

Placing his hands on his hips, Colonel Jefferson surveyed the carnage, and then said, "All of you horse soldiers round up your mounts. First Sergeant, prepare your men to march, because General Price has a very strict timetable for this attack. All four large units must be in place no later than dawn. The attack on Fort Davidson will start at sunrise tomorrow."

"Then we are to continue down Arcadia valley?" Watkins asked.

"No, I want ya and your men to circle north around the fort and destroy as much of the railroad as possible. You will make a force march, First Sergeant, and reach the rail line before the end of the day. Once there, rip up all the tracks you can find and burn anything that will catch fire. Your mission is essential to keep reinforcements from arriving at the fort from Saint Louis. Your job is not to go against the fort, but destroy the rail lines. If possible, take out at least a mile of rail."

"Suh, destroying that much line will take time. How long do you think the fort will hold out?"

Shaking his head, Jefferson replied, "Hard to say. They've some big cannon and we have no idea how many men. You just keep ripping line until you get different orders."

Snapping to attention, Watkins saluted and then called out, "Company C, form on me!"

# CHAPTER 3

**The** men formed and were soon moving north by east, and once well above the fort they'd head due east. The men were in a good mood, knowing they'd not be involved in the direct assault on the fort, only Bill wondered what awaited them. It was very unlikely the Union would leave the railroad unprotected, knowing it was their lifeline to the city of Saint Louis, and their only source of supply. He had ill feelings about the mission and so far, his feelings were always right.

James walked up beside him and asked, "What's goin' on in your mind?"

"I suspect this railroad work won't be as easy as it sounds. Seems to me it will be well protected."

"Likely, and I've given that some thought, too."

"The way I figure, iffen there are thousands of men at the fort, there will be a whole bushel-basket full of 'em near the tracks. Hell, that's the only way they can keep fightin' when the stuff hits the stump. That rail line can bring 'em supplies and more men iffen they need 'em."

"Do ya think Watkins has thought of all of this?"

"Sure, but we have our orders and there ain't a hell of a lot we can do, except follow 'em."

Silence followed and after a few minutes, James moved back to his spot in line. While the men were moving quickly, Bill wasn't sure how far the railroad was from Ironton. From what he'd seen on an old map and been told, the rail ended at Pilot Knob, but another brigade was attacking the town. If the attacking unit could take the town and then send another small unit north to rip up the rails, then things might go well. The maps the Confederates had of the area were over twenty years old, so many of the important places they were to attack or control weren't even shown accurately, like the railroad. Bill saw this mission as a good chance for him and his men to end up dead.

After walking for three hours, Watkins sent two men forward to find the railroad. The rest moved under cover of an oak forest to wait for the scouts to return. Most of the men catnapped, but a few nibbled on moldy cornbread or pieces of raw salt pork. Bill double checked his gear, ate a small piece of hardtack, and went to sleep.

Two hours later, the two men returned hot and tired, but they'd found the intended target and it was less than an hour away. Watkins and Bill had been sitting together talking about life before the war when the two scouts entered the woods.

"We didn't see no Yanks, except that don't mean there ain't none."

"Did ya walk up or down it a ways?" Watkins asked.

"Not on the tracks, but yep, we went up and down 'bout a mile. We didn't even see no footprints in the dirt around them tracks."

"Okay, on the way to the tracks we'll have a group of about ten men in front of us. If the way is clear, and it sounds like it might be, once at the tracks those ten will provide security for the rest of us as we do our damage."

"Sounds like a good way to do the job," Bill added, and realized Watkins was worried, too.

"This is almost too easy, and it makes me wonder why," James suddenly stated.

"Could be the Yanks ain't got as many men as we think they do. They might have pulled 'em all back to help defend the fort." Watkins was deep in thought.

"Well, it don't matter much, the way I see it." Bill said and then continued with, "We still have a job to do, so I suggest we get on it."

Standing, Watkins replied, "You're right. Men, let's go, we have a date with the devil and he's wearin' Yankee blue."

Isaac, who'd been quiet most of the day, walked to Bill and asked, "What if the Yanks are waiting for us?"

"Men will die on both sides then."

"And iffen they ain't waitin'?"

"We'll destroy every inch of track we can get our hands on."

Strange way to fight a war, don't you think?"

"Since this is my first war, I ain't real sure. Now, let's stop talkin' and start walkin'. We've got a railroad to destroy."

When they arrived at the tracks, all was quiet. Watkins immediately designated men to pull the rails, to burn ties, and others to guard working groups. On arrival, Bill had seen a small shed beside the tracks and inside they found all the tools needed to repair or destroy the railroad. The men started to work almost instantly.

By midnight, they'd torn up a good quarter mile of track, but they'd discovered the work was slow and time consuming at best. More than one man had injured his back prying the spikes from the ties, and it took the strongest of men to do the job. Then the rails were extremely heavy, and the ties were difficult to dig from the gravel and dirt holding them in place.

"We'll work for another hour, quit for the night and then start up again at dawn," Watkins said as he wiped sweat from his forehead.

A Private who'd had been down the rails about a mile ran to the First Sergeant and reported, "I got Yanks movin' this a ways, only it's too dark for me to say how many."

"They must have heard the rails being moved." A man Bill didn't know stated.

"What's that?" Watkins asked.

"I worked fer the railroad in Mississippi most of my life and iffen ya put yer ear to a rail, ya can hear a train a-comin' or a man workin' on 'em. The sound carries up and down the steel rails a long ways."

Bill moved toward the man and asked, "So our work could be heard iffen the Yanks had a man with his head to the rail?"

"As clear as a bell ringin', but they could've seen the light from the burnin' ties, too."

"Damn!" Watkins said. A few seconds later the First Sergeant added, "Okay, it ain't likely the Yanks will attack tonight.

They're liable to end up a-shootin' each other instead of us. How-some-ever, I expect 'em to hit us at first light, except we'll be ready fer 'em. I want half the men in the woods on the left of the tracks and the rest in the woods on the north side. Think of this as a big 'L' and you'll understand my idea. When we open fire in the morning, do not shoot any direction except straight ahead, or ya'll hit our men. I think one volley will greatly discourage our Yankee friends."

"Do we sleep first and move just before daylight?" Bill asked.

"No, I want all of the men to move to their ambush positions before they sleep. I want two squads at each of the lines in my 'L' and they can move into place right now. No talking, smoking, or noise until this is over, and for God's sakes, no fires."

"Iffen we work this right, there'll be a lot of dead Yanks come daylight!" Bill said with a smile.

"And, iffen things go to hell; we might all be the dead men. It won't work unless we gain total surprise and I want y'all to remember that. Now move!"

The remainder of the night passed slowly, as some men slept and some stood guard, while others couldn't sleep because they knew a battle would start with the birth of a new day. Bill slept for a while but awoke after a few hours. He pulled a plug of chewing tobacco from his pack and cut off a long piece. As he worked his chew, he thought of life up to this point and finally reached the conclusion he was no better off now than when he was a kid. He owned no land, owned no home, and his future looked bleak. Even if he survived the coming fights, what did he have, except Clara? Besides, if the South lost the war, the north was sure to strip the land and punish the men who'd fought against them. Only the

South was his home, and he didn't like the idea of running someplace else to live. He'd grown comfortable with the slow pace, even slower speech, and the Southern way of life, but what if he had to move?

He felt James elbow him in the side. When he glanced up, he saw it was dawn, the sun was rising, and there was movement on the railroad. He watched as the first Yankees materialized from a thick fog hanging like a veil over the land. He stopped counting when he reached twenty and still they came—right down the railroad tracks. Although the morning air was cool, he felt a trickle of sweat run down his spine and knew it was the sweat of fright.

When the head of the Union soldiers was but a few feet from him Sergeant Major Watkins yelled, "Fire!" A little less than a hundred rifles fired into the Union men and they fell like rag dolls, many of them to never stand again.

"Charge!" came the next command as boys in gray and butternut stood and ran toward the boys in blue, their long bayonets sinister in the early morning sunlight. Bill ran forward and as he left the cover of the brush and trees, a Yankee Sergeant Major moved for him. The man in blue must have expected the bayonet attack, because when Bill fired his rifle the man dropped to his knees with a look of confusion in his eyes. Keeping his eyes on the Sergeant as he quickly reloaded, he saw the man arch his back, giving a bloodcurdling scream and then fall forward. A rebel soldier stood behind him holding a rifle, the bayonet dripping fresh blood.

Bill recognized the rebel immediately; it was Isaac and he had a dazed look in his eyes. However, the young man lunged forward once more and the Yankee Sergeant gave his last scream.

Running to Isaac, Bill said, "Move, keep moving! If you stand still too long you'll become a target!"

"I killed! I have broken the ten commandments!"

"Look, they even had Christian soldiers in the bible, and we ain't no different than they were! Now move or you'll be the next to die!"

A burly looking redhead in blue moved toward Bill, raised his rifle and pulled the trigger, but nothing happened—a misfire! Screaming a loud rebel yell, he ran right for the man in blue and shuddered when his long knife struck the man in the chest and exited his back. The Yank grabbed the barrel of the rifle with both hands as he screamed. Raising his right boot, Bill had to kick the man twice before he finally slid down the long blade and landed on the gravel of the railroad. Looking around, he saw First Sergeant Watkins swing his rifle like a club, taking a lieutenant in the head. The man's head crushed and he fell to the ground twitching in his death throes. Out of nowhere, a Yank officer ran behind Watkins and ran him through with a saber. Bill was fascinated to see the bloody tip of the saber appear from the First Sergeant's chest like a magic act. Watkins threw his head back, screamed in pain, and then fell to the gravel. Bill quickly placed a new cap on the nipple of his rifle, sighted the Yank officer in, and squeezed the trigger. The man dropped instantly, struck in the chest.

Reloading as fast as he could, he had just finished when the Union color guard appeared from the fog. Lifting his rifle, Bill sighted in on the man carrying the stars and stripes, and pulled the trigger with a jerk. He saw the flag, with the man carrying it, drop to the ground and another man behind fall as well. Screaming loudly, Bill charged the remaining members of the color guard, only to see them run from the battlefield. In a matter of seconds, the remaining Yanks were right behind them, running as fast as they could. It was then he felt an almost unbearable pain in his back and turning his head, he saw a young drummer boy holding a bloody sword. Without a second of thought, Bill spun around and drove his bayonet through the young lad's body. It was after the boy fell screaming to the ground that he realized what he'd done —killed a child!

Bill, unable to remain standing, fell to his knees and then toppled over on his left side. His vision became blurred and after a few seconds, his world became gray, and then slowly turned black.

The next sound he heard was of metal striking metal. While he could not open his eyes, he knew by the smell alone he was in a hospital. He felt no pain or fear, and it was as if it was all happening in a dream.

It was then he heard a male voice, "Sergeant Sanders, can you hear me?"

He tried to answer, but his muscles refused to obey his mind, so he gave a slight nod.

"Good. You've taken what looks to be two bayonet injuries; one is very close to your kidney, and the other is in your left thigh. Additionally, you've taken a bullet to the skull, and we have no way of knowing the damage done there. It didn't shatter or break your skull, but as you know, it will be weeks before we will know the outcome."

The voice continued to speak but after a few more seconds the world turned black once more and Bill entered unconsciousness.

When he next came to, he was in a hospital tent, and he had no memory of the battle or of the doctor speaking to him. As he thought, he couldn't remember his name, where he was, or nothing of his past. When he asked for water, he heard his slurred speech and a slowness that had not been there before. An orderly handed him a dipper of water and after drinking, he fell asleep.

It was night when a doctor came to visit and he asked questions that Bill could not answer. He was unable to name his unit, the commander, his own name, or even from which state he'd enlisted. He could almost name them, but then the names disappeared in the fog of his mind.

"Sergeant Sanders, I'm afraid you'll be of little use to the Confederacy in the future. Your head wound is the cause of it and I don't think your memory will ever return, not completely."

Bill looked at the doctor with tears in his eyes and said, "Give . . . me . . . time."

"Understand, with time it usually gets progressively worse. No, I'm recommending you for an immediate discharge. Your war is over."

"When?"

"As soon as your other injuries heal, you'll be released to go back home, to Missouri."

"I . . . live . . . there?"

"That's where you enlisted, so you must live there."

"Will . . . my . . .family . . . be . . .notified?"

"Yes, a telegraph will be sent to the sheriff in Rolla and he'll contact your folks. You're a very lucky man, you survived, while many others died."

"I . . . have . . . pain."

"I'll have the orderly bring you a bottle of whiskey, that's the best I can do for you."

Days turned into weeks, until almost a month after he'd been injured the doctor visited once more. Kneeling beside Bill's cot, he said, "You're leavin' in the mornin'. I've a map here for you and some food for the trip back. It's a little over a hundred miles, but it shouldn't take take over a week to return home. I suggest you go to the sheriff in Rolla and have him take you home."

"Rol-la . . . right?"

"Yep, Rolla. I have written it on the map and circled it."

"Okay. Looks like I ain't got much choice."

"One more thing you should be aware of. Since you've been here, you've had four seizures. That means, Sergeant, something inside your head is injured. You could have another one at any time or not have anymore the rest of your life. But, expect more, so use caution crossing rivers, streams, or when around a campfire. You'll likely fall to the ground, and if it happens at the wrong place you could be injured or killed."

"Will . . . I . . . have gun?"

Shaking his head, the doctor explained, "Your gun is needed here, where the fightin' is goin' on. I don't think you'll need one anyway, because your discharge papers say you've a serious head injury."

Bill had been hiding some of his whiskey and after the doctor left, he downed about half a quart and fell asleep. He awoke once or twice, but after taking a long pull from the bottle he fell back to sleep.

Morning came with clear skies and a cool wind from the west. Though his leg was stiff and his head ached, he knew it was time to leave. Putting his old pack on his back, he stepped away from the hospital grounds, and started walking north. He had no urge to look back.

As he walked, the going was slow because of his leg injury. He discovered he tired quickly and had to take frequent rests. However, he was in no hurry, his war was over and all he had to do now was survive the trip home. Bill had no disillusions, he was moving through dangerous countryside and if the Yankees didn't kill him, partisans could. He knew his best bet was to trust no one until he reached Rolla.

When he stopped for his noon meal, he remembered a Yankee pistol he had in the bottom of his pack, and soon had it stuck in his belt. The box of bullets he placed in his coat pocket for easy access. He fried one small piece of pork and nibbled on a slab of cornbread, realizing he didn't have enough food to get him home. He'd have to forage at some point on the trip.

Wiping his skillet down with a dirty cloth, he placed it back in his pack, and then started walking again. He was impatient to get home, but he couldn't remember what it looked like, who lived there, or why he was in such a rush.

He covered mile after mile until darkness came, and then he moved a hundred feet from the road to make camp. His fire was small, about the size of a coffee cup. He then unrolled his blanket and sat by the fire. Pulling out his skillet and pork, he soon had supper on the fire. Hearing horses on the road, he pulled his meat from the fire and moved into the darkness.

"Fire on the left side of the road!" A voice spoke from the roadway.

"Patterson, Wilcox, and O'Brien, check it out!" Another voice ordered. Three riders broke from the main group and rode to Bill's fire.

From the darkness, Bill could see they were Confederates, so he stood and called out, "Over here! I'm a Southern soldier discharged from the army!"

"Come to the fire!" Patterson ordered as he pulled his pistol, while the other two did the same.

Walking from the darkness, Bill neared the fire and said, "Glad to see you boys."

"Colonel, we got a deserter on our hands!" Patterson called out and then said to Bill, "Move an inch and I'll kill ya!"

A few minutes later a Confederate Colonel rode to the fire and asked, "Why ain't ya in the army?"

"I was discharged from the army this mornin' and have the papers in my pack."

"Get them and be quick about it. We're out looking for deserters and we're to hang any we find."

Opening his pack and digging the papers out, he handed them to the Colonel as he said, "It's all on the paper. I took a ball to my head near Ironton a few weeks back."

Dismounting, the officer moved closer to the fire, read the papers and handed them back as he said, "Head wound. This man is no deserter; according to these papers, he was injured in the fight against Fort Davidson. Let 'em go."

"He looks like a deserter to me, suh," Patterson said as he turned to look at the Colonel.

"Damn it, Patterson, I said let the man go. He took a bullet to the head and discharged with excellent character! Now, get your ass back to the troop and fall in line."

When the men started moving, the Colonel lowered his head and said, "They're all good men, but we don't care much for this job."

"Sounds, suh, like your man Patterson loves the work."

The Colonel laughed and replied, "If so, he's the only one in the group who likes it. I'm sorry we bothered you, and have a safe trip home. And, thanks for your service to our country."

As the man mounted, Bill said, "I hope to have a safe trip, suh. Thank you for the kind words."

"You fought honorably, Mister Sanders, and should be respected for the job you did for the Confederacy. You should thank God that you live."

"I have and many times, suh."

"Goodnight."

Bill watched as the Colonel moved to the road and a few minutes later, he heard the troop riding north. He returned to the fire, placed his meat back on the coals to finish, and leaned back on his blanket. *It's a crazy world these days, when a wounded man is thought to be a deserter, and me without a rifle. Iffen I deserted, I'd damn sure have my long gun with me.*

That night he dreamed of the drummer boy he'd killed and awoke in the middle of the night soaked with sweat. As he stoked his fire back to life, he knew he'd see the boy's eyes the rest of his life.

# CHAPTER 4

## Missouri

**T**wo days later, he was out of food and he'd seen no homes, except for three burned out shells of what were once dwellings. He'd walked through the gardens looking for food, but little was found, except for a couple of withered carrots and a frost damaged cabbage. He'd eaten the last of it this morning and wondered where to turn next.

The morning was cold and he'd buttoned his coat, but it seemed to do little good. He'd hummed 'Rock of Ages' as he walked and when he rounded a turn in the road, he saw two Southern soldiers in a small camp off to his right. Waving, he called out, "Can I share your fire?"

Both men stood instantly, and he saw them pull the hammers back on their rifles. "Ya alone?" The tall skinny man on the left asked.

"Yep, I got discharged from the army and goin' home."

"Come, but don't make no sudden moves!"

Bill walked casually to the camp and kneeled beside the fire. As he held his open palms to the flames, enjoying the warmth, he asked, "Did you two get discharged, too?"

The heavier man on the right said, "Nope, we left."

Both men had long dirty brown hair and could have been brothers, except the thin man had a much longer nose. Neither had seen soap and water for months.

"Deserted?"

"Yup, we couldn't see stayin' where a man mighten get killed fer nothin'. Hell, the war's lost and we all know it. So why die when it ain't gonna change a damn thing in the end?"

"I saw some of our horse soldiers a ways back lookin' for deserters. Iffen they catch you, you'll hang."

The two deserters exchanged quick looks.

"My name's Bill, Bill Sanders."

"I'm Jesse and the fat man is Isham."

"Nice to meet ya."

Suddenly, Isham swung his rifle toward Bill and said, "Throw that knife I see to the ground and then move to the other side of the fire and sit down."

Dropping his knife, Bill asked, "Why? I ain't got no money or anything you'd want."

"We'll decide that, not ya. Besides, ya know we're deserters and that's enough in my book."

Jesse gave a crazy grin and said, "Can I kill 'em with my knife like I did that woman in Pilot Knob?"

"Not yet. We need to talk a spell."

"Then can I kill 'em?"

Isham shook his head and said, "Sure, but not right now. I'll let ya do the job directly."

When Jesse placed his rifle on a log near the fire, Isham leaned back against a boulder and asked, "How far back them riders lookin' fer us?"

"Full days ride would be my guess."

"Ya got any words to say to yer maker, get to sayin' 'em. I'm gonna turn Jesse on ya in a few minutes and he's hell with a knife."

"Can I have a cup of your coffee instead? I've had nothin' to eat for two days," Bill lied as he looked at the man.

Isham smiled and said, "Here, catch." He threw a tin cup.

He caught the cup easily. Reaching for the coffee pot, Bill picked it up slowly and then threw the contents in the face of Isham. The man screamed and brought his hands up to his eyes.

Bill pulled his pistol from his belt and fired once, seeing a black dot appear in the forehead of Jesse. The man fell to the ground and his body began to twitch and jerk as he died. He fired one shot at Isham and the man dropped hard to the ground.

Bill stood, walked to Isham and picked up his knife. Kneeling, he stuck the long blade up and under the man's ribs three times. With each thrust, the man screamed and his feet drummed on the ground. Finally, he stopped moving, gave a loud sigh, and died.

*Why in the world would they want to kill me? I have nothin' and I ain't never wronged 'em. Hell, I ain't even seen 'em before.*

Standing, Bill began to look the camp over closely. He found a huge piece of salt pork that must have weighed three pounds, a bag of cornmeal, three potatoes, a full jug of whiskey, and a bag of real coffee. All the food was in a burlap bag marked as Union property, so he knew where it came from. One of the rifles was an old muzzle loader, but the other was a .52 caliber Sharps. The Sharps was an excellent rifle that allowed the shooter to load a bullet into a breech at the rear of the gun. No ramrod was used and a man could fire two or three shots in a minute, even lying on his back. It was accurate too, often used by sharpshooters on both sides as a sniper rifle. The rifle was by far his best find in the camp.

Throwing one of the potatoes in the coals of the fire, he began to shave thin strips of pork into a large skillet, when it dawned on him—did these men have a horse? He started circling the camp and within ten minutes, he found a tired old mare tied to a limb on a big cedar tree. Her brand was CSA, so when they'd ran a horse had gone with them. Most mounts in the Southern army were in sad shape, and this one was typical of what he'd seen.

Leading the mare back to camp, he gave a silent prayer of thanks for all of the wonderful things he'd been given this day. He now had enough food to last the trip, as long as he was careful with the food, a new rifle, and a horse. As far as Bill was concerned, this was his lucky day.

At camp, he went through the packs of the dead men and found a poncho, a wool coat, two blankets, twenty cartridges for the Sharps, another pistol with a box of shells, four plugs of chewing tobacco, and ten dollars in Yankee greenbacks. He placed it all in his pack, finished his meal, and for the first time since the war started, he mounted a horse. Pulling her around, he moved to the road and started north, leaving the dead men where they'd fallen.

The day passed uneventfully, with the exception near dusk, when dark clouds started gathering on the horizon to the west, and he knew he'd have rain before morning. Stopping, he looked around and then rode about a hundred yards into the trees before he stopped to make a camp. Using the poncho, he quickly constructed a crude lean-to, and started a small fire. As his fire burned, he moved around the woods, gathering firewood for the night. Finally, he fried some of the pork and used the grease to fry one of the potatoes, the first fried ones he'd had in years.

It was just as he crawled under his shelter the rains came. There was a light gust of wind and then it began to sprinkle. Taking a sip of his coffee, a bite of his meat, he glanced skyward and knew a bad storm was coming. A bright flash of lightning filled the sky, followed seconds later by a loud report of thunder, which made the horse dance on the picket line. Leaning back on his blanket, he sipped his coffee and ate his meal. Bill realized, for the first time since the start of the war, he was content.

His meal soon finished and his fire put out by the rains, he rolled up in his blanket and lay listening to the rain beat a gentle tattoo on the taunt material of the poncho. Within ten minutes, he was asleep.

Dawn came with water dripping from leaves and branches. Having placed some of the wood in his shelter prior to the storm, Bill started a fire and put a pot of coffee on to boil, as he broke camp. Then, moving under the shelter, he drank four cups of the hot brew.

Suddenly, his vision grew gray and then faded to darkness.

When he next opened his eyes, the fire had burned out and the sun was fully up. He guessed he'd been out for an hour, but he wasn't sure.

*I had a fit,* he thought as he looked around to make sure his belongings were where he'd placed them. He felt weak and thirsty, so he took a sip from his canteen and lay back on the blanket. Within seconds, he was asleep again.

He awoke near noon, loaded his gear, and mounted. He decided he'd ride until after dark to make up for the time lost, and he did. It was a couple of hours after darkness before he finally moved into the woods and made camp for the night. He wasn't hungry, so he unloaded the horse, tied her to a picket line, and then rolled up in his blanket. He dreamed of the little drummer boy. They boy kept asking why Bill had killed him. Then the boy stopped talking and just stared at him with big sad eyes.

Bill swiftly opened his eyes and sat up; his heart was pounding, and he was sweat-soaked. Getting up from his blanket, he picked up a tin cup, moved to his supplies and filled it with whiskey he'd taken from the men. He quickly knocked back the first cup and then poured a second.

*I have to go easy with whiskey or that dead drummer boy will turn me into a drunk. I got enough troubles in life without adding drinking to the list. I will never have more than two drinks, that'll be my way with whiskey from now on.*

Sipping the second cup, he tried to remember the names of his ma and pa, but couldn't. He knew they were Sanders, because he was, but what were their first names? It's one hell of a mess when a man has lost all of his memories, except the one he wants to lose. *Why did I forget the names of those who love me, while remembering the boy I killed? Besides, that boy stabbed me with a sword before I ever knew he was around and killin' 'em was an accident.*

Finishing the second cup of alcohol, he rolled in his blanket and lay listening to the wind blow through the trees. *Am I still the man I was before shot? Or have I changed a great deal? Will those who loved me when I left for war, still love me when I return?* He was wondering about his future when he drifted off to sleep.

Three days later, he rode into the small town of Rolla. It was crawling with Union soldiers and he'd taken his gray coat off and placed it in his pack. He wore a Yankee dark blue shirt, tan canvas pants, and no hat. He'd just dismounted in front of the jail when he heard a voice call out, "You, with the tan pants, stop."

Turning, he saw a Yankee officer walking toward him. Giving the man an ill felt smile, he asked, "What can I do for you, Captain?"

"For starters, you can tell me why you're not in the army and what your business is in this town."

Pulling his discharge papers from his shirt pocket, he handed them to the officer and waited as he read them.

"Where do you live, if you're from Rolla?"

"I have no idea. When hit in the head, I lost most of my memory. I came here, to the jail, hoping the sheriff might know my kin."

"What's your name?"

"It's on the paper, I'm William Sanders."

Glancing at the paper, the Captain said, "Let's go see this sheriff and see if he knows you."

When they entered the small jail, the sheriff stood and said, "Well, I'll be damned, Bill Sanders! What're you doin' home with the war still goin' on?"

The Captain asked, "So, you know this man?"

"Hell, yes, and know 'em well. He and my boy grew up together!"

Gazing into Bill's eyes, the Captain said, "That answers my questions, Mister Sanders. I'm sorry if I seemed rude, but there is a war on."

"I understand, suh, and I would have done the same in your place."

As soon as the Captain left, Bill held his paper out to Rufus Williams and said, "I took a hit to my noggin and ain't right in the head yet. The doc said I might come around one of these days or I might be like this the rest of my life."

"How come ya didn't just ride home?"

Lowering his head, Bill replied, "I don't remember where home is, the name of my parents, or even your name. I've lost almost all of my memory and like the paper says, at times I go into fits."

"Good God, son! Well, my name is Rufus Williams, and I've known your folks since before ya was born. Your pa is Clyde and ma is Myrtle."

"I see. Could you tell me where I live?"

Picking up his hat, Rufus said, "I'll do you one better than that, I'll ride out there with ya."

The trip home took a couple of hours and during the ride, he asked as many questions about his family as he could think of. It was a strange feeling, going home to strangers.

"Your pa and ma are religious folks."

"I'm glad to know that."

"Yup, and your pa is a deacon in the First Baptist Church about half way to town. They're there four times a week as regular as clockwork."

"That's good. You said I had a brother, is he in the war, too?"

"Was, he was killed on the same day your pa lost his left arm. They were in the battle of Wilson's Creek, ya know."

Bill didn't reply, but wondered how his family would take the loss of his memory. Being Christians, he knew they would welcome him home, but it would take a lot of patience being around a man who had lost his mind.

Finally, they rode to the crest of a hill and Rufus said, "That's the place down there in the valley. I'll not go down with ya, 'cause I think your home comin' should be just between y'all." The man pulled his horse around and started back for town.

A few minutes later, tapping his horse in the ribs, Bill felt a trace of fear as he moved toward a home he didn't recognize, and people he couldn't remember.

Riding into the barnyard, he dismounted and as he stood by his horse, as old man with gray hair came out of the house holding a shotgun in his right hand. His left arm was missing from the elbow down, but the long barrel rested on the stub.

The man glared at him and asked, "What do you want here?"

Smiling, Bill replied, "I'm lookin' for Clyde Sanders, he's my pa."

His pa looked hard at him, then placed the gun against the side of the house and yelled, "Ma, come quick, our boy has come home! Good God, boy, you lost a lot of weight!"

As pa hugged him, his ma ran from the house and stood shaking in front of Bill. Tears filled her eyes as she moved slowly toward him. When her arms went around him, she whispered, "I thought I'd lost you, son! I prayed every night for your safe return and the Lord heard me. I'm so happy you're home!"

Pulling away from Bill, pa said, "Let's go in, get some coffee, and talk. Boy, I'm glad you survived the war."

Entering the house, nothing Bill saw brought back any memories. Sitting at the table, he smiled as his ma poured him a cup of coffee, and then said, "Folks, I got a problem."

His pa met his eyes and asked, "How so? Was you injured in some way?"

"I took a ball to my noggin and lost most of my memory," Bill spoke and then lowered his eyes.

His ma sat and then asked, "But, other than that you're okay?"

"I also took a saber stab or two in my lower back and a bayonet in my leg, only they don't bother me much. It's strange not to be able to remember things, places and people."

Pa said, "Head wounds can be tricky. I saw some in the hospital when my arm was took off and some of them boys wasn't never normal. Heck, we can bring your memory back, parts of 'er anyways. I'm just glad you're alive, son."

Ma just sat the table and silently cried.

Meeting her eyes, Bill asked, "Why the tears, ma?"

"I never thought I'd see you alive again in this world. I'm happy son, so happy."

Bill smiled and realized he had two wonderful parents, even if he didn't know them.

"I'd imagine you're pretty tired right now, ain't you?" Pa asked.

"Yup, I am, but if I sleep now, I'll not sleep tonight. Can we just talk a spell so I can learn a few things?"

Pa laughed, looked at Myrtle, and replied, "Sure, we can do that, can't we, ma?"

Ma didn't answer, she just nodded, looked at Bill, and then gave a loud sob.

Bill sat at the table and drank cup after cup of coffee, as his folks told him of his childhood and the mischief he'd gotten into. Seems he'd been an active child and had had a lot of energy. However, he'd lost most of that now and constantly felt tired. He knew it was from years of poor sleep, bad food, and no shelter. While still young, in his early twenties he thought, he felt like he was in his sixties most of the time.

Unexpectedly he asked, "How old am I?"

Ma met his eyes, blinked a couple of times and said, "You turned twenty-four on the 14th of September. Ya was born in 1840."

"September 14 ? That means my birthday passed maybe ten days, before I was injured. I ain't sure iffen I was hurt on the 26th or 27th of the month. My discharge papers were signed on the last day of October."

"Yep, it was the beginnin' of last month when the marshal brought us a telegram from the confederate army that said you'd been seriously hurt and not expected to live," Pa said and then pulled his pipe from his coat pocket. He started packing the bowl with tobacco.

"Didn't they let you know when I was discharged?"

Striking a match on his boot heel and then lighting his pipe, pa took a deep drag, exhaled and spoke through a white cloud of smoke, "Nope, not a blame thing. We had no idea if you yet lived or not. But, the army has always been slow. Now, tell me, how's the war goin' for the South?"

"It'll end soon and no later than next spring would be my guess. Pa, we ain't got uniforms, food, shelters or nothin', so it can't last long. I remember our boys goin' through the packs of dead Yanks, trying to find what they needed. For some reason, I can remember most of the war, it's just the years before that give me trouble."

"I figured as much. From the one battle I was in, them Yanks seemed to have all kinds of gear with em. Every damned one of 'em had a poncho, extra clothes and more food than a feller could eat in a day."

Ma suddenly said brusquely, "Clyde, watch your language at the table. I don't allow no cussin' at the table and you know it."

Pa lowered his eyes and replied in a meek voice, "Sorry."

"They're still like that and while the south has some food, we ain't got a way to move it to the men. Sherman's in Georgia, tearing up the railroad and burnin' everything he can get his hands on. Iffen he gets to the ocean, the south is lost."

"Can he do the job?"

"Likely, ain't much in the way of men to stop 'em."

"I thought as much. The south is high on determination but low on equipment and supplies."

"Yup, I heard that over 3,000 of our men went into the battle I was hurt in, with no guns or weapons at all."

"How many men were in on the attack?"

"Nigh on 12,000, but those men without guns was told to take 'em from dead Rebs or Yanks."

"Holy cow, that's a real mess, now ain't it?"

Ma asked, "Did the Southerners win the battle?"

"Nope, but I ain't got no idea why. I heard there was less than 2,000 Yanks in the fort, so we should have won."

Pa poured a little coffee in his saucer and said, "I saw enough of war to know anything can happen and likely will when you don't expect it. I'm sure stranger things have happened." He then picked his saucer up, blew on the coffee, and then took a sip.

"Do you remember your girlfriend?" Ma asked with a big smile.

He lowered his head and replied weakly, "No, I don't."

Pa pulled his pipe from his mouth and said, "Her name is Clara Sue Wade, and she comes from a good family. Son, you're to marry her when the war ends."

"What does she look like?"

Pa smiled and replied, "She's a small woman, close to five feet and two inches tall, thin, but with all the bumps and curves in the right places. She has red hair and green eyes. Pretty little girl, in my mind."

"Figures, your pa only mentioned her body!" Ma said with a chuckle and then added, "She's got a good mind too, son, with good common horse sense to go along with her beauty. You could do a lot worse than Clara."

Looking at first his pa, then his ma, he said, "I don't remember her at all."

"You met her when you did some work for her pa, oh, about two years before the war. He needed some timber cleared and you did the job."

"This ain't good that you don't remember her, because she'll come over here as soon as she hears you're back," Ma said, placed her coffee cup on the table, and gazed into Bill's eyes.

Without flinching, or moving his eye's from hers he said, "I don't remember her at all."

"Not even a little?" Pa asked.

"Nothin'."

# CHAPTER 5

The remainder of the morning, pa showed Bill around the farm. None of it brought back any memories, until they entered his old sleeping spot in the loft of the large cabin. He saw one of his brother's shirts, an old homespun brown one, and was instantly flooded with emotions. Kneeling, he picked the shirt up and held it in his hands as he asked, "Pa, did Matthew die a hard death?"

"I . . . I was with 'em when he died, but I didn't see 'em get hit. The battle was wild, with men fighting hand-to-hand, and I lost sight of 'em early in the scuffle. Less than an hour into the battle, I took slugs to the left arm and my thigh, at almost the same time. I laid there for hours, until some of our boys picked me up and carried me to the hospital. The next day, I woke up with Matt beside me, but I ain't sure iffen he knew me or not."

"Your arm was missin' by then?"

"Nope, not yet. They stopped the bleedin' and placed me aside to give the doctors time to catch up. Seems a bunch of fellers lost arms and legs that day. Hell, I saw legs and arms stacked up outside that hospital tent like cord-wood."

"Was he unconscious?"

"I ain't really sure, but he didn't speak to me then. He'd taken a minié-ball to the left side of his head, a bayonet in the belly and had two deep saber cuts to his shoulders."

"Sounds like he run into some horse soldiers, followed by infantry."

"That's what I figure happened, too."

"Did he die before you lost the arm?"

"Nope, that was one tough boy I raised, and he lived for three more days. Just before he died, he called out for me and I went to his side. He was hurtin' bad, son, and it tore me up to see 'em in pain like that. They'd kept 'em drunk, but hell, it didn't help 'em much."

Lowering his head, Bill asked, "Did you get to talk with 'em, pa?"

"Uh-huh, I did, and for a few minutes he was almost normal. He said he loved us all and told me he was sorry the war got 'em killed. Told me to tell Mary he loved her, that's his wife iffen you don't remember, and then gave a loud sigh. That's all there was to it, he died."

"He was a good man and I remember Mary, but how did she take it?"

"Hard. She's moved from their cabin and lives with her folks down on the Little Piney River."

Suddenly, Bill grew rigid, his body began to quiver, and he fell to the floor.

His pa stood watching his son a few seconds and then screamed with fear, "Ma, get up to the loft and do 'er now! Bill's havin' a fit or dyin' on us!"

A few minutes later ma appeared, looked down at her jerking son and replied, "It's a fit. My aunt used to have 'em at times and ain't nothin' we can do for 'em until it's done."

"Lordy!"

"Take your belt off and the next time he opens his mouth, slip the leather between his teeth so he don't bite his tongue off. No matter how much he twists or turns, keep that belt in his mouth," Ma ordered as she kneeled beside her last living son. She prayed pa would keep the belt between Bill's teeth.

Close to five minutes later, Bill opened his eyes and said in a voice just above a whisper, "I'm okay now."

Ma asked, "Are you feelin' weak and tired?"

"Yep, how do you know?"

"You had an Aunt May, who died years before you was born, who used to have fits. She died in a cabin fire, only not durin' a fit. Anyway, she was always tired after a fit hit her. Why don't you lay down a while and get some rest."

Moving to his childhood bed, he asked, "What caused her fits to come on?"

"She fell from a horse and her head hit a rock. It almost killed her, except she recovered pretty much, only the fits hit her at odd times."

Crawling onto the bed and then stretching out, Bill remembered the comfort this bed had given him growing up. He remembered its warmth during winters and how he'd laugh with Matthew at times late at night. Bill glanced briefly at his brother's bed, knowing he would never laugh with the man again.

"You scared me pretty good, boy," Pa said. "I ain't never seen nothin' like that before!"

"I have one every few days and they don't last as long now as they did at first."

Ma gave a warm smile, kissed Bill's cheek and said, "He'll come out of 'em fine, as long as we can get something between his teeth."

"Ma, I'm goin' take a short nap. Iffen anybody comes around, even Clara, tell 'em I'm sleepin'." His pa turned and went down the ladder, but his ma hung back a little and replied, "I'll tell 'em, but one of these days ya'll need to talk to her, son. She's a good woman and you don't want to hurt her. I think she'll still love you, along with your loss of memory, fits and all."

"We'll talk about it later, okay?"

"Sure, Bill, you get some sleep now."

Bill leaned back into his pillow and in a few short seconds, he was asleep.

Later that afternoon, he was outside splitting some wood for the kitchen stove when a woman rode into the barnyard.

At first glance, he knew it was Clara, his pa had described her perfectly, and he deeply feared the meeting. She was an inordinately beautiful woman.

Dismounting and running to him, she threw her arms around him and kissed him passionately, but the passion wasn't returned. Moving away from him a little, she asked, "Don't you love me any more?"

"Clara, I was hurt in the war. I took a bullet to the head and don't have much of my memory left."

"But, you know me, right?"

Bill, unable to speak, simple shook his head slowly. Finally, after watching tears fill her eyes, he said, "I'm sorry. I never meant for this to happen."

"You don't remember anything about us? Even that night at the barn dance the year before you left?"

He shook his head once more and replied, "I didn't know I even had a girl waiting for me until ma mentioned your name this morning."

"Will your memory return?"

"The doctor said maybe and then again, maybe not."

Clara walked slowly to her horse, mounted and rode from the farm without looking back. She'd not spoken another word.

❧ ❧ ❧

Days turned into weeks and then one morning as he was pulling a bucket of water from the well, Clara returned. She dismounted, tied her horse to the hitching post, and then walked to his side. Giving him a sweet smile, she asked, "Would you like to get to know me again, Bill?"

He put the bucket beside his foot and replied, "I think I'd like that very much, Clara; maybe something you will say or someplace we'll visit will bring memories back. When I first got home, I saw one of Matthew's old shirts and my mind flooded with thoughts of him. I could suddenly remember what we'd done together, his face and the fact he was dead."

"I cried when I heard of his death."

"I did too, but before I saw his shirt, I didn't remember a brother, except for what folks had told me. I hurt inside, Clara; not knowing is a hard thing to accept. You're a beautiful woman and the man you love is a lucky man."

Moving to him, she kissed him on the cheek and replied, "You're that man. The only reason I came back is because I love you, don't you see?"

"I'm a lucky man then. Let me take this water in to ma and then we'll go for a ride. We need to talk and this is not the place."

She smiled and said, "I'm glad to hear you say that, because the old Bill would have said that."

He laughed and replied, "I'm the same man, except I don't remember most of the past."

Clara gave him a seductive smile, lowered her eyes, and replied, "Well, maybe I can relive the past or at least help you remember it."

Blushing, Bill started toward the house and called over his shoulder, "I'll be back out in a few minutes."

An hour later, they sat in the grass under a large oak tree beside a small stream. Bill gave the stream a long stare and said, "The creek is named after an animal, but I can't recall which one."

Clara laughed and replied, "Yep, it's call Beaver Creek."

A smile came to Bill's lips and it made her heart melt with desire. She'd always found him a gentle man, with a warm heart and a seductive smile.

"See, I'm starting to remember more!" He said as he turned to her.

Leaning, Clara kissed him hard on the lips, her tongue dancing with his. Her kiss was filled with the passion of a woman who'd waited four years for her man come home. She felt his passion building and for a few minutes, it was like old times.

Then Bill broke the kiss, sat up and said, "I don't remember ever feelin' like this before in my life, but I like it."

Clara laughed and replied, "You used to feel like that almost every day."

Standing, Bill said, "Clara, we have to talk. Just a few minutes ago, I wanted you in the worst way and I would have taken you, too, but it would not have been fair. You would have been lovin' a man you've known for years, care about, and I would have been, well, takin' care of a need."

"A need! Is that all I mean to you! I love you, Bill Sanders, and want my old Bill back!"

"Clara, give me time. Your kiss brought back feelings of a love for someone, only I can't honestly say it was you. I felt a feelin' I've not experienced since I was shot and it was one of desire, love, and happiness, all rolled into one. It confused and scared the hell out of me more than jus' a little."

Clara smiled and said, "That's love!"

"But, is it for you or someone else?"

Meeting his eyes, she replied, "You've never been with anyone else. I was your first girlfriend and the first woman you ever loved."

"Love has a lot of different meanin's."

"Yep and you can take it any way you want. Don't you remember what we did at the barn dance, under the pines?"

Lowering his head he said, "No, I surely don't."

"Well, all I'll say about it is we worried about a child for months. Only it was worth it to me, don't you see? I want to have your child, our child."

"Still?"

"Yes, still. I love you with my very soul, and one day you'll love me again. I know, because I'm going to make you."

Bill smiled and said, "Maybe I'm not worth it anymore. I have fits, can't recall the simplest things, and my old war injuries pain me at times."

Reaching out and pulling him close, she replied, "You're worth it and a lot more. I'll help you remember things and I'll help kill pain when you hurt. Bill, we were once very close and shared our deepest secrets and desires with each other. A day will come, it might not be soon, but we'll do that again."

Shaking his head, he said, "I'm a lucky man."

"Not yet you're not, but if ya'll lie back on the blanket you will be in a few minutes. There's something I want to do for both of us."

An hour later, after they'd dressed, Bill was unable to meet her eyes.

Suspecting his thoughts, Clara said, "I'm not a whore, if that's what you're thinking. I just made love to the man I intend to marry. We'd planned to marry before the war and we will in the near future."

"How do you know?" Bill asked with a big smile.

"Because you called me by my pet name while lovin' me and nobody on earth knows that name, but you."

Giving a huge smile, Bill said, "Honestly, about half way through, it all came back to me. I remembered meetin' you, our years of datin', the barn dance, and even your pet name."

Pulling him close, she hugged him, gave him a kiss and then asked, "Do you remember lovin' me? I mean that you really love and care for me?"

"Yes, dear, I certainly do. I do love you, Clara, and I want you to be my wife. Do you recollect the time on this same crick when you fell in tryin' to catch a crawdad?"

Laughing she replied, "Yes and we had a sparkin' session that almost turned into fire! You got me so hot that day, for nights after I dreamed of makin' love to you."

He remembered now, he truly did and he thought, *I'm the luckiest man alive! Oh, how I love you, Clara!*

"What were you just thinkin'? You had a big smile."

"How much I love you."

"That's good, real good, 'cause after what we just did a while ago, we might have to rush the marriage."

"Fine with me, that'll mean I can have your lovin' every day!"

"Not every day, but a lot and you can be sure of that."

Standing, Bill said, "Come, we got to get back to the farm before pa calls the marshal. He might think I got lost or something."

"Well, it could happen."

"Not when I'm with you. Besides, I'm sure you know your way around this place."

"That I do, but it is gettin' late, and my folks will start to worry."

⇥⇤ ⇥⇤ ⇥⇤

Later that night after supper, ma said, "You remember Clara now, don't you? I can tell by the smile that's been on your face all afternoon."

Nodding, Bill replied, "We rode to Beaver Crick and it all came back to me. I recalled her ma, the wood cuttin' job, dances we'd gone to, and other small things."

"Be hard to forget a good lookin' young thing like that for very long," Pa said and then chuckled.

"Clyde! You know, you're the kind of man who'd pretend to remember, just to have your way with a woman like that!"

"Nope, I'd never do that," he replied and then laughed, "but the thought would enter my mind for sure. It'd be purely a temptation of the flesh. "

Bill shook his head, enjoying the gentle banter, but he had something serious to discuss with his folks.

"You both know I've been home for over a month now, and I think I'm ready to get back to work."

"Do you remember what you used to do for a livin', son?" Ma asked.

"Something to do with horses, I think."

Pa suddenly said, "By God, you was one of the best blacksmiths in the whole state! That's what you was."

"Do you think you can still do that kind of work?" Ma asked.

"I'll spend some time out in the barn tomorrow. I saw the anvil and tools, so maybe iffen I work with some hot metal for a spell it'd come back to me."

"Ain't many men that can take a piece of raw steel or cast iron and turn it into something useful like a knife blade, skillet, or a beautiful gate."

"I recollect seein' a few smiths in the army from time to time, and I always thought they did a poor job. Now, after the hit to my noggin', I ain't so sure I will be able to do as well as they did."

"Give it a try in the mornin' and see how it goes. If you cain't be a smith, there are lots of jobs now, with the war goin' on and most of the men gone."

"Like what?"

"Lawman is one that comes to mind."

"I can't do that. If I have a fit at the wrong time, I'm a dead man."

"How 'bout a logger?"

"Maybe, it don't take much to cut down trees."

Ma, grinned and offered, "You could run a store."

Pa's face turned scarlet and then he said roughly, "Ain't no man, unless he's starvin', gonna run no dog-gone general store. Hell, Myrtle, that's a job for a sissy."

Bill laughed loud and hard, and then said, "Pa, I could be a teamster, drive a coach maybe, or even work in the telegraph office. I learned to send code in the army, and I still remember how to do it."

"You learned all them dot, dot, dots? I ain't got no use for telegrams and such. A man wants to talk to me, why he can just come visitin'? Only, how would your fits affect workin' at any of those jobs ? "

"Pa, the last fit I had was a long time back, up in the loft. I ain't sure what causes 'em, so maybe early in the mornin' I'll ride to town and talk with Doctor Bodeker."

"Well, he's Dutch and went to some big fancy schools over there, so maybe he knows somethin' our doctors don't know. I doubt it, but he might."

Standing, Bill said, "Thanks for the talk, folks, but I'm headin' off to bed."

Doctor Bodeker leaned back in his chair, gave a weak smile and said, "Bill, your head took a serious injury and it damaged your brain. Now, the injury wasn't enough to make you drool or seriously affect your behavior, but medicine knows very little about the human mind. About all we know is inside the head is a big lump of gray matter and that's it. Oh, we can see sections, veins, and a mushy substance, but how does it work? What magic takes place in that gray matter and how does it happen?"

"That's all we know?"

"That's about it, really. I have learned on my own that if certain portions of the brain are injured, parts of the body stop working properly. Let us say a feller takes a bullet to the right side of his skull and part of the brain is blown away. Instead of affecting the right side of his body, if he survives, it will affect his left side. So, after seeing a lot of injuries like that, I've reached the conclusion that an injury to the brain affects the opposite side of the body."

"Okay, but what about me?"

"The bullet that stuck you appears to have fractured the front of your skull and damaged that part of your brain. Now, that part of the brain has a section in the very front that looks like a bunch of wires or thick hairs coming together. I suspect it either controls thinking or holds the front halves of the brain together. I have no way to see inside of your head, to tell the real damage done, but I think it controls thinking and that's why your memory was lost."

"Could those wire things carry current like a telegrapher's key?"

"Maybe, but some kind of impulse makes the brain work."

Then leaning forward, with a bottle of rye in his hand, the doctor asked, "Drink?"

"Just one."

After pouring two glasses and handing one to Bill he asked, "Have you ever seen a man with half of his brain missing?"

"Uh-huh, in the war, why?"

"A man with half his skull missing and a brain in place is an interesting observation, because his brain pulses with each beat of his heart."

"So, I saw that, too."

"To me that means the living organism, the human body if you will, must receive both electrical impulses and blood."

Bill laughed and said, "Ain't a battery in a man's body!"

"No, not as we know a battery, but some part of the body makes those impulses to the brain."

"So you think my brain impulses ain't workin' right?"

Laughing, Bodeker replied, "Seriously? I have no idea, but for some reason the part of the brain that stores memories was damaged, and severely."

"Well, what causes the fits I have?"

"Messed up impulses maybe? I don't know."

"What can I do about 'em then?"

Bodeker knocked back the rest of his drink, stood and replied, "Learn to live with 'em and maybe ya'll live long enough for us to learn more about the human brain. I doubt you will, because it's complex, but you might."

Finishing his drink, Bill stood and left the office, more confused now than when he'd entered.

# CHAPTER 6

**H**is attempt at working with iron was frustrating and after an hour, he gave the job up. Saddling his horse, he told his pa, "I'm goin' into town and findin' me a smith. I'm gonna work for that man free a few weeks and see iffen learnin' again brings back some thoughts on how to do the job. When I picked that big hammer up, I felt something inside, maybe a desire or knowledge, but I didn't have the slightest idea what to do with it."

Pa asked, "Did you make anything?"

"Nope, just dented some metal."

"Try ole man Hawkins, he knows us and will likely let you work for him. Iffen you say the word free I know he'll agree quick like."

Bill laughed and replied, "I'll do that, pa."

His ride to town was cold and a light snow was falling, but he didn't notice the weather. He pulled up in front of the livery stables, dismounted and made his way inside. An old potbelly stove in the corner was glowing red on the sides.

"Well, Bill Sanders, good to see ya, son!" a man he assumed was Hawkins stated in a cheery voice. The man was short, just a few inches over five feet, green eyes and brown hair. There was the start of a potbelly.

"Howdy-do and it's good to see you again, too. I'm lookin' for a place I can brush up on my smithin' skills for a couple of weeks, so do you think I could do the job here? I'll do the work for free."

"Sure, I've need of another smith and can use the help. I'll bet it was your ole man's idea to come see me, now wasn't it?"

"Well, he suggested I come see Mister Hawkins and here I am."

"Yep, me and your dad go way back, and he knows Isaac Hawkins would never turn down free help! People can call Isaac Hawkins many things, but I always know a good deal when I see one. Come on in the office, let's get some coffee, and talk a spell."

➔◄ ➔◄ ➔◄

At the end of two weeks, Bill had most of his blacksmith skills back, and opened his own shop at the family farm. He'd experienced no more fits and hoped he'd seen the last of them, but suspected they'd return. His ma and pa had stood in front of the barn, both wearing big smiles, as he placed a sign over the door that read, 'William Sanders, Blacksmith.' "

"You need to start on a home and new shop here directly," Pa said, standing with his hands on his hips and a smile on his face.

"I haven't got the money or land and it takes both to do something like that."

"Horse feathers, you got both and I'll bet you don't recollect either of 'em."

"Nope, I don't."

Ma smiled and said, "Son, when you were born, both of you boys, pa gave clear deeds to forty acres of land and five hundred dollars. Now, that money has been in the bank for over twenty-four years, just a growin' interest, and you added to it some before you went off ta war. It seemed to me every dollar you earned, half went into that savin's account."

Pa grinned and said, "I'd suspect you got over a thousand dollars in the bank right now and while that's a good amount, it ain't enough to make a plank wood house. Your first one, just like mine and ma's, will have to be log."

Thinking for a few minutes, Bill said, "I must owe some back taxes on the land then."

Leaning over, his pa sent a brown stream of tobacco juice to the ground and then said, "It's undeveloped and the taxes each year was small, so we paid 'em for you. Now, since Matthew ain't comin' home and his land touches yours, how about takin' 'em both?"

"Want to give 'em Matt's savin's, too?" Ma asked.

"Nope, remember, I done gave that to his wife, but the lands there and so's a nice house.  The choice is yours."

"I'll buy it from Mary, because I couldn't take it and not pay her for it."

"It does my old heart good to hear you say that, son, because I already bought it from her." Pa said and then added, "The price is two hundred dollars and you can pay me back as business grows."

Suddenly, Clara entered his mind and he said, "I got to tell Clara! We can be married as soon as I can arrange it all! I'll be back later this evenin', but don't wait up!"

He ran to the barn, saddled, and a few minutes later rode to see the love of his life. An hour later, he stood in the barnyard of Clara's house with her in his arms. As soon as they'd kissed, he whispered, "Want to get married next week? Some good things have happened we need to talk about."

"L . . . like what?" She asked.

"Let's walk down the road a piece and I'll tell you."

As they walked down the country lane, Bill explained about the home, land and money. He stopped, pulled Clara close and asked, "Will you marry me next week?"

Raising her head, she met his eyes and replied, "Of course I'll marry you! I love you and have been waiting for those words since the day you left for the war!"

"Have your pa take care of the things you'll need, and I'll take care of the rest of it."

"The rest of it?"

"The church, preacher, rings, best man, honeymoon, you know, the rest of it!" He broke out laughing and gave her a hug.

"I'm so happy we'll have a home ready and eighty acres of land is no small farm! My pa only has twenty!" Clara said with pride in her voice and love in her eyes.

Abruptly, Bill fell from her arms to the dirt road and began to twitch and jerk. His eyes rolled back until only the whites showed.

Clara screamed and began running for the house as fast as she could. She ran up the steps, into the house screaming, "Bill's dyin'! Someone help me! Please, pa! Ma! Bill's dyin'!"

Her father rushed into the room, took hold of her arms and said, "Simmer down some and tell me what has happened and where he's at."

"Just down the road, by the pond. He fell and started jerkin'! He's dyin', pa!"

Her father took off as fast as his sixty-year-old legs would carry him and was soon by Bill's side. He pulled off his belt, placed it between Bill's teeth as he said, "He's havin' a fit!"

"What kind of fit?"

"Must be from his head injury durin' the war. His pa said he had one when he first come home, so he's had 'em before."

"What can we do?" Clara asked filled with fear.

"I ain't got no idea! Clara, I ain't never seen one before!"

Her ma walked up, kneeled and began to wash Bill's sweat soaked face with a washcloth. She looked up at her daughter and said, "I've seen 'em and there ain't nothin' we can do. He'll come out of it— or die on us."

Clara fell to her knees and began to cry as she asked, "Ma, how do you know?"

"You had an uncle, but you never met 'em, and he used to drink so much he'd go into a fit. Well, one day, way afore you was born, he had a fit and never come out of it. He died that night."

"Bill wasn't drinkin'!"

"Well, I don't know how fits work on folks that don't drink. The only one I ever saw was my brother and he died."

Pa said, "His jerkin' is slowin' down and he's not breathin' hard like he was."

Ma turned her head to Clara and asked, "You sure you want to marry a man that has fits? I'd think on this a spell, iffen I was you."

While she was still crying, her mother's words were loud and clear and her mind began to wonder of a future married to Bill.

A couple of minutes later, Bill's eyes rolled back into place, his body quit jerking, and he closed his eyes tightly against the embarrassment. He'd just had a fit in front of his bride to be and her family!

"Are you okay?" Mister Wade asked.

"I'm fine, just had a fit. I'm so sorry."

The old man replied, "It's a medical problem, son, and there ain't nothin' you can do about it. Ain't no reason to be sorry 'bout it, neither. You served our country with honor, Bill, so don't let this get you down."

Standing and dusting his trousers off, Bill turned and walked to his horse. He mounted and rode away without another word. Clara wanted to yell for him not to go, but something deep inside of her wouldn't allow the words to come.

➡️⬅️ ➡️⬅️ ➡️⬅️

Three mornings later, Bill moved into his brother's old cabin and started cleaning the place. Mary had been out of the place long enough for dust to cover everything, cobwebs were starting to form, and mice had moved in. He'd brought an old tomcat from his ma and turned the animal loose in the house, while he used a broom to knock the cobwebs from the corners. He'd just started wiping the dust from the furniture, when he heard a horse nicker in the barnyard.

Putting his hat on, then checking the pistols in his belt, he walked outside, half expecting trouble. Instead, he found Clara sitting sidesaddle on her horse and looking as beautiful as ever. She was wearing a pink dress and carrying a pink umbrella in her hand against the bright morning sun.

"Mornin', Clara. I thought you didn't want to see me any more," Bill said, as he moved beside her horse to help her down.

Once on the ground, she lowered her eyes and said, "I thought that, too, but I cain't stay away from you, fits or no fits. Even though you'd told me about 'em, when I saw you have one, well, it scared me somethin' terrible."

"How'd your folks take it?"

"Rough at first and ma still don't like the idea of me gettin' hitched to you, but pa said, 'He was injured in the war, protectin' us, and his problem is a medical one. We all know he ain't crazy or dangerous, so iffen I was you, I'd think on that a spell. Most of the time he's as normal as the rest of us.'"

"Well," she gazed into his eyes and said, "I done thought on it and I still want to be your wife, iffen ya'll still have me."

Moving to her, he took her in his arms and replied, "I love you and while it hurt me not to see you durin' this time, I could understand your fear. I was afraid you'd not want me after you saw how the spells hit me. It was embarrassing, Clara."

Kissing him on the cheek, she said, "Well, I can live with 'em iffen you can. Only, ya'll have to give me time to get used to 'em."

He replied, "You'll have a lifetime to get used to 'em."

"You still want to marry me?"

"You bet I do and we'll do it this week. Let's get hitched on Sunday, right after church."

"Oh, Bill, I'm so happy!"

Taking her by the hand, he said, "Come and let me show you our soon to be home!" Matthew had kept the place up before the war, but it needed fixed up now. There was a loose board on the porch and the steps moaned when they stepped on them, but the house was solid.

Entering, the first thing Clara saw was a wood burning cook stove in the kitchen.

"A new kitchen stove! My ma doesn't even have one of those!"

"Come and let me show you the rest of the house. There's a bedroom in the loft, two others down this hallway and our bedroom is at the end of the hall. Opening the door to each room as they walked down the hall, Clara looked in each and said, "Fairly good size, ain't they?"

"Yep, but wait until you see our bedroom, it's the biggest and nicest, too."

Opening the door to the master bedroom, they stepped inside and she immediately said, "The bed is huge. And, look at the overhead lamps!"

The lamps, attached to a number of deer racks, were of a very unusual design. She counted four lamps over the bed and two on the night stands. Turning to Bill, she pulled him very close, kissed him deeply and then fell onto the bed. Her passion mounted as he kissed her and his hands began to move over her body.

Letting out a loud moan of desire, she said in a whisper, "I want you . . . now."

Bill replied softly, "You'll have me, my love."

⇥⇤  ⇥⇤  ⇥⇤

That Sunday they were married in a small Baptist country church and headed east, to Saint Louis, for their honeymoon. Their folks paid for the trip as a wedding present. Along with the honeymoon, Bill's pa gave them ten more acres of land, and Clara's pa gave them three cows and four horses.

They'd traveled by stagecoach to Saint Louis, the only available method of travel to the big city, unless they rode horses. While there was a train to and from the big city, the Union army used it to move men and supplies and civilian passengers were not allowed. The ride was long, chilly, and rough as the stage bounced over each rock and rut in the dirt road. The trip was a little over a hundred miles and took two whole days and a full night of constantly moving. Since the stage was full, neither Bill or Clara got much rest and even less sleep, due to people talking, smoking foul smelling cigars, or drinking whiskey straight from a bottle. Drunken laughter filled the stage often, and nothing could prevent it.

It was dusk, on the second day, when the stage pulled into Saint Louis and the tired passengers unloaded from the muddy coach. They both complained of sore muscles, so Bill flagged down a hack and had him take them to the hotel.

For Clara, who'd never been out of Rolla, except to some small neighboring towns, the big city beside the Mississippi River fascinated her. There were thousands of people on the streets and all seemed in a hurry to get somewhere.

"Bill, look at all these people! How can they live all bunched up like this?"

"Many were born here, so they don't know any better. I couldn't live like this, with a neighborin' house almost touchin' mine."

The clop, clop of the horse's shoes on the cobblestone street was all that was heard for a few minutes, until the driver called out, "Here's yer hotel, folks, and I hope ya enjoy yer stay."

Bill threw the driver a quarter and then picked up their suitcases. As he walked toward the door, he took in the splendor of the place. It was a huge multistory building, with large pillars along the front, and a thick red carpet ran up the steps to the door. An old black man wearing a red uniform stood by the doorway and when they neared, he opened the door for them.

"Y'all have a good stay with us!" The black man said with a smile as they entered.

"We will, and I'm sure of it!" Clara said as she made her way into the hotel, with Bill right behind with bags in hand.

Once at the desk, a tall thin man with little hair asked, "May I help you folks?"

"You should have reservations for a Mister and Missus William Sanders."

Looking through a small stack of papers, the clerk smiled and said, "Yes, I do. You're in room 214 and I see it's your honeymoon. The hotel has furnished a fruit bowl, bottle of champagne and complimentary dinner for two, in celebration of your marriage. Let me see, yes the room has been paid and for two nights, so all you need is a key."

Handing them a key the man continued, "Congratulations on your marriage, and I wish you many years of continuous happiness."

"Thank you," Bill replied as he took the key.

As they walked up the stairs, Clara said, "I think the first thing we need is a bath, some good food, and then a long nap."

"I agree. While a stagecoach might be much faster and more comfortable than ridin' on horseback, I'm just plain worn out." Then giving her a grin, he asked, "But when do we start the honeymoon?"

"I'm afraid it'll have to wait until after we clean up and get some rest. Neither of us is in any kind of condition to do what we both want to do. I think it'll be more meaningful for us iffen we're at least clean and rested. Don't you think?"

"Yep, and I was just teasin' you. I love you, but I'm in no rush, because I've got the rest of my life to love you."

"That you do, William Sanders, and I want you to live to be a real old man."

⇒⇐ ⇒⇐ ⇒⇐

Morning came with bright sunlight shining through a curtain they'd forgotten to close, the light striking Clara in the eyes. She turned and reached for Bill, but he wasn't in bed. Raising her head, she spotted him at a small table reading a newspaper.

Hearing her move, Bill turned and said, "Well, about time you woke up. Champagne got to you some, huh?"

"W . . . what time is it? And, no, the drink didn't bother me much."

"A quarter to seven."

"What time did you get up?"

"Close to five, just like I usually do."

"Why so early?"

"Pa always woke me near five when I was on the farm, and the army got me up at that time, so I guess I got used to gettin' up early."

Giving him a seductive smile, Clara said, "Want to come back to bed? This is our honeymoon, and I think some of your personal attention would be nice."

Standing as he smiled, Bill began to undress as he said, "I've always got time for my wife."

❧ ❧ ❧

An hour later they were in the hotel restaurant having breakfast, when Bill saw a man he thought he knew, First Sergeant Andy Watkins. He looked like the man, except his right arm was missing at the elbow. Only, it couldn't be Watkins, he'd seen him killed at the railroad battle.

Speaking in a low voice, he said to Clara, "I think I served with the man with one arm by the window."

"Well, go say something to him, he's all alone and maybe he'd like to join us."

Bill stood, pushed his chair under the table and made his way to the man. Stopping beside the table, he asked, "You wouldn't happen to be First Sergeant Andy Watkins of the Confederate Army, would you?"

The man placed his fork on the edge of his plate and said with a big grin, "I'll be damned, iffen it ain't Bill Sanders! Son, I thought you were dead when we packed you from the battlefield that day."

"I was almost dead. Want to join us?"

"I'd be honored to do so."

A few minutes later, they were at Bill's table, when Watkins said, "I guess you're wonderin' about my arm, huh? I lost it a few months after you went to the hospital. A cannonball came by and as it passed, it took the arm with it. I was one of the lucky ones, or so I like to think."

Bill knew from the comment that his old unit had had many dead and injured, so he asked, "Did we lose a lot of boys?"

"Well over half. We ended up attacking Fort Davidson, but the Yank cannons did a real number on us. Or so I heard. I was in the hospital gettin' over my saber injury at the time. I lost my arm when we attacked a battery of cannon south of the fort a little over a month later."

"Hell, I thought that sword killed you."

"Naw, just went through part of my left side. Hurt like all get out, but I was almost completely healed in a month."

"How did James and Isaac come out of it all?"

"James was killed and Isaac lost both legs. I saw James killed, and he died after taking three bullets to the chest and one to the middle of his face. Isaac I heard later took some cannon iron in his legs and they were taken off at the knees."

Slowly shaking his head, Bill said, "Both were good men. Isaac hadn't even served a week yet, I don't think."

"In war all kinds of things happen and few are good. I knew them both as good soldiers, but they went down fightin' hard and that says a lot about them in my mind."

"James was a brawler and loved to fight, so I guess he was up front when he was killed."

"Yep, our cannons had blown a big hole in the wall where those cannons were, and he was the first man to run inside, but quickly fell. The fire became so intense, I had to pull the men back, and once we were out in the open the Yanks opened up with all their cannons. That's when I lost the arm."

"I'm sorry about the arm," Clara said, and lowered her head not sure what to say to the man.

"Well, I'm lucky! Don't ya understand, I'm still alive. I can get by with one arm, but many men died that day and all for nothin'."

"Nothin'?" Bill asked.

"Yup, we never did take Fort Davidson or the wall, but eventually the Yanks withdrew to Saint Louis."

"We had over 12,000 men and we couldn't take a fort manned by 1,200 Yankees? What happened?"

"Price divided his men into groups and we were to all attack at the same time, except all the groups never showed up at the same time. The Yanks would fight one group, move their cannons and then fight off another group. If we would have all been in place at the same time and then attacked, we would have won the day, only we weren't and didn't."

Bill, wanting to change the subject, asked, "What brings you to Saint Louis?"

"Visiting family, and you?"

"We are on our honeymoon," Clara proudly announced, and then blushed.

"Well, congratulations! I hope the two of you have many long and good years together! You got a good man here, Missus Sanders. Bill was one of my best, and I could always count on him to do any job asked of him."

Pulling a watch from his coat pocket, Watkins said as he stood, "It's time I go. I have to catch a boat down river to New Orleans and it leaves in thirty minutes."

Standing, Bill shook hands with his old First Sergeant and said, "Best of luck to you, Andy."

"The same to the two of you."

As Watkins walked away, Bill thought of James and the young Isaac, feeling great sadness come over him.

Clara suddenly asked, "Are you okay?"

"Sure, why?"

"You just had a strange look on your face."

"I was just thinkin' of the war, my dear."

# CHAPTER 7

The honeymoon ended too quickly for the two of them, and a week later found them at home, settling into a normal routine. Bill was up hours before dawn, either working in the barn or feeding his stock, and then into the house as the sun rose for a quick breakfast or coffee. During the days, he'd spent his time repairing fence, clearing stumps, or countless other tasks requiring his attention. Since his brother had gone to war and died, the small farm had had no serious work accomplished, which meant he was busy from can see to can't see. He'd return to the house each night bone deep tired.

While the place was shaping up, he knew it would be a year before it was in good condition once more. Clara did her part as well, spending time making quilts, sewing clothes for the two of them, or taking care of their chickens and fowl. They'd bought twenty-five chickens and six geese, and just feeding them and collecting the eggs was time consuming. Bill had insisted on geese; not only did he like their eggs, he knew they were better than a dog at warning of approaching strangers.

Times were tough in Missouri, and small bands of rough murderous men rode upon cabins in the night to rob and kill. Some claimed to be fighting for the south, others the north. Bill suspected most were riding for themselves and had little interest in the war at all. He kept two loaded guns in the house at all times and rarely did he work around the farm without his pistol belt on. He'd spent weeks teaching Clara to shoot a shotgun, rifle and pistol and as a result, she was a better than fair shot with any gun.

One morning the geese began to raise a fuss while he was splitting firewood and when he glanced at the road, his pa rode up on his big bay, dismounted, and walked toward him. Bill could see something serious had happened by the look on his father's face.

"Pa, is ma okay?"

"She's fine, but your Uncle Ben and Aunt Faye were killed late last night."

"Killed! Who in the world would kill two old folks, and for what reason?"

"Raiders, from what the army said."

"Good God, do they know which side did the killing?"

"Yup, Ben made that part of it easy—there were four other bodies in the barnyard. The dead men wearing a mix of uniforms, which, accordin' to the Yanks, means they were confederates."

"That ain't always true. Raiders can be men from either side, and since neither army supplies 'em regularly, they might wear about anything."

"Why in the world would Southerners kill loyal Southern folks like Ben and Faye?"

"Pa, they're out to rob and kill, so what Ben and Faye believed mattered little. Did they pretty much clean out the farm?"

"Well, there ain't a single critter left, the house and barn were burnt to the ground, and the army found their bodies in the barnyard."

"Faye was used, too, wasn't she?"

"Yup and hard, then they shot her in the chest. The army Captain I talked with said it looked like Ben had been killed in a building and then pulled to the barnyard, but Faye was caught alive." Pa replied, turned sad, and then continued, "Why would they rape my sister? Hell, son, she was over sixty years old!"

Shaking his head and cursing under his breath, Bill slammed the ax down hard and the blade stuck in a large piece of oak. When he looked at his pa, the old man was crying and shaking.

Putting his arm around his pa's shoulder Bill replied, "They're soulless men, pa, and raid to get food and whiskey. Her age meant nothing to them. Did the army say what they were goin' to do?"

Wiping his eyes with the back of his hand, the old man said, "Said they got a bunch of raids to look into, and they have patrols out now lookin' for 'em."

"I know this ain't mayhap the best time to bring it up, but have funeral arrangements been made?"

"We're goin' to bury 'em tomorrow on their farm. They both worked hard to make that place work, and I know they loved the land, so it's best."

"Ya okay with this?"

"Me and your ma know this was God's decision and we'll learn to accept it, but it's hard, boy. It's mighty hard."

"You got time to sit a spell?"

"Nope, just wanted to come by and tell you what happened, and to let you know the funerals will be held in the mornin' at nine. We're all goin' to meet in the barnyard and do the buryin' on the hill."

"We'll both be there. I'm sorry this happened, pa."

Walking toward his horse, pa said, "So am I, son, but God works in mysterious ways, or so the Good Book says."

Bill watched until his pa turned his horse and started for the road.

➡️⬅️  ➡️⬅️  ➡️⬅️

When Bill and Clara arrived at the farm the next morning, a light rain was falling and winds were gusty. They climbed from the wagon, made their way to a small group of family and friends, and waited. Less than ten minutes later, a Baptist preacher arrived and the group moved slowly to the hill. Rain was still falling.

At the graves, men took off their hats, the preacher lowered his head, and after a few moments of silence he said,

> "I am the resurrection and the life, saith the Lord: he that believeth in me, though he were dead, yet shall he live;

and whosoever liveth and believeth in me, shall never die.

I know that my Redeemer liveth, and that he shall stand at the latter day upon the earth and after worms destroy this body, yet in my flesh shall I see God: whom I shall see for myself, and mine eyes shall behold, and not another.

We brought nothing into this world, and it is certain we can carry nothing out. The Lord gave, and the Lord hath taken away; blessed be the Name of the Lord. Amen."

A beautiful young woman began to sing, "Sowing in the morning, sowing seeds of kindness . . ."

Minutes later, just as the singing stopped, a bright flash of lightning flashed across the horizon and a sharp crack of thunder followed. Leaning close to Clara, Bill whispered, "We'd better get back to the house, it looks like a bad storm comin'."

At that point, pa said to the group, "I want to thank y'all for comin' and for those of you that want, dinner will be at my place at noon. Now, let's all get out of here before the bottom of the bucket falls out and we get soaked."

At the wagon Clara and Bill donned ponchos. He assisted his wife up onto the seat and then turned to look at the hill for a few seconds. Climbing upward and sitting on the wet seat, Bill said, "God help me, but death bothers me little anymore. I loved Ben and Faye, but their passing didn't bring any tears."

Taking his hand, Clara said, "Honey, that's because of the numbers of deaths you saw in the war. You've grown cold toward death, and burials don't affect you like it does other folks."

"It's not just the numbers, but the way men died that haunts me. I've seen 'em burned to death, bayoneted in the belly, shot in the head, and if you think of a part of a man's body, I've seen injury to it. War is horrible, and only a fool ever wants to have one. Even without my injuries, I've changed and will never be the innocent man I once was. I no longer fear death."

Glancing at the low clouds overhead, Clara said, "Let's get home before we're soaked. I'm starting to get cold, too." She'd had all the talk of death she wanted and then some. She knew the repugnancies of the war would haunt veterans for years, but she couldn't understand it and didn't like talking about it. To her, death was a frightening thing and not to be talked about.

As they neared the farm, the rain began to fall harder and high winds bent the tops of trees.

Yelling over the wind, Bill said, "I'm headin' straight for the barn! I think we have a twister comin'!"

Driving the wagon into the barn, he took Clara's hand; they jumped and ran for the cellar. Debris flew past them and a pebble struck Bill's right hand, stinging as it bounced away. At the root cellar, he pulled the doors open, although it took all of his strength, and they quickly entered. The doors slammed shut loudly from the wind and he placed a thick piece of wood in place, locking them closed.

Striking a match on his boot heel, he spotted a lamp and lit it. Then, pulling Clara close he said, "Ain't much we can do now, except wait the storm out. Are you okay?"

"I'm fine, just wet, cold, and scared."

"We're safe in here. Even if a twister comes, we'll survive. Let's shuck off these wet ponchos and we'll be in better shape. I'd make a fire, but it'd end up killin' us. We have to have a lot of movin' air for a fire."

A tremendously loud noise passed almost overhead, Clara screamed and hugged Bill tightly. When he looked down at her face, she was terrified. Patting her on the back, he prayed aloud, "Lord, protect us even though we are but sinners. We are good God fearin' folks and know you can keep us safe. In the Bible it says, ask and ye shall receive—we're askin' now, Lord. Amen."

There came stillness, but neither of them moved. Both were afraid to open the doors to the cellar, so they waited. Finally, after a long wait, Bill stood and made his way to the door. Removing the cross-brace holding the doors closed, he opened the left side.

While it was still raining, the storm had moved on. Turning he picked up his poncho, put it on, and stepped outside.

The house was still standing, but the barn was gone, as well as the smokehouse and outhouse. Walking toward their home, he scanned the area and saw most of the small structures they had were no longer there. Nearing the house, he saw most of the roof was off, windows were broken, and the chimney was leaning away from the building.

*We can't stay here tonight. Only the Good Lord knows when the rest of the house will come down.* The only livestock he saw was his plow mule, Chester; the rest taken by the storm, or ran away in fear. He shook his head, put his hands on his hips and made his way back to the root cellar.

At the door he called out, "Come on up, honey. We're safe enough, but put on your poncho before you do. We've lost most of what little we had."

Clara walked to Bill's side.  Many long minutes later, she said, "It's all gone! How can that be?"

"I have no idea."

"I guess we're lucky in some ways, the house is still standing."

"Yup, it's standing, but we cain't live in it. The twister broke most of the windows, took a big chunk of the roof and I don't think it's safe to live in. It'll have to be torn down and built from scratch again."

"What are we goin' to do?" Tears were forming in her eyes.

"For tonight we can either sleep in the root cellar or ride over to my folks. Then again, we could go to your folks.  That's the only options I see."

Sniffling, Clara replied, "I don't cotton stayin' the night in a cellar and your folks are closer. Any horses make it through the storm?"

"Not a single horse, but Chester made it."

"That's all that's left? All we have is an old mule?"

"Yep, Chester and our lives are about it. I'm thankful the two of us survived without injury." Bill said and then looking at the dark sky overhead he added, "Thank you sweet Jesus for keeping us safe."

Riding double and bareback on Chester, they soon rode to the hitching post in front of Bill's boyhood home. Bill dismounted first and then helped Clara down. His pa walked from the house holding his shotgun at the ready, but seeing his son, he placed the gun against the wall beside the door.

"Trouble?" Pa asked as he walked toward them.

"Twister came through just before noon and cleaned us out. The house is missin' most of the roof, windows broken, chimney leanin' way out from the house, and if a flea near the place passes gas, it'll collapse."

"Either one of you get hurt?"

"Nary a scratch on either of us, because we were in the root cellar when the twister passed."

"Not good about the house, only you're lucky both of you are still in good shape. Come on in and let's get out of this rain" Pa said, and then turned back for the dry house.

In the house, ma soon had a pot of fresh coffee brewing, and leftovers from the funeral dinner, in the oven warming. As she worked, ma told of the twisters she'd seen during her lifetime, and of the people she'd known who had been killed. From her talk, Bill thought a person had died every year of her life, only he knew that wasn't true. He knew of some folks killed, but death from a twister was rare in this part of Missouri. Since they lived in the Ozarks, the rolling hills and deep valleys made most storms either peter out or skip over most homes.

Over coffee, Bill decided to bring up a subject that had been on his mind for years. It was something he wanted to do while he was still young and so alive. While he knew his folks would be against it, there was no better time to let Clara know of his desire, too.

"What are you goin' to do now, son, with most of your place gone?" Pa asked and poured a little coffee in his saucer.

Pa had started to blow on the coffee, when Bill said, "I'm thinkin' of gettin' shed of the place and movin' to Montana territory."

His father's head instantly came up and he asked, "What did you just say?"

"I'd like to hear this, too!" Clara said in an angry tone.

"I said, I'm *thinkin'* of goin' to Montana. I didn't say I was goin'."

His father sputtered and stammered a few seconds, but then finally said, "Why in God's name would you want to do that? What in the hell has Montana got we ain't?"

Ma blinked her eyes rapidly and asked, "You mean to leave us? You ain't been home a year yet."

Grinning, Bill replied, "Look, all of you, it's just an idea. Ever since I was a kid, I dreamed of owning a horse ranch up that way. Now, since we lost most of what we had, I thought it might be a good idea. I'm more or less jokin'."

"Well, I don't like your joke." Pa snapped quickly.

"I don't know what I think. Bill, you've never said anything about this to me before," Clara said in shock. She'd spent her whole life in Missouri and had never remotely considered moving.

"It's just a childish idea, is all it is."

Ma, always the practical one, said, "Look, iffen it'll make you happy, move. Except before you do that, make sure it's what you really want. All I ever wanted for my boys was for both of you to be happy, and iffen movin' to that Montana place will do that then start packin'."

"Myrtle! Have you lost what's left of your damned mind?" Pa's voice was loud in the small room.

Ma chuckled and replied, "Maybe I have, Clyde, but you need to stop bein' selfish, and keep in mind Bill ain't little William no more. He's a grown man and can do pretty much whatever he puts his mind to do."

"Hell, I know that, woman!"

"Watch your language at my table or you'll finish your coffee on the porch!"

"I didn't say we were goin' to move, I simply threw out a dream I've always had. I read about Montana in some dime novel I bought when I was about nine years old, and the country has always stayed in the back of my mind."

"I guess what your ma said is right, but I still don't like the idea much," pa said, and then lowered his head.

Clara, still upset that he'd not discussed it with her first, said, "What makes you think this Montana is a better place to live than Missouri?"

Raising his coffee cup, Bill replied, "I don't know if it is or not. I really don't know much about the place at all. During the war I met a man who'd been there, and he said some things that led me to believe it's a place full of chances for a feller to make good."

"Like what?" Ma asked.

"Free land, water, good crop country, and the only bad thing about the place is the Injuns."

"I don't think you want to move to some place full of Injuns, do you?" Pa asked with narrow eyes.

"He claimed they was called Sioux and mostly friendly to the white man."

"Son, I lived for a spell in Texas and iffen them Sioux are anything like the Comanche, he's way off track."

Ma shook her head and said, "Why don't you ride into Rolla in the mornin' and see what the army can tell you about the place? If the Sioux are good folks, then the army should know."

"Sounds like a good idea to me," Bill replied, and then took a sip of his now warm coffee.

➡➤⬅ ➡➤⬅ ➡➤⬅

Morning came with a heavy dampness in the air from the storm and a light breeze from the west. It was chilly, but not cold. At full daylight, Bill entered the small town of Rolla.

Seeing a First Sergeant leaning against a hitching post as he talked to two men, Bill waited and once the men walked off he asked, "Y'all got an orderly room around here?"

"Are you a Johnny Reb?" The burly Sergeant asked.

"Used to be, but I ain't no more. Took a bullet to my head and was discharged."

"What do you need the orderly room for?" He asked as he walked toward Bill.

"I got some questions about Montana country."

Smiling, the Sergeant extended his right hand and said, "My Name's Roscoe, David Roscoe."

Shaking the offered hand, Bill replied, "William Sanders, only my friends call me Bill."

"What unit were you in?"

"The third Missouri infantry. I took a ball to the head near Fort Davidson and they sent me home."

"It was a rough fight. Me and my boys were there, but you Rebs fought a hard battle."

Smiling, Bill said, "I'm surprised you'd even talk to me, I mean with me fightin' with the South and all."

"The fight's between our two countries, and I don't take it personal. Now, my boys might think different, but I've been in this man's army for almost twenty years and to me it's a job. When the army tells me to fight Injuns or Confederates, I do the best job I can. If you want to know a bit about Montana country, I can help you with that. I spent a few years stationed up that way."

"They got army posts up there already?"

"Yep and have had for years. I was at Fort Baker the first year of the war, and it's just a little ways from the Smith River. It ain't much, but there ain't a war there."

"How's the Sioux up that way?"

"Most of the time they're quiet, but they have their hell raising times. Usually they attack lone men in back country, although they've been known to attack a remote cabin now and again."

"Would you say the land and such are worth the risk of livin' there?"

"Oh, of that I have little doubt. It's good farming land and you can't beat it for cattle or horses. I knew one old boy up there that raised and broke horses for the army and he made a mint of money. We was paying him thirty dollars a head for each broken animal. The year I was there we bought fifty or more head from him."

"That's a lot of money in a year!"

"It sure is, but if you're thinking of moving up that way, take a few men with you. One lone man, or a single family, won't last long. You'd be prime pickin's for any tribe of Injuns in the area, so have at least five fighting men with you—more if you can get 'em."

"What tribes? I thought the Sioux were it."

"Nope, ya got Oto, though they live a long way from where you might be going, they raid the area at times. Then just about any plains Injun you can imagine could show up at your doorstep early one morning. They don't know boundaries like we do and as far as they're concerned, the land is free to travel or raid."

"Thanks for the information, Sergeant, if I have any more questions I'll look you up. Is that alright?"

"I'm in charge of the supplies here in Rolla, so I ain't going anyplace soon. Just ask for me by name and they'll find me."

# CHAPTER 8

## Montana Bound

That night, as they lay in bed, Clara asked, "Are you still thinkin' of goin' to Montana?"

"It's always been a dream. I brought it up yesterday, because this would be a good time to leave. I could sell the land, buy supplies and life stock here, and we could go. I know I should have discussed this with you first, but it hit me sudden like when we were talkin'."

"Well, it did make me mad when you started talkin' about a long trip I knew nothin' about. In the future, you need to tell me your dreams and desires," Clara said as she snuggled up to his side.

"I promise to do that, iffen you'll forgive me this time."

Kissing him on the lips, she said, "You're already forgiven, my dear."

"What do you think of a move to Montana?"

"What's it like up there?"

"I talked with a Yankee Sergeant today, and he said the land up there is prime for horses or cattle. He also told me flat land runs for miles and iffen it was him goin', he'd get a place near the mountains. That way he'd be close to timber and water. He said it's a good place for a ranch."

"Sounds like a smart man, for a Yankee."

Bill chuckled and then turned serious as he added, "But we'll need at least five men along to keep the land we claim. The Sioux Injuns own the land, and they take poorly to squatters."

"I don't know iffen I like the idea of having to fight to keep our land."

"Baby, there will be a fight to keep what we own no matter where we live. I mean, look at what just happened to Ben and Faye."

Lowering her eyes, Clara replied, "It's rough times we live in. Only, how can you get five men in Rolla to move to Montana?"

"I cain't, so I'm goin' to put an ad in a Saint Louis paper to see iffen any men are interested there."

"Should be, the city has all kinds of men movin' through it."

"Yup, that's what I figured, too."

Rubbing her hand over his lower belly, she replied, "Do it tomorrow."

"I . . . I think . . . that's a good idea. I have a feelin' we're gonna be busy part of this night."

Smiling, as her hand reached for him, she whispered, "We will be."

⋙ ⋘　⋙ ⋘　⋙ ⋘

Ten days later, a man with his family pulled up in the barnyard while Bill was working in the barn. Hearing the wagon's wheels moan as it stopped, he walked outside with a shotgun in his hand and asked, "What can I do for ya?"

"I'm lookin' for William Sanders."

"Well, you found 'em."

"My name is Peters, Joshua Peters, but you can just call me Josh. We read your ad in the paper and would like to go to Montana."

"How many is we? And, call me Bill."

"There're two families, mine and John's. He has two older boys, twins they are, and they're close to twenty."

"Are there any youngsters in the group?"

"Nope, they've all grown up."

Moving toward the wagon, Bill asked, "How old are you and your brother?"

"I'm jus' shy of thirty-five and he's three years older."

Extending his right hand, Bill replied, "Had to ask, because I don't want some older men joinin' up with us. Glad to meet you, Joshua Peters. Where's your brother?"

Josh released Bill's hand and replied, "Camped near Rolla. I came alone to see what this was all about."

Turning, Bill said, "Let me saddle a horse and I'll ride with you back to where they're at. I'd like to talk to all of the men at the same time, that way I only got to say what needs sayin' once."

⇥⇤  ⇥⇤  ⇥⇤

Once at the campsite, the four men and Bill gathered at the fire to discuss the coming trip. He saw the twins, Sam and Luke, were both strong looking lads, with long blond hair, but little facial hair.

John was a portly man, and Bill wondered how well the man would do once on the trail. His hair, like Josh's was brown and cropped short. Of the two, only John wore a neatly trimmed beard.

Sitting on a log, Bill said, "The trip will be long and hard. Iffen you think you can't make it, I don't want you along. I want men that ain't got no quit in 'em and will fight, need be."

John grinned and replied, "I've lost some weight and size over the last year and it'll do me some good to get some exercise. Me and Josh both served in the war, for the Confederacy, and was discharged last month when our unit broke up. Those who still wanted to fight went to other units, and those that didn't were sent home. I don't think the war will last another month, iffen that."

"I was in the war, too, but I never heard of a whole unit bein' torn apart."

"They jus' started doin' 'er and it's a cryin' shame. We were a cavalry unit, with no hosses. The men who stayed on went to infantry units. Hell, they didn't even have a way to move the boys and they had to walk."

"Last battle I was in, many men didn't even have a gun or knife. They were to take what they needed from injured or dead men on either side."

Josh added a log to the flames and said, "We tried, and God knows it, but we've lost. Last I heard, General Lee was thinkin' about callin' it quits."

"Iffen he stops fightin' they all will. He's a respected man, you know," Bill spoke, as he took an offered cup of coffee from John.

"That's what we figured, too. I think that's the main reason our Colonel let some of us boys go home. He said there was no reason to die for a lost cause."

Bill nodded and said, "Smart man, your Colonel."

John gazed into Bill's eyes and asked, "What about you? How come you ain't still in?"

"Took a ball to the head and they sent me home. Now, I have to warn y'all, at times I have fits, but they don't last long, just minutes. Only problem is, I'm pretty tired after havin' one."

John quickly glanced at Josh and then asked, "How long do these fits really last?"

"Less than five minutes and I ain't had one in months."

Sam, who'd been quiet, suddenly asked, "What causes your fits?"

"The doctors don't know. I've noticed after I've been under a lot pressure, I tend to have one."

"After?" Luke asked.

"Yup, not during, but after something important happens. My home was destroyed by a twister last month and nothin' happened, so maybe they'll go away eventual like."

Josh spoke, "Mayhap, but don't count on that happenin'. I saw many head injuries in the war, and you're lucky to still be able to move and speak. Most of them jaspers had the minds of kids after bein' shot. Nonetheless, I still want to go with you, iffen you'll have me."

"I wanted to be up front with all of you and let you know before we started the trip. I intend to be fair and honest and expect the same in return."

"We're all good, God fearin' men and as honest as the day is long. I'm in for the trip, too."

"That's good to hear. I figure we need about a week to gather supplies and then we can leave, if the last man shows. Do you have any women comin'?"

"Mary and John's Susan are in the first wagon. Everybody jus' calls her Sue." Josh

John stood and called out, "Sue, can you and Mary come to the fire for a few minutes?"

"Be right there!" A female voice replied.

Two women emerged from the back of a wagon cover and started walking toward the fire. One was middle-aged, short, stout, and had dark hair, while the other was much younger, with blond hair and carrying no extra pounds.

"We've the man we read about in the paper here to meet you both."

Standing by the fire, the middle-aged woman said, "Howdy do. I'm Mary, the wife of John, and she's Sue."

"I'm William Sanders, but jus' call me Bill."

Both nodded and then Sue asked, "Are you goin' to take us to Montana?"

Bill laughed and replied, "No, not me! I have an ad in the paper for a guide or someone who knows the way. I'm just puttin' this thing together and hope to keep it organized as we travel."

"We'll need a ramrod, and I'm glad you volunteered to do the job," Josh said and then smiled.

Bill grinned and then offered, "Why don't all of you bring your wagon over to my place for supper and I'll let you meet my wife, Clara?"

"We killed a deer earlier this mornin', so we'll bring the meat. I don't like showin' up for supper without bringin' something," Sue said, and then smiled.

Bill, knowing it was not right, couldn't help but feel flushed at her warm smile. This is one fine woman, he thought. "Very well, just get there a couple of hours before dark. We'll cook outside and talk." Bill replied, stood and then moved to his horse.

As he mounted, he heard John say, "We'll all be there!"
When he returned home, a filthy man dressed in buckskins was waiting for him under an oak tree. Pa was talking to the man, but when Bill tied his horse to the hitching post, he was too far away to hear the conversation.

As soon as Bill was beside his pa, the old man said, "This is Jack Moses, and he's come to see you about your trip to Montana."

The dirty man stood, shook Bill's hand and said, "I'm your man iffen you still want to go. I spent a lot of years up that way and still got my hair, so I must be doin' something right."

He was a short man with long brown hair and a ragged beard of the same color. His eyes were the color of cold steel, and his gaze was steady as he looked into Bill's eyes.

"How many trips you made that way?"

"Four, and each time I spent a year or more livin' off the land. I did some lookin' for gold the last time I was there, but saw not a trace of color."

"Then why go back?"

"I've done some readin' on it and learned there's gold out that ways, only I was lookin' in the wrong places. I figure to go back one more time and iffen I don't find what I'm lookin' for, I'll come home for good."

"When do you want to leave? I ask because I've got four men with their families who'll go with us."

"Let's give y'all a week to get supplied and then we can start movin'. Keep in mind, the trip is right out of hell, especially with wagons, but others have gone before."

"I think we'll do okay, as long as the Injuns leave us alone."

"Ain't much goin' on up that way right now, but Injuns are notional folks. I speak Sioux, Comanche, and a little Oto. I know sign, so iffen they get close enough to talk, I can deal with 'em."

Looking at his pa, Bill said, "I have them other folks comin' over for supper later. Tell ma we don't need her kitchen, because we'll roast the deer they're bringin' on a spit outside. I figure the deer and some beans will do the job, and maybe a big pan of cornbread."

"I'll tell her when I go back in."

In bed that night, Clara asked, "Did you get the details on this trip worked out with those other men durin' supper?"

"Yep, I made some rules."

"Rules? What kind of rules?"

"No drinking whiskey, unless we're in a safe place, all of us will pull guard duty every night, and some others about sharin' supplies and food. They have to know from the start that we'll have to work together and contribute what we have in order to have a safe trip."

"How'd they take it?"

"Pretty good, but they're family. Nobody raised any hell, so at least that part of the trip is done."

"Are you sure you want to do this?"

Bill looked into her eyes and replied, "I do, but what do you think?"

"I'm your wife and go where you go, so I'll always be at your side. I love you, Bill Sanders."

"I love you too, only I want you happy."

"As long as I'm with you, I'll be happy," Clara said and then turned the lamp off on the nightstand. She kissed him passionately on the lips and then whispered, "I want you."

⇢⇠　⇢⇠　⇢⇠

The day they left for Montana, Bill read in the Rolla newspaper that General Lee had surrendered to Grant at Appomattox Courthouse, Virginia. He had an idea where Appomattox Courthouse was, but he'd never been there and had little interest, other than knowing the war would soon be over.

*All those lives lost and men maimed, for what?*

The day was clear, with just a few scattered cotton balls of clouds off to the west, and a light breeze rustled the leaves in trees overhead. Clara was dressed in a loose-fitting gingham dress and wore her blue bonnet on her head, while he wore canvas pants, a homespun brown shirt, hat and boots. His pistol belt was around his waist and his rifle was at his side. As he flicked the reins, the horses began to move.

He'd said his goodbyes to his folks that morning, and both had tears in their eyes as they left. They were good folks and Bill knew his leaving was hurting them badly, but it was something he had to do. They had visited Clara's folks the day before, only her pa thought they were both fools for leaving and said as much.

"We're finally goin'! We're on our way to Montana!" Clara said, and then broke out laughing.

Bill found it strange she was laughing when all of the men wore solemn looks on their faces, and the wagon wheels creaked and moaned in protest of heavy loads. *If she thinks this will be months of picnics and fun, she's in for a big surprise. I just hope we all make it safely.*

Things went smoothly, until they turned west and entered the open plains, when it suddenly turned rougher on people and livestock. Even with the openness of the prairie, they found the best they could travel was about twenty miles a day, which everyone thought was too slow.

Moses sat by the fire one night and said, "You're all overloaded. You all need to drop some stuff."

"Like what?" Josh asked as he pulled his old corncob pipe from his shirt pocket.

"Most of the furniture you're carryin' and anything else you don't need. If you don't, you ain't gonna make it."

"We'll do it," Bill said, and then met the eyes of the other men.

"Good, 'cause once we cross the Missouri River, the trail turns really rough."

Clara glanced up and asked, "Rougher than this?"

"Yep, after we leave where old Fort Atkinson used to be, she'll turn real rough on us. That's another reason to drop some stuff you don't need. Iffen you don't, I honestly don't think y'all will make it all the way."

"We'll dump some things in the mornin'," John said, then looked at his brother and shrugged his shoulders. To him there was no choice.

That night as they lay under a canvas shelter, Bill asked, "You sure you're up to this trip?"

"Well, I think so, but I have something important to say."

"Is there a problem?"

Giggling, Clara said, "No, not a problem, only I think I'm with child."

"Really?"

"I think so, because I've not had a period for the last two months. Last week I should have started, but I didn't."

"That's wonderful, baby, great news!" Bill replied and then in a more serious voice added, "Only I ain't got any idea how to be a pa."

"You'll learn, just like the rest of 'em have."

"We don't have a name!"

"We will by the time the baby arrives. You can relax a mite, we've months to pick a name for a boy and a girl."

"Girl? I'd never thought of that."

"It could be either, so keep that in mind when you're thinkin' of names. Not all babies are boys you know."

"Yes, I know that, but the Sanders clan runs high in boys."

"We'll have to wait and see what the Lord gives us. I hate to say this, but I'm beat and need some sleep. I ain't strong like you are."

Laughing, Bill pulled her close and said, "Sleep, my dear, and dream of our soon to be child."

When the sun rose in the morning, all were busy pulling items from their wagons, and Bill shook his head at the useless stuff in some them. Josh pulled a bookcase out and let it drop to the ground, where the wood shattered. John pulled out basket after basket of dishes, pots and pans, as well as a large dresser. Bill and Clara removed a China hutch and sat it gently beside the trail, hoping someone who needed it might find it.

Moses walked around the wagons saying, "Keep your clothes, food, and enough tools and other gear to keep us alive once we get to Montana. The rest you can get shed of."

"This bed has been in my family for years!" Sue cried out.

"Now, honey, it's gotta go. We won't make it to Montana iffen we don't drop the bed. It's made of solid oak and just too heavy," John said and reached for the headboard.

As her bed was pulled from the wagon, Sue walked off in tears. Moses, following the woman said, "It has to be done, Missy, there really ain't no choice in the matter."

"I know that, Mister Moses, only I don't like it. That bed is almost 200 years old and been in my family the whole time."

Moses, knowing she was angered, turned and walked toward the wagons. As he moved he heard a sharp crack of thunder to the west and thought, *It looks like it's gonna turn wet here in a minute or two, and I've got a bunch of pilgrims with me. I'm already doin' everything I can for 'em, shy of wipin' their rears.*

John suddenly said, "I wish I'd known a while back my wagon was overloaded, because some of this stuff could have been sold."

Moses laughed and replied, "Did you think you could take a whole houseful of stuff on a trip like this-un? Hell, we'll be lucky iffen we get there our own selves! Y'all knew we had many long miles to cover, and your livestock has to pull the stuff you're chuckin' out the back of them wagons right now. Ain't you got no concern for your critters?"

"Of course I do, but I had no idea the trip would be this rough!"

Moses laughed once more and said, "Rough? You ain't seen rough yet, pilgrim. The rough part is still to come and when it does, remember your words."

"Well, somebody is goin' to find some good furniture when they pass this way," Josh said and all could hear the frustration in his voice.

Bill, tired of the complaining, said, "Not likely. I'd imagine most will have to do just what we're doin'—throw things away. Let's get this done and back on the trail. We've lost enough time this mornin', I reckon."

# CHAPTER 9

**N**ear noon, Bill rode up beside Moses and said, "We're bein' watched by somebody, but I ain't got any idea who it might be. I get a feelin' when I'm bein' watched, and I've had it all mornin'."

"I got the feeling too, and it's most likely Long Grass and his group of Sioux."

"Friendly?"

Shrugging his shoulders, he said, "Depends on the time of the day it is, and the day of the month. Overall, he's a fair man, but his young bucks prove a handful for him to control at times."

"What do you want to do?"

"Keep movin'. Iffen it's Long Grass, he'll drop in for a visit. Then again, iffen it's somebody else, they'll come sooner or later. Tell the boys and men to keep their guns close, but not to pick 'em up. Unless they've had guns in their hands all day, because that'll tell the Sioux, or whoever it is, that we know they're around."

Bill told the men and boys, then rode by his wagon and said, "Clara, keep that shotgun where it is, unless one of us fires first, but me and Moses think the Sioux are watchin' us."

"Good God!"

"Calm down a mite, we've a good fightin' force. All but the boys have been in more than jus' a few scraps. Besides, Moses thinks it's a group of Injuns led by a Sioux he knows."

"Let's hope so. The thought of Injuns scares me."

"It should."

"Don't talk like that."

"This is not a trip for the weak, and you're not a frail woman. Toughen up a mite and you'll do fine. Ain't an Injun goin' to hurt you as long as a single white man lives, and you know that."

Lowering her head, she replied, "I know, but it's a fear I think most women out west have."

"It's a healthy fear, but don't let it get the best of you." Bill said and then rode to the point of the group.

Clara shook her head and thought, *You're a strange man, Bill Sanders. Here I sit, scared to death and you ride off and leave me alone.*

Bill knew Clara disliked the way he handled her fear, and he wanted anger in her right now. Fear, he'd discovered during the war, could spread like a wildfire if one person panicked, because others would soon follow. *Anger is the best thing for her right now. While I don't like her mad at me, it'll do for the time bein'.*

Moses rode up beside him and whispered, "It's the Sioux, for sure. I just saw a warrior a few minutes ago."

At that moment, a large Sioux war party appeared on a distant rise. As they watched, two warriors separated and moved slowly toward the wagons.

Turning, Moses said, "No matter what happens, don't let 'em know you're scared."

Giving a weak grin, Bill replied, "How do you know I'm scared?"

"I'm scared, too. Any man with half a brain would be scared in a fix like this."

"Well, that's me, half a brain."

Moses chuckled dryly and replied, "You'll do. A feller who can joke at a time like this is okay in my book."

"I either joke or crap my pants. Fierce looking group, ain't they?"

"Yup, but they're good folks to those they call friend."

"Does Long — "

"Yep, he calls me friend." Moses replied and then laughed.

"I'm relieved to hear that."

"Quiet, here they come. Remember what I said about fear."

The warriors stopped almost ten steps away and the youngest asked in heavily accented English, "Why on Sioux lands?"

*"We pass through your lands and do not intend to stay,"* Moses explained in the Sioux tongue.

*"You are known among The People as Shoots Much."*

*"I am. How is my brother Long Grass?"*

*"I am well, and you my brother?"*

*"Well."*

*"We did not know you traveled with these white people."*

"Bullshit." Moses said in English and then replied in Sioux, *"They are my friends and we go to the land of the buffalo grasses."*

"What's goin' on?" Bill asked, apprehensive by the comment made by Moses in English.

"Shut your damned mouth, unless you want to get us kilt."

*"Why does the young white man speak?"*

*"He wanted to know your name and I told him."*

*"Good. A man should know who he is speaking with, and he is wise to ask."*

*"That is true."*

*"You may pass, my brother, but the Oto are on the plains and I cannot offer protection as you travel. They are few, but I think they'd make only a small battle to kill all of these white people. We were seeking them when our scouts found you."*

*"Each of these white men has fought many times in the past. All are great warriors and if the Oto fight us, their lodges will fill with the cries of their women. Yes, they might kill us all, but they will suffer much to do so."*

*"Your words I think are true. Go, my brother, to the lands of the buffalo grass,"* Long Grass said, pulled his horse around and rode back to the hill at a trot.

Turning to the small group, Moses ordered, "Get them wagons movin', we're free to go."

The whip in John's hand snapped loudly and the wagons started to move. When the last wagon passed, Moses said, "I don't like the idea of what's goin' on out here."

"Huh? I didn't understand the conversation. What is it you don't like the idea of?"

Explaining to Bill what the chief had said, Moses added, "Oto are good fighters and iffen we run into 'em, ya'll wish we hadn't. Their as tough a bunch as you'll find."

"I thought this is Sioux land."

"See, they're movers, Oto are, and the bastards will fight at the drop of a coin. To come onto Sioux lands means little to them, and they might be lookin' for a fight."

"Never heard of 'em."

Placing his hand on his saddle horn, Moses leaned his head to the side and narrowed his eyes as he replied, "Let's jus' hope you never see 'em, 'cause iffen ya do, some of us will die."

Bill felt a shiver run down his spine.

They covered twenty miles and a couple of hours before dusk, Moses led them into a small grove of cottonwood trees running along the sides of a small stream. Gray clouds had moved in and most suspected rain before dawn. The air was cool and the winds light.

Dismounting, Bill said, "Luke and Sam, you two stand guard while we make camp. I want one of you on the north side and the other south."

Luke pulled his hat down and said, "I'll take the north side."

As the two walked to their guard posts, Bill watched his small group establish a camp. They'd been on the trail long enough now that each person knew their duties and performed them without a wasted effort. In less than fifteen minutes, the work was completed, except for caring for the horses and gathering firewood.

Within an hour of arrival, a large pot of beans and venison was cooking over the flames of a little fire. The wood cracked and popped as the flames ate at it like a hungry living thing. Glancing upward, Bill saw the wood was dry and no smoke was seen against the cloud cover. Sitting in the dirt by the flickering flames, he took his hat off and ran his fingers through his filthy hair. *I need a bath in the worse way, only it won't do any good. I'll just be like this again come tomorrow.*

Luke was running wildly for the fire. Bill stood, checked his rifle and moved toward the young man.

"I saw some big critters over the rise! I ain't seen the likes of these things before, but I suspect they're buffalo."

Moses grinned and asked, "Big, shaggy and cow lookin' things?"

"Yup, only one hell of a lot bigger!"

"Yup, buffalo herd. Bill, you and Josh come with me. We're gonna make meat."

Luke, looking downcast asked, "What about me, I found 'em?"

Laughing, Moses said, "Josh, you stay here then. We'll take Luke, because he's earned the job. Don't worry none, we'll see 'em lots of times on this trip."

Luke, glad he'd get to go, smiled at his pa and said, "I'll get us a big-un, pa!"

Slapping his son on his back, Josh said, "You just do your best, and I'll be proud of you, son."

"I see one small problem here. Ain't none of us ever hunted a buffalo before," Bill said as he looked at Moses.

"It ain't hard, pilgrim. We'll walk our horses down that way, but keep your horse between you and the buffalo."

"Ain't no horse got six legs!" Luke scoffed as he shook his head.

"Son, I've yet to meet a critter that can count. This'll work, because I learned it from the Sioux. When it comes time to shoot, just place your rifle over the saddle and aim right where you would shoot a deer. Now, he won't drop quickly, but he'll go down after a minute or two."

"How close we goin' to move in?" Bill asked.

Moses replied, "Close to a hundred feet. Buffalo got bad eyes, but good noses. We're down wind, so they won't smell us. When you see my rifle start to come up, brings yours up too, only do the job slowly."

The three meandered down to the large shaggy beasts, and when they were in close, Moses raised his rifle, sighted a large cow and pulled the trigger. Luke and Bill fired a second later and as the herd turned and started walking, three of the animals found it difficult to move. The cow Moses had shot walked a few feet and then fell to her side, dead within seconds. Bill's just collapsed and Luke's walked off, only to fall after fifty feet. It seemed to Luke it took the huge animals time to realize they'd been killed.

"Kind of dumb critters, ain't they?" The young man asked as he moved toward the fallen animals.

"Sort of, but they make some damned fine eatin'." Moses replied as he pulled his skinning knife. Then, added, "We'll quarter 'em and then take the meat back. Be sure to get the tongues, heart and liver of your animal. They make some dandy soup."

They'd no sooner returned to the wagons when rain hit with a gentle gust of wind. The rainfall was soft at first, but all knew it would soon be pounding on their shelters. The women went into the wagons, while the men took shelter under stretched canvas in the trees, and soon the storm was upon them.

Lightning flashed and thunder cracked loudly as Bill leaned back on his blanket and pulled an old corncob pipe from this shirt pocket. The meat from the buffalo was in the wagons and processing would have to wait for the storm to pass. All knew the storms on the plains passed quickly, most of the time in less than an hour, but occasionally they lasted much longer.

As time passed, Bill understood this was not a typical storm and it looked as if it would last the whole evening. Turning, he asked Moses, "That meat will be okay like it is, right?"

Nodding, the older man replied, "Yup, it won't turn green, because it ain't hot enough. We placed it far enough in the wagons it won't get wet neither, so it'll be fine."

"Must be well over a thousand pounds of meat off of them three critters, and I'd hate to waste it."

"Probably closer to two thousand, and don't give it no more thought."

"How much further do we have to go to find white people?"

"Butterfield's Tradin' Post is the next place, only she's a ways off yet. I'd guess we'll get there in about three weeks, iffen we keep makin' good time. You noticed the trail turned rougher this mornin', or did ya?"

"Not a lot rougher, but I noticed."

"She'll get a lot rougher before we get to smoother ground again. Most of the rest of the way to Montana will be about like this, except for one really bad spot maybe a month from now."

"Bad, huh?"

"Yep. We'll have to lower each wagon down some bluffs and then cross a river. The job's a tiring one and all of us will work up a sweat. Then, iffen the rivers down, we'll have to cross a wide cold-assed stretch of water. Poor doin's that is."

"We'll get the job done. Tell me," Bill spoke as he stuffed his pipe bowl with tobacco, "is Montana the place I've heard?"

"Good country, except it takes a real man to live there. I suspect you and Josh won't have no problems."

"What about John and the boys?"

"The boys got grit in their craws, but I don't think John will make a go of it. He seems too soft, only I could be wrong. I've seen men before I thought would go under, except they didn't and the ones I thought would make it didn't. This country changes a man, makes 'em stronger, or they die."

"What of our women, I mean, will they make it?"

"Well," Moses said and then grinned as he continued, "I ain't no fortune teller, but I suspect your wife and Mary will do fine. That Sue, now, she has some serious growin' up to do if she expects to live in Montana country."

"She's a small woman."

"It ain't her size, it's her mind. I think she's lived a soft life and likes her comforts. Out here, she'll find comfort hard to come by or it ain't found at all. When you come to Montana or any place to homestead, you have to change your whole way of thinkin'. See, iffen the Injuns don't kill you, a disease, critter, or accident might, so you have to keep your eyes and ears open all the time. I don't see her doin' that. It's a shame too, because she's a pert little thing."

"Yup, she's pretty enough, but like you said, it's all about survivin' out here."

Giving a big tooth-gapped grin, Moses said, "I've been wrong before. Hell, she might survive while the rest of us go under. Just remember to reload after you fire your gun and when the bugs stop makin' noise at night, something *big* is near. Always keep your fires small, too. That and with a lot of luck, you might be among the livin' when the sun comes up."

"I'll remember what you just said. It seems I have a lot of learnin' to do."

"You do at that, but since you know you need to learn more you'll be fine. It's them that think they know it all that die fast out here."

Pulling his blanket up and around his shoulders, Bill leaned back and said, "I'm goin' to get some sleep. There won't be a meal tonight, and I don't suspect Injun trouble with it raining like it is."

"You can rest, while I sit here and think a spell. Iffen the rains stop, I'll send guards out. Come an hour before dawn, I'll wake all of you up."

"That sounds good to me." Bill spoke and immediately drifted off to sleep.

➡️⬅️  ➡️⬅️  ➡️⬅️

An hour before dawn, Moses touched Josh on the leg and whispered one word, "Injuns." He then moved to each man and the boys, waking them and spreading the warning. The women moved from the wagons and prepared to load the guns for the men if a fight started, while the men knelt behind what protection they could find. At some point during the night the rain had stopped.

Moses moved from man to man and said, "Looks to be Oto and iffen it is, there'll be no talk. Don't shoot until I do, but make every shot count. They're a bad-ass bunch and not to be taken lightly."

While next to Bill, the man started to move away when a sound like a hand slapping leather was heard. Moses fell, crawled to Bill and said, "Arrow in my left shoulder. Burns like a bitch, too." Glancing down, he added, "Yup, Oto."

Bill was looking at the arrow when he heard a loud war cry and Oto rose from the plains and ran for the camp. Moses snapped the arrow shaft off, leaving about three inches, aimed and fired his rifle. A warrior dropped to the ground where he lay unmoving.

Bill spotted a warrior wearing more feathers than a Christmas turkey, took in a deep breath and as he released it, he squeezed his trigger. The heavy lead slug from his Sharps rifle caught the chief in the middle of his forehead and gore exploded from the back of his skull as he fell to the grass. His body quivered and jerked as it began to shutdown.

Three shots sounded from around camp, one of the women screamed and when Bill turned to look, he saw Sue fighting off a warrior. She was too close to the brave for him to risk a shot, so he ran toward them, knowing he'd have to use his pistol when he got closer. The sounds of the battle increased as Bill neared and he knew he had to kill this man and then rejoin the fight.

The Oto brave suddenly noticed Bill, threw a tomahawk in his direction, which narrowly missed, and then raised his rifle. Bill dropped to one knee and pulled his pistol. He quickly plucked the hammer back and fired three bullets into the warrior's chest. Before the man struck the ground, Bill was headed back to his position, knowing if they survived this attack, they'd be lucky.

Moses had another wound, this one across this forehead, and he was laughing as he fired at the charging braves, which made Bill think the injury had affected his mind. Then he remembered how each man reacted differently to stresses in battle. Some prayed, others cried, and a few laughed. He recollected one old man who'd shouted the word of God as he put Yankee after Yankee to the bayonet.

Suddenly—it was quiet.

"They've gone, by God!" Moses shouted in joy.

"Are you sure?" Bill asked as he reloaded his pistols.

"Yup and by rights they should've gone when you killed their chief, so they must have wanted our wagons pretty bad."

"Why? Hell, there ain't much in our wagons."

"Son compared to an Injun you're a wealthy man. You have pots, pans, cups, food, clothes and many other things they want. Hell, they'll kill a man just for his horse or guns, so a wagon is kind of hard for 'em to pass up."

Standing, Bill said, "Let's check everything out and see if we have anyone besides you hurt."

At that instant, they heard a loud scream and Moses said, "Looks like one of us didn't make it."

Running to the wagons, they found John lying beside the fire pit. He looked bad, but Bill knew that meant little.

His body was jerking and twitching as Moses leaned over to check his injury.

"He took a ball in his neck, but he ain't spurtin' blood. Somebody shut that damned woman up! I can't even talk with her making that racket! Move her to the other side of these wagons, and let us try to save her man! Luke, you do it now!" Moses yelled in anger.

Then, once Mary was out of the way, Moses continued in an even voice, "Like I was sayin', he ain't spurtin' blood, only I don't like this jerkin'. The bullet might have struck his neck bone and iffen it did, he'll die on us."

"Any way we can tell?" Bill asked.

Pulling the ramrod from one of his old muzzle-loading pistols, he replied, "Yep, by usin' this with a rag on the end. Iffen I pull it out and parts of bone are on it, he'll go under most likely."

A minute or two later the ramrod came out the other side of John's neck with no shards of bone on the cloth. Moses smiled and then said, "Clean shot and it looks to have missed anything important. He'll live, iffen he don't fester on us."

Turning, Bill called out, "Clara, bring me the whiskey jug!"

Once she brought the alcohol, Moses took the jug from her, pulled the cork from the bottle and tipped it just a little. As the strong drink struck his neck injury, John gave a heartbreaking scream and passed out cold. His jerking and twitching quickly stopped, but his breathing was deep and regular. Moses wrapped the injury with some cloth and then wiped his hands on his pants.

Clara, who'd been watching quietly, walked to the fire and ordered, "Take your shirt off, Moses, you need some doctorin' too."

"Don't reckon I can get it off, so you'll have cut it."

Picking up a large butcher knife, she started at his shirttail and cut a line to the neck. Then, she peeled the shirt from his upper torso and said, "Bill, you need to do the doctorin', except I'll help you. I need to know how to do this stuff in case you're hurt one day."

"Smart woman," Moses said, and then took a long snort of whiskey.

"This will be my first arrow. I don't think the job is any different than a bullet, is it?"

Taking another snort of whiskey, Moses replied, "Iffen the heads stuck in some bone or muscle, it will be more difficult. Your only choice then is to either cut it out or pull it out with a pair of pliers. I think I saw some in your wagon."

"Clara, iffen you'll get the pliers, I'll have a quick drink of whiskey and get this show on the road," Bill said, as he moved toward Moses.

"Nervous, are you?" Moses asked and gave a weak grin.

"More nervous over the battle with the Oto than I am about doctorin' ya up. See, I worked on many an injured man durin' the war, and they either lived, or didn't. Damned doctors weren't much good, and all they knew how to do well was cuttin' off body parts."

"I hear'd that a while back."

Clara returned, handed the pliers to Bill and asked, "What now?"

Looking at Moses he asked, "You need a stick?"

"Nope, I got me a folded up piece of leather to use. Let's get this over with."

Seeing a questioning look in Clara's eyes, Bill said, "To bite on. He's gonna have some serious pain in a few minutes."

"I see."

Minutes later, with some folded rawhide in his mouth, Moses nodded.

"Now, I'm goin' to remove this arrow. Watch and then ask questions later. Be ready to hand me a bandage when he starts to bleed heavy, and he will at some point," Bill said as he reached for the broken arrow shaft.

Grasping the shaft, he tried to pull the arrow out, but that just brought a loud moan of pain from Moses without any movement of the arrowhead. Must be stuck in bone or muscle, Bill thought and picked up his knife.

He inserted the knife blade, ran it up and around the arrowhead, only it was still stuck. Frustrated, he turned and said to Clara, "Hand me the pliers."

Grasping the shaft as low as he could, he pulled but the arrow did not budge even a little, so he began to rock it from side to side. Finally, after many long minutes, the arrowhead came loose and blood began to flow freely. Blood started to run down Moses' bare chest and he let the rawhide fall from his mouth. Giving a weak grin, he said, "That arrow was stuck in bone. There wasn't any other way to get it out, pilgrim."

Wiping his bloody hands off with an old towel, Bill ordered, "Clara, put the blade of your butcher knife in the flames. When it's red-hot, let me know."

Moses blinked rapidly and asked, "Can I get another snort of whiskey? I have a bit of pain to get shed of."

"You got a passel of pain comin', too, so take you a few good belts," Bill replied as he handed the jug to the man.

Moses took a good half-dozen deep and long drinks from the jug, knowing the pain he was about to receive would be severe.

"The blade is ready," Clara said in a fearful voice.

# CHAPTER 10

**B**ill placed the flat of the shimmering blade against Moses' wound, melting and smearing the flesh together. The bleeding stopped instantly, but the man gave a loud scream of pain, his eyes rolled back, and he passed out.

"What a horrible smell!" Clara exclaimed, as she fanned the air.

Bill placed the still hot knife on a large rock beside the fire. "Yup, but I've done it so many times I hardly notice."

"Will he live?"

"He should, unless he festers. This ain't good at all, because we've two injured men with us and either or both could fester."

"Do we go on or wait for the men to heal?"

"We move. Neither of these fellers will die because we move, and winter will be upon us any day now. Moses said winter comes early in this part of the country, which means we don't want to get caught out on the plains when the weather turns."

"This is turnin' out to be a bit of a trip, ain't it?"

Looking deeply into her eyes, Bill asked, "Are you sorry you came?"

"No, I'm not sorry at all. I did get scared durin' the Injun attack, but I suspect most folks would. I just miss not havin' water to bathe as often as I should. It's harder on a woman to go without water."

Placing his arm around her, Bill replied, "One day we'll have our own ranch, with lots of water."

"Do ya promise? Will we really have lots and lots of water?"

Chuckling, he said, "Yes, lots and lots of water, and just for you!"

"Good, now kiss me, because I have to go help the other women."

Pulling her near, Bill kissed her, broke away and then gave a big smile.

"What are you smilin' about?"

"Thinkin' about how happy and lucky I am. I love you, Clara."

"I love you too, Bill, and later tonight I'll show you just how much."

➡⬅ ➡⬅ ➡⬅

At dusk, Bill had the wagons move in close and started making camp for the night. A strong wind had come and with it dark clouds, hanging low overhead. Both John and Moses were feverish, but Bill knew that was normal for injured men. Their wounds were clean and the skin looked good—with no sign of festering. He gave a silent prayer of thanks to God.

Once camp was made, Bill scouted the area, found a small cold stream, and took a shot at an antelope, which he missed. Returning to camp, he informed the women of the stream and started gathering buffalo chips. The women hated cooking with the chips, and had complained loudly more than once about the idea of cooking over burning dung. While he worked, he saw Sue, Clara, and Mary moving toward the stream with buckets in their hands.

Less than five minutes later, Sue returned screaming loudly. Thinking they were about to be attacked, Bill cocked his rifle and ran toward the woman.

"Snake! A big snake just bit Mary on the leg!"

"Where is she now?"

"I killed the snake and she's about half-way to the water."

Bill took off at a run and found the woman lying beside the bucket. Her eyes were huge in fear and sweat was running down her chubby face. Seeing Bill she said, "Rattler, only he didn't rattle until after he bit me. It hurts somethin' fierce."

Glancing at the dead snake, he knew he had to act and quickly. Pulling his skinning knife, he raised her swollen leg and cut two deep marks over each fang bite. He lowered his head and began to suck the poison from her leg. Bill disliked the coppery taste of the blood and the sourness from the venom, but he didn't stop for almost twenty minutes.

Josh arrived, knelt by his wife's side and asked, "Is she goin' to be okay?"

Bill gazed into his eyes and replied, "I won't lie to you, either of you, this is very serious. I think it could go either way. A lot depends on her health. Iffen she has a weak heart, well, that's not a good thing."

"My heart is strong enough."

"Let's hope so. Can you stand?"

"I think so. Let me try, but I'll need some help."

Josh and Bill each took an arm and pulled the robust woman up, and then placed her arms around their shoulders. Walking to camp was slow, and Mary moaned most of the way. Nearing the small fire, Bill had Clara spread out a blanket and then they lowered the woman slowly.

"About all we can do is give her whiskey for pain and let her sleep," Bill said as he pulled his hat off and ran his fingers through his dirty hair.

Josh walked to the whiskey jug, brought it back to his wife's side, and poured her a full cup. Handing it to her he said, "I know you don't like spirits, but this is medicine for your bite, and you need to drink all of this."

Her first sip caused her to choke and sputter, but by the third drink, it was going down much smoother. She finished the cup and then asked for another, noticing the strong amber liquid killed most of her pain. A few minutes after the second cup was empty, Mary was asleep.

As Josh and Bill sat by the fire, Josh asked, "When do you think we can move again?"

"In the mornin', but I don't like the idea much. We've three hurt folks and mayhap they shouldn't be moved, only with the Oto in the area we ain't got much choice in the matter. If they catch us again, we might not make it with just the two of us and the boys."

"I hear you. No, I think we have to move. I can't see risking the lives of those unhurt in a situation like this. If those Injuns catch us out here we'll die."

"That's exactly what I was thinkin'. Is Mary in pretty good health?"

"Ain't nothin' wrong with her that I know about, other than her weight."

"Well, she took that snakebite pretty rough."

Josh grinned and replied, "It's the first time she's ever been bit. Hell, I ain't never been bit either, so I guess she was scared."

"I guess so, but her face turned pretty red and that's not usual."

"Was it her heart, do you think?" Josh grimaced as he asked.

"Un-huh, I do. Either she has a heart condition or fear caused it. Hard to tell, but we'll know by mornin'."

"I hope she lives. I love her to death and she's a good woman."

"It's out of our hands and God will decide, but for your sake, I hope she makes it, too."

The night was quiet, with nothing happening, which pleased Bill tremendously. He had expected the Oto to make a move for the horses and when they didn't, he suspected they'd left the area.

He started a fire, put coffee on to brew, and began checking the injured. Moses was awake and wanted to talk, but Bill had too much to do to stand and make idle chatter. John was breathing deep and steady, only his neck was badly swollen. Raising the bandage, Bill could see the beginning of festering in the wound. *Have to clean him again in a little bit,* he thought as he moved toward Mary.

Mary was still near the fire, except she wasn't breathing, and her unseeing eyes were rolled back in her head. Bill squatted at her side, lowered his head to her chest, but heard no heartbeat. Feeling her forehead, he noticed it was cold. *Damn it all, we're short a woman now, and Josh is goin' to go insane when I tell 'em. I suspected her heart was weak, only I didn't expect her to die on us like this.*

Hearing a noise behind him, he turned to see Josh approaching the fire. Getting up, he moved to the man and said, "She didn't make it, Josh. She must have died at some point durin' the night."

"Mary? You mean my Mary is dead? She can't be dead! Maybe she's just asleep!"

"No, she's passed on, Josh."

Running to his wife's side, Josh kneeled and began looking her over. Suddenly, a cry of anguish filled the early morning air—Josh knew she was gone.

The others ran from the wagons and other sleeping places to stand beside the fire. Clara asked, "What's happened?"

"Mary died last night."

Luke and Sam walked slowly to their uncle's side, kneeled, and Bill heard Luke say, "It's okay, Uncle Josh, she's gone to a better place. It hurts me, just like it does you, but she ain't got no pain now."

Josh nodded as tears ran down his face, and his body shuddered.

Sam glanced at Bill and asked, "How come she died from snakebite? I thought you said most folks don't die!"

"She must have had a weak heart, son, and probably didn't even know it her own self."

Standing, Sam yelled, "You lied to us!"

Before Bill could reply, Josh said, "No, he told me the same thing last night, after you boys went to bed. He didn't lie, it was her heart, son."

Bill lowered his head and said, "I'll get a grave dug."

➡⬅  ➡⬅  ➡⬅

It was mid-morning before they laid Mary to rest. The weather was clear with a light wind from the west and the skies pale blue. Bill said a few words over her and then began to shovel the dirt into the open grave. As he filled the hole, Luke placed a crude cross at the head of the grave, and Bill saw her name and date of death cut into the wood. *At least she's marked. So many folks out here unmarked, or so Moses once told me.*

After he'd filled the grave, Bill returned to his wagon, leaving Josh and his boys at the grave. An hour later, they returned, and Josh wiped his eyes and said, "We'd better move, we're wastin' daylight."

The trail turned rougher and Moses, never a man to stay in bed long, climbed from the wagon onto his horse. He rode up beside Bill and said, "I'm still weak, but I can't stay in a bed long."

"Try not to tear your wound open or they'll be hell to pay. I'll have to put you back under a hot knife blade again."

"That I know, so you can be sure I'll take care. How did Josh take his wife's passin'?"

"Rough, but they had a lot of years together."

"Yep, that makes it even rougher. He's a strong man, so he'll bounce back in a few weeks."

"I imagine."

Pulling his hat down low, Moses said, "I'm goin' to scout up ahead for a spell. The last thing we need is to be surprised by a bunch of Oto."

"You start feelin' poorly; you ride back here, okay?"

"Hell, I'm feelin' poorly right now, but we need a scout out. Iffen I start to get dizzy or start throwin' up, I'll be back."

"You do that. We need you strong and in good condition to finish this trip."

Moses waved and moved forward.

Dropping back beside his wagon, he smiled at Clara and asked, "You okay?"

"I'm just sad Mary died. It's a shame she had to die that way."

"Yep, it surely was, but death happens out here and I know I sound cold. Actually, her death was better than some I've seen."

"I'd imagine, only the twins, Sue, and me ain't never been in a war."

"I didn't mean I didn't care she was dead. I liked the woman too, you know?" He felt anger growing.

"I know what you meant and you're right, in your mind. Just try to remember only you men have fought and seen the horrors of war. To us, death is still a thing to fear."

"I don't know what I would have done iffen it had been you instead of her."

"You would have gone on, because that's all you could do. But, it could have been me, because she'd just moved in front of me when the snake jumped out."

Bill met her eyes and said, "Her heart was weak, and I suspect her bein' overweight helped weaken her heart. You don't have that problem."

"No, and it was God's doin's, anyway."

Scanning the countryside, Bill said, "I'm movin' forward. Iffen you need me, give a shout."

The afternoon passed uneventful, with Moses returning just before dusk. His eyes were tired and rimmed in red, but he acted as if he'd only gone for a short ride. After he dismounted, he carried a small deer to the fire and said, "Ain't much for the numbers we have to feed, but it'll stretch in a stew or soup."

Sue, who was preparing supper, said, "It'll do, and thank God we have it. The buffalo meat was goin' bad and there wasn't much of it, anyways."

"Did you see any sign?" Luke asked from beside the fire.

"'Bout four miles further on up the trail I saw the sign of eight unshod ponies, so we'll have to keep our eyes open tonight and tomorrow."

"Was they carryin' riders?"

"Yep, the tracks were deep, so there's a good chance we'll have visitors at some point."

"Which way were they movin'?" Bill asked, as he added more buffalo chips to the dancing flames.

"West, but it don't mean much. Iffen they see our fire tonight they'll come."

"Okay, then once full dark the fire goes out. Now, I know iffen they suspect we're in the area they'll look for us, but there ain't any reason to make it easy for 'em."

Moses laughed and said, "By God, you're learnin'!"

"I have to learn, iffen I want to live."

"All of you do."

Bill, hating to bring it up, said, "John is festerin' on us and doesn't look good."

"You need to scrape the scab from his neck, run a whiskey soaked rag through his neck again, and then cauterize 'em. He'll take it rough, but there ain't no other way to do the job."

"Luke, you come with me and let's get your uncle to the fire. We need to fix 'em up now, so the festerin' don't spread."

A few minutes later, John lay beside the fire as Bill removed the bandage and pulled his skinning knife. The man was delirious with fever and all hoped he'd stay unconscious as Bill did his work.

"Take the edge of your blade and scrape the scab away. Try to do it all at once, so you don't cause 'em anymore pain than need be.  Then use a ramrod, like we did before." Moses said when he saw some hesitation on Bill's part.

In one quick motion, Bill's knife blade flashed, followed by a scream from John, and blood began running down the injured man's neck. Turning the injured man's head, he repeated the process on the exit hole, but the injured man passed out. Picking up the jug of alcohol, Bill poured a healthy amount on the wound, which brought more screams of pain, and then pulled his ramrod. Attaching a whiskey soaked rag on the end, he began to push it slowly into the wound and twisting it as it moved.  John passed out again.

Once the task was completed, Bill bandaged the man, leaned back and sipped a cup of whiskey. His mind was tired and blank, as it usually was after doctoring someone.

Sue, who had watched the treatment asked, "Will he be okay now?"

Moses, knowing Bill was exhausted, replied, "We'll have to wait and see. He has about a fifty-fifty chance of survivin' the doctorin'."

"What'll I do iffen John dies?" Sue asked from beside the flickering flames.

"Hell, woman, you'll go on to Montana country. You really ain't got much of a choice in the matter."

"No, I realize that, but what about a man in my life? I love John and now that he might die, I don't see how I can survive alone. It scares me more than just a little." She began to cry.

Josh said, "You can live with us, iffen you want."

"No, that wouldn't look right, with Mary dead."

"No," Josh replied, "I guess it wouldn't."

"I wouldn't worry about it none 'til we see iffen he'll live or not. All your worryin' might be for nothin'," Moses said and then placed the coffee pot back on the fire.

"How's your shoulder?" Clara asked Moses.

"Fine, and it should be back to normal in 'bout a month. Oh, I imagine it'll be stiff for a long spell, but she's healin' nicely."

Luke, who'd been standing guard duty, ran into camp and said in a low voice, "I got movement coming up the trail!"

Bill sat up and asked, "Injuns?"

"I don't think so, it was makin' too much noise to be Injuns."

"Noise?" Moses asked and then met Bill's eyes.

"Big critter is what it sounded like to me."

"Grizz!" Moses said in an excited voice, "Good God! He must smell our horses and want a meal of horseflesh! I want all the women behind us. Men make sure your guns are loaded, and by God, I mean do 'er now!"

At that moment a plains grizzly on all fours meandered over a rise near the wagons, stood and sniffed the air, then continued toward the horses.

"Protect our horses at all costs!" Bill ordered in a loud voice and everyone saw the bear stop. The animal stood, sniffed the air, then turned toward the fire, and the small group.

"Don't fire 'til he's close or some of us will die! I'll tell y'all when to shoot!" Moses warned with a loud fear-filled voice.

The bear broke into a run, and ran right at the group. When he was twenty feet from the fire, he stopped and Moses screamed, "Fire!"

Five rifles belched flame and smoke, but had little affect on the big beast, other than making him roar in anger. Standing on his back legs, the bear walked toward the men and when he was near the first man, he swung a huge paw and Sam rolled from the campsite. Rifles fired once again and with the same results.

Bill moved forward, emptied his pistol into the bear's chest, and the big beast slapped him to the ground hard, where he lost consciousness.

When he next opened his eyes, the bear was laying still, Josh and Sam were down, and he saw no sign of the women or Luke. Moses was sitting by the fire, shaking his head.

"How much . . . damage . . . did the bear do?"

Moses looked in his direction and replied, "Josh is dead, as is Sam. Luke, Sue, and your wife are in a bad way.  I'm the only one unhurt."

"Clara's hurt?"

"I got the bleeding stopped, but she ain't pretty no more. She took a claw across her face and it almost cut her whole damned head off."

"The others?"

"Sue had most of her scalp ripped away, but I sewed it back on as best I could. Luke has a leg hurt from the bear's teeth, only he'll live, I'm thinkin'. Of the hurt ones, your wife is in the worst way."

Getting on his weak legs, Bill moved to Clara's side, only to see her whole head wrapped in bloody white cloth. "Why ya got her eyes bandaged?"

Lowering his head, Moses replied, "Because she ain't got any eyes, son."

# CHAPTER 11

**E**arly the next morning, just as dawn was changing from gray to white, Clara gave a loud sigh and her body began to twitch and jerk violently. A few seconds later, Clara Sanders was dead. Bill, who'd never left her side, cried out in pain, but the only one who heard was Moses.

"She's in the hands of God now." The older man said as he neared.

With tears dripping from his chin, Bill cried in anger, "Well, I ain't got much faith in God right now, or nothin' else!"

"We tried, we surely did," Moses said, knowing his words were as dead as Clara.

Bill didn't reply, he lowered his head and groaned. Suddenly, his body began to jerk and he fell to his right side, sliding into darkness as he fought to stay conscious. He lost his fight.

When he awoke, Moses was sitting beside him, sipping on a cup of whiskey. Seeing Bill's eyes open, he said, "I got four graves dug. We'd better see to the buryin' pretty quick like."

"I had a fit?"

"I reckon that's what you'd call it. I knew an old mountain man that had the same problem and his was just like yours."

"How long I been out?"

"Oh, about two hours, I'd guess. I stayed close to make sure you kept breathin'. Look, Bill, I'm sorry as hell about your wife and the rest that died today, but these things happen out here. I don't mean to sound like I don't care, only that's the way it is."

Ignoring the words of Moses, Bill asked, "Four graves? Did one of the others die, too?"

"Yep, John passed. After I covered you with a blanket, I went to check on 'em and he was dead as hell."

Tears swelled in Bill's eyes as he said, "My Clara dead! I thought we had a lifetime of livin' in front of us."

"You did, but the bear put a stop to it. Bill, you've seen death many times, or I expect you did in the war, so pull your head out of your ass and start thinkin' how we're goin' to move now. Luke and Sue, I think, will live, so you'd better give serious thought to how we'll move and what we'll take with us."

Getting upright, Bill wobbled on unstable legs and then said, "Let's get the buryin' done first, then we'll discuss the move."

At the graves, Moses said, "Lord, we're common folk, all of us. I ask you to take our people into your hands and welcome them into the kingdom of heaven. Like all men and women, they're sinners, but good folks each and every one. They lived a hard life, like you know, and they were all God-fearin' folks, too. Ashes to ashes and dust to dust, amen."

Silent tears ran down the face of Bill, but he no longer cried out. Death, he knew well, and now it had hit him close. The loss of Clara was hard, but he knew he had to get busy and stay that way or her death would ruin him.

Back at camp, a few minutes later, Bill ordered, "We take one wagon. We'll go through the others and see if there are things we can use. I want all the food and water taken, along with tools or supplies that we'll need. Anything we don't need, we leave."

"What of the extra horses?" Moses asked as he leaned toward the flames. The day had grown cold with gray clouds moving in from the west.

"We take 'em, just mix 'em in our small herd. We'll leave everything else. Can Luke and Sue move?"

Giving a dry laugh, Moses said, "They'll move, but really shouldn't. I think we should travel about forty miles, then let them rest for a couple of days."

"What's in forty miles?"

"Jackson's Tradin' Post, but it ain't much. We can rest there and then continue after a few days."

Moving toward the closest wagon, Bill said, "Let's get this started. I want to be on the trail come mornin'. I'll need you to ride herd, because you're the only person I got left."

Moses smiled and nodded, because the old Bill had returned and only after being gone a short time, too. *He'll do to walk the river with,* the old man thought as he moved toward the mixed herd. *He's got bark on 'em.*

The next morning, an hour before sunup, a lone wagon was moving north, with a single rider bringing up the rear with a mixed herd of cows and horses. Snow had started to fall, but it was falling in a lazy way, with small flakes. Moses didn't expect much on the ground and said as much.

"We'll go as far as we can and iffen it turns bad, we'll hunt a hole."

As he drove the wagon, Bill remembered Clara's fears and dreams, and tears formed in his eyes. *Why is life so unfair to some and generous to others? Why did God take her when there were so many bad men and whores in the world? 'All things God does are for a reason,'* he remembered his ma saying. *I wonder iffen she still thinks that since Faye and Ben died?*

Scanning the countryside, he saw nothing but falling snow. The temperature had gone down, so he pulled an old wool capote from the back of the wagon and put it on. After a few minutes, he pulled the canvas that covered the wagon top open, looked in at Luke and Sue, and saw they were sleeping or unconscious. They'll be lucky to live, he thought and no one saw his tears.

Four days later, they rode over a slight rise and in the valley below was Jackson's Trading Post. "Hell, it ain't much, is it?" Bill asked as he looked at Moses.

"Nope, but it's safe down there."

"How many men he got?"

"He has two Mexican's work for 'em and three slaves. Them slaves stayed on after the war started, because he treats 'em like family. One's a big black by the name of Able and he's a good man, to my way of thinkin'."

"How so?"

"He's a natural born fighter and one hell of a blacksmith. Me and him fit off a bunch of Oto one year, and I'll bet you he kilt five of 'em on his own."

"By hisself?"

"Yep, and I got a couple, too."

Bill gave a weak smile and said, "Let's get down there. We got two hurt in the back that would like a few days in bed, I'll bet."

When they rode to the barn at the post, a large black man, well over six feet tall, walked out smiling and said, "Moses, ya ole son-bitch! How ya be?"

"Fine as frog hair, Able, how 'bout ya?"

"I'm doin' good, doin' good. What brings ya heah? Last I hear'd tell ya was way down south."

"I was, but I missed your ugly face and come back to see you."

Able laughed deep and loud, and then said, "I doubt ya come to see Able, only it don't pay no neveh mind; it's good to see ya 'gain. The cap'uns in the post iffen ya need 'em."

"Serious like, we need a couple of beds for a few days. A grizzly attacked us a few days back and kilt three of us, woundin' two more."

"Good God, ya don't say!"

"Able, this is Bill Sanders, and he's a good man on all accounts. His wife was one of them killed."

Removing his hat, Able said, "I'm sorry to heah that, suh. A plains grizz ain't nothin' to take lightly 'round heah. They be mean all the time."

"Thank you for the kind words, she was a good woman."

"Mos' likely she was, suh, mos' likely she was."

"Come, Bill, and let's go in and see about a couple of beds. While they'll likely live, ain't no need to ride for a couple of days. All that would do is cause 'em more pain."

The trading post was a crudely made affair, constructed of logs and poor chinking. When they entered the small building, there was little improvement over the outside. Wide pine planked boards nailed to empty whiskey barrels served as a bar, the tables were almost square, and made from the same wood. *If nothin' else, this place has low overhead,* Bill thought, but said nothing.

The Captain was a smallish fellow, a little over five three, and portly. His face wore a worried expression, while his hands shook and trembled. *He's a man fond of drink, I'll wager,* Bill suspected right off and when the Captain extended his hand, they shook.

"So, lad, a grizz tore yer wagon train apart, now did it? They're mean bastards, and I kill every one I can find."

"Well," Bill said with narrow eyes, "Ya missed one."

"Aye, I guess I did at that. I'm sorry to hear about yer wife, except out here all kinds of death awaits us."

"I've noticed." Bill replied, not liking the man at all.

"Captain, we need a couple of beds for two days. We've injured in the wagon."

"The cost is two bits a room per day."

Pulling a dollar from his pocket, Bill handed it to the man and said, "If you're ever in need, don't bother comin' to me. Ya'll find the cost more than you can pay."

The Captain laughed and replied, "I'm in a business, and this ain't no hospital. This is how I make me livin', son."

"Uh-huh," Bill said and then moved to one of the tables. As he sat down, he groaned, because he was dead tired.

Moses sat as well and then said, "Bring us a bottle of good whiskey."

Then turning to Bill he added, "We'll have a couple of drinks, and then get them folks in their rooms."

The Captain walked to the table, placed a bottle and the change near Moses, and then said, "The whiskey's a dollar a bottle."

Moses pulled out a coin and laid it on the table. When the Captain picked it up, he asked, "What's the charge for me and Bill to sleep in the barn?"

Chuckling, the Captain replied, "It's free and the roof don't leak, unless it rains."

Two days later, Bill climbed on the wagon and moved north, just as the sun was coming up. The two injured were doing much better, but lying in the back.

Moses moved his horse to the wagon and asked, "Ya don't like the Captain much, do ya?"

"He's fed by greed. Every damn thing we used, ate, or drank cost us money, and us with hurt folks along."

"They're in no danger of dying, and he knew it. Iffen they had been hurt bad, he wouldn't have charged us. Like the man said, he's in business."

Gazing into the eyes of Moses, Bill replied, "Well, I don't like the bastard, and iffen I never see 'em again I'll be happy."

Moses laughed, kicked his horse forward, and was soon riding about a hundred yards in front of the wagon. Three hours out, Luke was doing well enough he'd taken to driving the wagon, but Sue was still paining from her injuries. The bears claws had gone deep and her recovery would be slow. As he drove, Luke hummed 'We shall gather at the river," and had a smile on his face.

"What are you so happy about, boy?" Bill asked.

"We're movin' again, and I like that."

"Yep, we are at that. I want you to keep your eyes scanning the country as we ride, because we might not be the only folks out here."

"You reckon we ain't?" Luke's face turned sober.

Bill chuckled and asked, "Don't you remember runnin' into the Sioux and the Oto out here?"

"Yup, but that was a ways back."

"This is still their stompin' grounds."

Dusk found Sue up and moving around the fire. She tried to cook, but tired too quickly and soon gave it up. Bill placed a pot of beans and salt pork on the flames and leaned back against his saddle. He was deep bone tired as well.

"We covered a lot of ground today, maybe twenty-five miles. We keep this up and we'll be in Montana pretty soon," Sue stated from her blanket beside the small fire.

"It will grow rougher the closer we get, so I don't think we can keep coverin' this much distance every day," Bill said, and then added a log to the fire. Seemed to him he'd spent most of his life beside fires like this, and he was growing tired of it. *One day I'll have a home with a fireplace, where I can prop my feet up, sip coffee and talk, without worryin' about rain, snow or heat.*

"It will get a lot rougher, but you're a tough bunch, and I suspect we'll do fine," Moses commented from his spot beside the dancing flames

Sue rose, picked up a wooden spoon, bent over and began to stir the beans. Her cleavage showed and Bill noticed, just as he had before, she was a fine looking woman—and suddenly felt a cloud of guilt. Clara hadn't been buried a month, and he was already drooling over another woman. *Forgive me Lord, because I have sins of the flesh on my mind.*

Moses pulled his pipe from his bag, stuffed the bowl and then asked as he picked up a brand from the fire, "You okay, Bill? Looks like you got somethin' on your mind."

"Oh, I'm fine, just tired, and wondering iffen we'll ever get to Montana."

"I ain't too worried 'bout getting' to the place, it's the weather that bothers me."

"We've been lucky so far, only that one snowfall and it didn't amount to much."

Lighting his pipe and taking a deep drag, Moses exhaled before he replied, "We're due a hard storm, and I got a feelin' it'll hit us pretty soon." White smoke from his pipe covered his head.

"Let's pray the Good Lord holds off a spell before that happens."

Sue moved from the fire, returned to her blanket and then asked, "How bad are the storms up here when they hit?"

"It depends, but I once spent two weeks unable to move as it snowed. It snowed for a week, then it was another week before it melted enough I could travel."

"Whooeee, we don't want that to happen on us," Bill said as he shook his head in amazement.

"No, we don't. I'm jus' sayin' it could happen, not that it will."

Luke neared the fire and asked, "Who's goin' to take my place as guard?"

"I'll take it," Moses replied as he picked up his rifle and adjusted his hat.

There came a call from outside the camp, "Hello! Can I share your fire?"

Everyone melted into the background, but finally Bill called out, "Who you be?"

"I'm Isaac and I'm on my way north!"

"Are you alone?"

"Yep, I surely am and have been for some time."

"Come, but keep your gun held high in your left hand."

"I can do that!"

A dark form slowly moved over the closest rise and walked toward the camp. He appeared to be a big man, well over six feet tall. He moved slowly, as a tired man would do. Walking to the small fire, he asked, "Where y'all be?"

Bill stood and made his way to the fire, with his rifle held at the ready. He trusted no one while on a trail.

"Put your rifle, pistols and knife by your feet and then move to the other side of the flames." Bill said.

"Not the most trustin' jasper out here, now are ya?"

"Nope, and I never have been. That's one reason my ass is still alive today."

"I understand, 'cause I'm the same way."

Gazing into the man's eyes, Bill asked, "Are you a runaway slave or a free man?"

"Does it make any difference?"

"It does to me. I'll not have a man around that can bring me trouble. Runaways mean slave hunters, and they're a mean lot. The last I heard only Lee had surrendered, but the war might still be goin' on."

"I'm free. I was born that way and grew up in Chicago."

Extending his hand, Bill said, "I'm glad you came to our camp then."

"I used to feel that way 'bout strangers, but I had two white men visit me last night and once I went to sleep they stole me blind. Took my horse, mule and just about everything else they could lay their hands on."

"Did you find 'em?"

"I'm on foot, so what do ya think?"

Bill laughed and then asked, "Have you eaten yet?"

"Nope, had a little deer meat for breakfast, but that was it for the day."

Turning his head, Bill said in a loud voice, "Come on out, he's safe enough."

Seeing the others moving toward the fire with guns in their hands, Isaac said, "Yer pretty smart. Ya had me covered even after I figured ya didn't. Ya'll do out here fer sure."

Moses walked to the fire, gave Isaac a good looking over and then exclaimed, "I'll be damned iffen it ain't Isaac Baker! How in the hell are ya? I ain't seen you in a coons age!"

"Fine, Moses, I see yer back on the plains again."

"Yup, and here to stay this time."

Isaac laughed and said, "Ya say that every time ya come back, only ya always leave."

Lowering his head, Moses replied, "I get a hankerin' for good whiskey and bad women. I'm usually good for three or four years before the urge gets too strong for me."

As they ate, Isaac told them of the Oto and other Indian out on the plains. All were angry because whites were taking lands the tribes had owned for generations, and most were on the warpath. "Blackened their faces, they surely have."

Moses grinned, glad to hear someone speak as he did usually, "Waugh, it matters little. Injuns are always pissed 'bout one thing or the other. Truth is they jus' like to fight."

Isaac laughed and added, "This time they've got good reason and the four of ya sitting right heah are proof. See, they've started attackin' every white settler they can find, so I'd rec'mend y'all stay together fer a long spell."

Bill looked up from his seat on the ground and replied, "We plan to do just that, because it's the only safe thing to do."

"Ya look like a fighter, or at least a man who knows his way around. Was ya in that big war back east?"

"Yep, I was, but it's about finished now."

"Good, I never did cotton to Americans fightin' Americans, and it jus' didn't make no sense to me a-tall. Some say it was to free black folks, but I don't see that neither. Ain't no white man, from the north or south, gonna die fer no slaves. There had to be more to it than that."

"Well, I fought for the south, but it wasn't to keep no slaves, it was for states rights. I'll bet you, out of all the men in my outfit, only one man owned a slave and that was the Colonel. The rest of us, from the Captain on down, were dirt farmers."

"Looks like them rich slave owners pulled the wool over your eyes then, because you can be damned sure them rich men was fightin' to keep their property. They didn't care a penny about states rights. For them, it was all about money, and slaves mean money."

With a puzzled look on his face, Bill asked, "Why is your English so good all of a sudden?"

Isaac laughed and replied, "I once was a slave and worked in the master's house. My job was to greet all his visitors and show proper respect when they arrived. Well, one night this ole boy showed up ridin' a huge horse, so instead of putting it in the barn, I took it north. I ain't stopped movin' since."

"Did they look for you?" Sue asked.

"I have no idea, but I imagine they did fer a spell. Iffen they come out here, the Injuns killed 'em or they got scared and went home. I ain't seen hide nor hair of any slave hunters."

Moses laughed and then stated with a joyful voice, "Them slave hunters never seem to get very far west of the Mississippi."

Bill grew angry and said brusquely, "You said you were born free and in Chicago! You lied to me!"

"No, sir, I did not. I was born free and in Chicago. See, when I was about ten years old, my ma went to visit a family that were slaves in Alabama, and once we got there, the master kept us both. I never saw my brothers, sisters, or pa again. So, I guess instead of being a runaway, I actually escaped from imprisonment."

"They cain't keep a free man as a slave, can they?" Sue asked as she met Bill's eyes.

"Once in the Deep South, who they gonna believe, a black or white man?" Isaac replied, and all at the fire knew the answer.

# CHAPTER 12

$A$t dawn, the wind howled and screamed as it scattered falling snow in all directions. The temperature fell and it was well below freezing as Bill led each horse, one at a time, to a small stream. He broke the ice so each animal could drink. He then hurried back to the fire to warm. By the time he'd watered all of them, he felt frozen through. Walking to the fire, he added a log and held his palms out to the flickering flames to warm them. He could not remember ever being so cold that it hurt to breathe.

Moses soon joined him by the fire and watching the falling snow swept by the wind, he asked, "Been like this long?"

"It has since I got up about an hour ago. I don't know when it started, but one of the guards will know. I think I heard the wind pick up on Isaac's shift, nigh on three this mornin'."

"I had an earlier shift, didn't see a cloud in the sky, but this just shows how fast the weather can change up this away."

"This could kill a man who isn't prepared, you know."

"I'm sure plenty of men have died here, and just for that reason. Never, and I mean never, ride from any place and not have what you need to survive. The weather here can turn bitch ugly in less than an hour, and kill you dead as all get out."

At that point, Bill shivered and placed the coffee pot on the flames. Pulling the collar of his coat up, he said, "Ain't no need to wake nobody, we ain't movin' an inch in this. Let 'em all sleep as long as they want."

A few minutes later, Isaac walked to the fire wearing a buffalo robe over his shoulders. He gave a weak smile and then said, "Been cold doin's standin' guard."

"Who relieved you, Luke?" Bill asked, noticing the black man was back to speaking like a mountain man again.

"Yup, and when I left 'em he was wearin' a buff robe and a wool capote, so he'll stay warm enough. With this snow I don't expect no trouble, but ya can never tell out heah." After warming his hands, the black man moved toward his shelter and warm blankets.

After Isaac left, Moses said, "He's got that right. In all the years I've lived up this a-way, trouble usually comes when I least expected it."

Bill pulled his hat down lower and said, "Stocks been watered and wood gathered up, but I suspect we'll need more wood in a couple of hours. How long does a storm like this last?"

Moses glanced at Isaac, laughed and replied, "Till it's done, son. Storms up here can last a few hours or go on for a week. There just ain't no way to tell."

"I'll be glad to be able to move again. Every day we stay in camp is one day longer until we reach Montana."

"Yup, it is, but it's safer to stay in camp on a day like this. How long do ya think the animals would last movin' in this kind of weather?"

"Longer than I would. I'd not last an hour out in all that snow and cold wind."

"I understand you wantin' to move, only, like I said, it's safer to stay here."

"I was just dreamin' about a new home. How well do you know Isaac?"

"I wintered with 'em a couple of times. He's a good man, but don't talk much. I'll bet you he'd go all day and never say a word, iffen I didn't ask 'em a question."

"Why is his English so good at times but he sounds like a mountain man most of the time?"

Moses chuckled and replied, "It's his life now. I guess usin' proper English reminds him of his days as a slave and he ain't the same man he was back then. You won't hear much out of him anyway, so don't worry about it."

"My brother was quiet like that. He got killed in the war, at the same time pa lost his arm, and it was real hard on ma."

"War never solves a blame thing in my eyes."

"It has a place, but this one wasn't needed."

"You've kicked that dead horse before and many times."

"Yup, I have at that. Hard to get it out of my mind, after all the years I served."

Moses gave a sad grin and asked, "Want some coffee? It sounds like she's about done brewin'."

Holding his cup out, Bill said, "Sure do, and it'll hit the spot about now."

Luke walked from the falling snow, squatted beside the fire and said, "We got visitors comin', and they look to be United States Army men to me. They're wearin' Yankee blue and on horse back."

Moses wiped his mouth with his hand and asked, "How far off?"

"Less than ten minutes, why?"

"Just wonderin' why them fools are out ridin' in this storm is all."

Bill laughed and said, "Because they're army men and they move when they're told to do the job. They ain't got good sense like most folks. Except, who are they lookin' for or where are they goin'?"

Luke shook his head and replied, "I ain't got no idea. There ain't much north of us, except Montana and Injuns, or so you two told me."

Pulling his robe tightly around his body, Moses said, "Well, I'm goin' to get a little rest before them boys get here. I figure they're out for a reason and I'm sure, knowin' the army, they'll make it known clear enough when they get here."

The campfire grew quiet, except for an occasional snap or pop of wet wood, as the men waited for the horse soldiers to arrive. A few minutes later, a Sioux warrior walked boldly into the camp and said in heavily accented English, "Army come."  Bill knew the brave was an army scout.

Bill threw another log on the flames, sipped his coffee, and watched as a double column of mounted soldiers neared the camp. A Sergeant and Major dismounted, leaving the rest of the men sitting on horseback in the cold.

Walking to the fire, the major said, "I'm Major Evans, and this is First Sergeant Todd."

Everyone at the fire welcomed the two men, and then Bill asked, "What can we do for y'all, suh? "

"Oh, you're a Southerner! I think you'll be saddened to hear the war is over, and the north was most victorious."

"Of your victory I have little doubt. When did it end?"

"Less than a month or so after General Lee surrendered. He called it quits in April of this year."

"Good to hear it's finally over."

"T'was a bloody fight, lad." Sergeant Todd stated with a flat Irish voice.

"I fought in it for almost four years. Took a head injury late last year and was given a medical discharge. I never did figure out why we fought."

"You're lucky to be alive if you took a wound to the head. I fought because I was ordered to fight and for no other reasons. I surely didn't fight to free no Nig   ," Seeing Isaac, the major stopped mid-word.

Isaac grinned and said, "What was ya gonna say, suh? No, I don't reckon ya would fight fer none of us, now would you?"

The officer lowered his head and replied, "I apologize, because my choice of words was inappropriate."

Isaac's eyes grew narrow as he asked, "Because I'm here? It's inappropriate any time and any place, suh, not just around a black man."

Sergeant Todd quickly changed the subject, "We're lookin' for Oto, lads. They've been raidin' the whole Missouri border, and we're to put a stop to it."

Moses, who'd remained quiet, asked, "Been a bunch of killin'?"

"We learned close to two hundred dead and kidnapped. Countless homes and farms burned to the ground," Todd replied and then looked enviously at the coffee pot.

"Care for some coffee?" Bill asked.

The old Sergeant looked to his Major, who nodded his head, and then said, "We have no cups with us."

Bill handed his to the Sergeant, while Isaac handed his to the major—and waited.

"Thank you for the use of the cups," Major Evans said as he extended his hand and Bill filled his cup.

Isaac smiled, but said nothing.

"Now," Moses said, "What in the hell are y'all doin' ridin' in this cold-ass weather? Anybody with any sense will be holed up."

"I thought we might find the Oto camp, and we've only been out a few hours. I figured to search for three hours, and then seek shelter."

"Waste of time," Isaac said and then continued, "Them Injuns are long gone and iffen ya found any, odds are it would be the wrong ones."

"I have little concern over which ones I punish. An Indian is an Indian, and they're all a bunch of savages."

Moses shrugged his shoulders and replied, "Think what you want, but some of 'em is friends of mine and good people in my mind. You ride around thinkin' like that, and you'll start the biggest damn war you've ever had on your hands."

"Surely you jest! What can a bunch of red savages do to stop the United States Army?"

"Either one of you two ever fight against a group of partisans or raiders?" Bill asked.

"No, I've been out here since the war started." Evans answered, and Sergeant Todd just shook his head.

"Well," Moses said with a grin, "Injuns are about the best fighters in the world when it comes to hit and run tactics. I also guaran-damn-tee ya, they're better fighters on horseback than your boys are. Hell, they're almost born on the critters."

"I doubt that," Major Evans said, and then laughed.

"I've heard the same, sor," Sergeant Todd said, and then added, "Only I've never battled Injuns."

"Do you know those *'savages'* are deeply religious folks, who feed the poor and pray at the rising of each sun?" Isaac asked and then pulled his old pipe from his coat.

Turning to Sergeant Todd, the major ordered, "It's time we ride, Sergeant."

Todd looked at Isaac and gave a wink as he replied, "Yes, sor!"

Evans bowed and said, "Nice meeting you gentlemen, but we've Indians to catch, and I'll not find them here. I hope you have a safe trip."

As they turned to walk away, Moses said, "Major! Watch your hair out there, because you're a loose cannon. Think and then act."

"How I run this troop is none of your business, sir."

The two men quickly mounted and the whole troop left. The small group watched until the snow made it impossible to see them any longer.

"He'll get men killed and pretty damned soon too," Moses said and shook his head.

Bill stared into the flickering flames of the fire as he said, "I saw a lot of officers like him in the war. They won't listen to anyone else and it's always their way or nothin'. If his troop is lucky, maybe he'll be the first to fall, and then the Sergeant will take over. Sergeants have good common sense."

Moses asked, "What was your rank in the army?"

Smiling, Bill replied, "Sergeant."

➵ ➵ ➵

Three mornings later, dawn came with no snow and a warm breeze. Stretching, Moses said, "We'll travel today. Most of the mud has dried and the sky is clear."

"Good, let me get the horses in harness before it changes again," Bill replied with a smile as he moved toward his draft animals.

Sue was at the fire, turning salt pork with a long fork, and singing as she worked. Bill paused a few minutes listening to her voice. Then, shaking his head, he walked to his horses.

After a quick breakfast, the small group moved north once more. Moses moved out front to scout, while Isaac dropped back to cover their back trail. Near noon, Moses came riding fast, pulled up beside Bill's wagon and said, "Them soldiers are just up ahead or what's left of 'em is, in a valley."

"Left of 'em? Have they been in a fight?"

"More than likely they were ambushed."

"All of 'em dead?"

"I didn't stick around to check, but it looked like it. It ain't safe for one man to be in a place like that long."

"Damn, Moses. Head down our back trail and bring Isaac back. Once you're both here we'll go check it out."

"I'll do that and be right back, because he ain't that far behind us."

As the man rode off, Luke rode up and said, "I overheard part of it. We goin' to bury them fellers?"

"Grounds too hard, son, but we'll do what we can for 'em."

"Must have been forty men in that group, how could they all die?"

"I don't know yet, but ask me that question in an hour. I'm pretty sure I'll have you an answer by then."

"Are we goin' to wait for Moses and Isaac?"

"Yup, we surely are," Bill replied and then pulled out a long twist of chewing tobacco. Cutting off a piece he began to work it as he wondered what could have happened.

A little later, he was jarred from his thoughts as Moses and Isaac rode up. The black man grinned and said, "Didn't take our major long to get his butt kilt, now did it?"

"We don't know who's dead yet. Let's move forward and see if there were any survivors," Bill replied as he pulled his rifle from the seat beside him and held it in his hand.

The area was as flat as a tabletop as they rode, but after a few miles, it began to dip and rise in places. Moses dropped back and rode beside Bill as he said, "Next valley is where they are, scattered to hell and back too. I'd suggest you leave the wagon here. Sue and Luke don't need to see this."

"Sue, you stay with the wagon, but keep the shotgun in your lap. Luke, I think you're big enough to see this and help us with these fellers."

Moses gave a look of surprise and said, "They're mutilated."

"It's time this boy sees what bein' stupid can do to a feller out here. I ain't doin' it because I want to do it, but he needs to know death can be hard."

Luke, wanting to see the bodies, said, "I'm old enough to handle it."

"We'll see, now won't we? They're an ugly mess, but you'll see soon enough." Moses spoke as he started for the rise.

The three men made their way slow over the crest of the slight rise and in the shallow valley below bodies were scattered in all directions. Vultures, the scavengers of the plains, circled casually overhead, waiting for their chance to pick the bones clean.

"Dismount and look 'em over closely." Moses said.

The smell grew so bad, each man had to cover their nose and mouth with a bandanna. The first man Luke saw had three arrows in his chest and was gutted like a deer. Long and deep cuts to the bone were on each arm and leg. He'd been scalped, and his penis and balls removed. The young man fell to his knees and began to puke.

"I knew that'd happen," Bill said, as he searched among the dead for the Sergeant or Major, seeing neither.

Isaac called out, "Major's over heah, but he ain't lookin' good."

"Any sign of the Sergeant?"

"Not yet, but it's hard to tell the way some of these boys are cut up."

Moses, who had walked around the dead men, yelled out, "Two got away!"

Bill moved quickly to his side and asked, "How can you tell?"

"Two horses broke through and moved north. Looks like the Oto didn't even bother to follow 'em, either. Guess they had enough plunder on their hands to keep 'em busy a long spell. Only, one of 'em was hurt bad."

Isaac walked to the two men and said, "Ya both know we can't bury these men. There's just too many of 'em, and the ground's too hard."

"I figured that out," Bill said, and then continued, "Looks like the Injuns rode over two rises and sandwiched the soldiers between them. I'll bet the fight didn't last five minutes."

Isaac scratched his chin and replied, "That's the way I read the sign, too. Good Lord, didn't that major have a point rider or a scout out front?"

"Don't look like it to me, from what little sign I read. We got two soldiers up ahead, but hell they could be dead by now." Moses commented, scanned the area and then spoke again, "Let's get out of here. I don't like the feel of this place."

Bill asked, "Because of the dead?"

"Nope, it ain't that, I feel them Oto."

"They've been gone for days."

"Do ya think? Mayhap they have and then again, they might have left a man back here to see who'd show. Ya ever think about that?"

"Nope, but I don't like this place either."

Isaac gave a sad grin and said, "Let's get the boy and return to the wagon. Moses can ride our back trail, while I ride ahead to see iffen I can track them soldiers that got away."

"Watch your ass out there then," Bill replied.

"Oh, I intend to do jus' that. God only knows where the Oto have gone."

Hours later, just as dusk was close, Isaac returned with a single rider at his side. They rode to the other horses, tied their mounts to the picket line, and dismounted. As they neared the fire, Bill saw the Sergeant lived.

"I found the Sergeant, but the Private that was with 'em died on the way back."

The burly Sergeant sat by the fire and blinked a few times before he said, "They came over both rises at the same time, and the battle was but a short one."

"I figured as much. Did the major have a point man out?"

"No, and no flankers either. I warned him earlier in the day, but he would not listen, and told me he was the commander and not me."

"A lot of good men died because of his stubbornness," Moses said as he stoked the fire.

Staring into the flames, the Sergeant replied just above a whisper, "Good men, dear mither of God."

Getting up and moving to his wagon, Bill returned with a jug of whiskey and said, "Isaac, you and the Sergeant have a good healthy snort or three."

Both took long pulls on the jug and when they handed it back, Isaac asked, "What will ya do now, Sergeant? Hell, yer miles from the nearest fort or post."

"There's a trading post, Butterfield's if I remember right, just a day or so ride from here. I guess I'll go there. It was a damned bloody shame! He killed those men just as if he pulled the trigger on a gun!"

Moses, not sure what to say, replied, "Aye, he did at that, but there's nothin' you can do about it now. He was the man in charge, not you."

Lowering his head to his big hands, the Sergeant began to cry.

Silence filled the campsite as each man felt the Sergeant's pain, but could do nothing to lessen it. It was something they'd all felt before and would likely feel again.

Suddenly raising his head, Sergeant Todd said, "Stupid son-of-a-bitch! He knew better, he surely did!"

Bill, handing the man the jug once again, said, "Well it's over and done with. I saw it happen too many times durin' the war."

"Finish your drink, Sergeant, and then get some sleep," Sue said, as she walked from the wagon with two blankets in her hands.

A little later, the Sergeant's snores started, and the men began to speak in low voices. "He took that pretty rough," Isaac said as he raised his coffee cup to his lips.

"A battle like that one is rough on any man! I've seen many a man killed and some whole groups of men wiped out by cannon, but Injuns kill up close and personal like," Bill replied, stared into the flames, and his memories started coming back.

"I'll bet ya have." The black man replied.

Jarred back to the present, Bill gave an ill felt smile and asked, "You want to see another battlefield, Luke?"

"Nope, seen all I ever want to see of killin'. Why in the world did the Injuns cut them fellers like they done?"

Moses met the young man's eyes and said, "The red man believes they'll be able to fight the spirit of a man they've kilt after they die. They cut 'em up so they'll not be able to fight, and to identify the man as the one they've killed. They cut off body parts so the man can't use that part of his body in the spirit world."

"Makes sense, in a twisted way."

"Well, sense or not, that's the reason they do the job."

"Ugly is what it is. Ain't no sense in killin' a man and then doin' all that cuttin' on 'em. Now, I know they have a reason, but it's not right to my way of thinkin'." Bill stood, and then moved toward his sleeping spot for the night.

# CHAPTER 13

## Montana

**The** wagon's wheels moaned and groaned in protest of moving as the sun came up. The day would be a cold one, but the sky remained clear and with the coming of the sun, it would warm up. Bill, mounted for over an hour, rubbed his hands together and then pulled his hat down lower against a light wind. He didn't mind the cold, as long as they could continue to move north. Sergeant Todd had left that morning, and while saddened to see him leave, Bill understood a soldier's responsibility to his unit and service.

Isaac rode to Bill's side and said with a grin, "We're now in Montana, and ya can start lookin' for a home. Moses said ya wanted a place near the mountains, so we'll move west tomorrow and start lookin'."

"Must be a long ways to the mountains, I don't even see a hill!"

"Oh, there's some rough country west of us, but this is the easiest way to travel. Most folks come up this way, then move off in the direction they want to go. A wagon won't go far once the mountains are reached, too hard to move."

"Where ya gonna winter at, Isaac?"

"Ain't thought about it much, to tell ya the truth. I imagine where ever I am when the snow starts to fly hard."

"You could stay with us, iffen you wanted."

"Nope, I appreciate the offer, but I'm a loner and always have been. I never winter with more than one other feller, because I like it quiet."

"Not much of a people person then?"

"Not really. Oh, I like to go to town at times and have a few drinks in a saloon, but to be around folks full time is too much work to me. A feller has to watch what he says, control his temper and go along with the group. I like to make my own decisions. No, I truly appreciate the offer, but I have to turn ya down."

"That's fine, just thought I'd ask. What about Moses?"

Isaac laughed, rubbed his wide nose and replied, "Who knows? He's a good man, but a strange one when it comes to his travels. I think ya'd better ask him, only most likely he don't even know."

"Now," Bill said with a smile, "that's freedom!"

Shaking his head, Isaac replied, "No, it's not freedom, not really. It's hunger and thirst, along with loneliness if ya ask me. It's poor planning and judgment, but that's the way a few of the men live heah. More than one man will start winter poorly prepared and be dead by spring thaw. It takes a lot of grub, firewood, and clothing to survive the winter and most of these old timers know this, but some still don't get ready."

"How come?"

"They ain't lazy, but they just don't do it. Oh, some do, but most of 'em live the life they want and don't think of the comin' seasons. It's almost like they're too busy living to plan ahead."

Bill thought for a few minutes and then said, "Sounds pretty dumb to me, except in a strange way I can understand it. I'd not be like that, I'd prepare. Only I can surely see where a man might be too busy livin' to get ready fer winter."

"I need to move off to the right a bit and look the country over. We're still in Injun country and it don't pay to get caught with yer pants down out heah."

Laughing, Bill replied, "You do that; I'll stay near the wagons and keep my eyes open." Isaac pulled his horse around, waved as he rode away, and was quickly lost from sight.

That evening, over supper, Moses said, "We're nearing a place I think ya might want to take a look at. It's nested near the mountains, got a shallow but wide stream, and the land's rich. I'll tell ya right now, iffen I was inclined to homestead up here, I'd take this place in a heartbeat."

Bill, who'd finally seen the mountains off in the distance at mid-morning, grinned and replied,

"Okay, we'll take a look at it in the mornin'."

"No, it ain't that close. I'd imagine we'll be near it at about dusk tomorrow. We'll spend the night there, and the day after tomorrow you can look it over. We're still a good twenty miles to the mountains proper, and tomorrow we have some streams to cross and hills to climb."

Bill turned his head to Sue and Luke and asked, "Do you two want to stay with me until we can get you two a cabin up? It'll mean spendin' the winter, but there ain't really no other choice."

Sue gave a shy grin and replied, "We need a place to stay, so I guess you'll have at least one winter guest."

"Luke?" Bill asked.

Smiling the young man said, "I could do worse than winterin' with you. I'll stay, but as soon as spring hits I want a place of my own."

Moses shook his head and said, "That won't work out heah yet, son, too many Injuns. I'd suggest y'all layout a large plot of land and share. You can make a cabin next to Bill's, and then if you're attacked y'all can gather at one point and fight 'em off. A lone man out here is soon a dead man."

Luke quickly replied, "I can do that."

After almost everyone had gone to bed, Bill looked over at Sue and asked, "Are you sure you want to winter with me? We are a man and a woman."

"I did a lot of thinkin' on that and we need each other," Sue said, and then lowered her head.

"Do you mean because we both lost our mates?"

Giving a low giggle, Sue asked, "How many women have you seen since we got here? You've seen the same number I've seen of men—none. It ain't like we got much choice."

Chuckling, Bill replied, "You're a practical woman, aren't you?"

"It just makes sense to me. Now, I know you don't love me and I hardly know you, but it'll come with time. See, I figure we need each other. Only don't expect no sweetness until we get hitched, because I ain't a whore."

"No, you're not a whore, but you mean to sit there and tell me you've thought this all out?"

"I sure have. God must have a hand in it, too, or else why is my man and your woman dead?"

"Have you talked to Luke about it?"

"Yup, some." Sue suddenly looked somewhat uncomfortable.

"What did the boy say?"

"Well, he said you'd never be his pa, 'cause he already had one of them, but he died. He respects you a lot and he didn't get mad about it, so I'd guess he's willin' to let it happen."

"Okay, we'll give this a try, except I'll talk to Moses in the mornin' and see iffen he knows a preacher here about that can marry us up." Bill added another log to the fire.

Grinning, Sue said, "He knows one, and told me as much."

Laughing, he said, "I'm the last one to know of your plan, huh?"

"Pretty much, because I wasn't sure how you'd take to the idea."

Moving to her side, Bill met her eyes and said, "You're a good hard working woman. You're very attractive, have a wonderful smile and radiating eyes. No, I could do much worse than take you as my wife. I, well, to be honest, just never expected things to work out like they did, that's all."

"Me neither, but they did."

Laughing, Bill asked, "So, when is Moses goin' for the preacher man?"

"At first light, and that's one of reasons we won't be at the place he wants to show you until later in the day. He wants us married first."

Standing, Bill gave her a grin and said, "We need to get some sleep. Daylight comes early in these parts."

➪⬅ ➪⬅ ➪⬅

Dawn was cold, with no wind, and Moses had been gone for over an hour. He returned a couple of hours after the sun came up, and with him was an old man who swore he was a man of God. His hair was long and dirty, his few remaining teeth rotted and his beard looked like a birds nest. He did carry a Bible in his right hand. Moses introduced the man as Deacon.

"Yer doin' the right thing by marryin' up, son. Mos' folks would jus' live in sin."

"We ain't like that. We just ain't sure you're a man of God, is all."

"Oh, I'm a preacher alright, but know I don't look like one. I come out heah nigh on thirty years 'go and ain't left since. This is my church now and at times I do weddin's, funerals, and at the odd time provide a church service," Deacon said as he sat down on an overturned wooden bucket.

"What church faith are ya?" Sue asked.

"I'm a good God-fearin' Baptist!"

"Can ya write? Because we'll need a weddin' paper," Bill asked as he met the man's eyes. Nodding, Deacon replied, "I can read, write and even cipher a mite. I'll write out a marryin' paper jus' as soon as I finish the job."

Turning to Sue, Bill asked, "Well, what do you think?"

Smiling sweetly, she replied, "Let's do it. I think he really is a man of God and after all, both Isaac and Moses have said he is. I've not known either man to lie."

Twenty minutes later, the marriage complete, Bill pulled two dollars from his pocket and handed it to the preacher, "For the services."

Holding the coins in his hand, Deacon said, "I don't want yer money, son. I did this fer ya out of the kindness of my heart and through the love of God. No, keep yer money, jus' be a good husband to this woman."

Taking his coins, Bill tilted his head and asked, "How come you don't want money for doin' the Good Lord's work?"

Deacon laughed and replied, "I never take money fer doin' a marriage. How some ever, I do take it fer a funeral, baptism, or other services rendered. Marryin' is special, and I think takin' money will bring the couple bad luck."

"Well, at least promise us ya'll come by our place for supper one Sunday," Sue stated with a big grin.

Looking confused, Deacon asked, "And where might yer place be?"

Moses laughed and said, "They ain't got a place yet. They're takin' a look over by Pine Hill Crick, near the mountains, later today. They might just end up there. It's a good place."

"Aye, it's good land and the water is clear and cold. She's spring fed is my guess. I'll drop by there in the spring and see iffen your cabin is up by then."

"It'll be up." Bill stated and then added, "We need to get movin' iffen we want to cover some miles today. We're wastin' daylight."

➡️⬅️  ➡️⬅️  ➡️⬅️

Bill drove his wagon with Sue sitting at his side as the small group moved west. Deacon had come along, saying he didn't have anything better to do for a few days. The going was slow, with many small streams from the mountains to cross, but most were shallow and lazy. It was near dusk when they topped a small hill and in the valley below, they saw the land for the first time.

Isaac was riding beside the wagon and noticed Bill stop as he took the view in. "Beautiful place fer a home, don't ya think?"

"Why, them mountains is almost at the back door!"

"Less than a mile would be my guess. Ya don't want to build too close to 'em, or it'll give the Injuns a chance to sneak up on ya."

"I figured that right off. See that lone tree at the end of the valley? Our cabin will go up about fifty feet to the right of it, or so I'm thinkin'."

"Good spot. Now, let's meander down there and take a real good look. Iffen ya don't like the place say so, because there's lots more around."

A little later, Bill pulled his wagon beside the tree, helped Sue down and asked her, "What do you think?"

"It'll do fine. Lumber is near, the creek runs across the land, and it's well sheltered from the wind. I like it."

Giving a loud yell, Bill said in an excited voice, "Let's unload the wagon then, we're home!"

Luke, along with Deacon, who'd been riding herd on the cattle and horses, came riding up and said, "I like this place! Lots of good grass for the animals and clean water, too." He quickly dismounted, full of excitement.

"We like it too, Luke, and we're stayin' right here!" Sue replied in an excited voice.

"Well, we ain't got near the critters we started this trip with, so it'll be lean times for a long spell," Luke said, pulled his hat off and ran his fingers through his dirty hair.

"How many did we lose?"

"Nigh on half would be my guess. Some horses was stolen by the Injuns and a few of the cows were either too old or in bad shape to make the trip. We can make do with what we have; only it'll take time for the herd to grow back to what it was."

"Well, I'll let you handle the critters for us. You can ramrod the place and what money we make we'll be split with you, with a forty percent goin' to you every year. How does that sound?"

"One day that will be a lot of money, do you know that?"

Placing his hand on Luke's shoulder Bill said, "I hope so, son, I really do. I've carried a dream of this place in my mind for years and it just wouldn't die."

"When do we start on the cabin?"

Smiling, Bill replied, "In the morning, right after we eat. It'll be hard work fallin' them trees in the mountains and then using the horses to pull 'em down here. I want a good number of logs ready to use before we start putting the house up. That means for the first couple of weeks we'll just knock down trees and drag 'em here."

"I'll stay with you, until the cabin is up, but I ain't doin' no tree cuttin' or draggin'. I'll stand guard over the place. How 'bout you, Isaac?" Moses said as he dropped the butt of his rifle to the ground and then grasped the gun by the barrel.

"I don't mind doin' a little hard work, unlike some old men I know, but I have to be paid in good food every night." Then glancing at Sue, he added, "And, I know that is one payment I'll enjoy. Yer a fine cook, Missus Sanders, and yer man is a lucky feller."

Moving to her side, Bill put his hand around her waist and replied, "I know well I'm a lucky man. She's not only an excellent cook, but a fine figure of a woman."

Luke, embarrassed, lowered his eyes and grinned.

Isaac entered the conversation with an idea, "I saw a small herd of buffalo back a ways, so how 'bout I take Luke and we go make some meat? We'll get a smokehouse up fer ya tomorrow, but today me and him can knock down maybe four of 'em. That'll give ya some meat while we work to put a cabin up. Once we start on yer house, we'll not want to take time off to hunt."

"What ya standin' there fer, boy, get yer rifle and stuff! Sounds to me like yer goin' on a buff hunt! And, ya two take at least five hosses, 'cause buff meat is heavy!" Moses spoke in mock anger.

Luke scurried off to get his ammunition and gear, giving a loud shout of joy as he neared the wagon. He was excited and for once, he realized, he was being treated like a real man, instead of some snotty nosed kid. Then he suddenly grew sober, if he was being treated like a man, he'd have to start acting like one. No more complaining about pulling guard, no whining when he had to get up well before dawn, and he'd have to learn a lot more about being a man.

The two rode toward a distant rise and once near the crest, Isaac said, "Get down and let's crawl up to the rise and have us a look see."

On their hands and knees, the two moved up the side of the hill and looked down into the valley. They saw thousands of the big shaggy animals grazing peacefully. Tapping the young man on the shoulder, Isaac motioned for them to move back away from the crest.

Near the horses, Luke said, "We can't kill just three or four. One shot will down ten of 'em the way their bunched up like that."

"Not if we pick off the critters at the end of herd. We'll ride down in a few minutes and scatter 'em, then shoot at the ones toward the end."

Suddenly Luke's eyes grew large as he said, "Injuns!" He then kneeled in the tall grass and cocked his rifle.

Turning, Isaac saw a party of warriors riding toward the buffalo and kneeling beside the young man he said, "Sioux, so we're safe enough. I know most of the chief's personal like, and some of the sub-chiefs as well. We'll let them start their hunt and they'll soon be out of sight. Once they're gone, we'll get our meat and leave. I don't expect any trouble and that means no shootin' unless I shoot first."

"I hear ya, but I don't like it much."

"I didn't say ya had to like it, but I expect ya to do it. We start shootin,' and we'll both be dead in less than five minutes. 'Sides, they're friendly folks most of the time, if they know ya."

"I'll do what you say, but it goes against my grain."

Smiling, Isaac replied, "Good, it takes a good man to admit he don't like somethin' and yet do the job. Ya'll do to walk the river with."

Within minutes, the herd began to move and hearing the noise, they crawled to the rise and saw the Sioux had started the hunt. Thousands of hooves were pounding the ground and dust hung like a huge rain cloud over the big shaggy beasts. Warriors were moving in and out of the mass of animals, but dust made it hard to tell if any buffalo had fallen yet.

"When do we go down?" Luke asked as he glanced at the black man.

"Pretty soon, just as soon as the dust clears. We'll do it like we did the last time and walk beside our horses. When I shoot, I'll go for two of them, so you do the same."

A few short minutes later the main herd was gone, but dust still filled the air and little was seen moving in the brown cloud.

"The winds pickin' up, so it won't be long now," Isaac spoke as he moved away from the rise.

Luke, excited over the hunt, backed away as well and when they were back at the horses he said, "Won't be long now."

Smiling, Isaac asked, "Now, how do ya know that, young coon?"

"I know 'cause you're gettin' ready to ride."

Laughing, the black man said, "Yer right, now check yer gun and mount yer horse. In a few minutes we're goin' to make some meat."

A few minutes later the two men topped the rise, walking beside their horses. When they neared a small group of buffalo, Isaac stopped, placed his rifle over the saddle and pulled the trigger. He reloaded, located a new target, and fired again, seeing both animals drop.

Luke fired, saw a large bull drop and then sighted in on another. He fired once more and another animal was down. He started to move toward the downed buffalo when Isaac warned, "We got company, and it's the Sioux. Let me do the talkin'."

*Hell, you have to; I don't speak no Injun talk,* the young man thought as he pushed a new round into his rifle breech.

As five warriors neared, Isaac called out in the Sioux tongue, *"Hello, my brothers! It has been many moons since I have last seen you!"*

The warriors stopped and were seen talking among themselves. Finally, a lone warrior wearing a long headdress filled with feathers neared. Twenty feet from the two he stopped, but said nothing.

*"We hunger, my brother, and like the mighty Sioux, we hunt buffalo."*

At last, the Sioux replied, *"I see your hunt was successful, as was ours. We heard the sounds of your rifles, and came to see who was on our lands. My heart is glad it is the raven man I call brother. Who is the young white warrior?"*

*"One I teach the old ways. He is a fast learner and a good listener, which is rare for one so few in years."*

*"Your words are true."*

Turning to Luke, Isaac said, "Say howdy to old Brass Buttons. He's the main man with the Sioux."

Giving the Sioux a serious look, Luke gazed into his eyes and said, "Howdy-do, Brass Buttons."

Brass Buttons asked, *"What did the young one say?"*

*"He said he is honored to meet the great warrior of the Northern Sioux, Brass Buttons, and your name is spoken much by the white man."*

*"The white man knows my name?"*

*"Yes, you are known among the whites as a warrior and wise man."*

Brass Buttons raised his head and nodded solemnly as he replied, *"You may take your meat and return to your people. I will visit this young warrior again; he is wise beyond his years and will do well in his lifetime."* The warrior then pulled his horse around and galloped back to his men.

As the Sioux left, Isaac said with a chuckle, "Ole Brass Buttons took a shine to ya, son. He said he'll visit ya again one day. Try to make friends with 'em, he'll keep a lot of trouble off of yer ranch iffen ya can."

"W. . . why visit me?"

"I ain't got no idea, but he likes ya. Injuns is like that, they like ya right off or don't. He could end up bein' all that keeps everyone on yer ranch alive some day. Never make an enemy of an Injun, iffen ya can be his friend. They're loyal to friends and will make life easier fer ya out heah."

Shocked, Luke said, "Well, I'll be damned!"

"Ya ain't damned, son, yer lucky. Now, let's get this meat on the pack animals and get out of here."

# CHAPTER 14

**In** a little more than three weeks a rough looking cabin, smokehouse, blacksmith shop, and outhouse was standing tall on the Montana plains. The men were all hard at work putting the last touches to a barn, except Moses, who was standing guard near the front of the house. The cabin, constructed from logs dragged from the mountain, had split pine shingles for a roof. Moses had suggested they cover the roof with sod, to help keep the risk of fire down. The chimney was made of rocks and clay, for the same reasons. Each window was glass-less; with shutters made with slits for gun barrels installed on each frame, which secured easily. In the event of an attack, the shutters closed and the men could fire through the slits in the wood.

The barn was a rough looking structure, made entirely of logs, but shelter had to be up for the riding stock.

Moses warned as the men worked, "In less than a month, winter'll hit ya full force. The wind will howl and snow will fall of the likes you've never seen before."

Bill grinned, knowing the older man didn't like manual labor, and replied, "We got the frame done and most of the roof, we'll be ready. Ya feel like givin' us a hand?"

Moving back toward the front of the house, Moses said, "Yer doin' fine and it'll be done in a few days. You don't need an old man's help to finish the job."

Isaac laughed and said to Bill, "Ya sure put ole Moses in his place! I ain't never seen nobody handle the man like ya do."

Laughing with Isaac, Bill replied, "He reminds me of a man I once worked for, so it's pretty easy to figure out what will make the man move!"

"Moses is a good man, he just don't like work of any kind."

"Yep, I knew a few men when I was growin' up just like 'em. They wasn't lazy, but you couldn't get 'em to do a blame thing that didn't need doin' right now."

"That's Moses. He spent all his time the last few days tellin' us how bad winter will be, and he don't want to help get ready fer it. He's like them mountain men I told ya 'bout a few weeks back."

"I remember," Bill replied as he nailed a pine shingle on the roof. He'd made the nails by hand a few days after they arrived in his new blacksmith shop. His shop was one of the first small buildings they put together, so he'd have a place to work. While he didn't expect customers, he could make anything they needed and that would not only cut down on expenses, but save a long trip to a town or trading post.

When the last shingle was nailed into position, Isaac stood and said, "By God, she's done! Hell've a job, but we did 'er quick like!"

"That we did. Let's get down and see how Luke is doing on the inside?"

"I'm sure the young man has done well. He's a hard worker and will do well in life, I'm thinking."

Inside the barn, Luke was finishing the last stall when the two men entered. Bill smiled and said, "By Golly, it's almost done inside, too!"

"I'll be done in less than thirty minutes and then we can move the critters in." Isaac gave a warm smile and said, "Ya did a good job in heah, son, really good."

"It's the best I can do. I've never done anything like this before, so it was slow doin's at first."

"You did fine, Luke," Bill replied and then smiled. "I can see now I've chosen a good man to go into business with. You did this job like you been makin' barns all your life."

Luke laughed, pulled his hat off and wiped his sweat soaked hair with a red bandana as he said, "You know it's my first one, but I learned a great deal. Next time I make one, I'll know what I'm doin'."

Moses stuck his head in the barn and said, "Injuns comin', and they look to be Sioux."

Bill turned and asked, "Do you think they want a fight?"

"Not likely, Brass Buttons is with 'em and he took a shine to Luke. I'd imagine it's just a visit to see the boy, after all, he said he'd visit some time." Moses replied, gave a tooth-gapped grin, and moved from the door.

Glancing at Luke, Isaac said, "Come on; let's go see your Injun friend."

Walking from the barn, Luke replied, "He ain't my friend, yet. I have an idea he likes me, only I ain't got no reason why."

Looking to the west, Bill saw a long line of Sioux moving toward his home. He wondered what they'd do once they saw he was there to stay, but he said, "Try to become friends with the man, he might be a powerful feller to know."

"I done thought some on that, and think it's a good idea, too."

Isaac added, "It's like I told ya a-fore, he's the main Sioux chief, so if ya can be a friend of his ya'll be a lot safer heah."

Moses saw the men approaching and said, "Now, that's a lot of Sioux, let's hope Brass Buttons has come to visit Luke, or we'll be up to our asses in warriors in about five minutes."

Bill laughed and then asked, "Would they be approaching like they are now if they wanted us dead?"

"Not likely. We'd never know they were near until an arrow pierced our skins."

Isaac chuckled and then said, "I done told ya, Brass Buttons took a hankerin' to Luke, and he's payin' the young man a visit is all."

All were watching the line of warriors when they suddenly stopped about two hundred feet away from the cabin and four riders approached.

When they drew nearer, Luke spotted Brass Buttons by a long tail of feathers that fell from his head and trailed behind his horse.

One more feather and his war bonnet will drag on the ground, the young man thought.

Isaac suddenly whispered, "Nobody touches a gun. We don't want to spook the man and end up gettin' killed when all he wants to do is visit."

Brass Buttons stopped about twenty feet from the white men and said in Sioux, *"I see my friend is still healthy."*

Isaac translated and then Luke spoke, "So is Brass Buttons. It is good to see you are well."

One of the warriors moved his horse forward and then the chief said, *"I bring you meat. We know you have killed buffalo, I saw it with my eyes, but this is elk from the mountains."*

*"The young man thanks you for the meat."* Isaac said after Luke spoke. Brass Buttons nodded, but said nothing.

"Tell 'em I'll be right back!" Luke said and then took off at a run to the cabin. A few minutes later, he returned, holding something blue in his right hand.

"What ya got, son?" Isaac asked.

"It's an old Yankee jacket I used to play with. I'm too big to use it now and surely don't want to wear it. I was gonna throw it away, but I think it'll fit Brass Buttons. Tell him I am pleased with the gift of the meat and want him to have this coat."

As Isaac spoke, Luke took the coat and handed it to the chief. Once Isaac had finished, Brass Buttons raised the coat, broke into a smile and said, *"Thank the young warrior for the long knife coat. I have many things, but no coat like this. It is a good gift to give a warrior."*

*"I am glad you like it."*

Brass Buttons grew serious as he asked, *"Why are many white men moving onto Sioux lands? I do not mind if my young white friend lives here, but countless others come and they are like a raging river."*

*"It is the way of the white men,"* Isaac replied.

*"Of what way do you speak? Do all white men steal land? Do they not know the land they take is Sioux land?"*

Lowering his eyes, Isaac said, *"They see the land is not used, so they take it."*

*"What does this mean, not used? The bones of our old ones are buried in our land."*

*"A white man grows most of his food and when he does not see food growing in the soil, he thinks the land is not used."*

His face reflecting anger, Brass Buttons asked, *"Are the white men not real men? Do they not hunger for meat like a true warrior?"*

*"They eat meat, but unlike the Sioux, the white man does not move to follow game. He grows his meat and food."*

*"I have seen his food! Pigs, cows and the bird that drops eggs! That is not the food of a real warrior! A warrior wants red meat!"*

*"I know your words are true, but the Sioux way is not the way of the white man."*

*"I think the white man is a weak man and will not fight."*

*"He will fight, if he must. Have you not heard of the white man's war where the sun awakens each day?"*

*"I have heard, but think it cannot be much of a true battle."* The chief replied with scorn in his voice. Isaac shrugged his shoulders and said, *"I have spoken with one tongue to Brass Buttons. You may choose to believe me or not, that is your choice."*

Shaking his head, Brass Buttons replied, *"I know you speak with one tongue, but it is hard to understand the ways of the white eyes."*

*"As it is for all red men."*

*"I have heard there are many white men where the sun awakens each day. Is this true?"*

*"Yes, more than blades of grass on the plains."*

Lowering his head, the chief thought for a few minutes and then said, *"What will become of my people if the white men keep coming? Are the old ways to die?"*

Neither Moses nor Isaac spoke, though both were fluent in Sioux.

Finally, Moses said, *"The days of The People are coming to an end. One day, all the Sioux call theirs will belong to the white men. These white men are not the hunters of the one who swims, or a family that wants to share a home on Sioux land, but the takers of land. They crave land like a true warrior craves horses, and they measure their wealth by how much land they have."*

Giving a confused look, Brass Buttons asked, *"How can this be? Land is land and has no value. A good horse can carry a man into battle, while a good woman can keep a man warm on cold nights, but land?"*

*"To the white man, land can be plowed or used for his animals, which gives the land value."*

*"Ripping the land open gives it value? Does the white man not care for the spirit of the land? What of the bones of our ancestors buried in the land?"*

*"The way of The People is not a white man's way. He does not think the land has a spirit, and his God tells him to plant his food in the soil."*

*"I must leave, but tell the young white warrior I will return in the spring and we can hunt buffalo together. I have learned much talking this day, but your words do not please me."*

*"It is good for him to learn the ways of a warrior from a Sioux. I will tell him and during the months of hunger, I will teach him sign language, so he can speak when you return. And, at times, spoken words do not bring us joy."*

Mounting, the chief nodded and then replied, *"That is good. May the Great Spirit feed you well during the cold moons of hunger. Until I return again, stay well."*

As the warriors rode away, Isaac said, "I'm glad ya started speakin', Moses, I was plum at a loss fer words. He was askin' some hard questions."

"Aye, he was at that, but the good thing is, he never told Bill to move. So, Luke, I think ya have a new friend."

The young man smiled and said, "Wait until I tell ma I got me a Sioux war chief for a friend. I'll bet she has a sissy fit over the whole she-bang."

Bill laughed and then said, "Most likely she will at that. Come, we all need and deserve a shot of whiskey, a hot meal and a good night's sleep."

Moses grinned and said, "I'm glad you stopped right there. For a second or three, I thought you was goin' to add a bath to that list and I'll draw the line right there."

"Nope," Bill replied, "baths are only needed by workin' men and you ain't done a blame thing since I met you, except stand guard."

Isaac added, "By God, ya got that right!"

"Look, now, I told y'all when you started I'd not do no work and I'm a man of my word."

Moving toward the house, Bill replied, "You're truly a man of your word."

⇒⇐  ⇒⇐  ⇒⇐

Two days later the wind picked up and snow began to fall. The wind was so high that just getting to the barn became dangerous because no one could see the way. Finally, Bill ran a rope from the barn door to the porch of the house, just so he could make the trips. It continued to fall, even after more than a foot of fresh snow covered the land. The snow did not stop until seven days after it started.

Isaac used the time to work with Luke, teaching him the customs of the Sioux, as well as sign language. While a fast learner, he often became confused if Isaac signed too quickly. Most mornings, like this one, they'd get up a couple of hours before dawn to practice sign language.

"I know the sign, but iffen you go too fast it messes my mind up some." He complained.

"A Sioux ain't gonna sign slow when he talks to ya. He'll go at a normal speed, which is what I've been doin'. Keep yer eyes on my hand and ya'll fig'er it all out in the end."

"Okay, let's try it all again," Luke said with a determined look in his eyes.

"While I sign, ya tell me what I'm sayin',"

*"I have many horses, uh, stolen from the . . . the . . . Pawnee. Do you like to eat bear meat? No, I like buffalo better."* The young man said and then asked, "Was I right?"

"Right as all get out. Always keep yer eyes on an Injuns hands, iffen ya trust 'em, when he uses sign. They think it's rude iffen ya don't."

Laughing, Luke replied, "That's the only way I can understand 'em, is to watch every little move they make."

"It'll come with time, son."

Bill, who'd been on the porch standing guard, stuck his head in the door and said, "I got movement about a hundred yards from here. Does one of you want to check it out, or what?"

Pulling his buffalo robe around his shoulders and taking his rifle from the wall, Moses replied, "I'll take a look, but be sure to cover me good. It ain't likely to be Injuns, not in this weather, only it could be."

"I see a form on the ground, so who ever it is, they're most likely hurt some."

Walking from the warmth of the house and out into the cold night air, Moses cursed the rudeness of visitors who showed hours before dawn. "It just ain't polite to show up at an ungodly hour like this and expect to be welcomed with opened arms."

As he got near the downed form, he saw it was a white man, had an arrow in his back, and lay unmoving. Kneeling beside the man, he felt for a pulse on the side of his neck. Feeling the man's heartbeat, he picked him up and placed him over his left shoulder. He then slowly made his way back to the cabin.

Bill ran out to meet him about half way back and together they carried the man inside. "It's a white man!" Sue exclaimed as they entered the cabin.

Luke asked, "Is he dead?"

Moses, taking his robe off, replied, "He lived outside, but I ain't sure right now. Sue, you boil me up some water and Luke, ya get my doctorin' bag over by the window."

Kneeling beside the man, Moses saw his eyes were open and he was breathing, so he asked, "Who are you?"

"Nathan B. Mossland, and we were attacked by Injuns near sunup today."

Bill, suddenly interested, asked, "What tribe?"

"Hell, I ain't got no idea. All I know is they were Injuns." When Mossland quit talking blood covered his lower lip.

Moses, growing angry, said, "Y'all leave the man alone until I finish doctorin' 'em up. Then you can talk for days, iffen you want."

A little later, the job was done and as Moses washed his hands in a wooden bucket the wounded man said, "Frank went out to check on the stock in the barn, but didn't come back. His wife, Nadine, she sent me out to check on 'em. I'd just entered the barn, turned to light a lamp, when I felt an arrow hit me in the back. At first I didn't know what it was, because I just felt something hit me and then some pain."

Luke asked, "Did you have a gun?"

"Shotgun, and the first savage I saw got both barrels, too! I ran back to the house, but it was just me and two women to fight 'em off."

"Good God!" Moses said and then asked, "How'd you get away?"

"A-fore me and Frank built the place, we made us a tunnel that ran from a trap in the floor of the livin' room to a small stream a ways from the cabin. Them Injuns set the place on fire, so I fired two shots and me and the women went out the tunnel. Just as we come out on the other end of that hole I saw the place collapse in flames."

"Where're the women?" Bill asked as he looked at Moses.

Lowering his head, Mossland replied, "I lost 'em in the storm."

Sue spoke before anyone else, "What kind of man are you? You left women out there?"

With tears in his eyes, Mossland said, "I looked for 'em, I surely did, but hell, you can't see nothin' out in that storm."

Bill stood as he asked, "Where's your place?"

"Nigh on twenty miles west of here."

Walking to his buffalo coat, Bill said, "Isaac, you and Luke come with me. I'm hopin' we can still find them women alive."

Moses asked, "What about me?"

"You stay here and keep the place safe." Then, turning to Sue he said, "Honey, we'll try to find 'em, but don't be surprised iffen we can't do the job."

Walking to Bill, Sue kissed him on the cheek and said, "I know you'll look, and that's all I ask. Don't come back here all froze up and hurtin', 'cause after this man left 'em they're most likely dead anyways. Just make a quick look and then come home."

The way was lung-hurting cold, with snow blowing in every direction, and Bill had a hard time staying in the saddle as they moved. Even wrapped up in a buffalo coat, buffalo hat with ear-flaps, and mittens of the same, he was still freezing. They moved slowly, to keep the horses from slipping on the snow and ice, which only made the trip more uncomfortable.

A few hours after dawn, Isaac rode beside him and said, "We're near the place, I can smell smoke."

"I can't smell nothin'. It's too cold out here."

Luke suddenly shouted, "Off to the left! I think saw movement."

Moving in that direction, they soon came to the remains of the cabin and found two women sitting beside a small fire. Thank God they had coats and gloves on before they entered the tunnel or they'd be dead right now, Bill thought just before he called out. "You're safe now ladies, we've come for you!"

Both women looked up and Luke could see fear in their eyes. One, who looked to be the oldest, raised a shotgun and called out, "That's close enough! Who you be?"

"I'm Bill Sanders, this man is Isaac, and the young man is Luke. Nathan Mossland told us you were out here."

"I'll kill that worthless sumbitch when I see 'em. He ran off and left us."

"He said he lost both of ya in the storm." Isaac replied.

"Lost, my ass! He ran, mister! He ran and left us out here to fend for ourselves! Well, by God, we did the job, but when I see 'em next he'll die by my hand!" the younger woman said.

Bill and Isaac exchanged looks and then Bill said, "Can we come to your fire? We've been ridin' hard to get here as soon as we could."

"You're Bill Sanders, right?" The woman with the shotgun asked.

"Yep."

"Come, but don't none of you make any sudden moves, or I'll blow you into two pieces!"

Beside the fire, the men removed their gloves, held their hands near the flickering flames and enjoyed the heat. Then, Bill said, "We've brought extra horses to take you back. Only before I do that, I need the two of you to promise not to kill Mossland in my home."

"My name is Nadine, and this young thing is Nancy. You've got my promise. I'd promise anything to get warm again."

Looking at Nancy, the young woman nodded and said, "Me too. But, I'll kill 'em later, after we leave your place. What kind of man would just run off and leave without sayin' a word?"

Isaac replied, "Maybe he lost ya, like he said. It'd be easy to do in a storm."

"I'll be damned," Nadine said, "You're a black man!"

Isaac laughed and said, "I've been one most of my life."

The older woman spoke once more, "No, Nathan is my husband, and he's useless as a man. He ain't got any grit, and I know he ran because he said he was goin' for help."

Luke said, "And, he did."

Laughing, Nadine replied, "Findin' y'all was an accident. My man couldn't find his rear-end iffen you put his hands in his back pockets."

"He's your husband. Do you still plan to kill 'em?" Luke asked, and then added a small piece of wood to the flames.

"Bein' my old man don't mean a blame thing. He ran off and left two women! He's no good as far as I'm concerned. He didn't care what happened to us, as long as he was safe."

Bill looked up at the sky, shook his head and then said, "We need to get movin'. We've more snow comin' and I hope we can get back before it hits. I want both of you to know the trip will be hard, with few breaks taken, because this weather can kill. Now, mount and let's ride."

# CHAPTER 15

The return trip was a ride right out of hell, with everyone feeling the cold, but Luke felt it more than the others did. About halfway back, he'd dropped his mitten in the snow and couldn't find it. He had to ride with one hand and keep the other one in his coat. After a short while, his covered hand began to chill, so he'd take his uncovered hand out for a few minutes and place the covered one in his coat pocket. Unknowingly, his uncovered hand was slowly freezing.

It was shortly after midday, when they saw the light from the cabin off in the distance, that all knew they were safe. Riding into the barn, Bill noticed the first of the new snow falling. As they made their way to the house, it was falling faster. Both women had been quiet during the ride, but Isaac suspected all hell to break loose when they confronted Mossland.

The heat in the cabin was almost more than the small group could stand when they entered and closed the door behind them. A fire was blazing in the fireplace and a large pot was hanging over the dancing flames. The smell of fresh soup filled the little structure.

"You found 'em alive!" Sue screamed and ran into Bill's arms.

"Just barely. I don't think they would have lasted the night," he replied.

Moving to the women, Sue said, "I'm Sue, Bill's wife. You two need to get by the fire and warm up some. I've coffee done, so take a cup from the table with you and help yourself."

Nadine suddenly asked, "I didn't get lucky and Nathan died, did I?"

"Good heavens, no! He'll be fine once his wound heals," Sue answered.

"That's just my blamed luck! He ran off and left us, you know."

Meeting Mossland's eyes, Bill asked, "Is that how it happened? You didn't say nothin' about that when you got here."

The man broke eye contact and just above a whisper, he said, "I was ashamed. I was so scared when we come out of the tunnel that I just took off runnin'."

"You'll leave as soon as this storm has passed. I'll not sell or give you a mount, so you'll have to walk to safety."

Silence filled the room, except for the clink of the coffee pot as it touched one of the women's coffee cups.

"Mister Sanders, it's well over a hundred miles to safety! Surely you'd not make me walk that distance."

Bill's eyes narrowed as he replied, "I just fought a bloody war and saw just about everything a man can do, from stupidity to bravery, but you know what? A coward bothered me the most. I got little use for a man with no iron in 'em and you're that kind of man. You should've stayed with your woman and your friend's wife, even if it cost your own life or at least brought 'em with you. No, you'll leave and on foot as soon as the snow passes. I don't want you in this house."

Mossland donned his cap, gloves, and coat, and walked from the cabin.

Isaac asked as he looked at Bill, "You know he'll die?"

"Probably, but he deserves it."

Moses, who'd been listening to the conversation, said, "It's not right, Bill. Let the man heal and give 'em a horse. I believe in justice too, but iffen you send 'em out on foot you might as well shoot 'em here. Either way he'll die."

Bill, thinking that maybe he was being too hard, replied, "Okay, I'll think on this a spell. Only, I warn y'all right now, I can't stand a coward."

"Fair enough, but let the good Lord guide yer decision," Isaac said.

"No!" Nadine yelled and turning from the fire she said, "He left us to die, so he deserves the same kind of treatment. He's no good, I tell you!"

"I said I'll think on it, now let me be. There ain't goin' to be no more talkin' about this and once I've made up my mind, it's final. This is my home, and I make the decisions here!" Bill replied in a loud voice.

Luke moved to Sue and asked, "My hand is burning something fierce, would you mind takin' a look at it?"

Sue saw the hand was dark red, and under the nails, she could plainly see frozen tissue. She gave a gasp of surprise and asked, "Moses, would you look at his hand, it don't look good to me. While Missouri gets cold, I've never seen an injury from the cold that looks like this one does."

Taking the frozen hand in his, Moses said, "Frostbite is what he's got. Son, why in the hell didn't you have your gloves or mittens on during the ride?"

"I dropped one and couldn't find it. I didn't think it was such a big deal at the time, except the hand kept getting cold."

"Well," Moses gazed into his eyes and continued with, "Let's hope I can save the hand. I'll make no promises and iffen I have to take 'er off, you might not survive the doctorin'."

"Take off my hand! I'll be damned! Ain't nobody cuttin' one of my hands off!"

Pulling his pipe from his pocket, Moses calmly replied, "Simmer down a mite, son. It could be the only way to keep you alive, young coon. Now, we'll try to save your hand first, but iffen that don't work, we'll have little choice in the matter."

Sue asked, "What do you need me to do?"

"Get me a bucket of warm, not hot, water."

"I've some by the fireplace right now."

"Get it." Then turning to Luke he said, "I'm gonna try to warm your hand up, only it'll cause you pain like you ain't never felt before."

"I'll handle the pain."

Bill walked to the table, picked up a clay jug of whiskey and handed it to Luke. As the young man looked at him, he said, "Take at least five long drinks. Make 'em good ones too, because it's all we got to kill the pain. I've seen what he's about to do and watched grown men cry like babies while the job's bein' done. Lot's of men in the war suffered from the heat and cold."

Raising the jug, Luke began to drink. The first sip of the raw amber colored alcohol stunned him and left him choking, but a few drinks later it went down much easier.

Moses moved to his side and ordered, "Put the jug down and let's get this done. I'm gonna stick your hand in this warm water and no matter how much you scream or cry, the hand will stay in the bucket. Do you understand?"

"Okay."

Taking Luke's hand, Moses stuck it in the water and immediately the young man began to cry, but he sat beside the bucket unmoving.

"Hurts, don't it, son?" Bill asked.

"Feels like fire . . . honest to God!"

Moses gave a weak grin and said, "You're doin' fine, Luke, just a few minutes more."

Sue poured a water glass full of whiskey and handed it to the young man as she said, "Sip on this as the hand thaws out. I'll hold the glass, so when you want a drink just let me know."

"I need . . . a drink . . . now."

Two drinks later, the glass was empty and Luke still cried. Sue filled the glass once more and handed it to him.

Pulling the hand from the water, Moses asked, "Does your hand still hurt?"

"Still . . . burns!"

"That's a good sign. It should hurt when took from the water. I think we might save this hand after all."

Luke took a long gulp from the whiskey glass and asked, "Does it have to go back in the water again?"

"Nope, we're finished with the water. I'm goin' to wrap you up and then it's off to bed for you. Keep drinkin' whiskey until you get tired enough to sleep. We'll know in a day or two iffen we saved your hand or wasted our time."

"You mean all that pain might have been for nothin'?"

"Son, compared to havin' a hand took off, the pain you just had was nothin'."

Luke stood and then Bill and Moses moved him to his bed. Sitting on the side of the bed, he sipped whiskey for a few long minutes and then suddenly fell over on his side—he'd passed out from the alcohol.

"He'll have a bad hangover in the mornin'," Isaac said from a rocking chair near the fire and gave a low cackle.

"A hangover is the least of his problems. I don't cotton to heavy drinkin', like he just did, but it has it's place in life. At least now he'll sleep a few hours." Bill replied as he covered Luke with a blanket.

Sue, glancing at Moses asked, "Do you think we saved the hand?"

"Hard to say really, but iffen we didn't, the hand will turn black with white dead skin on his fingers. If that happens, the hand has to come off fast."

Bill, sitting at the table poured himself a glass of whiskey, took a sip and then asked, "You ever done that before?"

"Just once."

Sue smiled and said, "See, he's done it before. How many days did it take the man to be up and movin' around again?"

Lowering his head, Moses said, "He never got up again. Rooster, that was his name, died the night I took his hand. He started bleedin', and I couldn't get it to stop."

"Did you cauterize it?" Bill asked, and then lowered his glass to the table.

"Sure, but it didn't stop the blood. Rooster died lookin' me in the eyes and it still bothers me, even after I tried all I could to keep 'em alive."

"Was it from the cold, like Luke?"

"No, far from it. He'd taken a Pawnee arrow through the hand and had made light of it when it happened. When I first treated 'em, he'd talked of how lucky he was. A week later, it was putrid and had to come off. Oh, I don't think Rooster blamed me for his death, but I did then and still do."

Sue, feeling the older man's pain asked, "Why?"

Shrugging, Moses replied, "I don't really know. Mayhap I knew the job was too much for me to take on, but I did it anyway, because I had no choice. Then again, I wasn't ready, not really, when I cut the hand off. I had no bandages, no hot knife blade, and never expected as much blood as there was."

Bill, knocked back his drink, poured another one and moved to another rocker beside the fire. Taking a small sip he commented, "You know, in the war I killed a young boy. I didn't mean to do it, but he'd stabbed me in the back and I turned mean on 'em. He was dying before I even realized he was just a kid."

Sue looked at him and said, "No!"

Nodding, Bill added, "To this day, I have dreams of that little boy and he still haunts me from the grave. I don't know how you feel, Moses, but I know how I feel."

"Bill, that's terrible. I never knew," Sue said in a low voice.

"No one knew. This is the first time in my life I've spoken of it."

Isaac said grimly, "Iffen he was old enough to stab ya, he was old enough to die fer not doin' the job right."

"Good God, Isaac, he couldn't have been over ten years old!" Bill all but screamed at the black man.

"In my mind, his age makes little difference, when he picked up a knife, sword or gun; he knew he could be killed. Hell, man, it was war! When he stabbed you, he became jus' another soldier in the war."

"Maybe, except I still see his eyes in my dreams."

Sue lowered her head and said, "I don't doubt you do see his eyes, but killin' of the boy was not your fault, no more than Rooster dyin' on Moses. Both were bad luck, fate, or God's will. You can call it what you will, it's still the same."

Bill remained silent, but took another small sip of his drink.

Morning came with Luke still in pain. He sipped whiskey most of the day, but by evening his hand had stopped hurting. Moses dreaded a look at the hand, only once uncovered the hand looked normal.

Grinning, Moses said, "By golly, I think your hand will be fine. I don't see any discolorin' on it, and iffen you can move the fingers okay it should be back to normal in a few days."

Moving his fingers, Luke said, "The fingers move okay and don't hurt when I do it. I was scared to hell and back you'd have to take my hand."

"Let me give you a warnin' right now. In the years to come, keep that hand extra warm. Iffen it ever gets cold like that again, you'll lose it. Once a body part's been froze, it freezes faster and with more damage the second time."

"I'll remember that."

"Good, now take another drink of whiskey and get some more sleep."

As Luke poured a glass of drink, the older man made his way to the fire, sat in a rocking chair and smiled. Sue, seeing the smile on his face, knew Luke would keep his hand and she was glad. A young man would take the loss of a hand harder than a grown man would.

Just then, the door opened, in stepped Bill, and he placed some wood in wooden box beside the flames. Hanging his coat up and taking his boots off, he sat near the fireplace to warm up.

"I'd say it must be twenty below zero out there right now."

Moses smile and replied, "Most likely it is and by the way, Luke will not lose his hand."

"Thank God, I was hopin' that'd end up the case."

"Where's Isaac?"

"He's outside splittin' wood. The man is usually the first up come mornin', and he told me my kindlin' is too big for him. He likes his nice and thin."

"Isaac, like most of us, got his own way of doin' some things."

Silenced filled the small cabin and then Moses asked, "Yep, I guess so. Did Sue tell you 'bout Mossland yet? He's gone."

"Died on us?" Bill asked.

"Nope, he stole a horse and rode out before any of us was awake. He took some bacon, beans, a large pot and one of your guns." Sue said.

"He needs to die, but, let 'em go."

Moses grinned and asked, "How come you ain't out lookin' for 'em?"

Bill laughed and replied, "Too damned cold for me to be out there right now. To tell you the truth, I don't think the man will make it to Jackson's Tradin' Post or Butterfield's either, because this weather will kill 'em."

"Mayhap, but it's hard to tell. You're just goin' to let it go then?"

"Yep, I am for now. Next time we're at one of the tradin' posts we can ask about 'em. If I ever get my hands on the man, he'll hang for takin' my horse."

"Hell that sounds fair to me."

Sue, who'd been knitting, asked, "Don't you think that's pretty harsh?"

Moses gave a light chuckle and said, "That's exactly what a court of law back in the states would do to the man."

"This is not the states, Moses."

Bill butted in and said, "No, it's not the states, and a good horse is harder to find out here than back home. Keep in mind, he didn't just take a horse, he took our food, blankets, a gun, and mayhap some things we ain't discovered missin' yet."

"They're all hangin' offenses out heah, Sue, every single one," Moses added.

"For stealin' a little food you'd hang a man?"

"Yup and I've seen it done, too. We usually only have one-way of dealin' with ser'ous problems out here. Either the man walks free or ends up on the short end of a long rope. See, we ain't got any jails, so it's all or nothin'."

Sue placed her knitting in a small basket, gave a tired grin and said, "I can understand that, but it looks to me, since we make and enforce the laws, we need to be very careful when we give out punishment to crooks."

"We are careful and most, if not all, of 'em deserve what they get. Iffen we're around a bunch of folks, we usually have us a court before we hang 'em, just to make it legal like."

Sue laughed as Bill said, "If I ever see 'em again, he's a dead man. I'll not have a man takin' advantage of my offerin' him a home, warmth and food, and then stealin' from me. He ate of my salt, you know."

"I hear you and that's pretty serious where I come from."

Shaking her head, Sue said, "Let's stop taking about Mister Mossland and figure out what we're goin' to do with these two women we have on our hands."

"Simple. Once the weather clears, somebody will take 'em to the closest tradin' post and drop 'em off," Moses replied.

"In the mean time, we're stuck with 'em. I will not send two women out in this kind of weather. It would not be the Christian thing to do."

Sue blushed and replied, "Of course not, Bill, and I didn't mean it that way. I just meant they're a handful and will be under foot for at least another week."

"Likely they will and mayhap longer. We'll jus' have to set some rules and make 'em live by 'em. Or, is there some other reason ya don't want 'em underfoot?"

"No, not really, but Nadine was quick to want to kill her husband."

"Hell," Moses said, "I don't blame her one bit. It was deathly cold out there and I agree with Isaac, or was it Bill, that said they would have been dead by nightfall."

"It was me, and I think she has a right to kill the man. You just don't run off and leave two women alone. It ain't a manly thing to do."

Standing, Sue replied, "I'll leave that up to you two to talk over, I've got to put a big pot of beans and ham on or we'll have no supper this night."

Moses said, as she walked off, "She's a good woman, but got some serious growin' up to do in my eyes."

"Uh-huh, she does at that. Now, tell about the first time you met the Sioux."

Moses closed his eyes and let his head lower to his chest. He was quiet for a few moments and then spoke.

"One day, way back when I first come out here, I was in my camp mindin' my own business, which was cleanin' beaver plews at the time, when I had some visitors—Sioux. They rode right into my camp and stayed mounted, without a word spoken.

Finally, this brave with a whole shit-load of feathers gets off his horse and says, "You come."

"Now, me, I thought they was takin' me captive and didn't see much of a choice, so I went to their village, expecting to be tortured to death. Only, it didn't happen that way. Once we got there, they give me a lodge of my own and treated me good.

Well, about the second day, a bunch of Ree attacked and all hell broke loose. I grabbed my gun and joined in the fight against them rascals. To make a long story short, Soarin' Eagle, he was the warrior who brought me to the village; asked me to take the women and children and run. I did just that and we hid in the mountains for over a week. Using my rifle, I kept us well fed, but wondered if there were any survivors of the attack.

Finally, Soarin' Eagle and two men tracked us to our campin' spot and said it was safe for us to return. The Ree had attacked them twice more in the time we'd been gone, but Sioux scouts later told 'em they was gone, so they came for us.

That night, in a big hoop-de-doo, the village adopted me right in and Soarin' Eagle made me his blood brother. I lived with that bunch for over three years and even took me a wife, but she died of small pox, like most of the tribe, a little over a year after we was hitched."

Bill, surprised, asked, "You were married?"

"Yup, she was a good woman, too."

"But she was an Injun, and that made you a squaw man."

Moses looked long and hard at him, and then asked, "You don't like Injuns?"

Lowering his head, Bill replied, "I ain't got nothin' against 'em, but they kill white folks."

"Yep, they kill us, but for a good reason."

Raising his head, he asked, "They have a reason to kill us? Now what in the world could that be?"

Giving a low chuckle, Moses said, "We're stealin' their lands and giving nothin' in return. But, Brass Buttons won't kill us because he likes Luke. Now, let me tell ya, that's the only reason."

Bill felt an involuntary shudder run down his spine as he thought of a fight with the Sioux. He already knew it would not be a fight they would win and the warriors would be ruthless in battle.

# CHAPTER 16

A few days later, Bill was in his small blacksmith shop shaping horseshoes, and he'd been working since early morning. The sound of his hammer striking metal filled the cool afternoon air. Snow still covered parts of the ground, but the lung hurting cold had disappeared.

"Dang noise is loud, ain't it?" Sue asked Isaac, who was sitting on the porch beside her.

"That's the sound of progress, don't ya know. Any time a man is makin' somethin' from metal, we're movin' forward."

"How ya figure?"

"Man's come a long way the last few years and can make mos' of anythin' he want's. It wasn't like that a long time back, 'cause back then a man had to work from can see to cain't see jus' to get enough food to survive another day. Now days, food ain't that big a deal, not since man learned to work iron and steel, so guns could be made. Now if we need food, we kill a critter, but back then ya just died."

"I never thought much about way back."

"Ya should some time, and think how lucky we are."

"What will they have in the future?"

Isaac chuckled and replied, "I ain't got no idea, but iffen I did, I'd get rich quick. There'll be changes, but they'll come slowly."

"Like changes to the red man?"

"Yup, them folks are livin' on borrowed time and some of 'em know it, too," Isaac said, and then pulled out a twist of tobacco.

Pulling out his pocketknife, he cut off a long piece, placed it in his mouth and began to chew.

"In some ways it's sad. I mean, we're takin' their land and they can't stop us."

Spitting a long stream of brown juice into the snow by his feet, Isaac replied, "Always been like that, since the beginnin' of time. The strong take, and weak do without. Years ago, I'm sure men fought over the best hunting grounds, women, water and the like. But, you know, the strongest are the ones who got it all."

"It's the gun," Sue said flatly.

"Nope, it really ain't. Now the gun will speed it all up, but iffen we didn't have guns, we'd fight with knives, rocks, or clubs. What's gonna hurt the Injuns is our sheer numbers. There are jus' too many of us and few of them. No, this land will one day be in our hands and grand cities like New York and Saint Louis will spring up outta nothin'."

Turning to look at the black man, Sue asked, "Do you really believe that? I just can't picture that in my mind. This country is wild and untamed, so I can't see it."

"So was the land around them big cities we got now. First, the settlers come in, then business, schools and churches. Once schools and churches come, it's a jus' a matter of time a-fore the town becomes a city or dies out. Some don't never die, except they stay small. Only, who knows what the coming years will bring 'em."

"What makes a city grow?"

"It's business and people passin' through the town. Now I don't know much 'bout New York, but Saint Louis and New Orleans grew because the mighty Mississippi passed by their front door. Folks started using the river fer travel and a-fore ya knew it, they was cities. They got traffic comin' and goin' on the river."

"I see," Sue replied, but really didn't understand much of what the man was saying.

"The fastest growin' cities are them that start near old river crossin's. London, way over in England and Saint Louie are two good examples of what I'm talkin' 'bout. Years ago, long a-fore towns was there, those spots were where folks used to cross-rivers. It was jus' natural fer a city to start quick like. Both are big places now, but sure to grow even bigger."

"How do you know so much about the world?"

Isaac grinned and replied, "I read a lot, Missy, and I don't think there's no reason fer a feller to stay ignorant, iffen he don't want to. It's a choice, jus' like gettin' outta bed."

While Sue said she understood, she was at a complete loss. How could a runaway slave know more than she did? It concerned her and real ignorance scared her, because dumb people died at an early age, especially on the frontier. If you made the wrong decision, you died.

Luke walked out of the house and asked, "Why do you two look so serious?"

Isaac glance up at the young man and replied, "Jus' talkin' 'bout the world in general. How ya feelin' this cold day?"

"Pretty good, I'd say. I was up at dawn and workin' in the barn long before the sun come up.

Off to the west it looks to me like we're in for some more rain or snow."

"Snow, most likely."

Standing and dusting her dress, Sue said, "Iffen you two will excuse me, I've chores to start."

As she walked into the house, Luke asked, "Bill out in the blacksmith shop?"

"Yup, been there since near dawn, workin' his tail off."

"What's he makin'?"

"Horseshoes, nails, hinges, and other things a small place like this needs durin' winter."

"Seems to be busy work to me, 'cause there ain't no reason fer a man to be out workin' his tail off when it's as cold as it is."

Standing, Isaac said, "Speakin' of cold, I'm goin' in for a spell. I been out here too long, and it has chilled me some."

"I'm goin' for a short ride around the base of the mountain. Iffen I don't get out of the house, I'll go nuts or kill somebody."

"Ya do that, but watch yer hair out there. Most warriors don't go out much in the dead of winter, but some might be out fer one reason or 'nother."

Laughing, the young man replied, "I'll keep my eyes open." He then walked to the barn, pulled his horse from a stall, and started saddling. A few minutes later, he rode from the barn and moved slowly toward the mountains.

Glancing up at the sun, he figured it was still a couple of hours until dusk, so he'd ride around the base of the mountain and then return home. Staying inside the cabin was making him short tempered, and he felt like lashing out at everyone. He knew a ride would be good for his mind and body.

Riding over a slight rise, he placed both of his hands on the saddle horn and looked around. It was then he saw four riders riding fast in his direction. A few minutes later, he realized they were Indians, but of what tribe he could not tell.

Kicking his horse in the ribs, he galloped to some boulders at the base of the mountain, dismounted and pulled his rifle from its sheath. Not knowing how long he might be in the rocks, he also pulled his canteen, saddlebags, and rope. He then slapped his horse hard on the butt, knowing it would return to the ranch way before dusk.

A bullet zinged off one of the rocks, just missing him, so he cocked his rifle and quickly moved behind the largest boulder. His heart was pounding hard in his chest and he felt fear starting to build in his mind as he scanned the plains looking for the warriors. A few minutes later he spotted a color that didn't seem to belong, so he lined up his rifle sights, took a deep breath and as he released it, he gently squeezed the trigger. The sound of his shot was loud, but he missed. When the warrior attempted to stand, Luke placed a bullet in the man's chest.

The brave fell and as he struck the ground, three more braves stood and started running right at him. He felt an arrow strike him in the left shoulder and ignoring the pain, he fired quickly. One man fell, but the other two continued running at him. It was then his rifle jammed, so he threw it to the ground and pulled his pistol.

Luke fired two rounds from his pistol and saw one warrior fall, but the last man was getting close, too close. The brave struck him hard; knocking them both to the ground, and the young man felt a searing burn along his left side. Dismissing the pain, he moved away from the warrior and raised his pistol.

The Indian moved at him in a rush and Luke fired, but felt a knife blade enter his chest as the warrior fell. Falling to his knees, he saw the warrior was down, but still trying to get on his feet, so he fired his pistol once, twice and then a loud snap as the hammer struck an empty chamber.

This time the brave was down for good, and Luke could see a bullet had struck the man in the head.

Reaching, he pulled the knife from his chest and instantly felt warm blood running down his torso. Untying his bandana, he pressed the cloth against the wound and then winced in pain. Feeling weak, he moved behind the large boulder and sat down, knowing his wound needed care and soon if he expected to live.

➽⬅ ➽⬅ ➽⬅

Bill had just come out of the blacksmith building when he saw Luke's horse run into the barnyard. Moving slowly, so he'd not frighten the animal, he took the reins in hand and looked the horse over closely. He saw no signs of a fight or blood, but he knew something had happened or the horse would not have returned alone.

Turning, he called out, "Isaac and Moses, I need you both out here, and now!"

A few minutes later, both men walked to his side and Isaac said, "I warned that boy 'bout keepin' his eyes open!"

"Mayhap he did, you don't know what happened yet!" Moses said his tone filled with anger.

"Nope, I don't know, but ya can bet yer ass it wasn't good."

"That's enough, both of you! It don't matter much iffen his eyes were open or not. We got a young man on his own and with bad weather comin'. Moses, I want you to go to the cabin and get what we need to stay out a couple of days, while Isaac, I need you to saddle three horses. While the two of you are doin' that, I'll get our rifles and ammunition. Let's move, we don't know iffen the boy's hurt or not."

Twenty minutes later the three men rode from the cabin, leaving Sue and the women behind. While she had attempted to be brave, Bill knew she was scared, but Luke needed him. *She has to become a frontier woman someday, and it might as well be today,* he thought as he moved toward the mountain.

As they rode, the temperature fell and a light snow began to fall as the winds started to blow. "Be dark directly!" Moses said as he rode up beside Bill.

Motioning Isaac forward, Bill asked, "Did the boy say where he was goin'?"

"Told me he was gonna ride at the base of the mountain, was all he said."

"Okay, we'll check there first."

"Be hard to see a man in this snow," Moses said, and then pulled his hat down in front to protect his eyes.

"We have to look. He's like a son to me and I don't like the idea of him mayhap bein' hurt with nobody around the help 'em."

A little later, Isaac rode beside Bill and said, "I see a small light off our right side." Then pointing with his right hand, he added, "See, ahead of us 'bout a hundred feet, maybe."

"I see it now. It's got to be him, ain't anybody else out here!"

Nearing the light, Bill shouted, "Hello the camp! It's me, Bill!" There was no response.

Turning to Isaac, Bill said, "I'm ridin' in. There's a chance the boys been hurt and if he has, he might have passed out."

"Watch yer ass; iffen he fought with some Injuns, he'll be trigger-happy."

"I already thought of that." Bill then tapped his horse forward.

Entering the camp, he saw Luke wrapped in a blanket near the fire, so he turned and called out, "Come on in!"

Dismounting, he walked to the man, kneeled and pulled the blanket from his body. He shook his head as he saw at least two injuries, but there could be more. *He's a tough lad, he surely is,* Bill thought as he walked to his saddlebags and pulled them from the horse.

Moses and Isaac rode into camp, dismounted and moved toward the fire. Both saw the blood on the young man. Moses asked, "He goin' to live?"

"It's too early to tell yet." Then handing the older man a broken arrow shaft, he asked, "What tribe is this or can ya tell?"

"That's an Oto arrow." Moses replied and then continued, " I'd guess a bunch was out huntin' and spotted the boy."

"Isaac, pour us all, includin' Luke, a cup of whiskey," Bill ordered as he placed his knife blade in the flames of the small fire.

"Only got three cups, so use mine to feed the boy some, then I'll pour me one."

"Okay, but only one drink apiece, to help fight off the cold," Bill replied and then turning to Moses he commanded, "Get us a shelter up, using some canvas tied behind my saddle. We'll not last the night iffen we don't get out of this wind."

Bill looked the young man over closely and a few minutes later Isaac asked, "How's he look?"

"He took an arrow in the shoulder, nasty cut to his stomach, and a few other cuts and bruises. I'm worried about the belly, because it broke the skin for about an inch."

"Ya gonna sew it closed or cauterize it?"

"Sew, I think, because a hot knife might burn his guts. I'll have to be careful I don't poke no part of his insides, but I ain't got much choice. Hell, we both know with a belly wound he's likely to die anyway."

"Ya got that right. Iffen he lives, he'll be the first I ever saw do the job."

"Get the alum from your saddlebags and bring to me. I'll need it to put on his belly after I sew 'em up."

"Okay."

When the man returned, Bill gave an ill-felt smile and said, "Time to start the dance." He then picked up the shimmering blade and pressed it against Luke's shoulder. The young man's eyes flew open wide, he screamed, and then fell back limply to his blanket.

"He passed out." Bill placed the blade back in the flickering flames.

"Best way to take some doctorin', don't ya know."

Picking up a needle, Bill threaded it and then dropped it all into a cup half filled with whiskey.

A minute later, he removed it and in the dim light of the fire, he began to sew Luke's belly together. All the time he worked, he figured the young man would still die, but he had to do all he could.

Finishing the bloody work, he glanced first at Isaac, then Moses, and said, "I've done all I can; it's up to the good Lord iffen the boys lives or not."  He then poured a cup of whiskey on the injury, which made Luke moan.

The remainder of the night was cold, with snow falling and strong gusts of wind shaking the canvas shelter. More than once, the group thought the wind was going to rip the canvas from the rocks, but it held.

Dawn was cold but the snow had stopped. Moses and Isaac rode from camp and scouted around the shelter to make sure they were alone. They saw no Indians, except the four Luke had killed, so Moses scalped each and tucked the hair in his belt.

"Hell," Isaac said as Moses mounted, "I thought that boy was hurt by a single Injun. Waugh! He put four of 'em under, he surely did."

"Yup, he did at that, and it means our teachin' did the boy some good. Not many full-grown men could kill four Injuns." Moses said and then added, "I just hope the boy lives, only belly injuries are bad doin's."

Isaac tilted his head to the left and replied, "Iffen his guts wasn't hurt or the sewin' don't fester, he'll be fine. I hope the boy lives, 'cause he'll be a great addition to this part of the country, as tough as his young ass is."

"Let's get back to the fire, I'm freezin'."

When they returned to the warmth of the small fire, Bill was changing the bandage on Luke's stomach wound. Both men figured the boy must be okay, because Bill hummed a no-name tune as he worked.

Pouring a cup of coffee, Isaac asked, "How's the boy?"

"Ain't no festerin' yet, so he's fine. You see anything out there?"

Moses grinned and replied, "Yup, four dead Injuns, all kilt by the boy."

Bill stopped working, met the eyes of Moses and then asked, "Four? Are you sure?"

Pulling the hair from his belt, he replied, "Pretty sure, I got the scalps in my hand."

Looking down at the child-like innocence on Luke's face, Bill said, "Damn, who would have thought? Looks like my stepson is a pretty bad hombre, huh?"

Moses laughed and replied, "Yup and we need his kind out here. He'll grow into a fine man, iffen he survives this belly cut, and we might end up some day bein' glad he's with us. Ain't many that can kill four Oto Injuns."

Bill looked at Isaac and asked, "Would you go back for a wagon? I figure we can move 'em by wagon, but a horse will get 'em bleedin' again."

"Sure, I'll leave directly, jus' as soon as I finish my coffee."

"That's fine."

"Iffen it don't start snowin' again we can have 'em back at the cabin way a-fore dark," Isaac said as he poured the dregs of his coffee into the flames of the fire.

Bill added a small log to the fire and said, "Tell Sue we'll be back today at some point, but we ain't got no idea when. Let her know we'll have to move slowly and it will take us some time.

Iffen the weather turns rough, we might not be back until tomorrow mornin'."

Walking to his horse, Isaac spoke over his shoulder, "I'll let 'er know."

Moses, still beside the fire called out, "Watch your ass out there, Isaac!"

"I always watch that part of my body, especially when I'm on a trail!" The man replied, and then broke into a loud laugh.

Watching him ride away, Bill looked down at Luke and said, "I know you can't hear me boy, but you'll soon be in a nice warm cabin."

Moses said, "Yup, God willin' and the snow don't start to fly."

➼⬻  ➼⬻  ➼⬻

When Isaac neared the ranch, he spotted trouble right off. A thick finger of smoke rose to meet the low clouds from where the ranch would be and it was too big to have come from the chimney. I hope one of the buildin's didn't catch on fire, he thought as he dismounted. Moving on his knees to the crest of a small rise, he looked down in the valley, and was surprised to see charred remains of the place. There was not a building standing.

*Damn me, I hope Sue's okay and them other two, but it ain't likely,* he thought as he moved away from the rise and started walking to his left. *I'll circle and come in behind the place. Them Oto must have struck right after we rode off.*

As he moved, he scanned the countryside, but saw no movement. About a hundred yards from his horse, he spotted sign of six shod horses and that surprised him. *What in the hell are six white men doin' way up heah this time of the year, unless it was Injuns on stolen stock. Ain't no way to tell yet, but iffen it was Injuns I'll find the women dead.*

Nearing the destroyed ranch, Isaac cocked his rifle and moved slowly toward what used to be the barn. Snow still covered the ground and he saw no tracks in the barnyard, so that meant to him the raiders had struck before the storm or during it. He saw nothing worth keeping, just smoke from the dying flames. He found no bodies and saw not a single arrow, so it confirmed white men had done the job. Every building was gone and he felt a deep dread, knowing he would have to be the one to tell Bill.

Placing his rifle on the log Bill used to chop wood, he thought, *Ain't but one white man knew we was here, and that was Mossland. Looks like the sorry jasper hired some men and came back. I had a gut feelin' we needed to find the man right after he stole the horse and left, but didn't say nothin'. I wish I had now.*

Picking up his rifle, he moved for his horse and unknowingly spoke aloud, "The women wasn't kilt, so that means they most likely took 'em fer sport."

# CHAPTER 17

**S**ue had never been so frightened in her life. She'd just seen Nancy brutally raped by six men and she shuddered, wondering when her turn would come. The air was cold, but the men had given them no blankets or even shelter. She sat by the fire, unable to move, paralyzed by fear.

Nathan laughed, looked at his wife and said, "You're next, wife! I'll teach you to call me a coward and try to make me look small in front of other men!"

Nadine, scared, but livid, yelled, "You'd turn me over to these damn animals to use? What kind of man are you!  You're my husband, you sonofabitch!"

"Keep yappin', and I'll cut your damned throat when we finish! You ain't nothin' but mouth and a pain in the rear! That's all you been since we got hitched."

James, one of the younger men in the group said, "I don't want none of her, she's too old. I'll wait for some of that younger stuff over by the fire."

Nathan laughed and replied, "You're a fool! While Nadine ain't much to look at, she's good, real good."

"Have at her then, I'll wait."

Before Nadine could move, the biggest man in the group, a dirty no account named Dodds, grabbed her from behind and threw her hard to the ground. Another man, called Stump, grasped the front of her dress and ripped it to her waist.

"Look at the size of them titties!" Dodds yelled and then began to unbutton his trousers again.

Two men held her down as the other three, including Nathan, raped her. She fought and cried, but the men continued, until each had taken her twice. Nathan was the last man and immediately after his climax, he pulled his skinning knife and ran the blade over her throat.

Nadine's eyes grew large with fear and her body began to twist and jerk, as a fountain of blood shot high into the air. She choked on blood, and Sue heard her feet kicking at the dirt as she died. The men stood over her laughing as her life's blood pooled under her head. Then, there was no noise, except laughter.

Good God, he killed his own wife! Sue thought and her panic grew—because what would they do to her?

⟶⟵  ⟶⟵  ⟶⟵

Isaac rode into the camp and tied his horse to the picket line. He dismounted slowly and made his way to the warmth of the fire.

Bill glance at him and asked, "Where's the wagon?"

"Ya ain't got one no more and the ranch is gone too."

"What in the hell do ya mean the ranch is gone?"

"Sign shows six white men hit the ranch right after we left, or during the storm, and burnt the place to the ground."

"What about the women?"

"Took 'em, to play with I'd say. I saw not a single human body, just some dead critters."

"What about our horses and cattle?"

"Scattered to hell and back would be my guess. Not a one of 'em on the ranch."

Moses scratched his chin and said one word, "Mossland!"

Isaac met his friend's gazed and replied, "That was my first guess, too. Ain't nobody else knew we were there, but him."

Bill stood, adjusted his gun belt and said, "Moses, you stay here with Luke, while me and Isaac go after the women folk."

Isaac asked, "How's Luke doin'?"

"He's healin' and we don't have a place to take 'em, so here is as good as the next place."

"I hear you, but don't kill Mossland out of hate, Bill. Bring 'em back, we'll have a fair trial and then hang the bastard." Moses said, and then looked into the dancing flames of the fire.

"I cain't promise that, but I'll consider it as I ride." Moving toward the horses, Bill added, "Keep your eyes open, because them Injuns might come lookin' for them missin' warriors."

The two men mounted, waved at Moses, and rode from camp.

➻➼ ➻➼ ➻➼

The two men rode all day and most of the night before they stopped. Too tired and cold for a fire or food, they just moved out of the wind, wrapped their buffalo robes around them, and went to sleep. Both were exhausted and slept the sleep of the dead.

It was near dawn when Isaac asked, "Did ya hear that?"

Bill, standing near the fire, looked up and replied, "Yup, it sounded like a scream to me."

"Woman?"

"Yep, it was a female," Bill said, stood and turned in the direction of the cry.

"I think we just found our men. We'd better leave the horse heah and go at it a-foot. We'll need our rifles, but I ain't sure how ya want to handle this."

"Well, from the sign you saw," another scream sounded and both men turned, "we're out numbered three to one, so we go in shootin'. Try not to kill Mossland, I'd like to take 'em back for a hangin' iffen we can. Watch your ass when we get close to their camp, because there aint' much cover out here."

"Sounds smart to me, now let's go before they kill that woman."

Nearing the camp a few short minutes later, Bill saw Sue on the ground with her dress ripped and breasts hanging loose, as she fought two men. Glancing around, he quickly located all six of the men.

Then, looking at Isaac, he whispered, "Ready?"

The man nodded and raised his rifle, knowing Bill would kill the two men holding his wife.

Two shots filled the cool morning air, and one of the men holding Sue fell to the ground unmoving. A second man fell into the fire, where he quickly stood and slapped madly at the fire burning his dirty clothing. Another shot rang out and a huge bear of a man fell screaming with a bullet in his gut.

Bill then shot the second man holding Sue and as he fell, she moved toward a boulder. Seeing her scurry out of the way, he moved forward, knowing four of the men were out of the fight. He spotted Mossland, fired, and watched the man knocked back hard by the heavy bullet. He'd taken the slug in his left thigh.

The last man began to run, but Isaac kneeled and lined his sights on the man's back. He squeezed the trigger and smiled when the man's head exploded. *Either this damned guns shootin' high or he moved at the last second,* he thought as he looked around the camp.

The big man was screaming in pain, the burning man was on his knees with the fire out but still smoking, while Mossland was on the ground with a large pool of blood under his leg.

Bill walked into the camp at a fast pace. When he neared the burned man on his knees, he fired into the man's head, sending blood and gore out behind him. The wounded big man tried to lift his pistol, but Isaac was faster and sent a bullet to the center of his chest. He fell back hard, gave a loud sigh and died.

Mossland, frightened, asked, "You gonna kill me?"

Bill gave an evil smile and replied, "Nope, not here anyway. We're takin' you back for a trial and then we're goin' to hang you."

"Hang . . . me?"

"Yep, it's a slow death iffen your neck doesn't break when you fall." Then, turning, he called out, "Sue, you can come in now, it's safe."

She appeared moving slowly from around the huge rock and Bill could see pure terror in her eyes.

Isaac walked to his side and said, "They're all dead, except for Mossland."

"Good. I see another woman in a blanket over by the horses, but where's the third?"

"She's dead," Sue said in a flat voice.

"Which one was it?" Bill asked.

"It was Nadine! Mossland had the men rape her, and then he cut her throat!" Sue screamed and then ran into Bill's open arms. After a few moments, Bill took her to the fire.

Isaac looked down at Mossland and asked, "You let these men use your own wife and then killed 'er?"

The injured man lowered his eyes, but said nothing.

Shaking his head, Isaac turned and walked to the fire, where the two women now sat.

Bill moved to Mossland and tied his hands behind his back. "I'll not dress your wound, because it ain't goin' to bother you for very long."

Isaac, who'd been looking the women over, said, "Bill, get me some whiskey from my saddlebags. These two need a cup to calm 'em down a mite."

As soon as the two had downed a cup of whiskey, Bill said, "Mossland, I've made a slight change in my plans about you."

"W . . . what change?"

"I've decided we're goin' to just hang you here. Ain't no reason to take a man like you back for a trial."

Isaac gave a weak grin and said, "My thoughts are the same. I'll get a horse."

"You can't hang me without a trial, it'd be murder!" Mossland screamed.

"You know all about murder, don't you Mossland?" Bill replied.

Isaac led a big bay to the camp along with a slightly smaller roan.

"In case ya didn't notice, there ain't any trees around big enough to hang no man, so we'll have to do this the hard way," Isaac said as he unraveled a long rope.

"How we gonna do the job with no trees?" Sue asked.

"Watch and learn." The man cut the rope in two, tied two hangman's nooses, and then walked to Mossland. As the man lay shaking in fear, Isaac placed one noose around his feet and another around his neck.

Then, the rope with the noose around his neck was tied to the saddle horn on the bay while the other rope was tied to the saddle on the roan.

"The idea heah is when the horses move in different directions it'll strangle the man. But, we have to move slow like, or we'll pull his damned head off," Isaac said from beside the bay.

"Pull my head off! Lord have mercy! Please, shoot me!"

"You move the bay while I lead the roan. And, Mossland, iffen you want to pray for forgiveness you better get started, because time's runnin' out."

"Please, don't hang me, please! I don't have much money, but you can have it all!"

"I'll take your money after you're dead, so that won't work," Bill replied, as he slowly led the horse a few steps. "See, you still owe me for a horse, gun, supplies and food you ate at my ranch."

As the rope grew taut Mossland screamed, finally realizing he was really going to die at the hands of the two rough men.

Isaac looked over his shoulder and said, "Pull up about three feet and then stop for a few minutes. Take 'er slow now and iffen I tell ya to stop, stop right then or his head will come off."

Mossland screamed in fear.

Bill moved the roan forward and then stopped. He could hear Mossland gasping for breath, and it bothered him, but then he thought of the man's wife and the way she'd died. The war had hardened his heart and while he didn't like critters to suffer, a man like Mossland deserved to die hard and slow.

Five minutes later, Isaac said, "He's dead."

Backing his horse a few feet, Bill untied his rope and let it fall to the ground. When he glanced around the camp, both Sue and Nancy were smiling.

"Can you two ride?" Isaac asked, and then moved to the fire. His rope, like Bill's, lay on the ground beside a horse.

Neither woman replied for a couple of minutes. Then, Sue said, "I can, but I think Nancy's mind is gone. She was raped a bunch, and the last time something snapped inside her head."

"Sue," Bill said softly, "did they bother you?"

"Nope, they started to, except you two showed up. Bill, I've never been so scared in my life. I wondered iffen I'd ever see you again." She lowered her head and began to cry.

"You know we don't have a home to go back to, don't you? They burnt it to the ground."

Suddenly, Sue raised her head, her eye's narrowed and she said, "By God, we'll rebuild then. It'll be a rough winter, but we'll survive!"

Bill gave a low chuckle and thought, *she's turnin' tougher, she surely is*, but said, "Let's mount, and Isaac, you drive those horses with us."

Bill placed Nancy on a horse, tied her securely, and then the small group began to move. Hours later she called out, "Untie me, I'm fine now."

She was untied, but Bill doubted her strength, so he asked, "Are you sure you can ride? "

"I can ride, I'm pretty sure. I guess my mind shut down for a spell after all I'd been through."

"I saw it in the war often enough. If you start to feel weak you'll let me know, right?"

"I'll tell you."

After riding a few more miles, Sue asked, "How's Luke? Did you find 'em?"

"He took an arrow to his shoulder and has a serious belly wound, but I think he'll live. We got us a tough boy there."

"I should have asked earlier, only so much has happened to me in just the last two days."

"I'm just glad you're both alive. I never dreamed when we rode out to check on our boy that raiders would hit. Hell, I thought nobody knew about the place."

"Mossland did, and I think he hated his wife. Those men stood over her laughing as she died choking on her own blood."

Seeing the pain in her eyes, he replied, "It's all over now, honey, except building us a place to last the winter. We'll build closer to the mountains, because we can't be draggin' logs to the old place; too far. Besides, we ain't got the time, so are you up to livin' in a tent for a spell?"

"A year ago I would have been shocked to have been asked that question, but now I can do it and know I can. This country changes a person, or they die. It toughens a person pretty damned quick."

"I know what you mean. I've grown tougher myself, and never thought that could happen to me. I know you must get sick of me talkin' about the war, but imagine thousands of men dying like Nadine did, violently by someone else's hand, and you'll have an idea of the impact it had on me. I saw horrible things and only the last few months have I felt almost like my old self."

"You're a good man, and I never thought it would happen this quickly, but I love you. While I waited to be raped, I almost lost my mind, just thinkin' of those nasty men touchin' me."

"You don't have to worry about them any more, they're gone. I felt a great loss when Isaac told me you were gone. I knew what they'd do to you and you know, I'd still wanted you even iffen you'd been raped. See, I discovered I love you, too."

Isaac rode up beside them and ordered, "Cut the love talk, we ain't got no idea who mighten be out heah with us. Last thing we need is to end up in a serious fight with jus' two men."

The rest of the ride back Bill was quiet and the only sound heard was the clop-clop of the horses moving.

◆◆◆◆◆◆

Moses cocked his rifle at the sound of horses nearing and as he moved behind the boulder, he heard a voice call out, "Moses, it's us, and we've the women with us!"

"Come, but make no sudden moves until I see who you be for sure."

Bill laughed and while Moses relaxed, he didn't look forward to talking with the man at all, especially if he had his wife along.

After they'd tied their horses to the picket line and walked to the fire, Bill asked, "How's Luke?"

Moses decided the best way to break the new was to just say it, "He ain't doin' good, and festerin' has set in his shoulder."

"Shoulder; I would have thought it was his belly."

"Nope, the belly is as clean as a whistle. Earlier this mornin' I scraped his injury and poured some whiskey on it, so we'll have to wait to see iffen it did any good or not."

"Think he'll live?" Sue asked with her eyes watering.

"No, ma'am, not really. When I opened the boy up, puss and tainted blood jus' poured out."

Bill looked over at Sue and said, "It's out of our hands now. He'll get better or he won't. I think it would be a good idea iffen we all prayed at some point today."

The night was quiet, with the temperature dropping to way below zero, and most of the small group spent their time by the fire. It was too cold to sleep, even under a shelter, so Moses said, "Come mornin' I'm goin' to look for Brass Buttons and his Sioux. I think I can get some buffalo robes to keep us warm as we wait out the cold season."

"Think ya can find 'em?" Isaac asked as he poured a cup of coffee.

"I'm pretty sure I'll find 'em a little south of here."

Sue, not liking the idea of going to Indians for help asked, "Why don't we jus' kill some buffalo?"

Moses laughed and replied, "'Because there ain't none up this way no more. See, each fall they start movin' south and by now they're all near Texas. Come spring they start movin' north again, so we're months from seein' any buff's."

"Sun will be up in an hour, is that when yer gonna go?" Isaac asked and then sipped from his cup.

"Nope, I'm goin' to leave right now." Moses stood and then moving toward the horses continued, "I'll take three extra horses, because robes are heavy and iffen I ain't back in a week, I'll never be back."

"Watch yer topknot, pilgrim," Isaac said with a smile as his friend moved toward the horses.

A few short minutes later the man rode from camp, leading three horses into the cold black morning.

A little after dawn, Luke woke and asked for water. As Sue gave him a drink he asked, "W . . . what are . . . you doin' here, ma?"

"Raiders struck the ranch and burnt it to the ground. Bill came and got me, and brought me here."

"So . . . tired," Luke said and his eyes closed.

Bill, who had been caring for the horses, walked to the fire and asked, "Was that Luke I heard speaking?"

"Yep, it was. Is that a good sign?"

Shaking his head, Bill said, "Not really, but it could be. I'll check 'em in a minute and we'll see how his injury is."

"But he spoke to me."

"Sue, durin' the war I saw lots of injured men speak and seconds later they fell dead. It don't matter much, the talkin' don't, it's the condition of the wound."

"I see. Can you check 'em now?"

"I don't see why not," Bill replied and kneeled beside his stepson. Pulling the bandage back, he smiled and said, "Looks good to me. He still has some redness around the hole, but I don't see no puss or purple lines in his skin."

"Then, he'll live?"

Smiling he replied, "Yes, Sue, I think our son will live. He's a good young man, and I'm proud of 'em."

She'd heard how hard her son had fought, and was proud of the fact he'd killed four braves, "I am, too. I never would have thought he had that much grit in 'em."

"Why not? His pa had it."

"Yes, John had grit, but he was gettin' old and couldn't do some of the things he used to do."

"He seemed okay to me."

"I was talkin' of things between a man and woman, not his strength. I loved him, you know, but it wasn't the same kind of deep love I feel for you."

Suddenly Bill laughed and said, "I'm sorry, but I find this a strange talk from a woman who just a day ago was worried about bein' raped."

Sue grew angry and replied brusquely, "I'm relaxed and talkin' with my husband! I was talkin' about love, not raw brutal sex. Sometimes, Bill, you frustrate the livin' hell right out of me!" She then stood and moved toward the horses.

*She's pissed, but will get over it directly.*

Suddenly, Isaac said, "We got visitors coming, and they're Injuns."

"Can you tell what tribe?"

"Too far away right now. I'll know in a few minutes."

"I hope to hell it ain't them Oto, or we're in some serious trouble with just the two of us."

"We'll know in a few minutes, I'd guess."

# CHAPTER 18

$\mathbf{T}$en minutes after spotting the Indians, Isaac said, "It's Sioux." He then gave a weak smile, turned to Bill and added, "Could be Moses run into 'em on the way to the village."

"How many?"

"Small group, I counted twenty riders."

"Let's hope it's Brass Buttons and his bunch, and not a group that doesn't know us."

A few minutes later, a lone brave rode to the rocks and said, *"Brass Buttons wants to speak to the young white warrior."*

*"The young warrior is weak. He fought the Oto and killed four of them, but he was injured,"* Isaac replied in the Sioux tongue as he held four scalps in his hand.

The brave gave a loud scream, turned from camp, and rode back to the Sioux.

Isaac grinned and said, "The big bug will be here in a minute or two. He knew Luke was a fighter way back, I'd guess."

Right then, Brass Buttons left the group and rode for the boulders. He stopped near the camp, dismounted and walked to the fire.

*"The young warrior has killed Oto?"*

*"Yes, as I said to your scout, four fingers of them."*

*"With no help?"*

*"No help and alone."*

*"He will be a great warrior one day and feared by all of his enemies."*

*"Yes, I think so. Did you see Moses?"*

*"He is with us, but we did not speak of the white warrior, we spoke of buffalo robes."*

*"Our house of wood is gone."*

*"Your words are true and that is why I am out riding in the cold. I have been to your lodge of wood, but fire has destroyed it. I search for my white friends. You need the help of the Sioux, because the moons of hunger will come."*

Isaac turned to Bill and the others as he told them what Brass Buttons had said. "We only need the robes," Isaac said a few minutes later.

*"You will have much need for food. I will have my braves bring you jerky and pemmican for the long cold months ahead, as well as robes."*

*"We thank you, my chief."*

Brass Buttons laughed and then said, *"I am not your chief, but I understand you are being polite. This is good. It says I have picked the right whites to be my friends. Will the young warrior live?"*

*"He will live."*

Turning and walking to his horse, the chief stopped after a few feet and said, *"I will have the food and robes to you when the sun is at it's highest."*

Moses rode into camp, dismounted and waved to Brass Buttons as the chief mounted and returned to his men.

"I see you got some robes," Bill said as he walked toward the older man.

"Yep, he gave me ten of 'em, and said he'd send more later today."

Sue smiled and said, "You were right, knowin' that man saved our lives."

"He's a good man, Sue, just fightin' to hold onto what God-gave to 'em."

"I think you just might be right, I truly do." She replied.

That night it was colder than the night before and come dawn, Luke was complaining about a pain in his right hand. When Bill looked it over, he threw a glance at Isaac, and said to Sue, "Luke has frost damage to his hand. I think at some point last night his hand was not covered by his robe, and it got pretty dang cold."

"What does all of that mean?" Sue asked as she moved toward her son.

"The last time his hands were as cold was the night he rode in the freezing weather. I warned him then iffen his hands ever got as cold again the damage would be worse."

"Is the damage really bad?"

"It's too early to tell, but I think so," Bill replied, picked up his cup, added an inch of whiskey from a clay jug to his coffee, and gave a loud sigh.

Her voice filled with fear, Sue said, "He's hurt and has little control over his body. I'm sure the hand fell from the robe."

"Honey, it matters little how it happened, only that it happened."

"He won't lose his hand will he?"

Lowering his head, Bill replied, "I won't lie to you, I don't really know. I suspect he'll lose a few fingers at least. See, once a body part has frozen before, it freezes faster the next time and the damage done is much greater."

"My God, and we can do nothing?"

Bill just shook his head.

"I cain't believe this! He survives a torn open belly, an arrow in his shoulder that festered, and now you tell me he'll lose some fingers!"

"Look, get mad iffen you want, but it won't change a blasted thing."

"I . . . I know, it just upsets me; he's a good boy."

"Sue, bad things sometimes happen to good people, but I cain't tell you why. I guess God is testin' folks at times."

"Maybe, but I don't like it," Sue replied and then walked off.

The men spent the day cutting logs in the forest and dragging them near the rocks. By darkness, four walls were almost five feet high and Bill said, "We should have this thing done by this time tomorrow. We'll not put shingles on it, we'll cover it with logs and then add some sod."

"It'll leak some, then" Isaac said, and then grinned.

"I ain't worried about rain as much as I am snow."

"I'll start on a chimney in the mornin', iffen you two can pull the logs," Moses said and then frowned. He'd been working all day with the logs, but hated the job. In this case, he worked, because all men had to work or it could mean the death of everyone of them. This was, according to him, a time when every man of them had to lend a hand in order to survive.

"That's a good idea. You know, with a little luck, we might be sleepin' near a warm fire tomorrow night," Bill said with a smile.

"Don't count on 'er yet, because God has a way of changin' the weather whenever he gets a notion," Moses said and then pulled his pipe.

"I hear you, but we'll be sleepin' by a fire."

Isaac laughed and said, "First we have to survive tonight! Last night was cold doin's and I froze my butt off, robes or no."

Bill took a sober look and said, "Tonight we'll stand guard on the fire and keep it burnin'. Luke will likely lose some fingers because of last night. His hand got pretty cold and since it froze before the damage was done quickly."

Moses said, "You should know tomorrow or the next day."

Pulling his old brier pipe, Isaac thought for a minute and then said, "Yep, freezin' shows damage pretty dang fast. Iffen the hand froze, ya'll no by tomorrow fer sure."

The night was cold, and snow started to fall about an hour before daylight. Bill and Isaac headed to the forest to cut logs, while Moses put a chimney up. The snow was light at first, but by mid-afternoon, it was a regular blizzard, with snow flying in all directions. The roof had been complete and most of the chimney when the men called it quits due to a lack of visibility. All that remained uncompleted was adding sod to the roof and finishing the chimney.

Moses said, "We can still burn a fire in the place, but we'll need to keep an eye on the flames."

"Well," Isaac said as he pulled his possibles bag around and removed his flint and steel, "let me start one right now. It's colder than a banker's heart in this place."

Within minutes, flames were dancing wildly in the hearth and Bill walked to the two men and said, "Luke's goin' to lose two fingers. They're black, swollen, and the tips are white. They'll have to come off in a few minutes."

Moses shook his head and said, "The boy won't like havin' the job done much."

"I figured that much, so Sue's been feedin' 'em whiskey all afternoon."

Placing a log on the flames, Isaac turned and asked, "Ya ever took a finger off a-fore?"

"Nope, but it cain't be too hard, just start cuttin' at a joint. Both can be removed at the second knuckle and still save the hand."

Moses pulled a plug of tobacco from his shirt pocket, pulled his pocketknife and cut off a piece. Placing it in his mouth, he worked his chew for a minute and then said, "Ya'll need to cauterize the stubs and keep 'em drunk over night."

Pulling his skinning knife, Bill replied, "I figured that too." He then placed the knife in the flickering flames to get hot.

An hour later, Luke lay sleeping deeply under a robe, because he'd put away most of a half quart of whiskey before the removal of his fingers. He'd taken to the cutting poorly, and the pain had caused him to pass out. He had awakened as Bill was wrapping his hand.

"D . . . did I lose t . . . the whole fingers?" Luke's words were badly slurred.

Giving a weak grin, Bill replied, "No, just about half of each. You know I had to do this, right?"

"I know."

"You lay back now and get some sleep. Havin' body parts took off weakens a man, and sleep is the best thing for you."

The young man closed his eyes and was asleep in seconds.

The smell of burnt flesh filled the room, but no one seemed to notice, because it was a scent they'd come to know well.

Sue stood, moved to Bill's side and asked, "Did it go okay? I mean, was all the bad flesh cut off?"

"Yea, I got it all. I poured a lot of whiskey on the fingers too, so it ain't likely he'll fester on us." Pulling Bill close, Sue whispered, "I need the both of you in my life. I was so scared when you told me his fingers had to come off."

"I can understand that, but I think he'll be fine."

Still whispering, she said, "I want you, Bill."

Giving a light chuckle, he replied, "That ain't likely to happen, until spring thaw. We got a house full of folks in here."

Kissing his cheek, she said, "Tonight, after all of 'em are asleep?"

Pulling her close, Bill whispered, "Yes! I want you too, very much."

Sue and Nancy prepared a meal of roasted rabbits and pemmican, and they washed it down with melted snow. While the meal was not much, it was the best the two women could do with what little food they had.

"Ain't much of a meal, now is it?" Sue complained.

Moses met her eyes and said, "Iffen Isaac hadn't put his snares out, we wouldn't have had the rabbits, and I've had less—many times."

"Me, too," Bill added and then picked up his coffee and took a sip.

"Hell, I've had nothin' to eat, lots of times over the years." Isaac said, gave a slight grin, and added, "When ya live in the woods and mountains, there are times ya have no food or yer forced to eat tree bark or whatnot."

"That's too hard a life for me," Sue said as she took the dirty plates from the men. They only had four plates, so they'd taken turns eating.

Both Isaac and Moses broke out laughing, and then Moses asked, "You don't think you're cut out to be no mountain woman, huh?"

"No," Sue replied, "not me. I like a full belly and the heat of a fire on cold nights."

"Like Isaac, it's the only life I know. I ain't got no learnin's and can't do most jobs, so I think me and him will die roamin' these mountains."

Bill gave a smile and said, "As long as you're happy, that's what counts most in life."

The small talk continued right up to bedtime and most were glad to be indoors, out of the freezing wind and snow. One by one, they moved to their robes, rolled in them, and went to sleep. Bill and Sue lay side by side in the dark room, with only the faint flickering light from a dying fire to see by.

She leaned forward and kissed him; he felt her burning passion, which only increased his own. Sue moaned and reached for him.

➡️⬅️  ➡️⬅️  ➡️⬅️

With dawn, the blizzard had strengthened, the wind was howling, and going out of doors was dangerous. Bill, with the help of Moses, soon had a rope leading to the woods and another leading to the horses.

Sue stood and as she moved toward the door, Bill said, "The rope on the right leads to the woods, iffen your goin' out for your mornin' toilet."

She nodded and left the cabin, but was back a few minutes later saying, "While I was out there I heard some loud cracks, but it didn't sound like gunfire."

Isaac laughed and said, "Most likely what ya hear'd was limbs snappin' from the cold."

"You're teasin' me!"

"No he ain't." Moses said and then added quickly, "It can get so cold that the water inside of trees freezes, and then the limbs give a loud crack when they break."

Sue glanced at Bill, but he sat on the floor by the fire, stone-faced. Finally, he said, "Makes sense to me. Durin' the war I didn't see none of that, because the south doesn't get that cold."

"Well, she does up heah," Isaac replied.

Moses, placing his empty pipe between his teeth said, "Now y'all know why I was workin' along side of you buildin' this cabin. I knew iffen we didn't get 'er up quick like, some of us would freeze to death."

A low moan came from Luke and he asked, "W . . . water?"

Sue moved to his side with a canteen of melted snow. She raised his head and let a little water run into his mouth. He still felt feverish, but not as much as the night before.

"My fingers off?"

"Yep, been off a spell."

"I can still feel 'em."

Bill, hearing the young man said, "In the war lots of fellers had body parts took off, and they still felt 'em. I asked a doctor about it, and he told me it was common for a man. He said it had something to do with nerve endin's, but nobody understands why it happens."

Moses' eyes softened as he said, "I was worried about you, son. You almost went under a couple of times."

Luke gave a light laugh, groaned and then replied, "Thanks, Moses, but I'm doin' fine now. I remember goin' under a hot knife more than once, only that's 'bout it. Right now I hurt all over."

"We can give ya some more whiskey tonight, but it's runnin' low and it's a long way to the nearest saloon 'round heah," Isaac stated, and then laughed.

"Where am I? This ain't our cabin."

Bill explained what had happened, shrugged his shoulders, and then asked, "Do you have a lot of pain right now?"

"Some," Luke replied, not wanting to be a kid and complain.

Looking at Sue, Bill said, "Give 'em another cup of whiskey. I know we're runnin' low, but I'll not have 'em in pain as long as we got a drop in the jug."

Moses added, "As soon as this weather breaks, me and Isaac will make a quick run to Butterfield's Tradin' Post and get some supplies. We ain't got much of nothin' left, and we need some more whiskey for our man, Luke. Besides, we ain't got no idea when one of us will be injured again and we'll need strong drink."

Sue gave a grave look and asked, "You think it'll happen again?"

Isaac placed his coffee cup beside his leg on the floor and replied, "Now, ya only been out heah a few months, but what do ya think?"

She paled and said, "We'll need it, from what I've seen."

Bill, concerned about bad weather trapping the two older men on the open plains, asked, "How far is the trader's place from here? And, can you both make the trip and not get snowed in?"

Moses, packing his pipe bowl with tobacco said, "Nye on a hundred and fifty miles, so it'll take us a little over two weeks to get there and return, barring any bad weather." He then pulled a brand from the fire and lit his pipe.

"That's a lot of days on a pretty cold trail, only I don't see any other choice." Bill didn't like the idea at all. Except he understood they desperately needed supplies.

Looking at his feet, Moses said, "And, there's the problem of money. Me and Isaac got a little, only it won't be enough at Butterfield's prices."

Grinning, Bill glanced at Isaac, and then replied, "Hell, money ain't no problem, for right now anyway. Seems them jaspers that took Sue was carryin' a good amount, and Mossland had the most."

"By Damn, I'd never thought of that!"

Isaac said, "We took over $800.00 off them six dead men, and iffen we take their guns we'll trade them, too."

Moses thought for a minute and then said, "There were five repeatin' rifles in the bunch and they'll trade fer over forty dollars a piece, while the old Hawken will only fetch about twenty. All of them pistols they had will go for 'round twenty, too."

Bill asked, "That's well over $300.00, will that be enough?"

Moses grew serious and replied, "Nope, not fer the number of people we gotta buy stuff fer. I'd think our bill will be closer to five or six hundred."

Reaching into his pocket, Bill pulled out a thick wad of bills, handed five hundred dollars to the older man and said, "Iffen ya see other things we need, pick 'em up while yer there."

Sue, the primary cook, suddenly said, "I'll write it all down a-for ya go, but we'll need a hundred weight of beans, flour, cornmeal, five pounds of salt and pepper, twenty or so in coffee, six tin plates, some more cups, knives, spoons, and forks. I'll leave the amount of whiskey to get up to ya, 'cause I don't know much 'bout that."

The two old mountain men exchanged looks and then Isaac said, "We'll take four or five extra horse's jus' to get that much stuff back heah. I know that's a lot of pack animals, but it'll be cold doin's and I want to try to keep the loads small on each critter, so we can move faster."

Bill nodded and replied, "Ya take what ya need to do the job without getting killed. I'd rather y'all took too many than not enough."

"We'll leave as soon as the weather breaks. Right now I need to go out and check on the horses," Moses said, stood and moved for the door.

# CHAPTER 19

$T$**wo** mornings later, right after dawn, the two men mounted and rode from the rough cabin, heading south by west. While the sun was up, it was still cold. The storm had blown for days, but there was less than eight inches of snow covering the ground, and both prayed they could make a quick dash to the trading post and return before the next snowfall.

As they rode, Moses moved up beside Isaac and said, "You get cold, don't play no mountain man games with me, let me know. I'll let you know when I need to stop, too. We won't do those folks back there a bit of good iffen we freeze to death."

Giving a light chuckle, the Isaac replied, "I'll let ya know fer sure, 'cause cold weather is serious business."

"You got that right. I fig'er we'll will ride until one of us gets cold or it gets dark. Most likely one of us will get cold a-fore it gets close to dark. Each time we stop we'll make a small fire and have something hot to drink, even iffen it's only water."

"Well," Isaac said as he pulled his hat down lower to cover his eyes, "at least there won't be no Injuns out. It's too damned cold fer a man with any sense to be movin'."

"Enough naybobbin', let's ride."

⋙ ⋙ ⋙

A week later, the two men sat on their horses looking down into a valley. In the center was a group of rough structures and they knew they'd made it to the trading post. The trip had been rough, due to snow and ice, as well as freezing winds most of the time.

They'd eaten jerky and pemmican until it was coming out of their ears, or so Isaac complained one evening.

"Sure as hell ain't much to look at, is it?" Moses asked, as he turned to look at his friend.

"Nope, it ain't. But, it's warm down there and he's got some good food to eat. I say we get down there, warm up, eat some and get to tradin'. I've got bad feelin's 'bout them pilgrims we left back there."

Moses snickered and replied, "You're gettin' like an old woman, ya know that? We left 'em in the best condition we could, and they got enough dried meat to live until spring."

"Mayhap yer right, but they're all good folks."

"Yup, they are at that, but we're doin' the best thing we can for 'em right now. Let's ride down and see iffen Butterfield has any deer meat on the stove."

They kicked their horses gently and moved toward the trading post at a walk.

A few minutes later, as they tied their horse to the hitching post, an old man holding a double-barreled shotgun walked from the building.

"Well, now, I'll be damned! Iffen it ain't ugly and uglier! How ya two boys been?" The old man asked as he placed his shotgun against the wall of his trading post.

"Doin' fine and still got our topknots. How ya be, Butterfield?" Isaac replied.

Turning angry, the man said brusquely, "Pissed is what I am. A while back six jaspers rode in heah and took all the money I had. Liked to kilt me too, but I got a couple of shots off at 'em as they rode outta heah. I don't think I hit none of 'em though."

Moses looked at Isaac, the man nodded, and then he said, "I think we got part of yer money on us. Who was the man leadin' 'em?"

"A no account sumbitch by the name of Mossland! I ever see 'em again I'll kill 'em on sight."

Isaac walked up the steps and said, "Can we finish this inside? I've spent the better part of a week out in this weather, and I don't cotton to it much."

Moving toward the door, Butterfield said, "Sure, come on in and tell me why ya think ya got part of my money."

Taking a seat at the closest table, Moses asked, "You got anything to eat, besides jerky or pemmican?"

Smiling, and knowing how a man felt after a long ride in the cold, Butterfield replied, "I sure do, but it's only deer meat simmerin' in gravy, fried taters and cornbread. Ya want me to get the two of ya a plate of it?"

"Yup, and bring some whiskey, too. Lordy, it's cold out there." Isaac was bone tired, and his face was so cold he felt it tingling from the heat provided by a small wood stove in the corner of the room.

"While I put yer plates together, tell me why ya think ya got some of my money."

Isaac explained the whole situation and then said, "The man we kilt was named Mossland, and he had a lot of money on 'em, jus' like all the men did."

Moses lowered his head and said, "But it puts us in a mess now. We'll give what we got on us to ya, but we got little cash, some guns to trade, and a bunch of cold miserable folks waitin' on us."

Butterfield placed the food on the table, turned and picked up a bottle of good whiskey, and then said, "I'll see yer people are taken care of. Ya know, it's not the loss of the money that pissed me off, but the fact they robbed me. I hate a damned thief!"

Pouring a glass full of whiskey, Isaac said, "I don't care much fer 'em, either. And, these are good folks waitin' fer us, John, some of the best."

"I'll take yer guns in trade and then give ya the goods ya need as a reward fer the job ya did with Mossland. Ya tell that Bill feller with ya to keep the money he has and not worry about sendin' it back.

"However, I will take what cash of mine ya got today."

Handing the old trader his money, Moses said, "We thank you, John, you're a good man."

"Bullshit and ya know it. I ain't always a good man, but I'll he'p anybody out heah that needs somethin' to live on. As long as I fig'er they're honest folks, I'll do what I can fer 'em."

Pulling a long list from his coat pocket, Isaac asked, "Can ya fill this order?"

Butterfield reached inside his coat, removed his reading glasses and then put them on. Looking the list over closely he finally said, "I got most of all of this, only I ain't got no mittens or socks. Hell, y'all make yer own, and I ain't never carried either."

"Throw in some deer skins and we'll make our own." Isaac then raised his glass of whiskey and downed about half of it. Wiping his mouth off with the back of his hand, he picked up his fork and started eating.

As the trader gathered up the supplies, he asked, "Ya got enough extree horse's fer all of this?"

"Yep, we surely do. Didn't ya see 'em when we rode up?"

"I saw something, but my eyes ain't what they used to be."

Isaac stood and asked, "Do ya have room in yer barn fer our animals?"

"Sure do, just put 'em in some empty stalls. When ya two headin' back?"

"Come sunup I want to be on the trail back," he answered, and then walked from the building to care for their horses.

"By damn, these folks must be good the way ya and Isaac wanna get back to 'em."

"They are, but they're a bunch of pilgrims, and he's scared something will happen while we're gone."

"It might, but ya gotta have supplies or something will happen to their asses fer sure." Butterfield said.

"Where are your worker bees?"

"They're in their cabins. This time of the year, we don't get many visitors, so they ain't got much to do after they milk the cow and make sure I got firewood. Now, come springtime, things are hoppin' around heah."

"Can you throw in a couple pounds of hard candy in them supplies?"

Butterfield chuckled and asked, "Got a sweet tooth, now do ya?"

"Nope, it ain't fer me, but for the women folk and young man we got with us. He's been through hell the last few weeks."

As he pulled candy from a jar, the trader asked, "How so?"

Moses explained what had happened to Luke and then asked, "Don't you think that's pretty rough on a feller?"

"It's enough to make a man think he ain't livin' right in the eyes of God. Ya know, I'm pretty lucky, 'cause in over thirty years out heah, I ain't never been seriously hurt. Oh, I took an arrow a couple of times, been shot four times, but I never had no festerin' nor in real danger of dyin'. Look, ya and Isaac sit and nurse that whiskey while I go in the back to gather up the rest of this stuff."

Smiling Moses replied, "Sure, we can do that."

A few minutes later, Isaac entered, pulled off his coat and said, "Temperatures droppin' like an old woman's chest out there. I suspect our ride back will be a lot colder than our ride heah."

"Let's jus' pray we don't get no snow. We get a big one, and we'll have to stop and hole up someplace fer a spell."

Isaac shrugged and replied, "Ain't nothin' we can do 'bout it iffen we do. They know we mighten be late if the weather turns bad."

⇢⇠ ⇢⇠ ⇢⇠

Bill looked around the fire and met the eyes of everyone there. He'd expected Moses and Isaac back days before, but a large storm had moved in and covered the land for miles with snow. They still had a lot of jerky and pemmican, so starving was out, except they grew tired of the same food day after day. Bill was getting to the point that just the sight of pemmican made him want to gag.

Luke was up and moving around, and not one complaint about the loss of his fingers. He was doing his share of the work too, watering horses, chopping wood, gathering pine needles to make tea, and countless other small tasks they did during a typical day. But, his favorite task was checking the snares that Moses had out and when he was lucky he'd enter the cabin with a big smile on his face, like he did this morning.

"I ain't eatin' no damned 'possum, and won't cook it neither!" Sue yelled as soon as she saw what he'd caught.

"Good," Luke said, "it'll leave more for me then."

Nancy looked ill as she asked, "Are we really supposed to eat that thing?"

"Nancy," Bill said, "you either eat it or jerky and pemmican, only the choice is yours. I'll force no one to eat what they don't want. Now a 'possum is covered with fat and right now yer body needs it."

"I'll pass, the thing looks like a big rat!"

Bill laughed and said, "I ate rat in Atlanta during the siege once. It ain't that bad, after ya get past the thought."

Nancy covered her mouth and ran from the cabin.

Sue, angry at Bill's teasing, yelled, "Bill Sanders, you stop that, and right now! You made 'er sick with your talk."

His eyebrows rose as he said, "I only told her the truth."

"Truth or not, that's enough," Sue turned and stormed from the cabin.

Luke, laughing, reached inside his bag and removed two sage hens. He placed them beside the fireplace. "I was gonna tell 'em 'bout the hens, but Nancy was so upset over the 'possum I never had a chance!"

Bill roared laughing and after a few minutes, he sobered up enough to say, "Let 'em lay. They'll see 'em when they come back and as cold as it is, they'll not be out long."

"What should I do with this 'possum?"

"Hang it in a tree, because we damned sure might need it in a few days."

Right then, Sue stuck her head through the door and said, "Riders comin'!"

Glancing at Luke, Bill ordered, "Get your rifle and come outside with me. Could be our supplies are here, or trouble's comin' to visit."

Picking his long gun from the wall, Luke said, "'Round here, it could be either!"

The sun was out and while still cold, the snow had stopped. The two men scanned the countryside and saw the riders immediately.

"They're back and the pack horses are packed high," Luke said in excitement.

The women yelled their joy, while Bill felt tremendous relief, because the two were returning alive, supplies or not. They were good men and the trip must have been right out of hell.

Twenty minutes later, the two men rode up smiling. As soon as they dismounted, Moses said, "There is a whole side of smoked bacon in the nearest pack on the first horse. Iffen one of you ladies would be nice enough to fry some, I'll pull it from the pack right now."

"I'll fry it, and love doin' it, too!" Nancy yelled out and then gave a little hop for joy.

Isaac moved to Bill's side and said, "We've a mountain of different foods and supplies on them horses."

"So, you spent most of the money and didn't bring back much change?"

"We didn't come back with a penny," Isaac said, and then explained about the robbery of the old trader.

"I'm glad you gave 'em the money. I don't want nothin' that ain't mine, and it's nice he let us keep the rest of it and gave us the supplies."

"Butterfield's a good man, but there ain't much nonsense in 'em. He was once a mountain man, but he grew tired of wadin' cold-assed streams and started a tradin' post. I know he's made more money tradin' than he ever would have as a trapper."

"Well, what did ya bring?"

"Everything Sue wrote down, except the mittens and socks, and a lot more. We've canned peaches, pears, jams, jellies, meats and all kinds of stuff. Hell, when he found out me and you killed Mossland, he called it a reward from the high country."

Bill laughed and asked, "Any troubles?"

"Some, but nothin' we couldn't handle. We didn't see a single soul during the trip, not a one."

"It's too damned cold out here, so come on in, the both of ya and warm up. I'll unload the packs and bring 'em in."

Seeing Luke, Moses asked, "How you be, son?"

"Doin' fine, only I cain't reach as far as I could last month."

"Men learn to live without body parts, and you were lucky the Good Lord didn't take your whole hand or arm. You should thank God next time you and him talk a spell." Moses said.

"Me and him already had that conversation a few days back."

"Good. Now let's get out of this cold and let Bill do some work fer a change!"

To the folks who'd waited in the cabin for the two mountain men, it was like Christmas morning. Bill brought in pack after pack, until the whole north wall was stacked high.

Once finished, he sat on the floor beside the fire and asked, "What did you two do, clean out the whole store?"

Isaac laughed and replied, "Nope, when Butterfield found out about our women, he sent things only a woman needs. Like a coffee pot, plates, cups, glasses, silverware, blankets, sheets, and a whole bunch of other things."

Moses injected, "That's Butterfield. When he helps a person he don't do the job half-assed, it's all the way. We got twice what we needed, and he didn't ask fer a penny. He said killin' Mossland was pay enough."

"He's either a good man or a foolish one," Bill replied, and then reached for the coffee.

"He ain't foolish by any stretch of the imagination. He's a pretty smart man, only he don't like the idea of women bein' with us and not havin' what they need. Hell, he ain't hurtin' fer money.

He's married to some rich old gal back east and they got a pile of money 'tween 'em."

"He sure as all get out don't act like a rich man. Most rich folks I've seen are pretty tight," Bill said, as he looked the stack of supplies over closely.

Isaac chuckled, in a good mood because he was home, and said, "He ain't like that. Ole Butterfield would give a needin' man the shirt off of his back."

Sue walked to Bill and asked, "Is it okay iffen Nancy and me start unpackin' the supplies? We'd like to see what we got to work with, besides the bacon."

Two hours later, the smell of bacon frying and cornbread baking filled the small structure. Bill felt his mouth water at the thought of bacon and cornbread, his first in over two months. While the pemmican and jerky had done what it was supposed to do, keep them alive, it got old quickly. Closing his eyes, he remembered the baked chickens, geese and ducks his ma used to cook during Holidays and smiled. And, at every meal, he was assured of biscuits and cornbread, as regular as clockwork.

Bill knew hunger from the war, but it bothered him when the women didn't get the kinds of foods they needed to stay strong. While pemmican had meat and some fruit in it, the layer of bear grease could not be good for a man or woman. His pa used to say only lean red meat was good for a body to stay healthy on and Bill believed him. He'd always felt stronger and healthier after a good meal of beef, deer, or buffalo.

"Bill, are you listenin'?" Sue asked from beside him.

"Uh, I was daydreamin' about my ma's cookin' to tell ya the truth."

Sue laughed and handed him a tin plate with cornbread and bacon. He held it to his nose took a sniff and savored the aroma. While it was a simple meal, it smelled wonderful to him. Taking a piece of bacon, he took a big bite, chewed it slowly and enjoyed the taste. Who would've ever thought a little piece of hog meat could taste so good.

That night, as they lay on the floor, instead of sleeping, they spoke in low tones.

"The tradin' post sent us all kinds of things. We got lots of food, and enough other supplies to keep us alive well through spring."

"We're lucky the owner is a good man. Actually, keepin' his money bothers me some."

"He told ya to keep it, so why does it bother ya?"

"After seein' all the stuff he sent us, I feel like I owe the man something."

"You don't owe him a thing, don't you see? He did what he did out of the goodness of his heart and that's rare. Just remember the man in your prayers and that'll be enough."

"Oh, I said a prayer of thanks right after them two got back. It was an act of God, and we both know it."

"Well, I have another act of God to talk to you about."

Feeling his body tense with her words, he hoped things were going as well with her as they were with him. "About what?"

"You're gonna be a pa by this time next year," She said and then laughed.

Bill gave a loud scream, but quickly quieted down when Sue asked, "Do you have a name picked out yet?"

"No, no I don't and, oh, this is not good. We got a baby comin' and no name!"

Isaac gave a loud laugh from beside Moses.

A few minutes later, the cabin grew quiet and Bill whispered, "I love you."

"I love you too, but right now we'd better get some sleep. Another loud scream and we'll have to fight our way outta this place."

Bill fell asleep, but only after thinking long and hard about his coming child.

# CHAPTER 20

**W**hen spring arrived, it came suddenly one morning with warm winds, chirping birds, and green buds on trees. Buffalo grasses, which surrounded them, suddenly appeared and grew at an astonishing rate. The gray-green grasses grew long and had a slight twist in the stem as it grew.

Moses, Luke and Isaac had left an hour before dawn, hoping to see a herd of buffalo or maybe a deer. While they still had a lot of food from the trading post, all agreed to save as much of it as possible, so it could be eaten at special times. Hams, sides of bacon, and other treats were too hard to attain to eat every day. Behind them walked four horses to pack the meat, if they were successful.

Near noon, Isaac rode beside Luke and said, "Over this next rise is where we usually find a large herd of buffalo this time of the year. Now, iffen they're there, we'll shoot from the crest and the shots will be long. When ya shoot, take a deep breath and as ya let 'er out slowly, squeeze yer trigger easy like. Ya find yer shootin' is better that-a way."

Luke nodded in reply, but said nothing.

Moses stopped his horse, turned with his right hand on the cantle, and said, "We go the rest of the way on foot. And, no more talkin' until we start shootin'. You got somethin' to say, use sign language."

They dismounted and they walked halfway up the rise. Then they fell to their knees and crawled to the top. In the valley below, they saw thousands of the big shaggy beasts, along with wolves moving around edges of the herd, looking for weak, old, or sick animals to feed on.

Luke gave a loud suspiration and signed, "Many buffalo!"

"Keep the noise down. They see poorly, but hear well. Get ready to shoot, but only kill the one's on the outside of the herd," Moses ordered with his hands and then lined his sights up on a big cow.

"I understand," Luke replied with sign language, filled with excitement of the hunt.

Isaac shot first and it looked as if he'd missed, but a few seconds later his buffalo fell to the ground unmoving. Mose and Luke's shots followed shortly and two more of the big animals fell to the grass.

"One more killin' a piece and that's enough."

In a matter of two or three short minutes, three more buffalo were on the ground.

Standing, Isaac said, "Now, when we walk to them critters, keep yer gun at the ready. Iffen one of 'em is only hurt, he might turn on ya. Go toward the beast from his ass, not his head. Iffen he quivers, put another round into 'em as quick as ya can."

Luke smiled; proud his shooting had equaled the two old mountain men, and replied, "Makes good sense to me."

"Let's go and get that meat. It's likely we ain't the only hunters out heah and we don't need to run into Omaha or Oto."

As the three men approached the downed buffalo the rest of the herd simply walked away, not frightened by them.

"How come them buff'alo didn't take off runnin'?" Luke asked, surprised the big critters didn't stampede.

"They have bad eyes. They see us, but not clearly and don't take us as a threat, and they ain't smart enough to realize we just kill six of their kind with guns. I've seen men kill a hundred of the big beasts before they panic and run." Moses replied.

Isaac, not to be left out of the conversation said, "Let's be glad they ain't real smart and taste as good as they do. We've enough meat heah to last us fer months."

While Luke had killed the animals before he was almost overwhelmed as he skinned the first buffalo. *It'll take me hours just to get this first one done!*

"Hard doin's, skinnin' a buff is!" Moses said with his voice hinting of humor.

"That's for sure! How in the world do Injun women do the job so fast and alone?" Luke asked.

Isaac pulled a bloody arm from a buffalo's chest and accenting the importance of his words with the knife in his hand, he said, "I don't know, but by God, they do the job and fast, too."

"Enough naybobbin', we ain't got no idea who heard our shots. Just quarter these things and let's get out of heah. I got me a squampshus like feelin' all of a sudden."

From out of nowhere, an arrow flew and Isaac fell to the grass, thrashing in pain.

"Injuns!" Moses yelled and then scurried behind his buffalo.

Luke grabbed his rifle, moved behind the beast he'd been skinning and cocked the hammer back with a loud click. Seeing Isaac still lived, but in pain, he ran to the man's side and dragged him behind his buffalo. Arrows flew, but none touched the young man. Turning, as soon as he was behind the dead animal, he ran back and picked up Isaacs' rifle.

"I count ten Injuns, and they look to be Pawnee!"

Gritting his teeth against his pain, Isaac said, "It's Pawnee, or at least this arrie is."

A warrior determined to count first coup on one of the men, jumped from the tall grasses and ran right for them. Luke lined up his sights and gently squeezed the trigger, smiling as a slug took the warrior in the center of the chest and knocked him back hard. The brave screamed a few times as his body jerked and twisted, then lay still—dead.

"Here they come!" Moses yelled but the warning was unneeded, because Luke had already lined his sights on a big warrior leading the group. But, before he could pull the trigger, the man's head exploded in a gory mist of blood and bone. The young man slid his sights over a few inches and fired twice, seeing two men drop. One he suspected was dead, but the second didn't fall in an uncontrolled manner and could very well be alive.

Hearing a loud grunt from Moses, Luke glance toward the man and saw a spear in his chest and a bloody point was out his back. Moses, meeting the younger man's eyes, gave a weak grin, pulled his pistol and fired five times into the Pawnee. He then dropped to his side and after a few seconds began to groan in the grasses.

"They're pulling back!" Luke yelled loudly.

Isaac, in pain, said with labored breath, "It . . . could be a . . . trick. Don't stand . . . yet. Wait . . . a spell."

Kneeling, Luke cut the front of Isaac's shirt and pulled the material apart to check the injury. The arrow had hit the man high and just a little off center of his chest. The blood was dark and not bright in color, which Bill had said in the past meant no inner organs were injured. Pulling his pouch to his side, Luke pulled out an old shirt and began bandaging the man. He decided to leave the arrow in, at least until he could return and have Bill look the man over.

A few seconds later, a group of about twenty Pawnee rode over a rise and disappeared from sight.

"They're gone . . . now, son. Check . . . Moses."

Luke stood and made his way to the old mountain man, knowing he was dead. When he neared he saw the man was still alive, but in a lot of pain.

"I'll . . . go under . . . this time," Moses whispered as the young man kneeled beside him.

"I'll get ya back to Bill, mayhap he can do something."

"Pull . . . spear . . . out."

Seeing no easy way to do the task, Luke placed his foot on Moses' chest and grabbed the wooden handle. The first time he pulled, it didn't move an inch, but on the second attempt it came right out. Kneeling, he cut Moses' shirt off, wrapped him with some white cotton cloth he had and then walked to the horses. He returned a few minutes later with a small jug of whiskey in his hand.

He fed the two men enough raw alcohol to help them sleep and then quartered the buffalo and loaded the meat on the pack-horses. As soon as the meat was loaded, he took each man, placed him on a horse and then tied him in place. He'd have to move slowly, or the men could slip under their horses and start bleeding again.

He grabbed the saddle horn, placed his foot in the stirrup, and as his leg went over his horse's back thought, *Moses will go under. The blood was bright red, and I know that's a bad sign.*

Getting comfortable in his saddle, he took the reins of the horses and began to move at a slow walk toward home.

Half way home, Moses called for him to stop.

Luke moved to the man's side and asked, "You hurtin'?"

"Yup . . . and . . . dyin', son."

"What do ya need from me, Moses, to help ya?"

"I want," he gave a long groan of pain before he continued, "another . . . drink."

When Luke returned with the whiskey, Moses couldn't raise his head, so the young man pulled his head up and let a good amount of alcohol run into his mouth.

"Thank . . .ya kindly fer the . . . " Moses never finished his sentence, because he gave a loud sigh, followed by a rattle in his chest, quivered violently, and died. Luke used his hand to close the man's unseeing eyes.

Isaac was unconscious, so Luke mounted and once more moved toward home.

*About all I've seen out here is fightin' and death, and we've yet to make a dollar,* he thought as he started remembering Moses.

It was dark when he rode up to the cabin and dismounted in front of the cabin door. Bill, hearing the horses, came out of the cabin and asked, "Did you find any meat?"

"We did, but the Pawnee found us shortly after. Moses is dead, and I ain't sure iffen Isaac will live."

"You hurt?"

"Didn't get as much as a scratch durin' the whole fight."

Shaking his head, Bill said, "Damn it all, Moses was a good man."

"It seems to me, any folks can die out here, too. I'll miss the man, but I've come to see death as a part of life."

"Well, let's get his body laid out straight, or we'll have to bury 'em curved."

The two lowered Moses from the horse and moved him to a crude barn recently constructed.

Straightening his body on an old horse blanket, Bill said, "We'll do the buryin' in the mornin'."

Isaac was taken into the cabin and Luke stayed inside to tell the tale of the attack, while Bill went back outside to move the meat to the smoke house and care for the horses.

"It's goin' to turn hard around here without Moses to help. You know that, don't you, horse? He was a man full of knowledge and he'll be missed." Bill said as spoke to the horses. He'd learned years ago to communicate with a horse and noticed if he spoke to one often enough, they grew closer.

He carried the meat into the small building and hung it on meat hooks he'd made while the men were out hunting. He'd gone back to the old ranch the day before and while walking through the ashes he discovered his anvil, hammerheads and most metal tools were still intact. The tools he brought back and installed new handles. He constructed a new work structure and within half a day, he was back in business again.

*We need to place some of this meat in some brine. I for sure don't want no more jerky for a spell, had my fill.*

When he entered the cabin, Isaac was moaning as he sipped a large glass of whiskey, and Luke was looking his injury over. The man's shirt was off and his huge black muscles glistened with sweat.

He raised his head and said, "I don't have much trouble breathin', but the damned thing hurts me."

Bill walked over to Luke and asked, "Do you want to doctor 'em up or have me do it?"

"I'd like to try, iffen you'll stay by my side and lead me a bit. I gotta learn how to doctor sometime, and this is as good a time as any other."

"Well, right off we know a few things about the Injun who shot 'em. First, the arrow wasn't pulled all the way back or it would have gone right through 'em. Second, the tip wasn't smeared with human waste or snake poison, because he'd already be festered. Now, the only way to get that arrow out, iffen it's stuck in bone or muscle, is to use them big pliers I got out in the barn. So, go fetch 'em and then you can start to work when you get back."

After four tries with the big pliers, the arrowhead finally came out and Isaac gave a light groan of relief, as Luke placed the bloody tool by his side.

Picking up a jug of whiskey, Bill asked, "You know what he has to do now, right?"

"I know the routine, jus' get 'er done."

Luke took the jug from Bill and poured about a half a cup on the black man's chest.

Isaac muffled a loud moan, but all in the cabin knew the man was experiencing pain and admired his grit.

As the whiskey ran down Isaac's chest, Luke said, "Next will be a hot knife." The black man nodded and closed his eyes against the coming pain.

As soon as the whiskey evaporated, Luke pulled the glistening blade from the fire and placed it against Isaacs' chest. The man's body quivered and his feet drummed on the dirt floor, but he never cried out. A few seconds after Luke removed the hot blade; Isaac slipped into unconsciousness and felt no more pain.

"The way you smeared his flesh together is just how it's got to be done. You want to move the flesh over the wound iffen you can, so the bleedin' stops. You did just fine," Bill said, as he turned his head away from the smell.

"Stinks, don't it?" Luke asked.

"Hell, you should know! How many times you had it done?"

Grinning, Luke replied, "Only the times you've done it, but it's hard on a man."

Nancy neared and asked, "Will he live?"

"I suspect he'll be fine."

Sue stood, wiggled her nose and ordered, "Let's open some windows and get the smell out of here. Ain't no way we can eat breakfast or even sleep with the stench of burnt flesh in this room."

With the shutters opened wide a cool breeze soon cleared the room. It was dark, with a million stars sparkling like diamond dust overhead.

⇒⇐ ⇒⇐ ⇒⇐

Isaac stood by the grave and said, "Open wide, O earth, and receive Moses that was fashioned from thee by the hand of God aforetime, and who returneth again unto Thee that gave him birth. That which was made according to his image the Creator hath received unto himself; do thou receive back that which is thine own."

Then taking a handful of dirt, he added, "The earth is the Lord's and the fullness thereof. Lord, he was a good man and well liked by most folks. We ask you to take him into your arms and let him know he's missed by us. This I ask in the name of Jesus, amen."

Amen echoed over the plains, as Luke and Bill picked up shovels and started filling the grave. Luke had spent hours the night before carving a wooden cross for the head of the grave and once finished he put it in place.

Sue read the words on the cross, "Jack Moses, born 1801, died 1866. A man with the h'ar of the b'ar!"

"That looks real nice, son," Bill said and then smiled.

"Yup, he would have liked it." Isaac added and grinned as well.

"Where'd you learn that fancy prayer?" Luke asked Isaac.

"I heard a preacher man say it once and I liked the sound of the words, so I kept it fer my own. I think it's fittin' fer a proper buryin'."

The small group began to move back toward the cabin, but immediately Bill sighted a large group of mounted riders moving toward them. After a few minutes, he saw they were Sioux, so he relaxed."

"Sioux comin'," Isaac announced.

"Likely Brass Buttons comin' to see how we did over winter."

Isaac replied, "That's my guess too, well, that and he might want to see Luke again."

Since the day was warm, Bill said, "Luke take yer shirt off, so the chief can see yer battle scars. That'll impress the livin' hell right out of 'em."

"And," Isaac added, "make sure he sees your two fingers are missin', too. It will all add to his respect for ya."

Removing his shirt, Luke asked, "So, what's all of this suppose to mean to us?"

Isaac gave the young man a soft smile and replied, "He'll know yer scars are from fighting your enemies and that will impress 'em. Not many braves yer age are scared up, so he'll know yer a scrapper."

The chief rode to the men and dismounted. Nearing, he suddenly stopped, looked Luke over closely and said, *"My eyes see my friend yet lives, but where is the old warrior?"*

Isaac said, *"He has passed over to the other side, my chief."*

*"All living things must pass over one day. It is the circle of life of all living things. The young one, he has more scars than when I last saw him."*

*"He is a warrior, so scars mean little to him. The old warrior died in a battle with the Pawnee, and our young warrior took three more scalps."*

*"Waugh! He will grow to be a warrior others will fear and that is good. It is unusual for one with so few seasons to have so many scalps and scars. I think he needs a Sioux name."*

Turning to Luke, Isaac said, "He's gonna give ya a new name. Or did ya catch that by watching his sign language?"

Luke, who'd been practicing sign with Isaac and Moses all winter, read the dancing fingers and hands very well. "I got that much from it all."

Turning to the chief, Isaac asked, *"What is to be his new name?"*

*"I have given his name thought and he will be known by The People as Scalp Taker. It is a name worthy of a great warrior and my young friend has earned it."*

Then seeing two fingers were missin' on Luke's hand, he asked, *"How has he lost two fingers? Has he been in mourning for loved one?"*

*"No, much cold came and his fingers froze. We had to cut them off."*

*"I have seen it before and how did my friend take the pain?"*

*"Like a true warrior. Not a sound was made, although it hurt him much."*

The chief walked to Luke, placed a hand on his shoulder and raised the other one to the sky as he said, *"Before the eyes of the Great Spirit, I give you the name, Scalp Taker!"*

Then, lowering his hands, he said to Luke, *"Your name is one of honor and truly a warrior's name. Live up to the name, because all you do from this sun on will reflect on you, and let your enemies learn to quiver in fear at the name Scalp Taker. I have spoken."*

Luke, using sign language, replied, *"I will do so, father, and thank you for the new name. I will make you proud of my name, because I only have one Sioux father."*

Brass Buttons smiled and replied, *"And, I only have one white son, who goes by a name I have given him."*

"Whoooeee," Isaac said, turned to Bill and blinked rapidly.

"What's goin' on," Bill asked because he knew no sign or any of the Sioux tongue.

"Brass Button's just named Luke, Scalp Taker, and that's fine doin's! He called Luke his son and Luke called 'em father. Hell, we're part of the Sioux family now."

Bill didn't speak, but he did give a huge smile.

*"Do you have hunger, my chief?"* Isaac asked.

*"No, I brought a gift to my son,"* Brass Buttons said and then raised his spear high overhead.

Off in the distance, a warrior broke away from the group and rode toward the cabin leading a horse. When the horse and warrior stopped beside Brass Buttons, Luke saw a large pouch on its back.

The chief walked to the brave, took the reins and said, *"The horse is yours as well as the pouch. It is a gift of the heart and not one needing repaid. I give this freely to you, Scalp Taker."*

Pulling the pouch from the horse's back, Luke opened it and pulled out a set of buckskins of the likes he'd never seen before. He saw the shirt was dyed a light tan, except at the shoulders where it was red. The red slowly blended into the tan near his chest. The pants were of the same color, except the red started at the bottom of the legs and blended into tan near his knees. There were four eagle feathers in the pouch as well, for the coup he'd counted on the Oto earlier. At the very bottom were beaded moccasins.

Seeing the young man smile, Brass Buttons said, *"I owe you three more feathers. I will send them to you today. We must go now."*

*"Goodbye, my father."*

Brass Buttons smiled and said, *"You are to come with me. I have another surprise at my village worthy only of the man called Scalp Taker."*

Luke was speechless and bit frightened at the thought of going to a Sioux village alone, so he asked, *"Can I bring my friend who speaks the Sioux tongue?"*

*"Yes, I think he might speak for us when sign does not work. You must wear your new clothes when we return to my village."*

Luke smiled and said, "Be right back, got go change into my Injun clothes." He then ran for the cabin.

Turning to Bill, Isaac said, "Me and Luke are goin' to the village. I don't expect us back fer a couple of days."

"Think it's safe?"

"He called the boy, son, now what do ya think? Relax, he jus' wants to show his people a young fightin' man, and no harm will come to us."

# CHAPTER 21

**L**uke turned some heads when he entered the village wearing his buckskins with four eagle feathers in his hair. All who glanced at him riding beside Brass Buttons knew the young man was a proven warrior. They rode through the center of the village and stopped at a teepee larger than the rest.

After dismounting, the chief said, *"Come into my lodge. We will eat and speak of my gift to you."*

The inside of the lodge was clean with a small fire burning in the center. A woman near the age of the chief dished out two tin plates of stew and then left. Luke wondered at Injuns having plates, but realized they must have gotten them from traders.

Minutes later, the simple meal finished, Brass Buttons pulled out his pipe and lit it. He moved the pipe in four directions and then raised and lowered it. Isaac leaned close and whispered, "He's movin' the pipe in the four main compass heading and then toward heaven and hell. Ya do the same when she comes to ya next."

Luke took the pipe, took a drag and then gave a light cough. He too moved the pipe and then handed it to Isaac. Soon the red man knocked the pipe clean, the ashes falling into the fire, and placed it on a buffalo robe.

*"Now we must speak of a gift suitable for a true warrior."*

*"I don't need or want more from you, father, the buckskins are enough."*

*"You speak like a man, but this is a gift I have given much thought. It would please my heart greatly to give this to you."*

*"As you wish."*

Isaac leaned toward Luke and said, "This is strange doin's. I ain't never see anything like this before."

*"My wife has gone for your gift and will soon return."*

Suddenly, Isaac gave a light snicker.

"What's so funny?" Luke asked.

"Iffen what I think is 'bout to happen, yer gonna crap!"

"What?"

"Wait and see, young coon, jus' wait and see."

At that point, the entrance flap pulled back and the wife of Brass Buttons entered—with a young woman behind her.

The wife and young woman sat on the left side of Brass Buttons as the chief said, *"This is my wife, Swallow and my daughter, Singing Bird."*

Luke and Isaac nodded to the women.

The chief cleared his throat and said, *"When a man becomes a true warrior and counts his first coup, it is an important time in his life. But, you, Scalp Taker, have taken more than a handful of scalps and I see no honor offered to you by your own people. Among the Sioux, you are a man of strength and prestige, unlike many others.*

*When a man takes his first scalp or counts his first coup, he is to move from the lodge of his family and take a wife. Until that first honor, he lives with his mother and father."*

Not sure what was goin' on, Luke signed, *"I understand and it is as it should be with The People."*

Brass Buttons raised his head and said, *"It's only when he takes a wife that he becomes a complete man. Only you have no woman and I see no young white women on Sioux lands. So, I thought long and hard over this and finally decided, if there are no white women, then Scalp Taker needs a Sioux woman. Singing Bird is to be your woman."*

Isaac gave a loud snort and then broke out laughing.

Turning to the black man, Luke asked, "Did he jus' say what I think he said? He's given his daughter to me?"

"Yep, he's surely done jus' that!"

"I don't want a wife! I'm not fully growed yet!"

"Simmer down some, or ya'll piss ole Brass Buttons off and right now he's in a good mood. There is no way ya can get out of this, so accept his gift and let it go. Iffen ya turn 'em down, and I'm serious heah, we could end up dead."

"Why would he kill us?"

"He'll think you don't want his daughter 'cause she ain't good enough fer ya. Do ya understand?"

"Yep, but how can I get out of this mess?"

"Ya cain't son, not really."

"Good God, me with a wife! What's my ma gonna say?"

Isaac just shrugged his shoulders.

*"Why the white man talk?"*

*"My friend was surprised you offered your own daughter to me, and he thinks I am too young for a wife. I told him I am a warrior, not a boy, and have need of a wife."* Luke had to say something and since he had no choice, he decided to accept the situation.

The chief smiled and said, *"It is good. You will find Singing Bird will keep you warm on cold nights, knows how to please a man under the robes, and will bring you many children."*

*"That is good!"* Luke signed but inside he was frantically looking for a way to keep from marrying the woman.

Standing, Brass Buttons ordered, *"Come, we will start the wedding ceremony."*

➡️⬅️  ➡️⬅️  ➡️⬅️

Two hours later, as they moved toward home, Luke rode beside his unwanted wife full of anger. He'd not wanted a wife, didn't need a wife, but he had one. Singing Bird had not spoken a word, not one, since she'd been introduced to him. He wondered what she thought of the mess they had now.

Riding up to the cabin, they dismounted, tied their horses to the hitching post and entered. When Singing Bird entered, eyes fell on her and all talking stopped.

"Who's your friend?" Bill asked after he'd pulled his pipe from his mouth.

Isaac broke out laughing and between gasps for breath said, "Ask . . . Luke."

Sue, suspecting something had happened asked, "Well?"

"Damn it! She's my wife!"

"Wha . . . at?" Bill's eye grew large with question.

"Brass Buttons gave our mighty warrior a wife, and she jus' happens to be his youngest daughter, too."

"Did you want her, son?" Sue asked.

"Ma, now what do you think? No, I didn't want her, but I had no choice in the matter and to refuse could have gotten me and Isaac killed. My refusal would have deeply insulted the man."

Bill, confused, asked, "What are you goin' to do?"

Shaking his head as he plopped down on the floor, Luke said, "Keep 'er I guess. Don't seem like I have much say in the matter."

Sue grew red-faced and said, "You'll not live in sin in this house."

"They was married by a shaman," Isaac replied, enjoying the situation.

"Isaac, you know me and Sue don't approve of no heathen marriage. If she lives with him, they'll have to be married in the eyes of God. Do you think Deacon is still around?"

"Deacon's around, 'less he was killed over winter. I've a good idea where he'd be, too, but it'll take me a week to ride fer 'em and return."

"You'll not go it alone. I'll go with you," Bill said, and then added, "I've not got out on a long trip since we got here and need some fresh air. They'll be safe enough, with Scalp Taker guardin' 'em, I'd reckon."

➡️⬅️  ➡️⬅️  ➡️⬅️

The two men left the next morning and the weather was clear, with only a couple of cotton balls of clouds off to the east. The winds were light and it looked to be a fine day coming.

Looking down at Sue, Bill said, "We'll be back in about six or seven days. Iffen we're a little late don't worry, especially if the weather turns bad."

"I won't worry, except you two watch yourselves out there."

Leaning over, Bill kissed her and said, "Take care of our baby. That means no hard work or heavy liftin'. Luke's man enough to keep all of ya safe, so listen to what he says if a problem comes along." Sue was just starting to show her pregnancy.

"I'll keep our baby safe, just hurry back to us."

As the two men rode from the cabin, all waved until they were out of sight.

An hour later, as Luke cared for the riding stock, Singing Bird walked up to him and asked in sign, *"Where do the men go?"*

Turning and meeting her eyes, he said, *"To get a Holy man for us, so we can be married."*

*"We are one already. We were married in the village."*

*"That is true, but only in the eyes of the Sioux. Since I am a white man, we must marry according to my customs, too."*

*"Why did you not sleep with your wife last night?"*

*"I cannot sleep with you until we are married in the eyes of my God."*

*"God?"*

*"You call him the Great Spirit or Great Creator."*

*"We were married in the eyes of the Great Spirit."*

*"Yes, we were married in the eyes of the Great Spirit, but not in the eyes of my God. I don't know if your God and mine are the same, but I cannot lay with you until we do this thing."*

*"If it is your wish, I will wait."*

*"I thank you. It is important to my mother and me, too."*

*"It is a small thing."*

*"No, it is a very big thing to white people."*

*"I know little of the ways of whites."*

Pulling his hat down to shade his eyes, Luke replied, "Ya'll learn."

⇒⇐  ⇒⇐  ⇒⇐

Three days later, the two men found Deacon high in the mountains, sitting on a log and sipping coffee, as bacon sizzled in a cast iron skillet on a small fire. A light rain had threatened all day, but so far it remained dry, which meant little to the two men. Both knew a storm could come quickly, and they were glad to reach Deacon and his shelter of canvas.

Looking up, Deacon saw Isaac and called out, "I'll be damned iffen it ain't ugly! Where's your no account partner?"

"Gone under, he has!"

"What injuns kilt 'em?"

"Pawnee, but they didn't get his topknot!"

"Come on up, and I'll add some bacon to the pan."

A little later, as they all sat by the fire, Deacon said, "Moses was a good man and I'm sorry he's gone under, but he was gettin' long of tooth. He wasn't as fast as he once was."

Bill, poured some coffee in his cup and replied, "He rode over ten miles after my boy pulled a spear outta his chest and never complained once about the pain."

"He had sand in 'em, always did have. Well, Isaac, what can I do for ya or is this a social visit?"

"Ya up to doin' a marryin' job in a few days?"

"Who's the lucky couple?"

Bill grinned and replied, "Seems ole Brass Buttons gave my boy his daughter, and he won't have 'er for a wife until they're married in the eyes of the Lord."

Deacon smiled warmly and said, "He's a good boy, then. Not many men would take a squaw and marry her before God. I'll do the job and the fee is the same as the last time."

"Nothin'?" Bill asked.

Nodding his head, Deacon said, "Yup, nothin'. God enjoys seein' folks married and I like to make my master happy. We'll leave when the cock crows."

"Ya ain't got no chickens!" Isaac laughed.

"Okay, we'll leave when my cock would crow iffen I had one. Are you happy now?"

There came a loud crack of thunder off in the distance and rain began to fall hard. There came a gust of wind and the canvas shook and twisted as the men laughed.

"Looks like a bad storm, so we'd better get under the canvas." Isaac yelled over the pounding rain striking the trees.

"Uh-huh, but we've had 'em a-fore. Might as well catch up on yer sleep or read a bit, iffen ya got a book." Deacon said as soon as he was under shelter.  Then, he leaned back against the trunk of a large oak.

"I left mine," Bill replied and then added, "only I'd read a Bible iffen ya got one."

Deacon reached into his possibles bag, pulled out a well-worn Bible and said, "I never come to the mountains without a Bible. I have to get a new one every year, 'cause my kind of livin' is hard on a book."

"It'll do, I reckon."

As Bill opened the book and began to read, Isaac and Deacon leaned back and closed their eyes.

The rain turned to hail and the small stones of ice began to beat a tattoo on the stretched canvas. An hour later, the storm stopped instantly, as if turned off by the hand of God. Deacon started another fire, placed the bacon back on to cook, and then made a fresh pot of coffee. He hummed a no-name tune as he worked and soon the men were eating.

The air had a slight chill in it, due to the passing storm, but it wasn't cold. Water dripped from trees and brush, while the men talked of many things.

Bill took a sip of his coffee and asked, "You ever think of buildin' a home and stayin' in one spot, Deacon? You could open a small church."

Deacon laughed, placed his cup by his foot and replied, "I've give 'er some thought at times, mostly when the weather turns bad or I ain't got no food, but seriously leave my mountains? I don't think I could do that, not really."

"Why not leave the mountains?"

The older man scratched his cheek and then said, "Son, these mountains have been my home for over forty years. Now, that doesn't mean much to you, but there is a pull in these mountains fer some men. I happen to be one of those men. See, I love this place, jus' like a man loves a pretty woman, and I could no more leave heah than a man could leave a good wife."

"But, at times you're hungry, thirsty and scared in these mountains, especially when the Injuns get on yer rear-end."

"Aye, yer right, only it's a small price to pay to live the life I do. I love the smell of pine early in the mornin' and the scent of wood-smoke in the evenin's. I can come and go as I please, and my nearest neighbor ain't close enough to hear me break wind. I love watchin' an eagle soar overhead and the deer eatin' in the valleys below me. No, son, I cain't leave my home, because, I guess, I see God heah."

"I can understand that, except what will ya do when ya get so old ya cain't move much or get sick?"

Gazing into Bill's eyes, Deacon replied, "Well, I guess I'll die heah, then. I cain't think of a better place fer a feller to die, can ya?"

"Yep, I can. I want to die with my family around me."

Pouring another cup of coffee, Deacon said, "I can understand that, but I ain't got no family left. I left Missouri right after my wife and two kids died of cholera. I couldn't stay. I thought to come out heah fer a few years, get my thinkin' straight, and then go back home. That was nigh on forty years ago, and I ain't been back since."

"You ever miss it?"

Deacon laughed and said, "I miss my family, but I don't miss people or the rush they're in all the time. I don't miss crowds, noise and the stink of a big city or town. See, when you grow up in places like that, well, you don't know any better. Once out heah, I found a life more to my likin'. Don't ya see?"

"Uh-huh, it makes sense to me."

Isaac, who'd been listening said, "I was out heah years a-fore the war started 'tween the north and south, and I feel the same way. I do have to admit, my reason for comin' was a whole lot different, but I moved jus' the same. Men learn to love these mountains, with a passion usually saved for a woman, or they hate the place and soon return home. It's a brutal life we live, and some men jus' ain't got enough sand in their craw to stay."

"We'll soon see more and more black folks comin' out heah, 'cause there ain't much left fer 'em in the Deep South. Since they're free, many ain't got no idea what to do, so free land will sound good to mos' of 'em." Deacon said and then continued, "Black folks can add a lot to the settlin' of this country, but only iffen white folks allow 'em to do the job. I 'magine lot's of small black towns will spring up, only I don't see no big cities comin'. They mighten be free, but mos' whites still don't like 'em."

Bill said, "I don't think most whites hate black folk, they're scared of 'em. I learned early in life to fear things or people I didn't understand. I was scared of the first blacks I met, 'cause I knew nothin' about 'em."

Isaac's eyes narrowed as he replied, "Hell, we ain't no different that mos' white folks. We even want the same things, a home, kids, a good job, and to be able to stand on our own two feet with pride."

"Oh, I know that now, but before I had no idea what a black man wanted out of life."

"Well, by damn, at least yer honest 'bout it."

Deacon thought for a few minutes then said, "I don't think the red man is much different than us either, except in his way of thinkin'. I figure he wants the same things we all do; only he places coups and horses at the top of the list."

Standing, Isaac said, "Well, time fer me to hit the robes. I want to get an early start in the mornin'."

Deacon grinned and said, "We'll pull two hour shifts overnight. I'll start first, then Bill and finally Isaac."

# CHAPTER 22

**B**ack at the cabin two days later, Deacon stood outside under a large oak tree and married Singing Bird and Luke. Most folks, including Sue, didn't approve of a mixed marriage, but she kept her mouth shut, because Luke had little choice but marry the daughter of Brass Buttons.

Deacon finally said the magic words, "I now pronounce ya man and wife. Ya may kiss the bride."

Luke leaned over and pecked his wife on the cheek.

As folks dispersed and started back to their jobs, Bill walked to his stepson and said, "Me and Isaac have made you both a small cabin back in the woods a ways. This way you can have some privacy on your weddin' night. It's back by the stream."

Luke glared at him and replied, "Ain't sure I want a weddin' night! The thought of havin' to get married still pisses me off."

"Don't take it out on her, son, she had little to do with it. I suspect her pa made the decision. Keep in mind, Brass Buttons thought giving his daughter was a way to honor you, not a way to make you mad."

Isaac, hearing the conversation said, "Yer married now, in the eyes of both Gods, so ya might as well be a fair man and a good husband. I think, given time, ya'll come to love that little girl."

"And in the eyes of God, your marriage ain't real until it's consummated," Bill added.

Lowering his head, Luke replied, "I know, but I just never dreamed of gettin' a wife this a-way."

"Well, young pup, ya got one, so be a man about it and do the right thing. Life ain't always fair and can be filled with surprises, but I think God had a hand in all of this. She expects a weddin' night, ya know?" Deacon said and then added, "Well, I'm headin' back to my mountains in a few minutes. Iffen ya ever need me, ya know where I be." He then shook hands with the three men and moved toward his horse.

As Deacon rode toward his mountains, Luke walked for his cabin, knowing Singing Bird waited for him. As he walked, he decided to take her as his wife, both in mind and body. He couldn't live with a woman and not make her an important part of his life, so it seemed this was his only option. *Maybe*, he thought, *we can learn to love each other. I'm sure more than one marriage started like ours, I mean look at ma and Bill. I can tell just by lookin' at her she loves him now.*

➤◄ ➤◄ ➤◄

The next day Luke and Singing Bird walked to the main cabin, hand in hand. Luke had found his wife to be passionate and loving, which rather surprised him, since he knew she didn't love him. He finally understood she'd decided, just like him, to make the best of a bad situation. Together they'd make a life and maybe, if they were lucky, they'd learn to love each other.

Entering the cabin, Luke walked to his ma seated on the floor peeling potatoes. He knelt at her side and asked, "Ma, would you mind teachin' Singing Bird English?"

His ma placed her knife in the small bowl she'd been using and replied, "I did me some thinkin' on that last night, and she needs to learn our language. I can help some, but Bill has the most education of all of us. Only with him makin' furniture and other chores 'round here, he ain't got the time to do the job."

"I was thinkin' you could teach her until the snows come and then Bill could take over. At that point, hopefully, she'll know a great deal."

Nancy, who was sitting beside Sue, said brusquely, "She's just a savage, and I don't think she's smart enough to learn our language."

Angry at her friend's harsh words Sue snapped, "Nancy, that'll be enough! She's the wife of my son!" She looked at Singing Bird, but suspected the woman knew no English. *I hope she didin't understand those cruel words.*

Nancy stood and walked outside.

"Son, excuse her, but she's scared to death of Injuns, and don't like 'em much."

"I ain't real comfortable with 'em my own self, but if I'm gonna be married to one, I'd like to be able to talk with her at times."

Sue laughed and said, "I can understand that. We'll start the learnin' in the mornin', right after breakfast. How's that?"

"That's fine, and since Isaac speaks pretty good Sioux, he's volunteered to be here until Singing Bird can at least understand a little English."

Ma broke out laughing and said, "Who would have ever thought I'd end up in a small cabin in Montana, teaching English to an Injun squaw, and usin' a black man as a translator!"

Luke joined the laughter, hugged his ma, and said, "Well, we gotta do what it takes, and I think Singing Bird will help us in ways we have no idea."

"Are you usin' sign language to talk with the woman now?"

"Yup and we can talk that way, but iffen she's to live with us, she needs to know our language."

"Tell her, right now, that I'll start teaching her our language in the mornin'."

"He does not need to tell me. I understand your words and I will be here."

Both Luke and ma's eyes grew large as they looked at each other, and then broke out laughing once again.

After sobering, Luke asked, "Where did ya learn English?"

"From a squaw man we had living with us and the long black robes that visited."

"What are long robes?" Ma asked.

"Catholic Priests, I imagine. They were busy in Injun country for many years. They wear them long black robes," Luke answered.

"I see." Ma replied and then asked, "Can ya read a little?"

"I can read very little of the talking leaves."

"Talkin' leaves?" Luke asked, and then suddenly added, "I remember Moses sayin' somethin' about the Injuns callin' paper with writin' on it talkin' leaves."

"Anyway, we'll start with the readin' in the mornin', just to see how much you know. Now, I got dinner to get ready, so you two go find something to do and let this old woman work."

The rest of the day, Luke worked on his small cabin, improving the roof, door, and fireplace. By dark, it was cozy. Singing Bird cooked a meal of buffalo, roots Luke didn't recognize, and a soup with rabbit. He turned the wick up on the lamp, pulled out his Bible and began to read.

Singing Bird, interested in the book asked, "What do you read?"

"The Bible. It is a book of words from God."

"Words from the Great Creator?"

"Yes, I guess so."

"Why did he give you a book and not The People?"

"I guess because most Sioux cannot read and he knew this."

She nodded at his logic and then asked, "Why did he not give the gift of reading to my people?"

"I do not have an answer. It was meant for the Sioux not to read, or the Great Creator would have given the power to ya."

"This reading is what will defeat the Sioux people. When one man's thought can be saved and then read by another, it is a powerful thing."

"Do the Sioux not paint stories?"

"Yes, we do that, but they do not speak like the leaves do, and it cannot tell the thoughts of the one who painted."

"I see."

"Can you read from the book to me?"

"Sure, I can do that." Luke replied, and then started reading about the creation of the world.

Later, after he'd finished, he glanced at Singing Bird and saw she was in deep thought. Picking up his pipe, he stuffed the bowl with tobacco and lit it with a brand from the fire. Inhaling deeply, he enjoyed the rich taste of the tobacco, and then let the smoke out slowly.

Finally, Singing Bird said, "I do not think the Great Creator and your God are the same."

"Oh, and why not?"

"Our story of creation is much different. In ours, old man coyote pulled all of the people from a hole in the ground. He did not make man or woman and then put them on earth."

"Well, mayhap our God is different than yours; I've never given it much thought."

Taking his hand, Singing Bird said, "Come my husband, let us see if you can bring me joy." As Luke followed her to the bed, his face turned red.

⇥⇤ ⇥⇤ ⇥⇤

A hard rain had fallen overnight, and the three women walked into the woods looking for mushrooms. Singing Bird, only reading for a little over a month, had already mastered one book, and started on the second. The books had been sent by Butterfield with the supplies. Nancy had change in her attitude toward the Indian woman and was nicer to her than before.

Morel mushrooms were spotted and quickly added to the baskets the women carried. It was near noon when Singing Bird stopped, scanned the countryside and whispered, "We are being watched."

Nancy raised her head, looked around and replied, "Nonsense, I see no one."

"It is the Pawnee. We must move deeper into the woods and then run for the cabin," Singing Bird suggested.

Sue, trusting the woman's survival savvy, whispered, "Let's go, but move slowly as if we're lookin' for mushrooms. We move too fast and they'll suspect somethin'."

The three women moved toward a grove of cedar trees, but before they could get there, a loud war cry sounded and six warriors rushed them. Nancy froze in fear, while Sue and Singing Bird ran into the trees.

Dropping their baskets the two ran side-by-side for over a mile, before Sue said, "I cain't run no more! I ain't as young as you are."

"You must run, or they will catch us," Singing Bird pleaded.

"I'll hide, you go on! I'm too tired and out of breath!"

Singing Bird glanced around and then ordered, "Get under that rock on the left, near the tree. It is like a small cave and may hide you. I will run to the cabin for help!"

No sooner had Sue started for the rock than the Indian woman took off running once more. She didn't stop until she saw the door to the cabin. Bill was splitting wood, Isaac was caring for the horses, and Luke was coming from the outhouse.

"The Pawnee attacked us! Nancy was taken and Sue is hiding!" She yelled out as she approached. She stopped beside Bill to catch her breath.

Isaac walked up and asked, "What's this about the Pawnee?"

"Is Sue okay?" Bill asked.

"The Pawnee attacked us. I think Nancy was taken captive, but Sue was okay when I left her."

The men ran for their long guns and other gear, returned to Singing Bird and Luke said, "Take us to where you were attacked."

When they returned to near the cedar grove, there was no sign of Nancy, but Isaac started walking in a small circle and finally called out, "They got 'er. I can see where she dragged her feet a foot or two in the dirt."

Singing Bird, worried about Sue said anxiously, "Come, we must find Sue."

They walked to where Sue had hidden but she was gone. Isaac saw drops of blood on the grasses.

"She's hurt or cut one of the Pawnee. This is fresh blood, only it's dark, so the injury is not very serious."

"Can you tell which way they went?" Bill asked as fear grew in his stomach.

"They moved north."

Turning to Luke he said, "Take Singing Bird to the cabin, and then send her to the Sioux for help. Tell Brass Buttons the Pawnee took your ma. Me and Isaac will try to foller this bunch, and let's pray we find 'em before they get to their village. You catch up when you can."

"But, that'll leave the cabin unguarded!" Luke replied.

"Send some Sioux back to watch the place. Iffen we don't hurry, we'll never get your ma back! Now move!"

➡️⬅️  ➡️⬅️  ➡️⬅️

Four hours later, Isaac said, "They're movin' pretty damned fast. They must suspect we're on their butts."

"What's that up ahead of us, on the left?" Luke asked, as he stood tall in his stirrups to get a better look.

"Cain't tell from heah, but move up slowly, it could be a trap."

The three men rode forward with their guns held at the ready and cocked.

Nearing, Isaac said, "My God, it's Nancy and she looks to be dead."

As he dismounted, Bill replied, "Maybe not, let me check."

The woman was on her stomach and when Bill rolled her over, he was shocked to see her throat had a jagged cut from side to side. Her dress was pulled up, and she'd been used before she'd died.

Isaac, from his saddle, asked, "She was used, wasn't she?"

"Yep, and then they killed her!"

"Mount up, we cain't do the poor woman no good. We'll fetch her body on the way back."

The men rode as fast as they could, only darkness found them in rolling hills country. It was just after dinner when Luke rode into camp, dismounted, and then walked to the small fire.   He said, "I see a campfire out in front of ya, about a mile. I think it's them."

Bill smiled sadly, looked at Isaac, and replied, "Good. You and Isaac check it out, and then come back and let me know what you find. From what we've seen, there are about ten of 'em and that's a lot fer three men to take on. But, I'll be damned iffen I'll let 'em have your ma!"

Isaac got to his feet and said, "Let's move now. We can look the place over, come back and talk 'bout how we want to do this."

The two men picked up their rifles, nodded to Bill, and disappeared into the darkness.

The walk was difficult because the moon hadn't risen yet, and Luke was surprised he tripped so often. During the day, the plains didn't seem to have many rocks, sticks or brush, but at night he found all of them. He finally decided they had been there all along, except on a horse he'd not paid much attention to them.

Nearing the Pawnee camp Luke went to the left and Isaac the right, so they could circle and count warriors. As he moved, he spotted Sue tied up beside the fire as the warriors ate and made small talk. He desperately wanted to call out to her, but knew it would mean his death and maybe hers— so he remained quiet. He continued to circle the camp and a little later met Isaac. The older man motioned for him to follow.

They didn't speak on the way back to camp, but once beside the fire, with Bill anxiously awaiting word, Isaac said, "I counted ten men, counting two guarding the horses. How 'bout ya?"

"Same count. I saw Sue, and she was tied up beside the fire."

"Well, relax some." Isaac said, gave a weak smile and continued, "She ain't been used, 'cause they ain't had the time to bother her and Nancy both. Nancy, in case ya two didn't know, was killed 'cause she couldn't keep up as they moved. Injuns on a raid let nothing hold them back, so they kilt her."

"Why'd they rape her, too?" Luke asked.

Shrugging his shoulders he replied, "Same reason a white man would have iffen he'd taken her captive, she was there. See, lot's of white folks think the red man is more savage than they are, but that jus' ain't true. A warrior raids to count coup and to move up in status within the tribe, not 'cause he's mean. A white man doesn't have that excuse. White men kill because they enjoy it or to get something that ain't theirs. Injuns have tribal rules they have to live by and most of the time they live by 'em, but they got their share of bad-asses, too."

Luke snorted and replied, "You make them Pawnee out to be good people!"

"Most likely they are, son, jus' different is all. They got friends and family that love 'em, they provide protection and food for the tribe, and, I know this will surprise ya, but many of 'em are gentle to their own kind. The thing most white folks don't understand is, when any Injun goes to war, it's all or nothin'. They are brutal warriors, mainly 'cause they're fightin' to protect their land or loved ones."

"I see those traits in Singing Bird, but I thought it was because she was a woman."

"Can you two have your Injun talk after we get Sue away from the Pawnee?"

Isaac gazed into his eyes and replied, "I wanted the boy to know we ain't killin' a bunch of animals, and those that die will be grieved by their mothers and wives."

"I don't care about the Pawnee, I want my wife back!"

"I understand that, so what we'll do is —"

➥⬅ ➥⬅ ➥⬅

It was well after midnight, and clouds moved low overheard as the three men neared the Pawnee camp. The campfire was nothing but red coals and all the warriors, except for the guards, were in their robes asleep.

Luke proceeded to the west side as Bill walked to the east. Isaac, the most experienced man of the three, moved toward the horses to silence the guards. Nearing the first brave, the man pulled his knife and prayed he'd make no noise. Throwing his left arm over the warrior's head, he quickly drew it toward his body, cutting off the man's air. His knife struck three times and then the brave's body went limp.

The second guard was a young boy, no older than twelve, and Isaac knew he couldn't kill him. Nearing the lad, he saw the boy was almost asleep, so he pulled his pistol and moved forward. When he was right behind the guard, Isaac struck him hard enough to knock him out, but not kill. The boy dropped as if struck by an ax handle. *Thank God, because I ain't got the hankerin' to kill no young pup, red, black, or white.*

A voice called out from the center of camp and knowing his Pawnee was not good enough to risk a reply, Isaac remained silent. A few minutes later, two warriors moved toward him. *Gotta let 'em get close, so Luke and Bill got time to get in position a-fore I start the dance,* he thought as he cocked his rifle.

Aiming, he waited, while the largest warrior never knew he was walking to his death.

Suddenly there was a loud cry from the middle of camp, followed by three shots, and Isaac squeezed his trigger. The warrior dropped screaming, while the second man ran right for him. Moving his barrel slightly, Isaac sighted in, took a deep breath, and gently squeezed the trigger of his repeating rifle. His target dropped without a sound.

Running into camp, Bill approached Sue as a warrior with a skinning knife in his right hand raised her head by her hair. *He's going to cut her throat!* Bill screamed in his mind and his Henry rifle came up, he squeezed the trigger, and saw the man go down. The Pawnee didn't remain down and was quickly on his feet as the white man ran toward him. Bill pointed his rifle at the warrior again, pulled the trigger, and saw his target fall once more, and this time he didn't get up.

Kneeling beside Sue, he pulled his knife and cut her bonds. Pulling the gag from her mouth he ordered, "Follow me, we ain't got much time!" Darkness swallowed them as they moved away from the camp.

Luke continued to fire his rifle, even after he'd seen ma and Bill escape, to cover them as they made for camp. He knew he'd hit three braves, but suspected they'd only been wounded, because he was firing too fast. His goal was to confuse the warriors and make them think a much larger group of white men was attacking. After about five minutes, he turned and ran for camp.

Isaac climbed on the back of a horse and moved the herd with him as he raced from camp. Knowing this herd might very well start Bill ranching again, he kept a close eye on the animals as he moved.

Traveling on horseback he was the first to return, and remained mounted as he waited. Soon Bill and Sue arrived, followed by Luke a few minutes later.

"I thought ya might want to go back into ranchin', so I brought ya a few hosses!" Isaac said as soon as Bill had caught his breath.

"Good idea, except we'd better get movin' or the Pawnee will be on our asses!"

Luke smiled and said, "Ain't but one or two that are in shape enough to foller us tonight. I put some lead out!"

Isaac gave a grim look and said, "Don't count on that, son. Odds are ya missed when ya thought ya hit. Ya can't count Injuns dead 'til ya see 'em with yer own eyes. Best fighters in the world, the red man is. And, yer right, Bill, we need to move."

# CHAPTER 23

**T**hey were half-way to the cabin when Luke pointed in front of them and said, "Good God, I hope them ain't Pawnee or we're dead."

Sue looked apprehensively at the approaching Indians, and her eyes grew large in fear.

Isaac gave a loud cackle and replied, "Them's Sioux, son. See the big curved lance the man on the left carries?"

Bill rode up beside Isaac and said, "Looks like Singing Bird found her pa."

"Yep, I'd say so."

"They're too late now. We have Sue back and horses to boot."

Isaac gazed into the young man's eyes and said, "Ya think so, huh? I'm willin' to bet ya old Brass Buttons wants to raid them boys now."

"Raid 'em, but why?"

"Teach 'em not to attack his family. See, when ya married up with Singing Bird, ya become part of his family, so he's got to avenge the attack."

Bill took his hat off, ran his fingers through his dirty hair and said, "Makes sense to me."

Isaac smiled at Luke and said, "You'll be expected to go 'long with 'em, too, since it was yer wife they tried to get. I don't think they'll ask Bill to go, since he done fetched Sue on his own."

Luke, tired, replied, "I'm beat, but I'll go given no choice."

"Good man, you'll stand taller in the eyes of Brass Buttons iffen ya ask to go along. He expects it, ya know."

"Hush, here they come," Bill warned just above a whisper.

Brass Buttons rode in front of twenty warriors, all wearing war paint, and when he stopped asked, *"Where is the other white woman?"*

*"She was killed by the Pawnee."*

*"That is not good. They must learn they cannot take women from the Sioux and kill them when they wish."*

*"Many Pawnee lodges will be filled with grief this night, father,"* Luke replied in his newly learned Sioux.

*"It is good the Pawnee have been taught a lesson, but they must learn to stay off of our lands. We will raid them, steal their horses and count many coups this night."*

Isaac asked, *"You have knowledge of where the Pawnee village is?"*

*"Our dog soldiers have found the village, and it is near."*

*"Your son and I wish to go along and do battle against the Pawnee."*

Looking at Luke, the young man nodded and the chief said, *"It is good my son is brave, but only we know he is. The Pawnee have had warriors die at the hands of my son, but they do not know him. No one lived after his battle the last time, and it is time they learn to fear Scalp Taker. You may both come."*

Singing Bird smiled.

Isaac turned to Bill and said, "Take Sue and Singing Bird home for now. Me and Luke are riding to the Pawnee village with these fellers."

"Ya two be careful at that village, those Pawnee are good fighters!" Bill said, and then turning to the two women he added, "Let's get back to the cabin."

"We'll be fine!" Isaac waved as the three broke away from the group and started home.

The day turned hot and not a cloud in the sky, as they rode north. Luke was tired, but knew he had to act as if all was well. A warrior didn't complain of hardship or the loss of a little sleep; his comfort was not important. What was important was making the Pawnee understand the Sioux would not tolerate attacks on their lands.

It was near dusk, when a scout appeared and rode to Brass Buttons, "The village is near. We can be there in less time than it would take to smoke a pipe."

The chief looked at his men and then said, *"Prepare for battle."*

Warriors checked weapons; some tied their horse's tails up, while others prayed. A few minutes later, Brass Buttons ordered, *"Lone Wolf and Dull Knife, take two hands of warriors each and go to the east and west sides of the village. I will take the remaining men and start the battle. Once we are fighting, bring your men to mine. We will catch them unprepared and many will die."*

The two sub-chiefs nodded and without a word spoken, they rode from the group.

Luke was scared, but tried not to look it, Hell, I was scared to death when I kilt them Injuns in the past too, but I did the job. The last thing I want to do is look the fool in front of Brass Buttons.

Isaac rode up beside the young man and said, "Jus' fight like ya normally do, and ya'll do fine. I always get a bit on edge jus' a-fore each fight, too."

Cocking his head to the side, Luke asked, "Ya do?"

"Why sure, any man with half a brain gets on edge."

"I thought it was jus' me." Luke replied, and then seeing the chief moving, he added, "Let's go; Brass Buttons has started the dance."

"I'll be right beside ya, son, or as close as I can be during the battle."

The countryside was rolling plains, with a few trees at times, and earlier hills had disappeared. Within a mile, Luke could see the lodges of the Pawnee and knew the fight was about to begin. Unlike on a horse-stealing raid, where stealth mattered, the Sioux rode right for the village. In the distance, he saw Pawnee warriors running and forming a defensive line facing the approaching Sioux.

*Lord, I ask you to protect me in the comin' fight. I know I ain't nothin' but a sinner in your eyes, but I'm a fair man and I believe in you with all my heart. Forgive me of my sins. I ask this in the name of Jesus, amen,* Luke prayed in his mind as rifle shots began to pop.

Suddenly, Brass Buttons gave a loud war cry and the warriors raced forward at a run. A warrior on Luke's left fell from his horse, but only after his head exploded, but no one slowed down or stopped. It was like a race, each man wanting to be the first to count coup on the Pawnee.

Luke's horse stumbled and fell, sending him to the ground hard. A Pawnee ran toward him and just as the warrior was about to spear him, he raised his pistol and fired one shot. The brave flew back hard and landed on his rear. Searching frantically, Luke spotted his dropped rifle, ran to it and as he picked it up, Brass Buttons fell wounded right beside him. Checking his gun first, he fired three rounds at the Pawnee, scampered to the downed chief and looked him over. He saw a bullet in the left side of the man's chest, but no other injuries.

The Sioux were starting to withdraw, but Luke stood and screamed, *"Brass Buttons is only wounded! Follow me to show the Pawnee the Sioux do not run from dogs!"*

The warriors turned and battle started again. The fight grew so loud it was hard to think, but all Luke did was aim, fire, and run forward. The two groups of warriors that Brass Button had sent in different directions suddenly struck hard.

The Pawnee began dropping to the ground injured and dying in large numbers, and then finally they broke and ran for their lodges. A few seconds, later women and children were running from the village to the safety of some nearby hills.

*"Let the women and children go! Do not follow them, because a true warrior only makes war on worthy enemies!"* Luke called out to the braves around him.

Isaac walked to the young man and asked, "Ya runnin' things now?"

"I . . . I guess I am. I had no idea I was givin' orders."

"Ya took over when yer Injun pa-in-law was hit, and that's good. Ole Brass Buttons will be smilin' like a small dawg passin' a big peach seed fer over a week! Ya did 'em proud, son!"

Dull knife neared and asked, *"The Pawnee are among the lodges, do we attack?"*

*"Attack once and then we will go home."* Luke spoke, raised his rifle and gave a loud war cry.

As he ran for the Pawnee, he saw Isaac go down followed by Dull Knife, but he led the warriors toward their enemy. A big Pawnee stepped forward, fired his rifle and a bullet clipped Luke's ear. A couple of seconds later, the young man struck the warrior running full speed. Both fell to the ground, where they rolled and rolled as the battle went on around them.

Finally, when they stopped rolling and the Pawnee was on top. Luke held the man's arm tightly to keep his knife away from him, only he expected his strength to fail at any moment. The brave was strong, much stronger than Luke was, so he knew he had to do something quickly or he was a dead man. Abruptly the Pawnee stiffened and fell to the right.

A young Sioux boy, named Toad, had stabbed the Pawnee in the back. Luke remembered that Toad was on his first raid and only recently had counted his first coup. Nodding his thanks, Luke called out, *"It grows late! Pick up our dead and wounded, it is time we return to our village!"*

The Sioux began an orderly withdraw, picking up wounded and dead men to return home. There were only four dead, but close to ten wounded. As they retreated, Isaac counted over fifty dead and seriously wounded Pawnee, and he knew most of the wounded would not last the night.

Those on foot mounted, all gave a piercing war cry and they turned their horses south, riding slowly away from the Pawnee village at a walk.

Brass Buttons was conscious and although his shoulder burned like fire, he rode beside Luke and said, *"My son, my eyes saw you in battle, and a fearless warrior led my braves into the fight. I am proud to call you my friend, but more proud to call you my son."*

*"It was nothing. I did what needed to be done."*

*"There were many men there, so why did only one man do what needed done? That man was you and no one else."*

*"Maybe, but I don't see it as a big thing."*

*"Waugh! You lead like a true chief, yet think like a young brave. Toad thinks clearer than you once away from the heat of battle."*

*"Toad saved my life today,"* Luke replied, and then told his story.

*"Then he must have a new name because of his bravery, and you must name him. Your life he saved and the giving of a gift is needed. According to our custom, you now owe him a life, and it can only be repaid by saving his life."*

*"I have thought of this and I wish to name him Bloody Knife, and I will give him a new rifle and two of my horses."*

*"This is good and will please him much. You must come to the village one hand and two fingers of suns from now for the name and gift giving."*

*"I will be there, father, only now you must rest. Do you wish a travois?"*

*"No, I will return to my people riding as a warrior. Pain I can take, a loss of respect I cannot."*

*"As you wish."* Luke spoke, and then tapped his horse gently in the ribs.

Riding beside Isaac, he asked, "You come out of the fight okay? I saw you go down durin' the battle."

Isaac gave a dry laugh and replied, "Tripped is what I did. Fell flat on my ass, but Dull Knife wasn't so lucky. He lost most of his head."

"That fight scared the livin' shit right outta me. Iffen Toad hadn't killed a Pawnee on top of me, I'd not be here right now. I come close to dyin'."

"Close don't count. Ya come out of it okay and that's all that matters. Ya'll need to give the boy some good gifts though."

"Brass Buttons and me talked on that a spell. I'll take care of the boy."

Scanning the countryside, Isaac said, "Well, this is where we break away from these Sioux and head fer the cabin."

Both men waved to the Sioux and made their way toward home.

At the cabin, they'd just tied their horses to the hitching post when Sue ran out screaming, "Bill has been having fits, and we can't get 'em to stop!"

The two men glanced at each other and then Luke said, "I don't know nothin' 'bout no fits."

"I know some, but there ain't much knowed 'bout 'em even by doctors, iffen what I hear'd was right."

"Hurry, come in the cabin and maybe you can help!"

Bill was on the floor jerking and twisting, and someone had placed a thick piece of rawhide between his teeth. His eyes had rolled back into his head and he slobbered as he moved, but there was no screaming from the man.

Isaac took one look and said, "Ain't a blessed thing we can do that ain't been done. Ya got the leather 'tween his teeth and that's 'bout all we can do fer 'em. We'll have to wait and see what happens."

Sue, so scared she was shaking asked, "Will he die?"

Isaac gave a quick glance at Luke and then replied, "I ain't got no idea."

Luke sat in a chair near the fire and asked, "What happened? I mean did somethin' bring the fit on? "

"He was workin' in the barn and fell from the loft. I was with 'em, but he didn't hit his head or nothin'," Sue replied.

Isaac thought for a minute and then said, "He must have hit hard and jarred his head. I ain't sure iffen that would bring a fit on, but I 'spect it could."

"His jerkin' is slowin' down a mite," Luke announced as he gazed into Isaac's eyes.

Bill twisted and turned a few minutes more, then stopped jerking. His chest moved with each breath, but it was not smooth breathing. Sweat covered his head and upper torso.

"Looks like the fits done stopped," Isaac said with a smile as he glanced at Sue. He held an unlit pipe in his left hand.

"It scares me, because one day he'll have a fit and never come out of it."

"Now, Sue, you don't know that. It's been a long time since he had one, so maybe he was due. I do think his fall caused this one, and he'll have to avoid falls or hits to his noggin in the future." Lighting his pipe, Isaac leaned back in his chair, inhaled and then slowly released the smoke.

Luke walked to Bill's side, removed the buffalo robe covering him, and said, "He's sweatin' somethin' fierce, so he don't need no coverin'."

Turning to Singing Bird, Luke said, "Brass Buttons took a bullet in his side, but it won't kill 'em. I'll tell you what; I almost got killed, but a youngster named Toad saved my life."

"Toad? Are you sure of this, husband? He is but a child."

"Sure enough I will give him two horses, a rifle, and a new name. He was fearless, and I was proud of 'em, with him bein' just a small boy, too."

"What name will you give to him?"

"I decided on Fast Eagle, except at first thought to name him Bloody Knife. He killed that warrior so fast; I didn't even know he was around. See, the Pawnee had me on the ground and I was gettin' weak. The warriors knife slowly grew closer to my chest, when suddenly he stiffened and when he fell I saw a skinnin' knife in his back. Little Toad was standin' there lookin' at the man—a grimace on his face."

"He is my cousin, and I know his bravery made my father very proud of him."

"Well, I like the little guy, and in 'bout a week we have to go the village for a big fandango. I'm to name him and give him his presents then."

"That is good," Singing Bird replied, and then went to help Sue prepare supper.

➡️⬅️  ➡️⬅️  ➡️⬅️

A week passed and Bill was long back to normal. He agreed that the fall must have caused the fit, so he promised to stay on ground level and try to avoid any hits to his head. But, later that night he didn't feel well and went to bed early. He felt feverish and his skin itched.

By morning, Sue and Singing Bird were with a fever, as the old mountain man sat by the fire with Luke at his side.

Luke asked, "Any idea what's got them sick like that?"

Lowering his head, Isaac replied, "I hope to God I'm wrong, except I think it's small pox and that's serious business. Bill has a horrible rash and his fever is high. We'll know in a few hours."

"Why's that?"

"Iffen Sue gets a rash, it's the pox almost fer sure."

"When will we know iffen it's small pox or not?"

"If they get pimply lookin' sores, it's the pox fer sure. Have you ever had it?"

"Nope, I ain't. I got an inoculation from a doctor when I was a kid to protect me, or so he claimed. All it did was scab up."

"I had it back 'bout twenty years ago, so me and ya are protected. That's why they're sick and we ain't. Didn't yer ma get treated by that doctor?"

"I don't rightly remember, only I don't think so. Mayhap it ain't the pox."

"I'm pretty sure it is. Could be some of them Pawnee we danced with had the disease, and we brought it home."

"Good God!"

"It ain't our fault, things like that happen. We couldn't know them Injuns had small pox, but I think some of 'em did."

It grew silent, with only the crackling of the fire heard, when Luke said, "The Sioux! They'll get it, too!"

"Yep, and it's likely they're already sick."

"Well, you stay here while I go help the Sioux. Do ya think Singing Bird is strong enough to ride?"

"Tie 'er to the saddle and ya should do okay and ya cain't hurt 'er no more than she already is, I guess. Ya jus' make sure ya give them Injuns a lot of water and broth to drink. The bad ones, the ones that will die on ya, will start passin' blood from all the holes in their bodies."

"Sounds like a nasty way to die."

"Son, I wouldn't wish a death by small pox of my worst enemy. It's a bad way to go and no man, black, yeller, red or white, should die from it."

→←  →←  →←

Less than an hour later, Luke was heading toward the Sioux with Singing Bird tied to her horse. He wanted to take her home, so she could be with her family, and hoped he was making the right decision. While she didn't have a rash yet, if it was the pox it would come next, and he hoped he was at the village by then.

While there wasn't a cloud in the sky, a light wind blew from the west, and the morning was cool. Singing Bird sat on her horse with a river of sweat rolling down her face.

*Please, Lord, don't take her from me. She's a good woman and I need her.*

# CHAPTER 24

**T**he village was quiet when Luke neared and even the dog soldiers did not challenge him, which made him think most were ill. He'd never been to the village before and not approached by a member of the dog soldier clan. Riding close enough to see the lodges, he noticed no one was moving around outside, and in a village this size there was always work to do. *Damn! They've come down with the illness!*

Pulling up in front of the lodge of Brass Buttons, he scratched on the hide covering the entrance and heard a weak reply. Untying Singing Bird, he packed her into the semi-darkened lodge. Placing her on a robe near the door, he added wood to the fire, sat on the ground and then looked around.

*"You have come, my son."* Brass Buttons said with a weak voice.

*"Yes, everyone at the cabin has sickness. I see the Sioux have it, too."*

*"Only one handful are not ill. I have had the illness before, so I will not get the red dots on my body. I am in my robes because of my injury, not the fever. I cannot help care for our sick."*

*"Have any of our people died?"*

Sitting up, the chief replied, *"Yes, we have lost two hands of people. Toad was one of those who passed over to the other side. He died bravely."*

Luke shook his head in sadness, but didn't reply, just nodded to show he'd heard the man's words.

Minutes passed and then Luke said, *"I must check the people and see who is sick, so I can take care of them."*

*"Antelope is doing this as we speak. It would be better if you cooked a large soup and then the two of you can feed the weak ones. I know cooking is a woman's work, but it must be done."*

*"It will be done."* Luke stood, went outside and walked to a huge cast-iron kettle. Making a fire, he discovered a fresh deer kill hanging from a nearby tree limb. Removing a rear quarter, he dropped the whole thing in the pot and filled it with water. As it boiled, he wondered how many Sioux would still be alive a week from now.

Overnight ten Sioux died, mostly the old and young, but the disease had not run its course yet, and Luke knew many more would die before the week's end. Singing Bird now had red spots on her body and if he'd not known better, he would have thought it was inflamed pimples. Her fever was high and while he wanted to stay by her side, he had a whole village to care for.

People were so ill the sounds of crying and wailing that occurred in a village when someone died were gone. Many were unable to lift their heads, while others passed blood from every hole in their bodies, as they moaned with high fevers. When Luke discovered a person in a puddle of blood, he knew death was near.

Finally, near exhaustion, he went to the lodge to sleep for a couple of hours. Brass Buttons said something to him when he entered, but he was too tired to respond. He awoke hours later, with his eyes burning and his back sore, so the sleep had done little good. He stood, stretched and went out to make water.

When he returned, the chief said, *"Please, look at my wife. I think she has crossed to the other side. When you came to sleep, you were too tired to hear my words."*

Luke knew the minute he saw her face she was dead. She was lying in a puddle of blood and her features had frozen in horror. He covered her head with the robe, checked on Singing Bird and then said, *"Your wife has left for the other side. Your daughter is doing better and I think she will live, as will as you."*

*"Why do some die and some live?"*

Shrugging his shoulders, Luke replied, *"I have no answer. I know we caught the sickness from the Pawnee, but I know little about it."*

*"We will have to start over again as a people. Many women and warriors are gone."*

Lowering his eyes, the young white man said, *"I spoke with Horse Running outside while making water and he told me over half of the village is no more."*

In a voice almost in a whisper, Brass Buttons asked, *"Oh, Great Creator, why did you allow this thing to happen to my people?"*

*"I must go and cook for those who will live. I will bring you a bowl of broth as soon as I can."*

*"Scalp Taker, it is not for a man to cook among the Sioux, but someone must do it.  I hope having you cook has not brought you dishonor."*

*"All of the women are too sick to cook. When one is strong enough, I will let her do the cooking."*

*"That is good."*

Luke turned and walked from the lodge.

➡️⬅️   ➡️⬅️   ➡️⬅️

Weeks later Singing Bird was up and moving around. The only sign of her battle with small pox was a few small scars on her cheeks, but she was not as strong as before the illness. Brass Buttons was sitting up and sipping broth when Luke entered.

Sitting beside the old man, Luke said, *"I must return to the cabin and see if my white friends still live. I worry about my mother after seeing so many die here."*

*"I understand and your fear is shared by me. In the history of The People, never have so many passed over so quickly. Go, my son, and see your white family."*

*"I fear what I may find when I return."*

*"Fear is normal for a man. It is facing fear that makes a man a warrior. We both know the fear of this illness is not like a battle, where you can kill what you fear. We cannot harm this sickness and yet it kills many of us. Only a fool would not fear something he cannot see, kill, or stop. Go and let the Great Spirit ride with you."*

Luke and Singing Bird left the village at dawn the next day, with stillness in the air that added a solemnness to their departure. Deep concern showed on the leathery face of Brass Buttons. The old man, aged greatly by the number of deaths suffered by his village, stood by his lodge and waved until the two were well out of sight. No one saw the tears on his coriaceous cheeks.

The ride back was fast, due to excellent weather and clear trails, so they rode to the cabin door a little after mid-day. Bill, who'd been splitting wood, sank his ax blade deeply in his chopping block and made his way to their horses.

Smiling, Bill said, "Dismount and then go in and see your baby sister!"

"The baby came while ya was gone, and they're both doin' fine!" Isaac said as he neared. He'd been caring for the horses when the two rode in.

"The baby has come?" Singing Bird asked in surprise.

"I just said so, didn't I?" Bill replied with a laugh.

Slipping gracefully from the back of her horse, Singing Bird ran wildly into the house, leaving Luke laughing with the two men.

"How'd the Sioux come out with the sickness?" Bill asked as his smile faded.

Shaking his head, Luke replied, "About six out of ten died, so the tribe ain't got so many folks anymore."

Isaac moved forward and said, "It's a hard death, small pox is. Only I suspect you know that by now, huh?"

"Yea, I do. I saw lots of folks die and all of 'em were bleeding something terrible, only there wasn't a thing I could do to help 'em."

"Now all them numbers ya read in the past in newspapers about people dying from sickness has meanin', don't they?"

"Sure they do, but now I wonder how the Pawnee came in contact with small pox."

Isaac glanced at Bill and then replied, "Deacon came through heah, oh, 'bout a week past and he claims the army gave the Pawnee infected blankets."

Luke's eyes grew large as he asked, "Our army wouldn't do that, would they?"

"Why not?" Bill said and then added, "They've done it before."

"No! You mean we've given infected blankets to others in the past? I didn't think our government would do such a thing."

Moving to the porch, Isaac sat and then said, "Every time we get ready to take over some land owned by Injuns, we give 'em infected blankets first. Why, I'll bet ya in a month they'll be settlers movin' all over Montana. See, the sickness will thin the Injuns out so much they'll not be able to fight the movers, and in a short time thousands of whites will have homes built. Once the whites are in place, they'll fight to keep what they consider to be theirs."

"But, that ain't the way a government should do things."

"I ain't no government man, so I can't say iffen it's right or wrong, only it ain't the Christian thing to do." Bill said, and then sat beside Isaac where he continued, "We did the same thing in Missouri, Nebraska and now Montana. Makes it easier for us to take over their land, don't ya know."

"But, it's wrong to kill using small pox!"

Isaac pushed his hat back on his head and replied, "Son, the army knows it's faster and safer to use infected blankets to kill the red man. Iffen the blankets weren't used, a lot of good white men would die in battle."

"It's murder!" Luke screamed.

"Aye, it is that, son, but simmer down a mite. It's been done now and there ain't nothin' we can do, but watch the settlers arrive. You can't take on the Federal government when most of the country would go along with the use of the blankets. Most American's don't even consider Injuns human, so they don't care what happens to 'em."

Lowering his head, Luke said, "I didn't care either, a year ago, but I surely do now. I learned a lot durin' my stay with the Sioux."

Isaac gave a tired smile and replied, "Glad to hear that, son. It's music to my ears and means yer finally becomin' a real man. Any man can learn to kill, just like a wild animal, but compassion is what makes us different from critters."

"I guess that's what Moses was tryin' to tell that Army Captain that got killed a while back, compassion and common sense," Bill said and then stood.

Luke moved toward the house and stepping on the first step he said, "Well, I can't change the world, but I can go see my baby sister."

With that said, he gave a light chuckle and entered the cabin.

As soon as the young man left, Isaac gave a big smile, looked Bill in the eyes and said, "I think Luke is finally all growed up. He left us a boy and returned a man. His thinkin' is good and he has a right to be mad about the killin', but the important thing is, he knows there ain't a damned thing he can do to stop it."

"Yep, I remember feeling that way in the war a couple of times. I thought our government would never do some of the things it did, but we have to remember the government is made of people, too. Some of 'em are good and some ain't, just like the rest of us."

"I hear ya and it takes a man to understand life ain't always fair and the good guy don't always come out on top. I've found just the opposite is more than likely to happen."

"Nope, life ain't always been easy or fair to me, but that's what makes it interestin'."

"Moses used to say, 'My life ain't never been easy, so why should I expect it to be now?' And, ya know, I agree with the man."

"Enough talk about life, let's go in and have some coffee." Bill said and then stood.

"Yep, better minds than ours have wondered about the meanin' of life, and I'll bet ya they didn't come up with no answer either!"

Both men laughed as they made their way inside.

→← →← →←

A little over a year later, as Luke was repairing some storm damaged shingles on the barn, two strangers rode to the hitching post, dismounted and looking up at him asked, "Who owns this place?"

"Me and a man named Sanders, why?"

"We'd like to talk business with ya, iffen ya got some time."

Pulling his work gloves off, Luke climbed down from the roof, dusted his pants off and replied, "Business?"

"Yep, I'm Horace Brown and this feller beside me is John Dents."

Brown was a short portly man, near three hundred pounds, while Dents was as skinny as a rail split three ways and tall, well over six feet. Neither had much hair, but Dents did sport a pencil-thin mustache. Luke guessed their ages as on the high side of forty. While wearing cowboy clothes, they didn't look comfortable in them, which meant they weren't what they appeared to be.

Bill walked from the barn, gave a smile and asked, "Now, what was this talk I heard about business? I'm Bill Sanders and you can call me Bill."

"I'll come right to the point, Bill." Brown said and then added, "I've done my lookin' and I know you don't hold a deed to this land, but I'm still willing to pay you a dollar an acre for it."

Bill looked as if Brown had just slapped him, but managed to say, "It's not for sale."

"Okay, two dollars an acre is my final offer."

"I said, it's not for sale, not for two dollars an acre or at any price!"

Brown chuckled and then said, "Come my good man, all things in life have a price. I want this place and I'll get it, one way or the other."

Pulling the pistol he always carried in his belt, Luke said abrasively, "You heard my partner, it's not for sale. Now, get on your horse and ride." The sound of the hammer locking back was loud.

Bent, who'd been quiet up to now said, "I think he means business, Colonel."

Brown, growing red in the face replied, "I'm leaving, but I'll be back and when I do, you'll not like my visit."

Bill stepped toward the man as he asked, "Is that a threat, Mister Brown?"

Brown placed his foot in his stirrup, threw his right leg over the horse, then as he got comfortable in the saddle said, "Oh, no, I never threaten, but I often promise."

Luke's eyes grew narrow as he said, "I ever see ya on our land again, and I'll shoot to kill on sight! Do you both understand that?"

Dent's eyes grew large and he said, "I . . . I fully understand, sir, and I'll not be back." Brown just chuckled, pulled his horse around, and rode from the ranch.

Isaac stepped from the barn, gave a sly grin and said, "I had ya both covered from inside. But, what did the man mean when he said ya don't hold no deed?"

"I got one, but I guess it ain't showing up in the record books yet. I think me and Luke might just visit Butterfield's place and see what the hold up is."

"Who signed yer deed?"

"Butterfield did, and he's the land agent for the government. It's legal as can be, but I don't think John keeps his books straight or up to date."

"Then don't waste yer time goin' to see the man. I suspect he'll add yer land when he gets the time. As long as ya hold the deed, ain't nobody that can take this place from ya."

"Luke, for the next few weeks, let's keep a guard posted around here. I get the feeling our man Brown is a bully, only I'd not be surprised if some of his men show up some dark night."

Isaac scratched his chin and then said, "I think that would be smart. He was dressed like a cowboy, but he ain't done no cow punchin' is my guess. I think he's a feller with money and used to havin' his way. That jasper Bent called him Colonel, didn't he?"

"Colonel or not, by God, he'll not get what he wants this time, because we'll fight to keep this place." Luke said and then asked, "Bill, what makes you think Brown has men ridin' for 'em?"

"The rich never get their own hands dirty, since they hire others to work for them. If he was a Colonel during the late war, he'll be used to having men jump to his orders. I suspect he's got a dozen no accounts that rough folks up and do his nasty jobs. Hell, all of 'em together wouldn't add up to one pissed off Oto warrior."

Isaac gave a low chuckle and said, "Let's pray you're right Bill, or there will be hell to pay around here."

⇥⇤ ⇥⇤ ⇥⇤

The weeks passed, with no sign of Brown or anyone else around the ranch. Isaac had taken to scouting each morning just after dawn and while he'd spotted a few unshod ponies, he'd seen no sign of white men. The men had continued to work the ranch as usual, but now Luke wasn't the only one wearing a pistol belt around his waist.

Over breakfast, Sue asked, "There ain't much this Brown can do except try to run us off, right? I mean, he ain't got a legal stand has he?"

"No, I own the land and have the papers to prove it and besides, a bunch of papers mean little to a man like him. If he was a real Colonel during the war, he's used having a lot of power and respect, so if he has some money, well, he'll be a handful."

"I don't understand what you mean."

"People say money corrupts, and maybe it does, but power does, too. If he's been powerful the last few years, he's grown used to giving orders and having people obey, so he might think it'll work with us."

Sue laughed, put the baby to her breast and then said, "He's goin' to learn a thing or two iffen he comes around here lookin' for trouble."

Raising his coffee cup, Bill hesitated to take a drink until he said, "He'll find he's bit off more than he can chew." Finishing his coffee, he stood, bent over and kissed Sue on the cheek.

"Now, what was that for?"

"Nothin'. I love you is all. I'll be out plowin' iffen you need me." Putting on his old Confederate gray hat, he stepped from the house.

"Bill," Isaac said, "I was just comin' to get ya. We got a passel of trouble comin' and it'll be here directly. I spotted ten mounted white men movin' toward us nigh on two hours ago."

"Is the army comin' or some of Browns toughs?"

"I honestly ain't got any idea, but we'd better get ready for trouble."

"Where's Luke?"

"In the barn loft, where he claims he can keep an eye on things."

"Tell 'em I don't want no shootin', unless I start the dance or go down with a bullet in me. I hope it's some honest men, but you're right, we need to prepare for a fight."

"I never take any man's threats lightly."

"Neither do I."

Less than an hour later, ten white men rode into the barnyard and remained mounted. Bill, knowing they were waiting for him, finished his coffee and made his way outside. He wore his pistol and carried a sawed-off double-barreled shotgun.

When he stepped from the porch a thin man with red hair and filthy clothes asked, "Ya Sanders?"

"Maybe, then again, maybe not."

"I'm lookin' for a dirt farmer named Sanders."

Bill gave an ill-felt grin and replied, "You found 'em, so speak your piece and leave."

"I'm Jesse Harlow and I work for Mister Brown."

Bill just glared at the man.

Harlow asked, "Didn't ya hear me?"

"I heard ya just fine."

"Then why didn't ya answer me?"

"You didn't ask me a question. What did you expect me to do at the mention of Brown's name, quiver? I fear no man."

"By God, ya'll learn to fear this one!" a man beside Harlow shouted and when he started to pull his rifle barrel up, a shot rang out and the man flew from his horse. He hit the ground hard and lay unmoving.

"Wilson, see to Hinds," Harlow ordered.

"I wouldn't do that if I were you, Hinds. If you move, I might just get the notion you want to kill me and pull the triggers on this old Greener. I do that and most your saddles will empty mighty sudden like."

Harlow raised his hands and Hinds relaxed in his saddle.

"So, ya got a couple of men with ya, huh?"

"Enough. I don't think it takes much to fight the likes of you and this worthless bunch."

# CHAPTER 25

$H$arlow was angered, but ignored it, and asked, "When ya leavin' this place?"

Bill gave a light laugh and replied, "I ain't, but you and these men of yours are in a few minutes."

"Look, Sanders, we're both Southerners, so why don't I give ya some advice. Pack up and leave now. If ya don't, Brown will have all of ya killed. He wants this place, and he'll end up with it in the end."

"Oh, I disagree with you there, Harlow, because like most Southern men, I'm hardheaded and not about to leave my home. If your boss wants a fight, he's found one. But, tell 'em he'll need tougher men than you and your bunch to run me off."

Livid, Harlow pulled his horse around and as he rode away, he called out, "We'll be back, but the next time there ain't gonna be no more talkin'."

The dead man lay where he'd fallen, but they'd taken his horse.

When the dust cleared, Isaac asked, "What about the body?"

"Drag it out on the plains a few miles and leave it."

Luke, surprised by Bills coldness asked, "Do you think that's the Christian thing to do?"

"Yep, I do, son. See, critters on the plains need to eat too, right? I just hope eatin' pole cat don't make 'em sick."

Reaching for the rope on his saddle, Isaac said, "And a slow pole cat to boot."

Sue, who'd watched the confrontation from a window, ran into the barnyard and asked, "Will they be back?"

"More than likely they will, why?" Bill replied.

"We don't need trouble, Bill."

Walking to Sue's side, he placed his hand on her shoulder and asked, "Do you really want him to have our ranch, after all we've done to stay here?"

"Of course not, but there must be some way to talk with the man."

"I tried talk, but it didn't work. Sue, there are times in a man's life when fighting for what is his is the only choice. I did that during the war, I did that to make a ranch here, and I'll do it again if I have to, just to keep my home."

Turning, she moved into his arms and said, "I'm scared I'll lose you. I don't want to be alone again now that I've found you."

"Everything will turn out fine, you wait and see."

"Could the Sioux help us?" She suddenly asked.

"No, I'll not even ask Brass Buttons, and for two reasons. He's having a hard enough time keeping what land he's got left and second, the army would go after him if he so much as pointed a finger at a white man. Besides, they were almost destroyed by small pox, and he ain't got but a handful of warriors."

"What can we do?"

"Stay close to the ranch, keep our guns close at hand, and kill every one of the sons-of-bitches that come near. I'm not an easy man to anger, but I am now, and Mister Brown will soon discover he's messin' with the wrong man."

Later that night, as they lay sleeping, Sue awoke to the smell of smoke. Getting out of bed, she saw nothing, but the smell grew stronger. She made her way to the front door and when she opened it, she saw the barn was aflame.

"Bill! Bill! The barn is burning!" She screamed and a few minutes later Bill, along with his shotgun passed her in a dead run, heading for the barn.

Bill threw the main barn door open, allowing a couple of colts and a milk cow to run out, then he entered, only to come back out a few seconds later. Coughing, he fell to his knees and said something Sue could not hear.

Running to his side, she asked, "What's wrong?"

"The smoke is too thick and I can't reach the back of the barn!"

"It's okay, there's nothing there but some tools and such."

Looking up and into her eyes, he said, "You don't understand, Isaac was sleeping there!"

"Oh my God, no!"

Standing, Bill looked around and just above a whisper he said, "Maybe he got out! Maybe he's safe!"

Luke and Singing Bird ran into the barnyard, spotted the couple and ran to them.

"What happened?"

"Your ma smelled smoke, I guess, and woke me. Luke, Isaac was supposed to be sleeping in there! I tried to get in, but the flames were too high and the smoke too thick!"

"Bill, he's not in the barn, he went out tonight to keep watch."

"Why didn't he warn us then?"

"I don't know, but it's not going to be good news when we find 'em. He's either hurt bad or killed, would be my guess."

The barn gave a great shudder, like a living thing, and then the roof collapsed into the flames. The heat was intense, so the four moved back toward the cabin, where Bill sat in the dirt and watched his hard work burn to the ground. His anger was mounting, because he suspected Brown was behind the burning, but he had no proof.

"Was Brown behind this?" Luke asked, as if he was reading his mind.

"I don't honestly know. I suspect he is, but I can't point a finger without some kind of proof."

"Well, we'll look around after this fire dies down a mite. Right now it's too hot to even get near the place."

"We've got time."

At that point, Isaac stumbled into the barnyard, fell on his knees in the dirt and then toppled face-first to the hard packed soil. The back of his shirt was soaked with blood and as Bill moved for him, he suspected most of it belonged to Isaac.

Looking the man over, he turned to Sue and ordered, "Get me some water boiling and pull my medical stuff from under the bed. He's taken a knife in his back and it don't look good."

Luke said, "Had to be an Injun, ain't no white man that can sneak up that close to Isaac."

"Don't matter who it was, we got to get the bleeding stopped or he'll die on us. Take his feet and let's move him into the house. Lay him beside the fireplace where I can work on 'em."

The two men moved Isaac and the only sound the injured man made was a slight moan when they picked him up. Bill was worried, because he suspected the black man was dying, and he was their last link to real survival. He was also a good friend and they were hard to come by in Montana and even harder to keep alive, or so it seemed.

They placed Isaac beside the fire and Bill cut his shirt off to check the injury. *Yep, knife is what did the damage, hunting knife most likely. Close to his kidneys, too, so I can't do much except cauterize the injury and hope he lives.*

"Luke, place your knife blade in the fire and let it heat up. Ain't nothin' we can do but close the cut and hope he gets better."

"Think it'll work?" The young man asked as he pulled his knife and placed the blade in the flickering flames.

"I can't say, not really, but I don't know enough to doctor his guts. All we can do is seal the wound and pray he heals."

As his knife heated, Luke said, "Brown is behind this, and we both know it."

"Maybe, only I ain't sure. Many different things can cause a barn to burn, including hay that's been put up too green. We'll take a look at first light and see what we can find. Don't jump the gun on this; iffen it was Brown, I'll pay the man a visit."

"If Isaac dies, the man will be dead before you get to see 'em—because I'll kill him."

Shaking his head, Bill said, "That would be foolish, until we know what happened. Hell, for all we know, the Oto might have ambushed Isaac, so wait until he comes around."

"Oh, I'll wait that long, but not a minute later. If he names Brown or Harlow, one or both of them will be dead pretty damned quick."

"Hand me the knife, the blade's red," Bill ordered.

➻ ➻ ➻

The night passed slowly, with Luke sitting in a rocking chair beside Isaac, sipping on whiskey. Near dawn, Bill walked into the room and said, "You need sleep more than whiskey, but it ain't none of my business what you do."

"I can't sleep until I know what'll happen with Isaac. He's a good man, and I hate the thought someone ambushed 'em."

Pouring a cup of coffee, Bill replied, "Hell, it might be days before we know if he'll make it or not, so get some rest." He then moved to the sofa.

Luke grunted and threw back his drink.

Sitting, Bill continued, "He's an old mountain man and knew the risk when he went out to stand guard, but it was his turn. Now, I know we owe him a lot, more than we can ever repay, but this is rough land we've come to and he knew it."

Lowering his head, Luke replied, "He knew the risk better than any of us. I can't for the life of me, figure out who got close enough to knife 'em."

"Son, lots of men out here are good and not just Injuns. When I was in the army, why, we had one ole boy that could take a sentry out in no time and not a sound heard. He moved like a big cat. I figure a man like that knifed Isaac."

Luke took a sip of his whiskey, gazed into Bill's eyes and said, "Had to be a quiet man. I guess you're right about the sleep, but I'll wait until we check the barn before I go to bed."

"Sleepy now, are you?"

"No, not really, only my eyes are dry and tired."

"Well, as soon as I finish my coffee, we have a barn to look over. I suspect the barn was a warning and the next time it will be the house."

"I do, too. I did some serious thinkin' on that while everyone was asleep. If it had been the house, I don't think both of you would have gotten out."

Finishing his coffee, Bill stood and said, "That's hard to say, son, but I hate to even think about it. Come; let's take a look at what remains of the barn."

The air was cool, but not cold, as the two men moved around the blackened skeleton of what was once the barn. Smoke still lingered in a few spots, but the fire was long dead.

Shaking his head, Bill ordered, "Ya check the other side, while I look this side over."

Luke moved to the other side and suddenly yelled out, "I see some clay jugs in the trees, want me to check 'em out?"

"Check out everything!"

A few minutes later, the young man shouted, "I smell kerosene in these jugs!"

"I'll be right over there!"

As Bill neared, Luke held one of the jugs out to the man, "Take a whiff of this and tell me what you smell."

Bill raised the jug, sniffed and replied, "Yup, it's kerosene for sure. Okay, so we now know how the fire was started, but we don't know who did the job."

"By damn, Bill, I can't believe you'er so dumb you don't suspect Brown right off!"

Grinning at the young man's anger, Bill replied, "Oh, I suspect him, but that's all. We have no real proof he did a thing wrong. All we have are some empty kerosene jugs, a destroyed barn, and that's about it."

"You know it was him!"

"We just had this conversation, and I'll not argue the point with ya. When I go after Brown, the man will die and I don't take killin' lightly, son, neither should you. That's why I want to be sure before I face him."

Luke wanted to call Bill a coward, but deep inside he knew better. The man had been in countless battles, fought Injuns, and made a home where others had not dared to even come. *No, he's no coward, only why the hesitation?*

The young man glanced down at his feet and then said, "Well, Isaac will know who did the job."

"Mayhap he will and I hope he does, but he might not know, either. It was as dark as a whore's heart, he was tired, and there's a good chance he didn't see who attacked him."

"You reckon?"

"Yup, sadly, I do. Keep in mind, Luke, killin' is serious business and I'll kill no man without solid proof he's grievously wronged me. If you kill every man you suspect of wrongin' you, why eventually you'll kill the wrong feller. Then you'll either stretch some hemp or have to live with it the rest of your life, and I have enough demons."

Lowering his head, Luke replied, "I understand, Bill, but it makes me mad."

"Of course it does and it should. We put a lot of work into this barn and now it's gone, except killin' a man won't bring it back. Now, let's go inside and see if Isaac is doin' any better."

The cabin was hot after being out in the cool air, but Isaac was awake and talking with Sue as she feed him broth.

"Bill, Isaac said it was one of Brown's men who knifed him and he saw the man clearly—it was Harlow. What scares me is that Isaac didn't hear a sound as the man approached."

"Harlow must be a seasoned outdoorsman if he did the job."

"I ain't got no idea about all that, but he overheard the man say they had to hurry, burn the barn and get back to Bannack."

"That's a town to the west of us, Bill," Luke said with an eager voice.

"I know where it is and it's been there almost thirty years, iffen I remember right." Bill replied, kneeled and asked Isaac, "Is what Sue told me true?"

Tired from his talk with Sue, Isaac nodded.

Luke asked, "What now? We have a name and a town."

"Gather your gear; we'll leave within the hour for Bannack." Luke ran from the small cabin.

Sue gazed into his eyes and asked, "Do you have to go?"

"I have no choice now. If the word ever gets out I knew Brown burned my barn and didn't face 'em, why, we'd not be able to live out here. Folks talk, and you know that."

Growing sober, Sue replied, "Be careful, Bill, he'll have men around."

"I don't intend to face Brown in the open where his men will have a chance to bushwhack me."

"Oh?"

"Nope, me and him will have a Private chat and get to the bottom of all of this."

"What of Harlow?"

With a serious look in his eyes, Bill replied, "Him, I'll have to face in public. I want people to know they can't come around and stick a blade in anybody they find here. I'll make sure before the fight that people know my reason for starting it. Then I'll kill him."

"Can't ya go to the law in town?"

"Not from what I've heard. They had a jasper by the name of Plummer doing the law, about ten years or so back, and he was as crooked as a snake. The town ended up hangin' the man."

"Maybe the law there now is honest."

"Maybe he's honest and then again, maybe not. I'll have to wait and see."

"I got my gear!" Luke yelled out as he entered the cabin.

"Sue, this is something I have to do. I suspect we'll be gone near on ten days or so."

"May God protect you and Luke."

Pulling her into his arms, he kissed her passionately and replied, "I'll be back, baby, it may be earlier or a few days later, but I'll be back. I love you."

As Bill broke from her and began to gather his supplies, Sue said just above a whisper, "I love you too, William Sanders."

➽⬅  ➽⬅  ➽⬅

The day turned warm as the two men moved west at a walk, but gray clouds were gathering on the western horizon, which might mean rain later in the day. Buffalo grasses covered the plains and small herds of buffalo were moving in different directions.

Moving to beside Luke, Bill said, "Keep your eyes out for Sioux, Pawnee, or Oto."

Luke gave a light laugh and replied, "Oh, I'm doin' just that. Iffen I ain't learned nothin' else out here it's to keep my eyes open."

"Remember, the Sioux we see won't be part of Brass Buttons village and may not know us. None-the-less, you speak the language, so that'll be a help."

"I hope we don't see a single Injun the whole trip. Every time I run into 'em they almost kill me."

Bill chuckled and replied, "Yea, you're right about that."

The morning and afternoon passed quietly, only with the coming of dusk rain began to fall in gentle drops. Both men donned rubber ponchos and continued to ride until full dark.

An hour later, Bill said, "Let's move off to the right and find a place for the night. I'll get a shelter up and fire started, while you gather wood and water."

Luke, tired and wet, simply moved to the right.

There were no trees near them, but small brush lined a narrow creek near the campsite, so Luke gathered as much dead wood as he could. He knew the buffalo chips were too wet to burn and left them alone.

Dinner was cold deer meat and coffee, along with a slab of cornbread brought from home. While meager, compared to most meals they had at the ranch, it filled them. Little talking took place as they ate.

The meal finished, Bill asked, "Why so quiet?"

Luke gave a dry laugh and said, "I was up all night, rode in this rain today and jus' don't feel like talkin' much. Too tired, I guess."

Smiling, Bill replied, "I figured as much. You go to bed and I'll keep watch most of the night. I will wake you a few hours before dawn and then I'll get a little sleep. I don't need much, maybe three hours and I'll be as good as new."

Standing, Luke picked up his buffalo robe, blanket and rifle, and then moved under the shelter. A few minutes later, he was asleep.

Morning came with dark skies and rain still falling; only it was a fine mist. After making a pot of coffee and slicing some bacon into a large cast-iron pan, Luke woke Bill. The older man moved to the edge of camp, made water and returned looking red-eyed.

He kneeled by the fire, glanced at Luke and said, "We'll ride long and hard today. Iffen we put a lot of miles behind us, we'll be in Bannack tomorrow evening, maybe. You feelin' better now you've had some sleep?"

"Yup, a lot better. I was just beat yesterday and should have known better than to stay up all night sipping on whiskey."

Luke laughed and replied, "We had no idea we'd be goin' after Brown so quickly. Brown don't worry me much, but Harlow does. He's sure to be a scrapper and he's woods savvy, so that makes him dangerous in my mind."

"Well, iffen you don't kill the man, I damned sure will. He's a mean jasper and he needs killin' as far as I'm concerned."

"Aye, he does need killin', but iffen you brace the man, don't worry about no fast draw. Take your time and hit 'em in the center of the chest with your first shot. Fast don't win fights, but where ya place your bullet damned sure does."

# CHAPTER 26

**B**annack was a rough looking place in the middle of nowhere, and Bill didn't like the look of the place right off. Most of the buildings wore bare unpainted pine boards on the sides or made of logs. He'd heard the town was established after gold was found nearby, so he suspected it was put together in just a few days—and it looked it.

"Where to now we're here?" Luke asked from beside him.

"We find a hotel for a few days."

"We got money for that?"

Bill laughed and said, "I still have over five hundred dollars that Butterfield didn't want back, remember?"

Pointing, Luke said, "Looks like a hotel over there."

"It's the Meade and it looks pretty fancy for this town. It'll probably cost us a pretty penny to stay in a place like that, but we could both use a good night's sleep. Let's give it a try, at least for one night."

Tying their horses to the hitching post, they walked up the stairs and into the building, both noticing the winding staircase to their right as they entered.

As they neared the front desk, a small man with little hair asked, "How may I help you two gentlemen?"

Bill asked bluntly, "How much are your rooms?"

"Fifty cents a night, but I can remember a few years back when it would have cost ya two dollars for the same room."

"Is that for the two of us?

"Yup, we've fallen on rough times since the mining died."

"I'd guess so, hell, there ain't nothin' here that I could see that would bring folks out this way."

With questioning eyes, the clerk said, "You're here."

"I'm here on business. I'm to see a man about a horse."

Lowering his head and pulling out two keys, the clerk replied, "I see. Well, let me warn you, we have a vigilante group in town and they don't care much for trouble. So, I hope your conversation with the man is peaceful."

Bill laughed and said, "I don't see how buying a horse will get me in trouble." He then placed his money on the counter and added, "Have a bottle of good rye sent to our room in a few minutes, along with a tub. We both need a good cleanin', sip of whiskey, and a hot meal."

As he made change, the clerk replied, "If you want a good hot meal, try the Blue Bird Restaurant, but if you just want to snack and have a few drinks try Skinner's Saloon. Skinner's not there anymore, the vigilante's hanged him a few years back, but it still goes by that name. Skinner's has ham, pickled eggs, pig's feet and cheese for paying customers. There's more stuff, but I don't go in the place very often, I'm a married man." Handing the change and keys to Bill, the clerk gave a fake smile.

As the two walked up the stairs and down a long hallway, Luke said, "Ugly paint in this place. Who in the world would paint the walls a dirty bird shit yellow?"

"It might have been the only color of paint available in town. As I saw riding in, there ain't many buildin's painted, so I don't suspect the general store keeps much of it in stock. Besides, when did you start to bein' picky about the color of a wall?"

"I got picky when you paid the man at the counter. I'd figure a place like this would be painted up nice, instead it looks like dirty bird crap."

Stopping in front of their room, Bill unlocked the door, entered and said, "Furnishings are old, but look to be in good condition."

He walked to the bed and sitting down he added, "Mattress is still firm too, so we got lucky on this trip."

"This is the first hotel I've ever been in, so I wasn't sure what to expect."

"Usually the bed sags, the furniture is in poor shape and I've even had rooms with the windows broken. Of course a cracked mirror or dirty water in the wash basin is typical for most rented rooms."

"People put up with that? I mean, at least the hotel can make sure the water is fresh."

"Most travelers are too tired, just like we are, to really give a damn about the furniture or the water. They just want a bath, hot food and some sleep."

"I guess," Luke replied just as a knock sounded at the door.

Pulling his pistol and cocking the hammer back, Bill walked to the door and asked, "Who is it?"

"Room service, and I have your bottle of rye."

Opening the door slowly, with his pistol held at the ready, Bill saw the young man holding his whiskey and lowered his horse pistol.

"Sorry about pullin' a gun on you, but I wasn't sure who you were."

The young man laughed and replied, "Hell, mister, I get that at almost every room I visit. These are rough times and this town ain't too tame either, so don't worry about it."

After the young man left the room, Bill gave a shy grin and said, "Well, the water will be up next, so lets have a few drinks before it gets here. Then, after we scrape off four days of beard, we'll go to Skinner's place and nurse a couple of beers. I think that would be a whole lot cheaper than buyin' a meal some place. What do you think?"

"That'll work for me. What I want the most is a bath and some sleep."

"You'll sleep better with some food in you first. After we eat we'll come back and rest a mite. Now, I'm goin' down, unload our horses, and take them to the livery. If the tub arrives while I'm gone, go ahead and get your bath out of the way first." Bill spoke, turned and walked from the room.

He was able to find a livery that charged him a dime a horse, which he knew was low, and left his mounts with the man. As he moved toward the hotel, he saw Brown ride out of town with a group of about ten men. I'll have to get my Greener out, he thought as he continued to walk.

When he returned to the room, Luke was shaving and the water in the tub had a narrow ring of scum around it.

"Got your bath and shavin' done I see, so once I get ready we'll leave. I didn't realize how hungry I was until now." Bill said as he moved to their supplies, where he pulled his sawed-off Greener shotgun from the back.

Turning at the noise, Luke asked, "You think we need that shotgun?"

Opening the breech and inserting two shells, Bill replied, "I just saw Brown ride out of town with ten no-accounts with 'em, which means we've got to be ready at all times. This gun will even the odds a bit, or so I think."

"Well, you take the scattergun, I'll have my two pistols, and we should be fine. That double- barrel clears a big path when she goes off."

As he undressed, Bill replied, "Yep, can't beat a shotgun for in close work. Let me get cleaned up and then we'll go eat."

An hour later they were at the bar sipping on beers as Luke down pickled egg after egg. Finally, Bill said, "You eat one more of them damned eggs and you ain't sleepin' in the same room with me, not after drinkin' beer."

Luke laughed, but suddenly his face turned grim. Leaning close to Bill he whispered, "That Harlow man just walked in."

"Give 'em a few minutes to move to the bar and then we'll leave."

"I'm still hungry!"

"We'll go to a restaurant and eat. I don't want to face the man right now, because we need to talk with Brown first," Bill said as he stood and started for the batwing doors of the saloon.

Luke followed and half way to the door Harlow turned toward him, but didn't seem to recognize the young man.

Outside, Bill said, "We need to get our hands on Brown pretty damned quick, or I'll end up in a fight with Harlow first. I think we need to buy some food at the general store tomorrow and stay in our room most of the time. Our window's right over main street, which will allow us to watch Brown's comin's and goin's."

"The watching Brown will be easy, but the store's closed right now and won't open until dawn." Knowing the young man was hungry, Bill said, "Let's find a diner or restaurant and grab us a meal. Only, from now on we'll eat in the room."

They spotted a restaurant called the Blue Goose, entered and made their way to a table. A few minutes later, a young woman appeared to take their order.

"We'll have two beef steaks, burnt on the outside but still bloody on the inside, taters with gravy, and some biscuits."

"Drinks?"

"We'll have coffee."

"I'll be back when your order is ready. If you need anything just let me know."

"We'll be fine."

Luke watched her walk away and then said, "Pert little thing, ain't she?"

"Yep, but we're both married."

"I know that, I was just lookin' is all."

As soon as the meal touched the table, Luke started eating like a starved man and didn't speak again until he'd moped up the gravy from his plate.

Bill smiled and asked, "Were you hungry, son?"

"I was starved. That was a pretty good meal, but I wonder what it'll cost you?"

"More than it's worth, except we have to eat."

"Yup, but a feller could go broke livin' in town with the prices they charge."

"That's another reason we'll be eatin' in the room from now on."

The woman brought the bill, poured more coffee and then walked away.

Bill picked the tab up, glanced over it and said, "Not too bad, only two dollars."

"Two dollars to eat!"

"Yep, so the bill comes to a total of four dollars."

"It cost us two dollars a piece to eat! I thought two dollars was for both of us!"

Bill laughed, dropped four dollars on the table, and replied, "When I got married the first time, our meals in Saint Louis were over ten dollars. Of course that includes some French wine, but it was a lot of money."

"Ten dollars! I'd never pay that much to eat, and I don't care how fancy the place is."

"My pa paid it as a wedding present, so it didn't really come out of my pocket. Nothing in life is free, boy, not a blamed thing."

"I'd rather ride out onto the plains and kill me a buff."

"Then ya'd still have the price of the powder and lead."

Tired of talking about the high cost of living in town, Luke stood and said, "Let's get back to our room and get some sleep."

Over the next three days and nights, one of them was always perched near the window and every move Brown made noted.

Finally, Bill said, "The only time he ain't with somebody is early in the mornin' when he runs to the outhouse. We'll nab 'em in the mornin', but we can't come back here once he's in our hands. We'll have to have the horses loaded, get a spare for Brown, and ride out of town as soon as he's ours. I suspect this is the first place they'll check."

Luke, who sat at a small round table eating smoked meat and canned peaches, gave him a grin and replied, "Good. Are we goin' to kill the man?"

"I ain't sure yet, it all depends on what he tells me when we talk. Iffen need be he'll die."

"What now?"

"We quit the watch, catch up on our sleep and rest, and then move into place an hour before dawn."

➡️⬅️ ➡️⬅️ ➡️⬅️

Morning brought light rain, but Luke welcomed it this time, knowing it would wash away their tracks after they ran with Brown. He'd just pulled his slicker up and was cutting off a chunk of chewing tobacco, when a long crooked flash of lightning moved over the dark sky and a sharp crack of thunder sounded. *Good, heavy rain will help us*, he thought.

Suddenly, their target appeared and he was walking toward the outhouse. Brown held an umbrella in his left hand and was whistling an unknown tune as he walked toward the small building. Since both men were near the door of the small structure, they moved forward once the door closed, so they could take the man when he stepped outside.

A few minutes later, the door began to open. As soon as Brown stepped out, Bill placed a gun in his back and said, "Mister Brown, you're safe enough, but me and you are goin' to have us a little talk."

"If it's money you want, take my wallet, but I'll find you."

"It's not your money we want, Mister Brown, it's you."

Turning his head slightly, Brown glanced at Bill and replied, "Oh, Mister Sanders, how have you been?"

"I've been pissed, really pissed. Enough talk, move to your right and don't stop until we're near the horses."

Once at the mounts, Luke checked Brown for weapons and removed a loaded colt pistol, two knives and a straight razor. He then tied the man's hands behind his back and helped him onto a horse. Taking a rope, he ran it from around Brown's neck to the pummel.

"You can't tie me like this! If I fall I'll hang."

Luke smiled and replied, "Then don't fall, and pray your horse don't slip in the mud. I wouldn't worry too much anyway; you might end up hangin' regardless."

Bill, growing nervous said, "Enough jabber, let's ride and do it now."

The ride out of town was uneventful and instead of moving east, toward home, they turned south by west. They did not intend to go very far, maybe twenty miles and while it would be a full day's ride, they would question Brown later this evening.

Mile after wet mile passed, with breaks taken only for the horses. Finally, near dusk, Bill moved back into some trees and said, "Let's get a camp made. Once we've eaten, we'll have our chat with Brown."

They dumped Brown beside where the fire pit would be and the two men started to work. As Bill gathered firewood, Luke made a small fire and put up a canvas shelter, and in less than thirty minutes supper was cooking on the open flames.

After a meal of beans and bacon, Bill looked over at Brown and asked, "Why'd ya burn my barn? Don't try to deny it, I know the truth."

"I didn't burn your barn."

Bill suddenly stood and looking down at the man, he said in a low tone, "Don't lie to me, because I have a witness it was your men!"

"Okay, I wanted to scare you into leaving."

Pulling Browns wallet from his coat, Bill said, "I figure that barn was worth close to a hundred dollars, so I'm takin' it from you." After counting the money, he placed the wallet back.

"Can I leave now?" Brown asked, hoping that was what the ignorant farmer wanted, payment for his barn.

"Nope, you seriously hurt one of my men and ran off my stock. Now, before you even try, money will not make this up."

Feeling a knot forming deep in his belly, Brown asked, "What do you want?"

Bill grinned and then said to Luke, "Place his pistol back in his holster. Once he is armed, cut the ropes on his hands and feet. Me and Mister Brown are going to have us a good old fashioned gunfight."

Once his wrists were free, Brown rubbed them with a big grin on his face. All he had to do now was kill two stupid dirt farmers and ride back to town. It was too easy.

Slowly standing, Brown said, "I'll kill you and enjoy every second of it. See, I'm very good with a pistol."

"Are you plannin' to talk me to death?"

Before another word, Brown's hand came up filled with iron and it spat flame twice.

Bill jerked under impact of one slug, but the second missed. He raised his right hand, squeezed the trigger and had the satisfaction of seeing Brown knocked to the ground.

Brown lifted his gun, only to have Bill place two more heavy slugs into his chest. His body quivered once, he gave a loud sigh, and died.

Luke, seeing Brown was out of the way, moved to Bill's side and asked, "How bad are you hit ?"

"I took his bullet in my upper left shoulder, so I'll live."

"Move over beside the fire and let me doctor you up."

The injury, while not serious, was painful and likely to keep Bill from facing Harlow for some time.

"Damn it all!" Bill exploded when informed.

"You knew that when you told me about a hit to the shoulder."

"What do we do now? Should we stay here until I'm healed, or go back home? Iffen we wait too long, Harlow and the rest will move on us. Especially now, with Brown dead."

Kneeling beside Bill, Luke handed him a cup of whiskey and said, "Don't think on it right now. Drink this and get some sleep. We'll talk it over in the mornin'."

Bill gulped two cups of whiskey before he finally dropped off to sleep.

Morning came with Bill fighting a high fever, and Luke dragging Brown's body out onto the plains with his horse. After he cut the rope to the man's feet, he removed his pocket-watch, diamond stickpin, rings and wallet from him. Placing them in the saddlebags, he said, "Ain't no use to leave this stuff out heah. You wronged us, Mister Brown, and while you paid Bill in full, you ain't paid Isaac for his pain and sufferin'. I'll give this stuff to him when I get home."

When he returned, he found Bill having a seizure and as the man jerked and twisted, Luke held his thick leather belt between his teeth. *Good God, what in the world brought this on? When I left he wasn't even awake.*

Bill's attack lasted less than five minutes and he didn't awaken. Placing his belt on his saddle, Luke sat by the fire deep in thought. *I can't let Bill face Harlow when he's injured and might have a fit at any time. I'll have to do the job myself.*

Standing, the young man moved to his horse, saddled and rode out onto the plains. *Before I leave, I have to make enough meat for Bill to eat while he heals. I hope, unless I'm killed, to be back before he even knows I've gone.*

Soon back at camp with a small yearling buffalo calf, Luke cut the meat and placed it in the sun to dry into jerky. He added the liver and heart to a large pot and made a strong broth for Bill to sip. It was late before he finally rolled up in his robe and called it a night.

Early the next morning, he packed his gear, saddled his horse and checked Bill once more. The man still had a fever, but not as high as the day before.

Standing beside his stepfather, Luke said, "Pa, you're shot, so it's up to me to protect the family name. I'll remember what you said about making my shot count and not to worry about bein' the fastest draw. Well, I have to go now and I hope to see you again tomorrow. If not, I'll meet ya in a better place."

Picking up Bill's shotgun, Luke mounted and rode toward Bannack, knowing death awaited for one of them. As he rode, he thought, *Harlow is fast, but that's not as important as hitting the target. He's woods savvy, but that won't help him in town. He'll think I'm young, so it'll all be a big joke to him. I have to turn my youth into an advantage.*

During the rest of the trip, he thought of Harlow and evaluated the man's skills. Luke knew his chances of surviving were slim, but with his family wronged, he had to make it right.

# CHAPTER 27

**I**t was late afternoon when the young man dismounted in front of Skinner's Saloon and tied his horse to the hitching post. He pulled the shotgun from the boot and checked the loads. Turning, he walked up the steps and into the saloon.

There were only a few customers in the place, so he took a table in the back against a wall. As he took a seat, he noticed a clear view of the windows and the batwing doors. Laying the shotgun down on the table, he ordered a beer. He then pulled back both hammers on the gun, so it was ready to shoot when needed.

A portly bartender with a dirty rag in his hand brought the beer to his table and said, "That'll be a nickel. You new here?"

Handing the man his money, Luke replied, "Uh-huh."

"Where you from?"

"Hell, barkeeper, I'm from hell. I came here special like to take one of y'all home with me!"

The bar keeper shook his head, rolled his eyes and made his way back to the bar. He met all kinds in this business, so what was another crazy? As long as Luke had money to pay for his drinks, the fat man didn't care if he was a nutcase or not.

Luke was on his second beer when Harlow walked in, made his way to the bar and ordered a double rye. By now, there were a good dozen men in the place, most of them miners or store owners, still working in the dying town. While most knew it was time to move on, as long as the miners stayed looking for that last mother lode, so would the merchants.

After his third double, Harlow slowly turned and looked the saloon over. When his eyes spotted Luke, he grinned, put his hands on his hips and asked, "Well, now, it looks like I have a visitor!"

Luke remained seated, but replied, "You didn't kill the old black man, Harlow."

Harlow laughed and said, "No? Well, I sure as hell tried!"

"You're goin' to answer to me for what you tried to do. Some killer you are, when you can't even kill an old man."

Harlow laughed loud and hard before he said, "Kid, you should be home with your ma and not in a saloon drinkin' beer; it ain't good for you. It'll stunt your growth, or don't you know?"

"I'm goin' to kill you, Harlow." Luke said with a flat voice.

"Son, I can chew you up and spit you out without workin' up a sweat. Now, get up and go home to your momma."

Luke's chair screeched under him as he stood, gazed into Harlow's eyes and replied, "I'll get up, but I won't go home until I send you to hell. You almost killed a friend of mine and burned our barn to the ground!"

"Maybe I did and then again, maybe I didn't do those things. You got any proof?"

"The man you knifed identified you and did it by name."

"He's a liar," Harlow said as he went for his gun.

Luke brought the shotgun upward, lined up the barrels, and squeezed both triggers, just as he felt a bullet take him in the thigh. The double blast was loud in the saloon, and he heard a scream as his leg collapsed and he fell to the sawdust-covered floor.

Lying on his side, Luke opened the breech and slid two fresh shells into the gun. He then glanced toward Harlow, and saw Harlow was face down on the floor.

Forcing himself up, he limped to the fallen man and saw his shot had taken him in the middle of his belly. Harlow was dead. No movement came from the body.

Looking at the bartender, Luke ordered, "Get me a doctor, and do it now!"

The big man gave a loud gulp and moved for the door.

Leaning against the bar, Luke poured a glass of bourbon and placed his money on the bar. He'd taken one sip when the batwing doors flew inward and a sheriff entered, carrying cocked pistols.

"What happened?"

One of the cowboys sitting at a table said, "Harlow made a move for his pistol and the kid killed 'em with one shot from that big scattergun."

"What's your name, boy?"

"Luke and I ain't a boy. I've fought Injuns, righted a wrong and I'm married. I guess those things make me a man. You got a name, sheriff; I like to know who I'm talking with in situations like this."

"Name is O'Brien, Tim O'Brien."

A few minutes later, after Luke explained the reasons behind his fight, the sheriff shook his head and said, "You're a man alright. I've been waitin' for Harlow to be killed, figurin' it was just a matter of time. But, what happened to Brown?"

"A feller by the name of William Sanders killed 'em in a fair fight. Like I said a few minutes ago, Brown was behind the burnin' of our place, had the money to hire men, and needed killin'."

O'Brien laughed and replied, "The railroad is comin' and I suspect they'll want to lay some line across part of your land. Brown knew the land would increase in value, so he's been buyin' and forcin' folks off their farms. Since I'm just a town sheriff, I had no authority to lock him up."

"I don't understand."

"I can't do a blame thing about what they do once they leave town, because I don't have any authority outside of town limits. But, by God, you surely did the job!"

The doctor entered, glanced around and moved to Harlow first. Shaking his head he said, "Can't help his feller none, because that scattergun blew him almost in half." Then moving to Luke's side, he said, "Now, you're a different story."

The bullet had gone completely through the leg and while Luke was in pain, the doctor smiled and said, "You'll be back to normal in about six weeks. Change the bandage every day and keep it clean, so festering don't set in, and you'll do fine."

"How much do I owe ya doc?" Luke asked.

"Since you got rid of Harlow, there ain't no fee. I never did like the man." He then closed his black bag and left the saloon.

O'Brien moved to Luke's side and said, "You'll need a room for a few days, because you'll come down with a fever before mornin'. Do you have money enough for a few days in a hotel?"

Remembering the money he'd taken from Brown's body, Luke nodded.

Turning to the bartender, O'Brien said, "Give me two bottles of rye and put 'em on this man's tab. He'll be around after he heals to pay you. Now, when I get you in a room, you drink all the whiskey you can get down, it'll help you sleep. Do you understand?"

"Yep, and I've done some doctorin' in the past. But, I need somebody to go and fetch my pa out there."

"How can I find 'em?" The same cowboy who'd spoken up about Harlow drawing first asked.

"He is nigh on twenty miles west and near a small stream in some trees."

"I think I know the place. Is it in some rolling hills?"

"Yep."

"I'll leave now and have 'em back by mornin'. Come on, Too Tall, ya ride with me and we'll go get that feller."

An hour later, Luke was in a hotel room sipping straight whiskey against his pain. While his wound hurt, he was glad he didn't have to face a hot knife again. For a long time he stared out the window, not really thinking of anything at all. He suddenly realized, it was the second time since he'd started the trip to Montana that he was in a comfortable hotel bed. While he had a bed in the cabin, the mattress was stuffed with corn stalk and not feathers. Even the frame was made of roughly cut logs. Most hotels had beds that had been there for years and felt like it, too, from what Bill had told him. This bed was fine, mighty fine.

He picked up the newspaper from beside his bed and scanned the front page. There had been a double hanging in town last night with neither man given the benefit of a trial. Seems one was a horse thief, while the other was suspected of a killing, both hanging offenses according to the vigilantes.

An editorial spoke of people leaving and rough times ahead for Bannack, with the mines dead and no reason for others to come or stay. According to the writer, over half the town's original population was gone, and the rest would soon follow. At most, he gave the town two years and then Bannack would be a ghost town.

*Must be terrible to put your life and money into a town, then watch it die,* he thought as he put the paper down and leaned into his pillow. Within minutes, Luke was asleep.

"Ya goin' to sleep the day away?" He heard a voice ask.

When he opened his eyes, Bill was standing beside his bed, "Well, I guess that drunken cowboy found ya."

"Yup. They found me yesterday, late evening. I suspected you'd run back here to kill Harlow and according to them two cowboys, you did a real fine job of it. They said that Greener almost cut the man in half."

"He got off the first shot; only I took my time and placed my shot right in the middle of his belly."

Bill grew serious and asked, "Why'd you try it alone, son? He could have killed you."

"He wronged us and you were hurt, so I figured the killin' was up to me. He needed killin' or who knows who he would have killed next. He's the one that hurt Isaac, too; he bragged about it before we fought."

"Speakin' of Isaac, as soon as you're able, we need to head back to the cabin. I suspect Sue and Isaac are a mite worried."

"I hear you, and I think the day after tomorrow I'll be able to ride."

"Do you need anything?"

"Some more whiskey would be good. How's your injury?"

"No festerin', it's startin' to scab over, but I'm as sore as all get out."

"I got a tab at the bar, so tell the bartender it's for me."

Bill said, "If I ever have a blood son, I pray he'll turn out to be just like you, Luke. You're one hell of a young man and I'm proud to be your pa." He then turned and walked from the room.

At dawn, two days later, they walked from the hotel and mounted their horses. The morning was cool, with low gray clouds off to the west, and to Luke it looked like snow.

"Got bad weather comin' at some point today," Bill said as he tapped his horse lightly in the ribs.

"Who cares, I'm goin' home!"

"It's a good feelin', ain't it, son?"

"Uh-huh, but Lord you must have really been excited when you returned from the war!"

Bill shook his head and replied, "I didn't feel a thing. See, I didn't know anyone or anyplace when I got back. My head injury had cleaned out my memory, so I didn't remember a blasted thing."

"That sounds scary to me."

"I wasn't scared as much as confused. Hell, I didn't know my own ma and pa, girlfriend, dog, or nothing. I had to relearn it all."

Well, getting' to know your girlfriend again could have been fun."

"Oh, it was, it surely was. Now, let's quit the jabberin' and cover some miles."

Both men scanned the countryside as they rode and Bill noticed Luke had a smile on his face. *I never seen a man so happy to be goin' home,* he thought and found himself smiling as well. Moving his rifle to the other side of his horse, Bill spotted two riders nearing from the open plains.

"Riders comin'."

"I see 'em. Let's hold up and give our horses a short rest, in case we have to make a run for it."

When the men neared, Luke saw they were filthy. The man on the left had long brown hair, while the other had red. They were thin, wore untrimmed beards, and looked to be lazy no accounts in his mind. He trusted them about as far as he could toss his horse.

The two men stopped ten feet from Bill and the man with red hair said, "Howdy-do. My name's Redman, James Redman, and this other jasper's William Thomas."

Bill gave his name and waited, because he knew the man was going to say more.

"The plains are pure hell right now, with the Sioux out in force. Me and William liked to never got away from 'em."

"That right?"

"Yep," Thomas replied.

Silence followed and Bill and Luke kept the barrels of their rifles pointed in the general direction of the two men.

Redman gave a tooth-gabbed grin and asked, "Ya two don't talk much, do ya?"

Luke sent a brown stream of tobacco juice to the dirt and answered, "Nope."

Looking over at his partner, Thomas said, "Let's move, iffen we want to be in Bannack before dusk."

As they rode away, Luke said, "We've not seen the last of those two."

"I figured as much, too."

"Let's ride until near midnight and then hunt a hole. I think those two would kill a man in a minute and for a dime."

"That much?"

While both were sore, it felt good to be out on the open plains, moving toward home. They rode at a walk, neither feeling like talking, and it was shortly after their nooning that Luke said, "I just caught a flash of sunlight behind us, and I suspect it's those two yahoos' we met earlier."

"Keep ridin', they'll not try anything until we stop for the night. I suspect then they'll move in close and try to ambush us."

"Hell, we ain't got enough for a man to kill us over."

"We got more than they've got and they know it, too. Our horses will bring forty dollars each, the guns near the same, and we're both carryin' a little cash money."

"We'll just let 'em ambush us?"

"Nope, we'll have a surprise for the boys when they show up," Bill said with a big grin.

They continued to ride at a walk, knowing the men behind them would wait for darkness. Near dusk, the clouds moved in and the sky turned gray, bringing a risk of rain or snow.

"We'll stop for the night down in that valley, near the trees." Bill said with a smile.

"Good, I'm about worn out. I've got a little pain from my injury and need me a good shot of whiskey."

"You'll have it, along with more if you want, just as soon as we take care of those two behind us."

"Still goin' to surprise 'em?"

"Why not? They'd kill us in a minute, so they'll deserve what they get."

A little less than an hour later, a fire was burning, a small shelter was up, and firewood for the night was stacked under canvas.

Luke placed a pot of beans on the coals, leaned back and said, "Ain't there no way I can have a drink now? I'm in a mite of pain here."

Squatting beside the fire, Bill nodded and replied, "No more than three fingers worth. I don't want you roostered when those two show up. Drink just enough for the pain."

Luke Reached into his saddlebags, removed a quart bottle, and knocked back a good healthy snort. He then grinned.

"You're looking tired too, so get a little sleep. I'll keep an eye on things and get my trap ready. I'll wake you when the beans are done."

Stretching out on his blanket under the shelter, Luke said, "I'll do that, but iffen you need me, just yell."

Bill laughed. "Hell, iffen I need you, you'll hear the shots. I'll take no chances with those two jaspers."

➡️⬅️  ➡️⬅️  ➡️⬅️

Later, with supper finished, the two men sat in the darkness waiting for their visitors. It was just after midnight when a slight whisper of noise was heard and looking to his left, Luke saw a dark form moving toward the center of camp. The stillness of the night was suddenly broken by six loud shots.

"By God, this was too easy!" Thomas yelled and then broke into a loud laugh.

"Let's get their gear, see iffen they got any money and get to Bannack. I'm tired of eatin' beans and bacon every night. Hell, I'd kill for a whiskey," Redman replied.

"Ya just did, son! Now, let's take their money and get the hell out of here."

The camp suddenly erupted in a huge explosion and debris flew high into the air. Screams sounded, with a long silence following.

"Cover me as I check those two out," Bill ordered as he stood and made his way to camp.

Minutes passed and then Luke called out, "Is it clear!"

"It's clear, but it ain't pretty! The dynamite tore those jaspers to hell and back."

Standing and then walking to camp, the younger man said, "They got what they had comin', after all, they simply shot into our bedrolls. They were murderers, so as far as I am concerned they died too quickly."

The two dead men were torn apart and Luke was glad the fire had burned down enough he could not see the gore. As it was, all he could see was a few dark lumps scattered around.

"Let's mount and move camp down the trail a few miles."

"It's a good thing you picked up some dynamite for the ranch or we would've had a shoot out."

"I got it to clear stumps, route streams, and move hills, not to kill fellers with. Only it does that too, if need be."

They rode for a good hour and then Bill said, "Let's call it a night. I'll take the first watch."

Pulling up in a line of willows beside a small stream, the two made camp and shared a pot of coffee.

Bill looked across the fire, gazed into the eyes of the younger man, and asked, "Does how we killed those two bother you much?"

"No, not really. I was kinda shocked when they shot into our blankets, but I feel they got what they deserved, just like I said at the time.

"It bothers me some. It brought back thoughts of the war and of men I'd seen killed with artillery fire. Looks like a man could eventually forget or learn to live with the killing I saw, but I can't. I don't know why, but I can't forget."

"It was bloody business and not something easy to forget, I'd imagine. I think any feller who fought on either side, will remember it for the rest of their lives. Hell, how in the world could a person forget something like that?"

"I can't."

"No, I don't imagine you have, but you'll learn to live with it better. I ain't very old, but I've heard folks say the older you get the less of the past you remember. Like your memory dims or something."

Standing, Bill laid his rifle in the crook of his left arm and said, "I'm movin' off a ways to stand guard. I'll wake you in about four hours."

# CHAPTER 28

It was early morning, and the two were sitting on their horses on a slight berm above the ranch.

Luke said, "It sure looks good, doesn't it?"

"Yup, it does, but home always looks like that. Has a special glow, you know?"

"Uh-huh, and I'm glad to be back."

Bill grinned and replied, "Come on, let's hurry down there, because everybody probably thinks we ran away from home!"

When they rounded the house, Isaac stood in the barnyard holding a shotgun in his hands. He gave a big warm smile and asked, "So, ya two Jay birds finally decided to leave the big city and come home, huh? How did it go?"

"We'll have no more problems," Bill replied with a flat voice.

"Done?"

"Done, and Luke did the job."

"Good to see you on your feet again," Luke said as he dismounted.

"I'm still sore as all get out, but I'll live. I spotted y'all about a mile out and waited fer ya. I didn't know who ya was."

Tying his horse to the hitching post, Bill asked, "How's everybody?"

"All are as fine as frog hair!"

"Good, I was worried. When we left you were near death."

Issac gave a light chuckle and lowered his head as he said, "Singing Bird is the one who fixed me up. She made a medicine from some flowers and bear fat that had me moving in a few days. Now, I still can't dance, but I walk good enough."

The door flew open and out ran Sue into Bill's open arms, "Thank God you're safe! I was so worried, you've been gone so long."

"I couldn't help it. We both took some lead, none of it was serious, but we had to heal before we could ride. The important thing is it's all over."

"The Sioux came by here two days back, and ole Brass Buttons said he needed to talk with you. Seems he has a treaty to sign and wants you to speak for the tribe," Sue said.

"Speak with who, the army?"

"Nope, some feller from the Indian Bureau or some such thing. I never hear'd of 'em before," Isaac replied.

Bill shrugged, looked over at Sue and said, "You and I will go tomorrow. We'll leave at first light and most likely have to spend the night."

"Why don't we all go?  I know Singing Bird wants to see her pa." Luke added, and then asked,

"Where is she?"

Isaac, laughed and replied, "In the cabin, but she'll not come out to welcome ya back, iffen that's what you think. Injun women don't do that sort of thing. They see it as a weakness, and the wife should be as brave as the husband."

"Well, I'd better get in there, I missed her and she needs to know it, too."

As Luke entered the cabin, Bill said, "He's one hell of a man, and I'm proud of him. He went to town and confronted Harlow on his own, right after I caught a bullet. He did the job right too, like a man would. As far as I'm concerned, he's a man's man."

"He's got the bark on 'em, and I think he grew up the day he killed them four warriors. He's not been a kid since." Isaac said, smiled and then asked, "Feel like some coffee?"

"As a matter of fact, I do."

"Want me to fix something to eat, too?" Sue asked as she slipped her arm around his waist.

"No, no food. We ate a heavy breakfast, but some hot coffee would hit the spot about right now."

➨➨ ➨➨ ➨➨

Brass Buttons sat in his lodge surrounded by his white friends and usually he would have been content, but on this day, his mood was sour.

"*So, white men have told The People you must move?*" Bill asked.

"*No, they have not, but we must move. The whites want us to turn over a right of way for a trail leading to the setting sun. If we do this thing, we will move away from the trail, and that is what I meant. The white man said nothing of moving; only I expect that to be his next wish.*"

Luke thought for a few seconds and then asked, "*Will allowing the travelers to cross your lands be such a bad thing that you must move?*"

Brass Buttons gazed into the young man's eyes and replied, "*The white man will not stay on the trail, and he will soon be digging for gold on Sioux land. White people say this, but they do that. I have found with the white man, if you give him a tree, he soon wants the forest.*"

"*I think agreeing is better than a war with the white man. If you fight them, it will be a war you cannot win.*" Bill stated.

"*If they move into our Black Hills, war will come and I will be helpless to stop it. The hills are sacred to my people, with many of our ancestors buried there, so it will become a thing of honor.*"

It was quiet in the lodge as the fire snapped and popped, and then Brass Buttons said, "*Will you speak for my people? Will you see the talking leaves we sign do not have two tongues?*"

Bill cleared his throat, knowing the Sioux had but a little time left, and replied, "*Yes, I will speak for you. You do understand a time is coming when the white man will own all the Sioux now call their own?*"

Lowering his head, Brass Buttons answered with a voice filled with emotion, "*Yes, even I see the future and I am not a shaman. I hope to keep what is ours a little longer and avoid a war, but a day will come when I must say enough is enough. On that day, blood will flow like a river across Sioux land. Sitting Bull and others are speaking of a fight to come; even now we pray for peace, but prepare for war."*

*"You will stop no war, only postpone it,"* Luke spoke and then met Bill's gaze.

Bill, feeling the weight of the younger man's words replied, *"Your son is right. You cannot avoid a war with the whites."*

*"This we know well, and all I hope to accomplish by signing the treaty is to buy my people enough time to prepare better for battle. We are not fools, but this is a hard decision and not something to take lightly. Once we go to war, we will be a ruthless enemy of all white people."*

Bill nodded and said, *"This I understand and it is as it should be in a war. When are you to sign this treaty?"*

*"In the morning, and it makes my heart glad to know you have returned to help us."*

Isaac, who'd not spoken suddenly ejected, *"Hell, Brass Buttons, I can't read good, not that legal mumbo-jumbo, but I would have gone if Bill hadn't returned."*

Smiling the old chief said, *"This I know to be true. You said you would do it only if Bill did not return in time. He has returned."*

*"We'll spend the night and meet with this jasper come the time tomorrow."*

*"It is good."*

At that point, they knew the conversation was finished, so they stood and walked from the lodge, each man knowing the end had started.

"Shit done hit the stump this time," Isaac said as he shook his head.

"Well, all of us, even the Sioux, know they are living on borrowed time. I'll bet you right now, ten years from today the Sioux will be living on a small chunk of land the white man doesn't want."

"Likely." Luke stated but then continued, "Only that don't make it right."

"No, it don't make it right, but where do you think the land back east came from? We either traded some junk for it or took it by force from the Injuns. I think in fifty years or less, the United States will own all the land from the Atlantic to the Pacific oceans, while the Injuns will be stuck some place they can't cause any trouble."

Isaac leaned over, spat a brown stream of tobacco juice and interjected, "Hell, Bill, it won't be that long. Cut that time in half and you'll be closer to a real date. The Sioux are goin' the way of the mountain man and it won't be in too many years, either. Then, the only way to find out about either of us will be in some history class at school, but they'll mess it all up, too. We've had our time, but it's over."

Luke spoke, "It's always been like this, I mean, the strong take what they want from the weak."

"Yup, pretty much, but that don't make it right in my eyes."

"No, I guess it ain't right, but it's part of life and there ain't a damned thing we can do to stop it."

Isaac replied, "Ya got that right, young pup. As long as people back east want Sioux lands, it's only a matter of time."

➡️⬅️  ➡️⬅️  ➡️⬅️

Dawn came with a slow drizzle and a chilly wind that promised a wintry day to come. Low gray clouds moved overhead and Luke felt he could reach up and touch them, but his mind was not really on the weather.

Isaac walked to his side and said, "The government man is here, and the talkin' will start directly."

"Let's get to the meetin' place then; I don't want to miss this."

Near the village in an open field, four tents stood and the American flag waved in light gusts of wind. Uniforms abound and a number of well-dressed men, who Luke took to be government men, stood near a large table. One was louder and displaying more self-importance than others were. *He must be the big bug,* the young man thought.

Brass Buttons stood in front of the table, with most of the village behind him. Isaac moved quickly to the chief's left and Bill positioned himself to the right.

"Here is the treaty, Brass Buttons, so sign it and we can all go home." The loud man said as he placed a thick document on the table.

"Not so fast, government man. My name is William Sanders, and I speak for the tribe and myself. You got a name?"

"Nathan B. Powers. Are you a squawman?"

"Nope."

"What's in this for you?"

"Nothing's in it for me, but mayhap a little peace of mind."

"Have him sign this, because I don't have all day."

"Well," Bill replied with a chuckle, "it'll take at least three days before the chief will even look at this treaty. See, Injuns don't work like we do, and they like to think things out before they act."

"Three days! Good God, man, I don't have three days to wait for a damned mark on a paper!"

Bill started to turn and walk away, but suddenly Powers called out, "Okay, okay, tell the chief to take the document, look it over and then get back to me. Try to hurry this if you can, I'm in a bit of a rush."

"Injuns ain't in a rush," Isaac said.

Frowning, Powers asked, "Who said you could speak to me, boy?"

Isaac moved forward, but Bill blocked the way with his arm and whispered, "Let it go, Isaac. We don't need government trouble."

"I'll let it go, but this is the last time," Isaac answered, and then turned to Powers and said, "I'm here on the behalf of the Sioux nation, and I'll speak when I have something to say. If you dislike me or my kind, I'll take these good folks back to the village directly."

Powers, needing the signature of Brass Buttons, gave in. "Stay then. While I don't like it, I desire this treaty. I'm here to avoid future violence."

"You'll get it, I think, as long as this document reads fairly for the Sioux." Bill spoke, picked up the papers and walked away.

→← →← →←

Three mornings later, they met once again at the table. Powers was strutting around with his hands behind his back and yelling orders to everyone. When the Sioux appeared, he grew quiet and gave a fake smile.

Seeing Bill he asked, "I take it the treaty met your approval, Mister Sanders?"

"Since I spoke last time, it's only fair you speak to my partner, Isaac, this time. He's the big black man you don't care much for."

Appalled at having to negotiate a treaty with the black man, Powers sputtered and stammered.

"To answer yer question, we only made one change to the treaty," Isaac spoke before Powers could.

"Come now, what did you want changed?"

"The amount of trade goods offered fer use of the road."

"You want more, of course."

Isaac laughed and replied, "Much more. I may be a black man, Powers, but I ain't stupid. This open trail will generate money from every corner of America, and businesses will make huge profits. What ya offered the Sioux is about five hundred dollars in junk. Brass Buttons and his tribe want ten times that amount and an annual payment of ten thousand dollars."

"Ten thousand dollars! Are you damned insane?"

"Nope, just black, and that doesn't make me a fool. Either they get it, or they'll not sign the treaty."

"I imagine you're behind all of this. You and *your Southern friend*, Mister Sanders."

"Ya guessed right. We don't know how much the trail is worth, but we do know it's worth a hell of a lot more than yer offerin'."

"We could just take it, you know."

"Of course you could, but you'd pay for it in blood," Bill said.

Shaking his head as he walked in circles, Powers finally replied, "Okay, we'll increase the trade goods and I'm offering you eight thousand a year."

Isaac smiled, toying with the white man, and said, "This ain't no horse trade, we said ten."

"Damn it, do you know how much money that is?"

"Nope, not really. I guess I ain't made but a fifth of that in my whole life, but these Sioux will get it."

Growing angry, Powers said, "If I promise this, will you take my word or does the whole treaty have to be redone?"

Isaac laughed. "Your word? I might do that iffen I knew what kind of man you are, but I suspect we'll have to redo this heah treaty. See, I trust you about as much as I do a rattlesnake, white man."

"Just amend the damned thing, Powers, and let's get this over with." Bill added brusquely.

"Yes, yes, we'll amend it."

"While this ain't really part of the treaty, I thought I'd let you know if any white men are found in the Black Hills, they will be killed. The hills are sacred to the Sioux, and my warning is serious as hell."

"The agreement states the only place whites are to be is on the trail. Now, as stated in the treaty, a distance of three miles on either side of the trail is open for hunting. I see no reason a white person would be in the hills."

"I'm not disagreeing with the hunting distances, and neither are the Sioux, only warning you."

Giving a weak smile, Powers replied, "Okay, consider me warned. Give me a few minutes to amend the treaty and then you can have old Brass Buttons sign for the Sioux."

"Huh?" Isaac said.

"I said in a few minutes the chief can sign for the Sioux tribe."

"Hell," Isaac replied, "Brass Buttons ain't the leader of the whole Sioux nation. He just runs this one tribe."

"He can be the head cook for all I care. I simply want a man to sign for the Sioux people and if he's a chief, the better. One savage is as good as another."

⇥⇤ ⇥⇤ ⇥⇤

Six months passed and on the day the trade goods arrived, Luke and Singing Bird were in the village. The wagons delivering the supplies had an escort of two troops of cavalry, which made the Indians uncomfortable. The men in blue were white warriors, or long knives as the Sioux called them, and they watched them cautiously. As he stood beside Singing Bird, Luke prayed no young Sioux brave or inexperienced soldier would do something stupid. If either side fired a shot, all hell would break loose instantly, because neither side trusted the other.

A big white man wearing homespun clothes and a leather hat dismounted from a wagon and said, "My name is Lester Poor, and I am lookin' fer a Sioux chief called Brass Buttons."

Brass Buttons moved to Luke's side and asked, *"Will you speak for us?"*

*"Yes, I will speak for the people,"* Luke replied, and then turning to face Poor he called out, "He is the man beside me."

Poor walked to Luke, extended his hand and said, "I've things from the government for Brass Buttons. I need someone who represents the tribe to check items off as we unload them."

Luke's eyes narrowed as he asked, "What's the value of this stuff?"

"Nigh on ten thousand dollars, or so the paperwork I have states. Now, there ain't no food in this mess, but lots of blankets, knives, pots and pans, and whatnot."

"Any guns, ammo or powder, so these folks can hunt?"

"Uh-huh, close to two hundred rifles from the war, single shot muzzleloaders, but they're in good condition from what I could tell. There's also four hundred pounds of lead and close to the same in powder." Poor replied and then added, "Can we unload, 'cause I ain't real comfortable 'round these Sioux."

Luke laughed and said, "I'll do the checking items off, so you can start right now."

➡⬅ ➡⬅ ➡⬅

Later, after Poor left with his troopers, Luke shook his head at the quality of the gifts. The blankets were old and thin, the pots and pans used, the knives were cheap and not likely to hold an edge, and only the guns looked to be of fair value. Of course, there were the normal trinkets white men always gave to Indians, beads, mirrors, awls, face paint, and so on. Except Brass Buttons now had barrels of the useless items and would have to distribute them fairly.

Picking up a moth-eaten blanket, the old chief said, *"I can see now why the Great-Father gives his gifts freely, they cost him little."*

*"Father, it's likely the Great-Father in Washington has never heard of this treaty. I suspect Powers made this deal and pocketed the difference in cost."*

*"I do not understand."*

*"Powers may have paid three thousand dollars for all of this, but charged the Federal Government ten thousand. He kept seven thousand for himself."*

*"Has he no honor?"*

Luke laughed and replied, *"When it comes to money few men working for the Great-Father have honor."*

*"I do not understand this. How can a man say one thing and do another?"*

Luke gave a sad grin and replied, *"With your people wealth is measured by the number of horses a man has, but the white man counts his wealth in money. The white man seeks money like a Sioux warrior does horses."*

*"I understand greed, my son; I do not understand how a man can speak with two tongues."*

*"Powers did not lie, not really. The papers I have say the value of these items is correct, but I suspect he made a healthy profit in the deal. I do not think the quality of these goods is worth what he says he paid."*

*"Or, perhaps he made a poor trade with the one who furnished the goods?"*

*"Could be, and it would be hard to prove either way."*

*"Then do not worry about it, because some men are poor traders."*

*"I must go to Singing Bird,"* Luke replied and as he walked away, he thought, The Sioux are like children when dealing with the government. They trust when they shouldn't and believe what they want to hear.

# CHAPTER 29

**T**he next couple of years were productive years for the ranch. While the place was still not bringing in much money, it was producing enough to be self-efficient and the herds had grown in size. As Bill said, "It's just a matter of time, more settlers will come, and then this will become a busy place." Luke and Singing Bird built a home a mile from Bill, and filed claim to five thousand acres. Their futures looked bright after years of fighting just to survive.

Bill's blacksmith job had a long line of customers, most long distances from the ranch, so he stayed busy from dawn to dusk turning out knives, plows and other special order items. While not growing wealthy, the money was enough to furnish them things they couldn't grow or make, like salt, coffee, pepper, whiskey and flour.

This morning, Bill stood in the barnyard watching a troop of U.S. cavalry riding toward his ranch. He wondered what they were doing out on such a warm and beautiful day, and why they wanted to talk to him. *Lord, I hope Brass Buttons hasn't picked up the war hatchet,* he thought as he removed his hat and wiped his sweat-stained hair with an old rag.

"Who's comin' to visit?" Isaac asked as he walked from the house.

"Army, and I hope the Sioux ain't started to killin' folks. Except iffen it ain't started now, it will some day soon."

"Yep, we got folks all over the Black Hills."

The horse soldiers rode into the barnyard and a young Captain called out, "Are you William Sanders?"

"That I am."

"I'm to tell you the Sioux have risen and massacred over 200 men under General Custer's command."

"Where'd this happen?"

"Near the Little Bighorn River, just east of here."

"Did only the Lakota attack?"

"Hell, no, had all the Sioux bands and Northern Cheyenne together, along with a few other tribes, too. Things been goin' to the devil since miners found gold in the Black Hills."

"Damn me!" Isaac ejected.

Bill suddenly exploded, "Damn it all! Brass Buttons told Powers to keep whites out of the hills or there'd be blood! He warned the man fair and square!"

"Well, I'm told you know the area well and the United States has need of your services."

Bill stopped prancing, tilted his head to the right, and asked, "Oh, and exactly what services are they asking of me, sir?"

"We are hiring civilian guides to help us track down the Sioux. The pay is a hundred dollars a month and we provide your rations."

"Son, I think not," Bill replied and then gave a little chuckle as he continued, "See the army was warned years ago to keep whites out of the Black Hills, but you didn't listen. Besides, the last time a country asked for my services I barely lived through four years of pure hell, fighting for a lost cause. I was sick, hungry and so damned tired most of the time that I gave up soldiering for a lifetime."

The Captain fidgeted on his saddle, gazed into Bill's eyes and said, "I can understand how you feel sir, but those were white men killed. I'm prepared to offer you two hundred dollars a month, only that's as high as I am authorized to go."

"Captain, why would I want to lead you to a group of people who were just protecting their homes, like you and I would do?

The Sioux knew the Black Hills were in danger, and Powers agreed to keep the whites out, but here you sit in my barnyard making it look like the Injuns are evil. They did what they warned years ago. No, I'll not be a part of it."

"Sergeant, form the men in columns of two and then move 'em out at a slow walk!" The Captain yelled and then turned to Bill as he said, "I advise you to keep your views to yourself on this matter, Mister Sanders. The killing of General Custer and his men has the whole nation in an uproar demanding justice."

"And, you agree with this?"

Giving a light grin the Captain said, "I am just a soldier, sir, and do as ordered."

As the cavalry rode from his ranch, Bill gave the man a sharp salute and whispered, "Good luck, Captain. You're goin' to need it."

The Captain returned Bill's salute, pulled his horse around and rode after his men.

⇥⇤  ⇥⇤  ⇥⇤

A few short weeks later, Brass Buttons and ten of his people showed up at the ranch under the cover of darkness. The night was warm and a light wind blew, while a huge full moon glowed brightly overhead.

Luke stood by the old chief on Bill's front porch, "He says his people have known no peace since the killing at Greasy Grass Creek. I reckon that's the Injun name of Little Bighorn. The long knives have not allowed them to rest, and his people grow tired."

"I cannot deny shelter and safety to Brass Buttons or his people, except this will put us in one hell of a bind."

"How so?"

"Helping an enemy of the United States is a crime and right now, Brass Buttons and all Sioux are listed at the top of America's enemies."

"Damn. Let me tell the old man," Luke replied and then spoke to the chief. Brass Buttons spat out a few words, nodded and the looked sadly at Bill.

"He says, if you'll let him have a steer he'll head into the mountains and not cause you any trouble."

"Tell him I'll give him two beef and some other foods I have in the house. I've got blankets, clothing and a few boxes of ammunition I'll give him. Tell him I'd like to help, but I can't do any more than I am."

"He already knows you're between a rock and hard place, so I'll leave that part out."

Once again the chief replied, and to Bill the man looked to be near the end of his road.

"He said that's fine, and he thanks you for helping his people."

"Take 'em and find two big cows and while you're doin' that, I'll gather up some things in the house."

Sue, standing beside the door, rushed around the house gathering up things to give the Sioux. She remembered the cold nights filled with hunger when they were new to the land and the time she was a captive, so she would have given the house away, if the old man had only asked.

"Sue, we have enough. I'm going to give him five horses too, so they can be used as pack-horses. They can only take so much."

"Will they be okay?"

"No, I suspect not. The army won't allow them to rest, not for a minute. The only chance Brass Buttons has is to surrender, but he'll not do that."

"Why not?"

"He's lost all his trust in white men."

"The Sioux are good people, Bill."

"But, don't you see, they're the wrong color. The white man has little use for people of different colors. Besides, even if Injuns were white, it would not change the outcome. They have land, we want it, and we'll have it."

"I got the steers!" Luke yelled from outside.

Stepping through the door, Bill handed the supplies to Luke and a couple of women, and then said, "Tell Brass Buttons if he needs my help to send someone for me and I'll come. But, warn him to do so only in an emergency."

"I'll tell 'em and thanks—pa."

It was the first time, since his father's death, Luke had ever called Bill pa, and both men realized it.

Bill overcome with emotion asked, "Are . . .you . . . goin' with 'em?"

"I'll go with 'em for just for a ways, and I'll not be gone long."

"I want you back before sunrise."

Luke nodded and moved toward Brass Buttons.

# Conclusion

**Bill** lived to be an old man, dying in 1942, at the age of one hundred and two years. The ranch prospered and he was a very wealthy man at the time of his death, with almost half a million dollars in land and cash. Sue died before the turn of the century of an unknown fever and was buried beside two of her children that never reached adulthood. Their only surviving biological son, John Moses, took over the ranch at the time of Bill's passing, but sold it in the early 1960's and moved to California to retire.

Isaac died in 1895, when he was shot and robbed out on the open plains. While Bill never found his killer, he brought him home for a Christian burial. Deacon, one of the last surviving mountain men, did the burial rites.

Deacon died less than six months after Isaac, killed by a grizzly bear, his body never found and his cause of death never discovered by anyone. He simply rode away one morning, never to return.

Luke and Singing Bird had five children that lived, two of which moved to the reservation to be with their Indian families. One, Stands Tall, became a lawyer and worked to achieve a better agreement with the government and while his success was limited, he never gave up. He died in the mid 1970's and many Sioux yet today respect his name.

The other three children followed the trail of whites, and all were productive in their own ways. May Lynn married an army Captain and followed her husband from post to post until he retired in 1909. She had no children and died in 1953.

Isaac David moved north to Alaska in 1896 during the gold rush and was lost. The last word Bill had said all was well and he was leaving the boat the next morning to where he could move up the Chilkoot Trail. Neither Bill nor Sue had the faintest idea what that meant. Years passed, and finally the family accepted he'd died on his quest for gold.

Patrick Moses was the scholar and went back east to school. He attended a good university, got a solid education in business, and then returned to the ranch. His knowledge was helpful when Bill and Luke sold some land to the railroad, so a line could be laid to Billings. Additionally, Patrick was constantly finding ways for the ranch to bring in more money. He was the reason the ranch went from breaking even each year to flowing well in the black during the later years. Luke willed the place to Patrick knowing he'd worked hard to make the place a success and was deserving. Patrick never married and died on the ranch in 1970 of a heart attack.

After years of sickness, Singing Bird died of cancer in 1900 and Luke never remarried, dying himself in 1903. Many local folks said he died of a broken heart, but the doctor said it was pneumonia.

On July 28, 1878, the United States Army discovered Brass Buttons and his small group of Sioux hiding in the mountains. Without warning, they surrounded the Indians and as dawn broke, they fired into the lodges. In a matter of a few short minutes, all the Sioux were killed. Brass Buttons died in his lodge, tears running down his cheeks, remembering the white man's lies.

**The end**

# About the Author

**W.R. Benton**, a pen name, is an Award Winning and Amazon Best Selling Author. He has previously authored numerous books of Fiction, Non-Fiction, Young Adult, Science Fiction, and Southern Humor.  Such notable authors and actors as, Matt Braun, Stephen Lodge, Don Bendell, James Drury, *"The Virginian,"* actor Robert Woods, and many others have endorsed his work. His Amazon Best Selling Western, *"War Paint"* is being developed into a movie.

His hobbies include hunting, camping, fishing, hiking, cartooning, and reading.  Mister Benton has an Associates Degree in Search and Rescue, Survival Operations, a Bachelors Degree in Occupational Safety and Health, and a Masters Degree in Psychology complete, except for his thesis. Sergeant Benton retired from the military in 1997 with over twenty-six years of active duty. Benton lives in Mississippi, with his wife, Melanie C. Benton, and four dogs and two cats.

You can visit W.R. Benton online at http://www.wrbenton.net More of his books can be seen at: http://www.amazon.com/author/wrbenton/

 Visit him on Facebook at www.facebook.com/wrbenton01

## Nate Grisham
### Black Mountain Man

*Available in paperback & Ebook editions*

After a storm tossed night in the Rockies, Nate Grisham encounters a lost Army captain and his family far from any civilized town. And something doesn't seem right about his story of having been ambushed by Blackfoot warriors. After escorting them to the nearest Army post he discovers the Army is looking for an imposter—and murderer.

**W.R. Benton** and newcomer **Grady Clark** team up to bring another rip-roaring mountain man western to life in this new book. This story is inspired by real historical examples of blacks, both freed men and runaways, that moved west before and after the Civil war.

## Nate Grisham
### Book 2, Renegade Trapper

*Available in paperback & for the Kindle at Amazon.com*

**The continuing saga of Nate Grisham, Black Mountain Man**

When fellow trapper, Coon Turner, turns renegade killer to steal the plew of his friends, Nate and Cotton decide justice must be served, and they will go to any length to see the job completed. Coon knows if he can reach Missouri Territory, where the United States law has no jurisdiction, he'll be a free man. But making it safely to Saint Louis, with Nate and Cotton hot on his heels, isn't going to be easy.

Gathering up some men, he moves west once more and this time he discovers gold, while trading guns and whiskey to the Indians. Overtaken by his own unrelenting greed, Coon butchers his own men, one by one on the way to Missouri. Coon hopes to escape his trackers by becoming a gentleman, but soon he's visited by two mountain men, one white and the other black, both determined to kill him, but he escapes west once more.  Nate seeks to challenge Coon to a fight to the death and by tribal law, only one man can survive.

**Frontier action abounds in this new saga in the story of Nate Grisham!**

## Bad Man



Nate Grisham, his son Little Nate, and a group of their fellow trappers join up to take their pelts east to the big city. It's been a long trapping season and everyone's ready for a little recreation. In a sleepy little saloon along the way they find way more action then they bargained for. A handful of St. Louis dock scum, real no good, vile tongued, hot-headed types spark a nasty bar fight. During the ruckus Nate is badly injured, and another of the trapper's friends now lies dead, gunned down by the barroom thugs.

Now 14 years of age, Little Nate may still be young but he is fully capable of handling this kind of trouble. The group splits up and Little Nate gives chase alongside One-Eye Jack. Following the murderous trail of innocents the low-lifes leave in their wake, the pair need to track down the killers fast, before more people suffer, or the killers might disappear forever. It's not easy tracking these men down, however Mountain Men know a thing or two about making their own justice, and they're not about to let the murderers of a friend go unpunished.

*A fast-paced and exciting mountain man adventure, with raw gut-wrenching frontier action. The next must read installment for fans of the Nate Grisham: Black Mountain Man series.*

## Nate Grisham
### Book 5, Whispers the Wind

*Available in paperback & for the Kindle at Amazon.com*

The adventures of Nate Grisham continue in *Whispers the Wind*. Nate's former trapping patrner, One Finger Sisson, is out for revenge. A dozen years back he and Nate were forced to choose between dying at the hands of a Pawnee war party or leaving behind an entire year's harvest of beaver pelts. The Pawnee had made it clear at the time either surrender the plew taken from the tribe's streams, or die. His friend wanted to fight, but the 20 to one odds didn't look good to Nate, so he gave the plew away. They'd been left with nothing. The tribe had also taken their horses, guns, and supplies. And they were forced to walk a hundred miles to Butterfield's so they could get a grubstake for the coming trapping season. Sisson had sworn to kill Nate then, but he'd simply been run off. Nate found it hard to believe a man who he once called friend wanted to kill him so badly he'd kidnapped his wife. But his wife, Mist, is no ordinary squaw...she has powers of sight and is what the indians call a 'seer'. She will use this gift to her advantage, until Nate can track and rescue her.

# DAMASCUS STEEL

**A new Mountain Man saga
featuring reader favorite *Nate Grisham*.**

The War of 1812 is over, but tensions between England and the U.S. simmer. Political intrigues and divided loyalties lurk within the dark corners of America's capital. Barnshill, an English-born spy for the U.S. has plans for bright political future, and fierce White House aspirations.

With killers on his trail, he is lucky to befriend some turn mountain men, men with integrity and grit; Blade Williams, One-Eyed Jack, Nate Grisham, as well as braves Fire Eyes and Eagle. With the help of these stalwart heroes, Barnshill stakes his survival on their backwoods knowledge and unwavering loyalty.

*Available in Paperback & Kindle*

## Audiobooks by W.R. Benton

Available now at Audible.com and iTunes